LEE BROOK

Beneath the Surface

First published by BrookHarvey Press 2024

Copyright © 2024 by Lee Brook

All rights reserved. No part of this publication may be reproduced, stored or transmitted in any form or by any means, electronic, mechanical, photocopying, recording, scanning, or otherwise without written permission from the publisher. It is illegal to copy this book, post it to a website, or distribute it by any other means without permission.

This novel is entirely a work of fiction. The names, characters and incidents portrayed in it are the work of the author's imagination. Any resemblance to actual persons, living or dead, events or localities is entirely coincidental.

Lee Brook asserts the moral right to be identified as the author of this work.

Lee Brook has no responsibility for the persistence or accuracy of URLs for external or third-party Internet Websites referred to in this publication and does not guarantee that any content on such Websites is, or will remain, accurate or appropriate.

Designations used by companies to distinguish their products are often claimed as trademarks. All brand names and product names used in this book and on its cover are trade names, service marks, trademarks and registered trademarks of their respective owners. The publishers and the book are not associated with any product or vendor mentioned in this book. None of the companies referenced within the book have endorsed the book.

First edition

This book was professionally typeset on Reedsy.
Find out more at reedsy.com

For Mrs Wood—
For your support with my novels.
And for your support with my children.
Thank you.

Contents

Chapter One	1
Chapter Two	10
Chapter Three	20
Chapter Four	26
Chapter Five	35
Chapter Six	45
Chapter Seven	56
Chapter Eight	66
Chapter Nine	76
Chapter Ten	86
Chapter Eleven	96
Chapter Twelve	107
Chapter Thirteen	117
Chapter Fourteen	126
Chapter Fifteen	138
Chapter Sixteen	148
Chapter Seventeen	158
Chapter Eighteen	166
Chapter Nineteen	174
Chapter Twenty	182
Chapter Twenty-one	192
Chapter Twenty-two	200
Chapter Twenty-three	209
Chapter Twenty-four	220

Chapter Twenty-five	228
Chapter Twenty-six	237
Chapter Twenty-seven	245
Chapter Twenty-eight	255
Chapter Twenty-nine	266
Chapter Thirty	272
Chapter Thirty-one	281
Chapter Thirty-two	289
Chapter Thirty-three	298
Chapter Thirty-four	306
Chapter Thirty-five	316
Chapter Thirty-six	326
Chapter Thirty-seven	336
Chapter Thirty-eight	346
Chapter Thirty-nine	356
Also by Lee Brook	360

Chapter One

Esme Bushfield stared at her reflection in the antique mirror that hung in her room at Brandling House, where she'd spent the first day of her educational retreat. Her parents' idea.

She leaned in closer, carefully applying another coat of mascara to her long blonde lashes, making her bright blue eyes pop even more. Her parents would hate the dark, dramatic makeup, but that made Esme love it even more. She was so tired of living up to their strict expectations.

Tonight, she was going out with Ashley to have some real fun for once. Ashley Cowgill had been her best friend since they met in year seven. Where Esme was blonde, preppy and usually obedient, Ashley had the darker complexion of her dad, with chestnut brown hair and matching eyes that always had a mischievous twinkle. Ashley came from a broken home, her mother struggling financially and emotionally, her father coming and going as he pleased. As a result, Ashley had far more independence than Esme. She could come and go as she pleased, staying out late with friends while Esme was under strict curfews. Ashley represented everything Esme yearned for—freedom, adventure, living life on her own terms without parental constraints.

Esme sighed, putting down the mascara wand and checking

her daring outfit in the mirror. The red mini dress with the plunging neckline was sure to shock her conservative parents. Esme rarely wore anything so bold. Her mother preferred she dress modestly, in classic styles and muted colours. But not tonight. Tonight, she and Ashley were going to a party. They were only seventeen, but they'd managed to buy some alcohol during their lunch break. And Esme couldn't wait to lose herself in the pulsing music, to dance wildly without judgment, to feel young and carefree. To get pissed like never before.

Esme's mind drifted back to the first time she and Ashley had dared to sneak off on their own. It was a couple of years ago when they were in Year 11.

Esme had been waiting at the bus stop after school as usual, dreading the boring ride home to start on homework. Then Ashley came bounding up, flashing a mischievous smile.

"Hey, let's go into town for a bit instead of heading home right away!" she suggested with a nudge.

Esme hesitated. "I don't know... I'm supposed to take the bus straight home like always. My parents will worry if I'm late."

Ashley waved her hand dismissively. "A little adventure never hurt anyone! Come on, it'll be fun. We can window shop, grab milkshakes at McDonald's, just hang out."

Esme chewed her lip uncertainly. Part of her did want to join Ashley, to embrace that sense of freedom and spontaneity she'd never experienced before. But the dutiful part held back, knowing she should obey the rules.

Sensing Esme's hesitation, Ashley hooked arms with her reassuringly. "I'll get you home before your curfew, I promise. Live a little!"

CHAPTER ONE

Esme took a deep breath, then slowly nodded. "OK, let's do it." Ashley let out an excited squeal and pulled Esme towards the parking lot before she could change her mind.

Soon, they were walking through town, hand in hand. The nervousness Esme initially felt melted away as the sun tingled on her skin. Being with Ashley felt easy and natural like she could truly be herself.

They whiled away the afternoon, poking through quirky shops, trying on outrageous outfits and giggling. Over milkshakes, Ashley regaled Esme with hilarious stories about her family, so different from Esme's own. And Esme found herself opening up about her insecurities and dreams in a way she never had before.

Glancing at her watch eventually, Esme was shocked to see it was nearly 6 pm. "Oh fuck, I need to get home! My parents are going to kill me."

Ashley just laughed, unbothered. "Chill out; I'll get you there. Always an adventure with me!"

Ashley's carefree spirit was contagious. Despite cutting it close, Esme arrived home, buzzing with excitement. She knew her mother would scold her for being late, but she didn't care. For the first time, she had ignored expectations and just enjoyed the moment.

From then on, Ashley's daring attitude captivated Esme. Being with Ashley made her feel alive in a way she'd never experienced before. Their adventures became a secret ritual Esme lived for. Ashley brought out a bold, carefree side Esme didn't know she had.

Esme did a final check of her makeup in the antique mirror, making sure her smoky eyes and bold red lips were perfect.

Grabbing her clutch and doing a final spin in the mirror,

Esme attempted to push aside any nagging concerns. She was through with following rules and doing the safe, sensible thing. Tonight called for adventure and rebellion, not caution. And she had already kept Ashley waiting long enough. Their night of fun awaited!

Esme stood at the threshold of her room, the doorknob cold under her clammy palm. This was it—the point of no return. Once she stepped through this doorway to join Ashley, there would be no more obeying her parents' suffocating rules and expectations.

Her eyes landed on the thick medical textbook sitting neatly on her desk. Advanced Biology—the challenging volume her parents had gifted her just last month. "Study up!" her father had said proudly. "This will give you a head start for medical school."

Medical school. The path that had been chosen for Esme since she was barely old enough to read. Her parents were both doctors, and they expected nothing less for their daughter. Top grades, gruelling study schedules, extra chemistry lessons... it had all led to this predetermined climax—following in their esteemed footsteps.

Esme closed the distance, dropped her clutch, and traced her fingers over the embossed title, feeling the weight of that future pressing down on her. This book represented everything her parents wanted for her. Everything they had worked and sacrificed tirelessly for. And she was about to throw it all away for a night of teenage rebellion.

Guilt and longing battled within her. She loved her parents, and a part of her did want to make them proud. But an even bigger part longed to break free, to make her own choices, to embrace spontaneity and adventure with Ashley instead of rigid studiousness.

Esme took a deep breath, squaring her shoulders. She couldn't keep living her parents' dreams. This was her life, and she needed to start taking control of it. They would just have to understand.

A knock at the door made Esme jump. She crossed the room quickly, opening it to find Ashley standing there looking fierce in a shimmery black halter top and dark jeans. Her makeup was just as dramatic, with smoky eyeshadow and blood-red lips.

"Damn, girl, look at you!" Ashley said with an approving nod and wolf whistle. "Almost didn't recognise you for a second. Your parents would die if they saw this look."

Esme laughed. "Don't I know it? This outfit totally breaks all my mum's rules. No exposed shoulders, no visible cleavage, no skirts above the knee..." She rolled her eyes before giving Ashley another once-over. "I love it, though. We look fucking hot!"

The girls giggled with excitement and nervous energy. This was the farthest they'd ever gone to break the rules, and Esme still couldn't believe she was going through with it. She knew if she got caught there would be severe consequences, but the thrill of rebellion was too powerful to resist.

Esme grabbed her clutch and followed Ashley quietly into the hallway of the house, carefully closing the heavy oak door behind her without a sound. At nearly midnight, she knew everyone else was asleep, but the adrenaline coursing through Esme's veins kept her wide awake and alert.

Esme tensed as she noticed Ishaan Sadiq lingering in the corridor, leaning against the wall. With his greasy dark hair and tanned complexion, he had always creeped her out. Ishaan was obsessed with Ashley, constantly trying to impress her with inappropriate suggestions and risqué jokes.

Ashley grabbed Esme's arm, whispering harshly, "Ugh, not him again. Just ignore him."

But it was too late. Ishaan had spotted them and strode over eagerly.

"Well hello ladies, sneaking off somewhere?" he said with a sly grin that made Esme's skin crawl.

Ashley rolled her eyes. "None of your business, Ishaan. Shouldn't you be in bed like a good little boy?"

Ishaan just chuckled. "Maybe I want to be bad too. Mind if I join you? The more the merrier, right?" He winked in what he clearly thought was a flirtatious manner.

Esme recoiled, looking at Ashley pleadingly. She wanted nothing to do with this creepy guy tonight.

Ashley scoffed. "Yeah right, this is girls' night. No boys allowed. Why don't you scurry back inside before you get into trouble?"

Ishaan smirked, undeterred by Ashley's disgusted tone. "Come on, I promise I'll make it worth your while," he said suggestively, reaching out to stroke Ashley's arm.

Ashley jerked away from him sharply. "Get lost, perv!" she spat. Looking at Esme, she said, "Let's get out of here."

They turned and hurried away as Ishaan called after them tauntingly. "But I know it's not a girls' night. And plus, I've already been invited!"

Esme felt shaken. She couldn't believe how persistent and pervy he was. Ashley was right—he was bad news. She only hoped he was lying about being invited to the party.

Esme and Ashley crept down the grand staircase, their heels clicking loudly on the polished wood steps. The cavernous front hall of Brandling House was shrouded in shadow, the only light coming from the moon pouring through the towering, mullioned windows.

As Esme peered into the darkness, she recalled the chilling tales her fellow students had told over tea earlier that night. They spoke in hushed voices about the house's ties to the infamous Middleton Witches, two sisters who practised magic and ate little children. Legend had it their spirits still haunted the halls of Brandling House, seeking vengeance for their demise.

One girl even claimed she'd seen the ghost of Gwendolyn herself—a pale spectre floating down this very staircase late one night. The apparition's eyes glowed red with hatred as she glared at the terrified student before vanishing. Esme had brushed off the story at the time, but now, enveloped in the shadows of the cavernous hall, she felt a shiver of apprehension.

Just then, a loud creak echoed from the landing above, followed by a whoosh of frigid air. Esme startled, gripping Ashley's arm. Had the witches heard her doubting their existence? Were they already cursing her audacity to sneak out and break the rules? Esme's wildflower perfume seemed cloyingly out of place in the ancient house with its scent of dust and secrets. She longed to flee the oppressive atmosphere for the lively anonymity of the nightclub.

Ashley grinned wickedly, clearly relishing Esme's unease. "Don't worry, I'll protect you from the scary ghosts," she teased. Arm in arm, they hurried across the foreboding hall, the click of their heels punctuating the silence like a countdown to their rule-breaking escape.

Tonight was about freedom and fun, not childish ghost

stories. Linking her arm through Ashley's, Esme headed towards the exit.

But something felt wrong.

She couldn't relax despite wanting to be safely outside, wanting to close the heavy door firmly on the house's haunting legends.

So Esme stood frozen with her hand on the ancient iron door handle of Brandling House.

Ashley shifted impatiently beside her, brown eyes gleaming with rebellion.

"Come on, we need to hurry if we don't want to be late," Ashley whispered.

Esme chewed her lip. "Ash, are you sure this is a good idea? Sneaking out is risky enough without going to the woods."

Middleton Woods had a sinister reputation, rumoured to be haunted by a headless horseman. Local youth dared each other to spend a night there, though only some actually followed through.

Ashley scoffed, flicking back her chestnut hair impatiently. "Don't tell me you're scared of some silly ghost stories."

Esme bristled at the condescension in her friend's voice. Ashley constantly pushed her to take more risks, to rebel against her sheltered upbringing.

Sneaking to the woods to party was Ashley's latest attempt to pull Esme into her world of freedom and danger. Esme wavered, part of her longing to embrace the thrill of defiance even as her ingrained caution resisted.

Sensing her hesitation, Ashley gripped Esme's arm, her eyes entreating. "Come on, live a little! It's just one night. The men are waiting for us!"

Esme wavered a moment longer, then exhaled sharply. "OK,

fine, let's do this." Ashley's face lit up. Hooking her arm through Esme's, she pushed open the heavy door.

As Esme stepped across the threshold, a shadow flickered at the edge of her vision. She whirled around, her heart pounding, but only empty darkness met her gaze. Probably just a tree branch, she told herself, shaking off the unease.

Just then, a cold gust of wind slammed the door shut with a bang that shattered the stillness. Esme jumped, startled. Ashley let out an exhilarated laugh.

"That's the spirit! Welcome to adventure." Grinning, she pulled Esme down the stone steps into the waiting night.

Apprehension and anticipation warred within Esme, but she resisted glancing back at the looming silhouette of Brandling House as she plunged into the unknown. The chill wind seemed to whisper perilous mysteries just beyond the reach of her senses... but she quickened her pace to match Ashley's confident stride, ignoring the unease needling at the back of her mind.

Chapter Two

Police Constable Ella Nightingale navigated the police car through early morning traffic, her partner Omar Khan studying the briefing notes beside her. Two missing teenagers from a local academy—likely just a couple of rebellious kids off on a lark. Still, procedures had to be followed.

"So the programme head, Wayne Wardman, reported them missing first thing this morning," Omar summarised. "Seventeen-year-olds Esme Bushfield and Ashley Cowgill failed to show up for breakfast roll call after supposedly being in their rooms all night."

Ella nodded. "Standard protocol is to interview Wardman first about circumstances and mindset before the disappearance. Then speak to the parents."

They pulled up on Town Street outside Brandling House, the imposing gatehouse looming ahead. Ella noted the expansive grounds surrounded by wrought iron fencing—plenty of ways for savvy teens to slip out undetected.

Wardman greeted them anxiously in the library, sporting heavy bags under his eyes. Clearly, the disappearance plagued him.

Constable Nightingale studied Wayne Wardman carefully as he answered their questions about the missing girls. His tired eyes and slumped shoulders spoke of a burdened conscience.

"Let's walk through the timeline," Ella prompted. "What was the schedule on the day they disappeared?"

Wayne rubbed his chin. "Lessons as normal until 4 pm. Then independent study. Dinner at 6. Lights out at 9 pm sharp. When I checked the next morning, Esme and Ashley were gone."

Omar jotted notes. "Did they seem distressed or express wanting to leave?"

"Not at all," Wayne said. "Esme was a model student, excited for an upcoming field trip. Ashley was her usual indifferent self lately, but nothing ominous. That girl has such potential."

Ella leaned forward intently. "What about security footage? Any clues there?"

Wayne grimaced, shamefaced. "The owner has them switched off. They cost too much money, apparently."

Making a mental note to follow up with the owner, Ella moved on. "Any past history of disappearing or sneaking out?"

"Once or twice for Ashley," Wayne acknowledged. "But never for Esme. She followed the rules, focused on her studies."

Ella finished by collecting the attendee list and contact info for all students and staff. Wayne promised to call immediately if anything else surfaced. He saw them out, shoulders slumped with the weight of responsibility. Ella felt confident he'd assist however he could to find the girls.

Back in the cruiser, Ella voiced her thoughts. "He seems genuinely concerned. I don't think this is just teen rebellion. Something feels off."

Omar nodded grimly. "I agree. The parents' statements will give us more to go on. But my gut says we need to take this case seriously."

With a last glance back at the imposing facade of Brandling House, Ella started the ignition.

* * *

Constable Ella Nightingale surveyed the shabby terraced house, noting the overgrown garden and boarded-up window. This didn't bode well for what they'd find inside.

A tired-looking woman answered the door, her eyes red-rimmed. "Sandra Cowgill? We're here about your daughter, Ashley."

Sandra nodded numbly and led them inside to a cluttered living room. Her husband, Johnny, sprawled on the sofa, irritation flashing across his handsome, tanned face at the interruption.

After brief introductions, Ella said gently, "When did you last hear from Ashley?"

"Two days ago," Sandra said, voice cracking. "I've called and called, but she won't answer. It's not like her to disappear without word for this long."

"Has she done this before?" Omar asked.

Johnny snorted derisively. "All the time. That girl has no sense of responsibility. Just takes off whenever she feels like it."

"That's not fair!" Sandra rounded on him. "You're never here, always off on your own adventures. No wonder Ashley acts out with the example you set."

As their argument escalated, Ella shared an uneasy look with

Omar. This volatility surely impacted Ashley. They managed to interject a few more questions before intervening.

"Please, let's just focus on finding your daughter," Ella implored.

The Cowgills fell silent, looking abashed. After a few more terse responses, they relinquished a photo of Ashley. Ella's heart lurched imagining the teen alone and adrift with no one searching for her.

In the car, Ella turned to Omar. "That poor girl. No wonder she's always running away."

He nodded. "Makes you wonder if she's in real trouble this time, with parents too distracted to even notice she's gone."

Ella frowned, sliding the crumpled photo into her pocket. Finding Ashley suddenly seemed much more urgent. However strained things were at home, that girl deserved to feel missed—and right now, Ella was the only one looking out for her.

* * *

Ella gazed up at the imposing high-rise apartment building, a stark contrast to the run-down Cowgill residence. A doorman escorted them to the penthouse flat.

The door opened to reveal an immaculately decorated interior. A petite, well-dressed woman greeted them—Esme's mother, Dorothy Bushfield. Ella noted her red-rimmed eyes and trembling hands.

"Please come in, officers. Thank you for coming so swiftly." Dorothy led them to the sitting room and offered tea from a maid.

Settling onto the plush sofa, Ella asked gently, "When did

you last hear from Esme?"

"She called Sunday evening, just before leaving for Brandling House from school. She was so excited to spend time with her school friends," Dorothy said, her voice breaking.

Ella continued through the checklist of questions. According to Dorothy, studious Esme had never shown any signs of unhappiness or rebellion. She'd been her usual cheerful self right before departing.

Dorothy twisted a silk handkerchief, clearly struggling to maintain composure. "Esme's always been such a good girl. Gets top marks, helps around the house, never any trouble. Not like some hooligans out there!" For a moment, anger flashed across her delicate features.

Sitting forward, Dorothy continued earnestly, "Let me tell you about her last piano recital. She practised for months to perfect this beautiful piece as a surprise for my birthday..."

As Dorothy described Esme's thoughtfulness and talent, Ella felt her case notes fade into the background. She was gaining invaluable insight into Esme as a person—complex, motivated, deeply loved and reawakening Ella's fierce determination to reunite this family.

They wrapped up the interview and stood to leave. Dorothy grasped Ella's arm, eyes pleading. "Please find my daughter. She's everything to us."

Ella covered Dorothy's hand with her own. "We will do all we can," she promised. And she meant it.

* * *

Constable Ella Nightingale drove steadily back towards Brandling House, mulling over the missing girls' case. Her partner

CHAPTER TWO

Omar studied the notes from their interviews.

"Quite a difference between those two homes," Omar remarked. "Reckon Ashley's lack of supervision explains her habit of wandering off?"

Ella nodded grimly. "I'd wager both girls face pressures at home, just different ones. Might've reached a breaking point."

Her radio crackled to life. "PC Nightingale, this is Sergeant Greenwood. What's your status?"

"Just leaving the Bushfield residence, Sarge," Ella responded. "Heading back to Brandling House now."

"Copy that," Greenwood said. "After comparing backgrounds, I'm classifying both girls as high-risk missing persons. We'll need all hands searching ASAP."

Ella's grip tightened on the wheel. "Do you think they're in danger, Sarge?"

"Hard to say for sure," he admitted. "But Esme's vanishing is highly irregular for a studious kid. And Ashley's lack of parental oversight is concerning. I'd rather overreact than risk lives."

That sealed it for Ella. "Understood, Sarge. We'll get statements from everyone at Brandling House right away to assist the search."

"Good. I'm mobilising teams for house-to-house checks focused on Town Street, the Manor Farm estate, Lingwell Avenue, Mount Pleasant, and North Lingwell Road. See you soon."

The radio fell silent. Ella felt energised knowing they had the full force of the department behind finding the girls now. She glanced at Omar. "Let's get these interviews done quickly so we can join the ground search, yeah?"

He nodded, flipping through his notes with renewed vigour. Ella pressed harder on the accelerator. Every minute would count for those girls relying on them for help. She just prayed they could reach them in time.

* * *

Later, Ella Nightingale trudged down yet another residential street, glancing occasionally at the photos of Esme and Ashley as she knocked on doors. The same questions, the same concerned but unhelpful responses from locals. No signs of the girls.

At the fifth house, an elderly man answered, peering closely at the photos. "Haven't seen 'em. But strange folk've been lurking around lately. Young thugs up to no good if you ask me."

"Can you describe them?" Ella asked, intrigued.

The man shook his head. "Just shapes moving about at night. Gave me an uneasy feeling."

Ella pressed for more details, but he couldn't provide any. She made a note to canvass the area after dark. Still, this could be a dead-end lead fuelled by a suspicious mind.

At the next house, a tired mother holding a fussy toddler shook her head apologetically. "Wish I could help. I'll be praying those girls turn up safe." Ella thanked her and moved on.

She was beginning to lose hope when an older woman answered the last door. Squinting at the photos, recognition flashed across her face.

"I've seen them! Walking together last night, towards 'top of the ave."

Ella's pulse quickened. "What time was this?"

"Around half eleven. Thought it odd to see young ones out so late."

Ella took down the details, finally a solid lead. She hurried back to relay the tip, hoping this breakthrough would direct the investigation down the right path. There had to be more people who had crossed paths with Esme and Ashley that night. And Ella was determined to uncover every last shred of evidence to find the missing girls.

* * *

Sergeant Greenwood rubbed his temples wearily as he ended another fruitless call with the local transport services. No bus or train operators had seen any trace of Esme Bushfield or Ashley Cowgill in the time frame around their disappearance from Brandling House.

Jotting a few last notes, Greenwood sighed and glanced at the clock. Nearly ten hours since the girls had been reported missing, and they were no closer to answers.

The radio on his desk crackled to life. "Greenwood, this is PC Ramirez. We've finished canvassing Town Street."

Greenwood grabbed the radio. "Any luck?"

"Negative, Sarge. Locals haven't seen them."

"Copy that. Regroup at Brandling House for new assignments." Greenwood's shoulders slumped.

The search of nearby streets and public transit inquiries had led nowhere. He stared at the photos of the smiling girls on his desk, determination steeling his nerves.

Esme and Ashley were relying on him for help. He wouldn't let them down. There had to be a clue they were missing, a witness who saw something.

Rubbing his chin, Greenwood considered options. Officially, the girls were runaways, limiting the resources allotted. But his gut said this was more sinister.

Picking up his radio again, Greenwood called dispatch. "Notify all units to proceed with missing persons investigation as high priority. We need full canvassing and search efforts continued urgently."

He knew the higher-ups would resist expending maximum resources on runaways. But sometimes you had to take risks and trust your instincts. And Greenwood's told him these girls' lives depended on going full force, protocol be damned.

Grabbing his keys, he headed out. Somewhere in those woods or streets was the lead to find Esme and Ashley. And he wouldn't sleep until he did.

* * *

That evening, Sergeant Greenwood rubbed his temple wearily as he ended another call with the missing girls' parents. Their desperation was palpable, even through the phone. He couldn't blame them—if it were his child missing, he'd move heaven and earth to find them. But the police had to be strategic, which didn't always align with a parent's urgency.

He'd asked them to hold off on media appeals for now, not wanting to spook any potential suspects into hiding. They'd reluctantly agreed, though he knew they were anxious to utilize every resource possible.

Greenwood gazed at the incident board, considering options. Expanding the search perimeter was prudent, though staffing was limited. He picked up the radio to call in reinforcements from neighbouring districts when an officer knocked sharply.

"Sarge, there's a group gathering in the car park of the woods led by the Bushfields. Looks like they're organising a civilian search effort."

Greenwood sighed, grabbing his jacket. He should've known the parents would mobilize on their own, police advice be damned. Their desperation was understandable, though it complicated the investigation. There was no use fighting it now—he'd need to integrate their efforts smoothly.

In the car park, a sizeable crowd milled about as Dorothy Bushfield issued instructions through a megaphone, her face pale but resolute. A woman with a similar appearance handed out flyers depicting the girls. Seeing the photos of young, smiling Esme and Ashley reignited Greenwood's determination.

He stepped up beside Dorothy. "I know you want to help. My team will coordinate with your search parties—we'll find them together." Dorothy managed a tremulous smile while Sandra squeezed his arm in silent gratitude.

Greenwood gazed out at the volunteers, touched by their support. With the community and police working side by side, surely the girls couldn't stay hidden for long. "Let's bring our girls home," he declared, rallying the searchers. Hope wasn't lost yet—not by a long shot.

Chapter Three

George awoke with a pained groan, the ache in his shoulder both a harsh reminder of his past injuries as well as another night spent tossing and turning. He sat up slowly, rubbing the joint that had plagued him. The physical therapist said it would heal in time, but patience had never been George's strong suit. Especially not when the nagging pain compounded the sleepless nights tied to the all-consuming case filling his thoughts.

Padding to the bathroom, George avoided glancing at his haggard reflection in the mirror, not needing visual confirmation of his exhaustion. It had been this way since returning to Middleton and the unsettling loose ends left in the wake of his last case.

He stepped into the shower, letting the hot water soothe his sore muscles. But nothing could wash away the unease coiled in his mind. George kept revisiting those final moments, when he had cornered Detective Chief Inspector Alistair Atkinson, exposing him as the murderer of fellow officers. The last he'd seen of Atkinson was in the ambulance, supposedly to get treatment. But he never made it to the hospital alive, declared dead en route under ambiguous circumstances.

George scrubbed harder as if to scour away the gnawing

feeling that the surface truth did not reflect the dark depths below. Atkinson had clearly been involved in something sinister, but with his sudden passing, the rot within their own ranks remained unexplored.

Was Atkinson really acting alone? Or did the corruption spread beyond what George uncovered? Atkinson's suspicious death signalled loose ends, hidden dangers within their own force. Sweeping it under the rug to save face would only let the decay fester.

George shut off the water, bearded jaw set with resolve. He would keep digging, keep pushing until the whole truth was laid bare, even if it meant tearing down facades and exposing uncomfortable realities. It was the only way forward for the victims already lost and those still at risk.

After showering, brushing his teeth and dressing, George headed to the kitchen to make his morning coffee, slices of bright sunlight spilling across the counters. As the rich aroma filled the quiet kitchen, his mobile rang, shattering the peace. George tensed, his pulse quickening—early calls seldom brought good news.

"DCI Beaumont," he answered briskly, cradling the phone on his shoulder.

"Morning, George. It's Jim," came the urgent voice of George's boss. "We've got a situation—two seventeen-year-old girls, Esme Bushfield and Ashley Cowgill, have gone missing from Brandling House near you in Middleton."

George's mind raced, immediately immersed in the investigation. "When did they disappear, sir?" he asked, grabbing a pen to jot details.

"Sometime Monday night, according to the head lecturer of the study programme at Brandling House," Smith said.

"They were last seen leaving the premises around 11 pm by another student. Didn't show up for breakfast queue yesterday morning, so the head lecturer raised the alarm."

George pictured the scene—two teenagers full of laughter and mischief slipping into the shadows of night, oblivious to the danger lurking ahead. "Any indication of why they left or where they were headed?" He paused. "And why am I only hearing about it now, sir?"

"We assumed we'd find them yesterday, George, but the parents have put pressure on us to get a detective involved." Smith sighed heavily. "No solid leads yet. They have some history of minor rebellion—sneaking out to parties and such. Working theory is just youthful mischief gone wrong at this point."

George's gut twisted with unease. In his experience, these situations seldom involved mere mischief. "What action has been taken so far?"

"Uniform began interviews and searches yesterday. But Detective Chief Superintendent Sadiq is taking a personal interest given the girls' elite status. He wants HMET on it straight away."

George's brow furrowed. The head of the Homicide and Major Enquiry Team's direct oversight was unusual. These must not be typical runaways. Powerful forces were invisibly moving the game pieces.

After finalising coordination procedures with Smith, George hung up, feeling the weight of expectation. Two young lives depended on his team now.

* * *

CHAPTER THREE

As George navigated the slick roads on the brief drive to Brandling House, windscreen wipers working furiously against the relentless downpour, his mind drifted down memory lane. He knew this area like the back of his hand, having spent a good chunk of his boyhood roaming these streets and fields with mates. Life seemed simpler then—carefree afternoons of footie in the park, perilous bike rides down steep slopes, pretending to be detectives solving imaginary crimes.

George smiled wistfully. If only his youthful self could see him now, returning as a real-life Detective Chief Inspector to investigate a serious case. Though he sobered quickly at the thought of the missing girls depending on him.

Looming ahead through the misty rain sat Brandling House, just as imposing as George recalled with its peaked gables and tall mullioned windows. Ivy climbed the aged stone walls like the hands of time, grasping at history.

Brandling House held such mystery then, dark tales of witches and ghosts whispered by local youth keeping them at bay even in daylight.

It had been abandoned when he'd been a child, and there was a time he'd have given anything to explore the abandoned manor after hearing chilling tales from older kids. But his cautious nature won out, even then.

Now, pulling up on Town Street years later, George surveyed his surroundings with a detective's keen eye, cataloguing potential evidence trails. If they'd gone down into the woods, they may never find them. He just prayed this blasted rain hadn't already destroyed those last fragile forensic traces. There would be no do-overs or second chances at gathering delicate fibres or boot imprints if this deluge had its way.

Stepping from the vehicle into the downpour, George turned

his face to the weeping grey sky in frustration. "Always making my job harder, eh?" he muttered with grim resignation, shaking his head. "Fucking hell." But there was no point complaining about the uncontrollable elements—he had to play the hand he was dealt. And right now, time was his most precious and swiftly draining asset.

George strode up the path towards the stone architecture of Brandling House. Though built as a gatehouse, its grandeur evoked images of nobility and intrigue. Lantern sconces flanked the thick oak door, cold and empty now. But George imagined how often their fiery glow had welcomed carriages bearing such eminent guests like barons and dukes over the centuries.

The tap of approaching shoes drew George's gaze upward to the ancient balustrade lining the upper gallery. For an instant, he glimpsed a pale face peering down, dark eyes boring into him. George's breath caught, goosebumps rising. A ghostly visitor come to assess the interloper?

No. His pulse resumed normal cadence. Just a student paused on the stairs, no doubt curious about the police presence. Still, the watching eyes kindled an eerie memory from George's youth.

He must've been thirteen or so, biking home late from the park on the winding lane known as The Drift. The night breeze threw sharp daggers at George as he pedalled harder past the wrought iron gates of Brandling House. He couldn't resist glancing up at the stone facade. And in that instant, he saw a face glaring from an upper window—wild dark hair, malevolent eyes boring into him.

Young George's heart had seized in terror. Was it the witch? Come to curse him for spying on her lair? He squeezed his eyes

CHAPTER THREE

shut and pedalled madly until his lungs burned. For months after, his dreams filled with visions of being hunted by a witch, always waking before she caught him.

    Now, standing beneath that same balcony, listening to his own shoes echoing the rush of years, George steeled himself against the resurfacing childhood fear.

Chapter Four

Stepping into the dim foyer of Brandling House, rainwater dripping from his coat, George scanned for the officer in charge of the scene. His eyes landed on a slim brunette conferring with a search team member. As he approached, she dismissed the officer briskly and then turned to George with an alert gaze, clearly ready to take command.

"Detective Chief Inspector Beaumont?" she asked crisply, extending a hand. "I'm Constable Ella Nightingale, first response."

George noted Ella's firm handshake and direct hazel eyes radiating competence. Her neat uniform and tightly plaited hair projected professionalism and discipline despite clearly pulling an all-nighter if her smudged eyeliner was any clue.

"Constable," George greeted with an approving nod. "Catch me up to speed. What measures are already underway?"

Ella withdrew a leather notebook, swiftly summarising efforts so far—initial interviews with the house warden, security sweeps of school grounds, canvassing nearby streets. As they talked, George sensed a sharp intelligence and bold determination beneath her polished veneer. She was clearly invested in finding the girls, not content to leave it as a routine missing persons case. George felt doubly assured of having

CHAPTER FOUR

such a driven asset directing initial operations.

"No signs yet in perimeter searches," Ella was saying, "but we have officers canvassing wider areas and transport hubs in case—"

A rumble of thunder shook the windows, drawing their eyes to the grey deluge outside. Ella's gaze clouded with worry.

"This blasted storm isn't making it easy. Ground evidence will be compromised quickly." She glanced back at George. "We're working against the clock and elements here, DCI Beaumont."

George noted the fierce glint hardening her eyes. "We'll find them, Constable," he said with gruff assurance.

George knew that the steely resolve in Ella Nightingale would not relent until those girls were safe. Together, they would find out the truth, no matter the obstacles.

Following Constable Nightingale's brisk footsteps, George was led to the stately library of Brandling House. Warm wood accents and rows of leather-bound books evoked an old-world scholarly grandeur, belied by the anxiety etching the features of the man rising to greet them.

"Detective Chief Inspector Beaumont?" The man extended his hand, forehead creased with tension. "Wayne Wardman, head lecturer of the student programme."

George noted the crisp suit and political smile straining professionalism over deeper concerns as he shook Wardman's hand.

"Please, have a seat," Wardman urged, gesturing at the chairs clustered by the carved marble hearth, cold and dark like the winter morning.

As they settled in, Wardman leaned forward intently, hands wringing. "Have there been any developments in locating

Esme and Ashley?"

George heard the quaver beneath the cultivated tones. This was more than a generic concern for student safety—Wardman clearly feared implications.

"My team has only just been assigned the case, Mr Wardman," George said. "Why don't you tell me about your experience with both girls? It will help us establish their state of mind prior to disappearing."

Wardman nodded sharply. "Of course, whatever you need." He painted a picture of Esme Bushfield—an exceptional student, focused, cheerful. Parental expectations drove her schedule of rigorous academics and extracurriculars like piano and riding lessons outside school.

"And Ashley Cowgill?" George prompted when Wardman hesitated.

"Not as..." Wardman parsed his phrasing delicately. "Traditionally ambitious but quite clever in unconventional ways. Passionate about photography. Her home situation is rather unstable, unfortunately, which seems to impact her... reliability at times."

"You mean she has a history of wandering off," George interpreted bluntly.

Wardman flushed. "On... occasion, she has demonstrated lapses in judgment regarding punctuality and attendance. But never prolonged absences before this."

George studied Wardman shifting uneasily as he continued. "The circumstances suggest she may have instigated this disappearance, swaying the more responsible Esme."

Does Ashley resent school or authority?"

"I cannot speak to her psychological state with certainty," Wardman demurred. "Her marks are adequate, and she's generally pleasant, if prone to occasional obstinance when avoiding mandated activities."

The political phrasing only solidified George's suspicions that Ashley had been a burr in Wardman's orderly programme vision.

So George decided to prod the man further. "With your programme's reputation, two students inexplicably vanishing during your watch will no doubt spark uncomfortable inspection, Mr Wardman."

Wardman visibly paled, confirming George's hunch about the undercurrents at play. "It's my sincerest hope that this situation remains discreet without damaging repercussions," he said carefully. "I will assist your investigation in whatever capacity necessary, Chief Inspector."

George leaned back, satisfied he had accurately gauged the interplay of powers and fears compelling Wardman's version of compliant cooperation. The man clearly worried how Esme and Ashley's disappearance might impact his career.

"I appreciate that, Mr Wardman," he said smoothly, then stood to take his leave, signalling to Ella that he'd had enough of Wardman for now. They still had much ground to cover interrogating other persons of interest before shadows stretched too long, and another day was wasted.

Pausing in the hallway as Wardman retreated swiftly towards his office, George met Ella's eye, seeing his own suspicions reflected back.

Back in the oak-panelled hallway, George conferred quietly with Constable Nightingale while Wayne Wardman made urgent calls regarding the searches.

"Wardman confirmed another student named Ishaan Sadiq was the last to see Esme and Ashley before they disappeared,"

Ella updated George briskly. "Apparently around 11 pm Monday night, heading towards the gardens."

George rubbed his jaw pensively. "We'll need to question this Sadiq lad straight away before he forgets anything."

Ella nodded. "Agreed, sir."

Just then, Wardman approached, pockets jangling nervously. "Chief Inspector, I should clarify—Brandling House itself belongs to a Eugene Garforth. He oversees renting the facilities. Perhaps he knows something that could assist?"

George's brows rose with interest at this new information. "OK. What's Garforth's involvement with the educational programme?"

Wardman waved a hand vaguely. "Minimal. He owns several historic properties and was convinced to host the academy for rental income but leaves operations entirely to me. He's rather eccentric and keeps odd hours. With all the coming and going, who knows what he might have witnessed..."

George shared a telling look with Ella. A reclusive owner. Great.

"We'll need Mr Garforth's statement next, Constable," George said. "Best to cover all angles."

"Of course," Wardman agreed readily.

George frowned, but Wardman continued. "Let me fetch Ishaan from his room first. Hopefully his information on when he last saw Esme and Ashley may provide direction in pinpointing where to focus search areas before weather further erases traces."

Wardman hurried off while George observed Ella noting details in her pad.

"Possible financial duress for our Mr Garforth, suddenly

amenable to housing unpredictable youths," Ella murmured. "And this student last to see the girls. It seems those might prove telling threads to pull."

"My thoughts exactly, Constable," George concurred approvingly. "Apply some pressure and see what he tells us, Nightingale."

Soon, Ishaan Sadiq accompanied Wardman downstairs—a tall youth wearing an overly casual smirk and expensive trainers. George observed closely as Ishaan described chatting to Ashley and Esme around 11 pm Monday, allegedly last seeing them slip out the front door and down towards the woods.

"They mention any particular plans?" George asked pointedly.

Ishaan shrugged. "Just sneaking off for a secret smoke or snog session, I assumed. No idea it was a big deal."

George frowned at the lad's blasé tone and didn't comment. "And you saw them head down into the woods?"

"I think. Does it matter?" Ishaan looked mildly annoyed by the questioning.

"I need to know their movements, Ishaan," George said evenly. This cocky teen likely knew more, and George needed to figure out what he knew and why he was being a little prick about it.

For now, though, he knew he needed to speak with Garforth. See what secrets he could ease from the elusive owner.

So George followed Constable Nightingale up the winding stone staircase, footsteps echoing the countless soles that had tread these steps over centuries. At the first landing, Ella paused outside an oak door bearing a tarnished nameplate reading 'E. Garforth.'

At Ella's brisk knock, a tall gentleman with salt-and-pepper hair answered, surveying them down an aquiline nose. His tailored suit and signet ring marked old money sadly faded. Sharp eyes assessed the unwelcome guests.

"Mr Garforth? I'm DCI Beaumont; this is Constable Nightingale. We'd like a word regarding the missing academy students."

Garforth raised one sardonic brow. "Ah yes, the troublesome teens creating such drama. An inevitable nuisance hosting this little school, however financially prudent. What is it you wish to know?"

George noted the dismissive tone, hinting at deep resentment towards the programme and teenage 'nuisances' in his precious historical home. Interesting for an allegedly absent landlord.

Ella opened her notebook businesslike. "We understand you've had limited interaction with the students, but we're following every lead. Have you witnessed any unusual activity or individuals that seemed out of place?"

Garforth blinked lazily. "My dear, I seldom involve myself in the rabble's affairs unless disturbances impact my quarters. Youth, by definition, fail to comply with etiquette and schedule. Beyond that, I leave Mr Wardman to police unruly behaviours."

"Understandable," Ella replied evenly, though George spotted her jaw tighten. "But surely you or your household staff may have incidentally noticed questionable patterns?"

"My valet Langton handles the tedium of comings and goings." Garforth checked an ornate pocket watch. "I prefer privacy to pry into tenant affairs. Now, might we speed this tiresome process along?"

George crossed his arms, interest deepening at the clear brush-off. "I need to ask you some questions regarding your finances, Mr Garforth."

Garforth's eyes hardened. "My financial affairs are quite in order. And I'll thank you not to go nosing through private matters merely because two truants have gone larking about causing trouble."

His posh accent grew more clipped with irritation. George watched him closely. "Oh, we'll be conducting a thorough financing review, sir," he said mildly, relishing the flash of nerves across Garforth's face. "Standard procedure in cases with possible criminal complications. I'm sure you understand."

Whether grudge or money weighed heaviest in Garforth's motivations, George knew both could drive a person to desperate measures.

They conducted the rest of the interview with growing contention as Garforth dodged questions on his financial straits and relationship with Wardman. All while projecting an air of entitled impatience rather than genuine concern over events.

What a prick.

George snapped his notebook shut with an air of finality. "That will do for now, Mr Garforth; thank you for your time." He didn't bother reigning in the sarcasm. In fact, he was hoping he'd made it clear he'd taken an instant dislike towards the shifty peacock. Garforth had made no attempts to hide his drive for profit and disdain of rowdy youths, and his priorities had reeked of self-importance.

Again, what a prick.

Descending the stairs, George met Ella's knowing look.

"What a prick," she remarked wryly.

George grinned. "My thoughts exactly."

"I hope I'm not overstepping, sir, but I think we need to look further into his finances," Nightingale said as they headed back downstairs.

"I agree, Ella," George said firmly. "I'll get a forensic accounting team assigned as well as having this Langton brought in." He suspected the valet knew more about Garforth's affairs than his employer realised. They always did.

"Wardman and Garforth are tangled up in this somehow," George muttered.

Ella nodded. "I agree, sir. The owner's financial straits seem our most promising vein to tap. And Wardman likely fears damage to his program's reputation."

"Exactly," George said as he glanced over to where Wardman anxiously greeted the Bushfields and Cowgills. "The parents arriving complicates matters. They'll be demanding non-stop updates and full access while we question staff."

Ella followed his gaze sympathetically. "Agreed, sir, that will prove distracting. Though also possibly insightful if we observe interactions with persons of interest."

George sighed, steeling himself for the tempest of high emotions and demands swirling through those doors. "I better update the families on progress so far before things escalate..."

Squaring his shoulders, George crossed the hall, hoping to stabilise the understandably frantic parents enough to strategically utilise their insights rather than hinder the investigation.

Chapter Five

George crossed the oak-panelled library, Constable Ella Nightingale on his heels. His pulse kicked as he spotted three figures waiting tensely—the missing girls' parents had arrived.

He first approached the petite, graceful woman cradling a monogrammed handkerchief. Her elegant features were pinched with distress, but she attempted civility.

"Mrs Dorothy Bushfield?" George asked gently. At her faint nod, he took her trembling hand. "I'm Detective Chief Inspector George Beaumont. We will do everything possible to find your daughter, I promise you."

Dorothy's composure wavered. "Esme is such a good girl, always responsible. I just don't understand..." She turned pleading eyes to her husband. "Stanley, tell him!"

The distinguished older man gripped his wife's shoulder. "I apologise, Chief Inspector. My wife is rather shaken, as you can imagine." Stanley's tone remained polite, but George glimpsed fiery urgency below the surface. "What progress have you made thus far?"

Before George could respond, a distraught voice interjected. "Progress? They've likely made none! The police just fuck about while our girls are missing!"

George turned to see a tired-looking woman confronting PC Nightingale—Sandra Cowgill, Ashley's mother. Johnny, Sandra's agitated husband, stood behind her, jaw clenched.

The officer spoke calmly. "Ma'am, DCI Beaumont has only just taken over. Rest assured, we're exploring every avenue."

Sandra looked unconvinced but backed down at her husband's murmur. Ella gestured discreetly at George—better diffuse tensions swiftly.

Drawing a steadying breath, George stepped forward, addressing the group. "Let's move this discussion to somewhere more comfortable quarters, OK?"

Once settled around the library's imposing mahogany table, George walked through actions taken, clues uncovered, and the next steps. He trod the line between candour and caution. An emotional spark could ignite an inferno without progress.

"So these persons of interest—the head lecturer and owner," Stanley Bushfield clarified, stone-faced. "You believe they are involved somehow?"

George chose his words carefully. "They are assisting our investigation. But it's standard procedure to scrutinise all angles."

"Well, I, for one, applaud such thoroughness!" Dorothy declared shrilly. "Leave no stone unturned to find my Esme!"

"Here now, let's keep calm," Stanley soothed, though his taut jaw showed her fiery reaction aligned with his inner unrest.

George observed Sandra Cowgill sitting silently, twisting a crumpled photo of Ashley. Her softly trembling hands worried George—a storm brewed behind that fragile restraint.

"Mrs Cowgill?" George prompted gently. "We will utilise every resource to bring Ashley home safely. You have my word."

Sandra stared back hollowly. "She's run away before, but never like this. Not for this long..." Her voice cracked. "She has to come back this time!"

As Sandra dissolved into muffled sobs, George and Ella exchanged an uneasy look. They had defused the immediate powder keg by showing fierce commitment to the case. But the parents' fragile hope could ignite without swift answers. The missing girls' lives weren't the only ones at stake.

Steeling himself, George turned back to the distraught parents with relentless determination blazing in his eyes. "Now then, let's discuss how you can best assist the investigation..."

* * *

As the storm-drenched daylight faded outside the library windows, George observed DC Candy Nichols perch on the sofa's edge, taking careful notes as distraught parents described their missing daughters. He was impressed by Candy's compassionate focus despite the tense emotions swirling.

"When exactly did you realise the girls were gone?" Candy asked Dorothy Bushfield gently. "And do you know whether they took any personal items from their rooms?"

Dorothy dabbed her eyes with a monogrammed handkerchief. "I... I'm not certain. When that useless head lecturer called, I suppose!" Her flash of temper quickly dissolved into anxiety. "Oh heavens, I didn't even check what she packed!"

Candy patted her hand reassuringly. "Not to worry, we'll have the rooms searched straight away. But any insights you can provide will help. For example, did Esme normally carry a mobile or purse?"

"Of course!" Dorothy leaned forward intently. "She had an iPhone 15 in a pale purple case. And a small cross-body bag, tan leather..." She paused, almost in disgust. "From New Look, I remember."

As Dorothy described Esme's favoured items, Candy recorded diligently, blue eyes radiating compassion. George knew these personal details would prove invaluable to their investigation. As well as to search teams should the worst scenario unfold...

He forcibly redirected his thoughts. Speculation did no good now. Just meticulous extracting of each fragment that might comprise the truth.

Stanley Bushfield cleared his throat loudly in the tense silence following Dorothy's recitation. "Please inform us the instant anything of Esme's is located, Constable. Or if..." His permanent look of patrician restraint faltered slightly. "Well, I needn't elaborate on our fervent hope for a swift reunion."

Sandra Cowgill hadn't contributed yet, gazing numbly at the carpet. Candy leaned towards her, tone infinitely gentle. "We'll stay in close contact regarding any developments. Now, can you tell me if Ashley tended to keep her mobile or purse with her?"

Sandra blinked rapidly as if emerging from a trance. "I'm not sure... She was always losing things around the house. But that cute little backpack she decorated with the flower patches? Ashley took that everywhere." Her eyes flooded. "It was special to her..."

Candy nodded, jotting descriptions. "I understand. We'll be certain to look out for that."

Dorothy made an impatient noise. "This is all well and good, but what actual progress has been made? You detectives are only just getting involved when two days have already been squandered away!"

"We are exhausting every available option, Mrs Bushfield," George interjected smoothly. "I assure you, my team will uncover whatever clues remain despite precarious timing."

"See here, no one faults your competence, Chief Inspector," Stanley said. "But we, the parents, deserve transparency regarding efforts taken thus far."

Before tensions could escalate again, George walked through investigative actions step-by-step, weathering the barrage of frightened questions. He understood fear manifested as misplaced anger. As long as cooperation was maintained, he would bear the brunt of it. He had to if he was going to find the girls.

Candy eventually redirected the discussion. "Could the girls have had a secret reason for slipping away that night? Any particular friendships or meetups they referenced?"

The parents exchanged uneasy looks. "Esme rarely socialised outside school events," Dorothy said carefully. "Her studies kept her quite occupied…"

"Whereas my daughter has habitually demonstrated questionable judgment regarding male company and reckless behaviours," Sandra finished bleakly.

"Anyone specific she mentioned lately?" Candy pressed Sandra gently. "Even seemingly minor details could prove useful."

Dorothy gave an incredulous laugh. "With all due respect, Constable, I think we can agree if anyone would have instigated something ill-advised, it would be Ashley dragging my impressionable daughter along!"

"Dorothy!" Stanley chided as Sandra flinched.

"It's the truth, and you know it!" Dorothy declared shrilly. "Esme is a model student, reliable and conscientious. If your delinquent daughter pressured her into some foolish prank—"

"How dare you!" Sandra exclaimed through tears. "At least I pay attention to Ashley instead of ignoring her existence until I can mould her into the perfect pedigree! A prized bitch!"

As mutual animosity exploded, Candy and George exchanged an uneasy glance.

Later, conferring in the hall as rain lashed the windows, George asked Candy's impression on gaining background from the girls' inner circles.

"The friends paint Ashley as a daredevil, coaxing Esme to break the rules now and then," she mused.

George nodded grimly, unsurprised. "And Esme's academic drive?"

"Oh, genuine, by all accounts. But lately she... Her roommate mentioned secret moodiness and fighting more with mum. Sleeping instead of studying. That kind of thing."

George nodded, and he crossed his arms pensively. Something, or someone, pushed those very different girls over the edge together. Their best chance of revelation lay with someone who knew them both well.

But who?

* * *

As the missing girls' parents were escorted to guest quarters for a break, George observed Programme Head Lecturer Wayne Wardman pouring himself a stiff drink, hand trembling. His polished veneer of control appeared to crack without an audience.

George approached casually. "Rather a stressful time for us all, I'd wager."

Wardman started, composing himself quickly. "Oh, I suppose so. But truly, Chief Inspector, this annoying disruption shall resolve itself soon, I imagine. Teenage girls slipping off on foolish adventures... absurdly common and selfish, diminishing the important affairs of others."

His flippant words clashed with the tension evident in his posture as he gulped his scotch.

George simply nodded, allowing silence to amplify the unspoken truths. Finally, Wardman burst out in an angry rush: "I've devoted my whole career to this academy! Long nights shaping brilliant minds while short-sighted bureaucrats and overindulged children attempt to unravel it all."

He turned to George beseechingly. "You must understand, Chief Inspector. One small misstep, the slightest whisper of scandal or impropriety... all my years of tireless work erased in an instant!"

George studied the man who had gone from smooth politician to exposed nerve in moments. Not indifference then, but rather fear for his career that bred Wardman's outward dismissiveness. How far might that dread push a proud man clinging to his life's meaning?

Then again, why would he be involved if his career was at stake?

Unless he'd managed to do this before without being caught?

George made a mental note to look into any other missing teenagers.

"I understand well the cost of reputation, Mr Wardman,"

George said carefully. He understood far too much. "And the lengths some travel to maintain their masks."

Wardman's eyes sharpened, perhaps hearing the layered implication. Masks had their purpose but too often served to conceal inconvenient truths. And this case reeked of long-simmering secrets. And George would peel back whatever layers necessary to solve this case, no matter what feathers he ruffled and no matter who fought to keep old shadows thriving.

* * *

George gathered his team in Brandling House's library. Gazing at their fatigued yet determined faces, he felt confident his group could conquer whatever challenges arose.

"Right, briefing on where we stand," George began briskly, arms crossed. "The storm's compromised potential evidence trails outside. And searching all 600-odd acres of Middleton Woods for clues is implausible without direc—"

"All of it must be scoured straight away!" Dorothy Bushfield interrupted shrilly from the doorway, clutching her silk robe. "My Esme could be out there frightened and cold!" Stanley laid a calming hand on her shoulder as she dissolved into sobs.

George steeled his expression into patient sympathy. "Believe me, we would if we could. However, strategically applying resources based on evidence ensures higher chances of locating your daughter." Seeing Dorothy waver, George pressed his point. "I swear to you, we will utilise every skill and tool possible to bring the girls home. But throwing poorly planned staffing at acres of untamed woodland risks missing crucial signs. Please trust my team's approach."

CHAPTER FIVE

His earnest appeal finally penetrated the mother's frantic haze. She nodded grudgingly before allowing Stanley to guide her away.

George scrubbed a hand down his face, feeling the strain. Ella touched his arm reassuringly. "Well conveyed, sir. You've won their cooperation."

"For now, Ella," George sighed. "I'm afraid if I don't give them answers soon, they're going to revolt." He shook off gloom, refocusing. "Right, where were we…"

Candy picked up seamlessly. "Channelling search efforts once we've traced the girls' precise exit path based on eye-witness accounts and evaluations. Also analysing their social connections for clues." Candy paused. "We've alerted the banks, and they will inform us of any transactions, sir. And DC Blackburn is working with DS Fry at the station, monitoring their mobile phone records." Candy hesitated. "The woods don't have great signal, and so the last place we can place the girls is here at Brandling House via triangulation."

"Brilliant, Candy," George said. "In the meantime, let's revisit statements from the student who saw them last. I don't fully trust him if I'm honest."

Candy nodded, flipping open a leather pad. George had always appreciated her methodical nature despite her vibrant appearance.

"Preserving chain of custody for anything removed is paramount," she noted.

"Indeed. Document everything thoroughly—we'll need evidence uncompromised if it comes to trial." An ominous possibility George preferred not entertaining yet.

He focused back on Candy's upturned face as she asked about canvassing known offenders. He felt immense pride in her development into a fiercely skilled investigator under his wing this past year.

"My thought exactly. Let's prioritise area searches on any recently released individuals with a history of targeting youths," George said approvingly.

Candy grinned, cheeks flushing under the praise before schooling her features. "Consider it done. We'll find them, sir."

Her shining confidence buoyed George's nerves as she hurried off.

But then Head Lecturer Wardman burst from his office, face tense.

"Chief Inspector Beaumont, my apologies for interrupting, but Detective Chief Superintendent Sadiq has just arrived unexpectedly. He's most eager to receive an update on progress thus far."

Wardman's strained expression hinted at deeper concerns than a superior officer's sudden appearance. Likely dreading his elite program's reputation under official scrutiny by the department commander himself.

"I see," George said neutrally, thoughts racing. "Please show Detective Chief Superintendent Sadiq to the library, Mr Wardman. I will brief him on our ongoing efforts."

Wardman's relief was palpable as he hurried to oblige. George exchanged a loaded glance with Ella. Sadiq's intense personal interest escalated pressure exponentially, though perhaps he could provide additional investigative resources. They would need to strategically persuade their formidable boss that George's team had currently pursued all prudent avenues.

Chapter Six

George blinked in surprise as Detective Chief Superintendent Mohammed Sadiq strode authoritatively into the grand foyer of Brandling House, expensive Italian loafers clicking on the marble tile.

What was one of the highest-ranking officers in their division, and the head of the Homicide and Major Enquiry Team, doing here personally? George swiftly masked his astonishment, stepping forward to meet the unexpected guest. Over Sadiq's shoulder, George glimpsed Constable Nightingale's eyes widen briefly before she smoothed her features.

"Sir," George greeted formally, shaking the powerfully built man's outstretched hand. "How can I help you?"

Sadiq's smile seemed more predatory than pleasant, white teeth flashing in his tanned face. George suppressed a shiver at the almost feral intelligence burning in the man's dark eyes.

"DCI Beaumont," Sadiq drawled in his distinctive posh accent. "Let us have a chat, shall we?"

Without waiting for a response, the imposing DCS gestured for George to lead the way towards the stately drawing room at the back of the house overlooking rainy gardens. George exchanged a loaded glance with Ella as they followed in Sadiq's wake. The man commanded any space through sheer force of charisma and confidence.

Settling in an ornate armchair by the cold hearth, Sadiq studied George intently, fingertips tapping the polished mahogany arms as if playing an invisible piano.

"I want real-time updates on the investigation," he pronounced abruptly. "Every development, no matter how minor. Understood?"

George straightened under that piercing stare he recalled so vividly from five years back working a high-stakes abduction. Even then, newly promoted Detective Sergeant Beaumont refused to cower before the legendary detective. A lesson Sadiq evidently hadn't forgotten.

"Of course, sir," George replied evenly. "With respect, may I ask your interest in this case?"

Sadiq waved a large hand idly. "Let us simply say I have personal reasons for keeping a close watch, Beaumont."

George read between the lines easily enough—Sadiq had a tie to the case he aimed to keep neatly buried away from deeper scandal. But what was it?

"You may rely on my team's discretion regarding sensitive issues around the case, sir," George assured smoothly. Anything to keep this formidable ally and asset appeased.

Seemingly satisfied by George's tactful cooperation, Sadiq rose abruptly, checking a gleaming Rolex.

"Excellent. Wait here for a moment, Beaumont."

With that, the imposing figure swept from the room, designer coat flapping. The very air seemed to relax in his wake. George pondered the new complexities Sadiq's protective presence hinted towards. But he couldn't deny the man's influence and skill could greatly aid the investigation if lever-

CHAPTER SIX

aged advantageously.

Moments later, George blinked in surprise as Detective Chief Superintendent Mohammed Sadiq entered the room trailed by a familiar lanky youth—Ishaan Sadiq, the cocky student who last saw the missing girls.

Before George could process this unexpected development, Sadiq pinned him with a piercing look. "Beaumont, allow me to introduce my son, Ishaan. When I learned of the disappearances, I deemed it prudent to bring him directly under police protection."

Ishaan rolled his eyes. "Honestly, Father, I've told you everything already."

Sadiq silenced his son with a sharp gesture before turning back to George. "Naturally, questioning my own child raises biases. So, I am entrusting oversight of Ishaan's formal statement to your clearly capable team."

George read genuine concern beneath Sadiq's professional facade. This formidable leader contended with layered conflicts—commanding the urgent investigation while parental worry gnawed at his legendary composure. George imagined that strain.

"Of course, sir," George replied briskly. "Detective Constable Nichols will start a thorough follow-up interview straight away regarding Ishaan's account. We will apprise you directly on any developments." George winced at the word apprise. Why did he talk funny when talking to officers higher up the chain?

Candy stepped forward, leather pad ready. "If you'll come with me, Ishaan."

Ishaan sighed loudly but followed Candy from the room, Ella following closely behind.

George studied Sadiq's rigid jaw as he watched his son depart. "Witness statements often evolve remembering nuances, sir..." George offered diplomatically.

Sadiq's mouth twisted wryly. "Ishaan can be selectively truthful when situations displease him. I expect your team to pursue any discrepancies fully." His sharp gaze bore into George. "I want the truth, Beaumont, no matter the personal cost."

George heard the unspoken emphasis—Sadiq would accept no corrupted favouritism clouding the investigation, even with his own child now a confirmed Person of Interest.

"You have my word. We will uncover precisely what happened to those girls, sir," George vowed gravely.

Sadiq gave a terse nod and then seemed to deflate slightly, bracing himself against a leather chair back. The initial fiery energy fuelling his dramatic entrance dissipated, exposing profound fatigue and worry.

"Esme and Ashley... they weren't Ishaan's typical social circle," Sadiq murmured. "Why would he engage those girls specifically minutes before they disappeared?"

George posed the question gently. "Would Ishaan have any reason to harbour resentment against the victims?"

Sadiq passed a weary hand over his eyes. "I doubt it, Beaumont. But my work keeps me from home frequently, and adolescence brings much conflict..." His typically commanding voice flagged with shame. "Perhaps I don't fully know my own son."

The admission clearly pained Sadiq. George grasped his shoulder bracingly. "We'll get to the bottom of it, sir."

Sadiq managed a faint smile. "Thank you, George."

Just then, George glimpsed movement through the mullioned windows where search teams continued scouring the stormy darkness. He was sure he saw two small shapes clutching each other against the elements before the vision dissolved.

George blinked hard, resurrecting his professional manner, dismissing the trick of light.

* * *

Now seated across from cocky teenager Ishaan Sadiq in Brandling House's stately study, George kept his body language neutral, not betraying the scepticism mounting behind his impassive expression. According to Ishaan, missing students Esme and Ashley were simply rebellious party girls who likely ran off with older men. But George sensed blurred lines between fact and adolescent judgment.

"So you claim Esme and Ashley seemed... overly flirtatious with you?" Detective Constable Candy Nichols asked, head tilted dubiously.

"Oh yeah, always touching my arm, making excuses to talk," Ishaan said, lounging indolently in the leather chair. "They clearly fancied me. Can't say I blame them," he added with a smirk.

Candy lifted a brow, unimpressed. "Specifically, when and how did this alleged flirtation occur?"

"I don't know—at meals, in halls, whenever. Esme played hard to get, but Ashley was always up for a snog." Ishaan winked exaggeratedly. "That one would climb any bloke like a tree. No standards at all. The Leeds Bike, apparently."

George kept his face neutral despite distaste at Ishaan's crass words. "And this was your impression whilst spending time with them personally?"

"Nah, they weren't in my social sphere," Ishaan said smugly. "But I overheard things at parties... how Ashley was hooking up with a university lecturer. Like I said, no standards."

George doubted university staff would endanger their careers by consorting with teenagers. And Ishaan clearly parroted rumours to boost his own juvenile ego. But he would still check. Thorough should have been George's middle name.

"These seem rather personal assessments from an impartial witness," Candy remarked coolly, echoing George's thoughts.

Ishaan just shrugged, unaffected. "I call it like I see it. Everyone knows how those girls operated 'round here. Now they've run off with some older blokes, most likely. Prob'ly didn't take much convincing if you ask me."

His leering expression curdled George's gut. Pushing aside instincts to throttle this arrogant little prick, he rose abruptly. "That's enough for now, Ishaan. Constable Nichols will escort you out." But as Ishaan stood up, George eyed the young man. "You'd better not be lying to me."

As Candy firmly steered a protesting Ishaan away, George struggled to calm his disgust. The opportunistic teen was all too willing to feed toxic stereotypes and even distort serious tragedy. But why? What did Ishaan have to gain?

Whatever it was, George would find out. And he had a great idea.

* * *

Seated in Brandling House's opulent drawing room, Detective Chief Superintendent Mohammed Sadiq watched through

CHAPTER SIX

hooded eyes as his son Ishaan swaggered under questioning about his interactions with the missing girls.

"So you were not personally close with either Ashley or Esme prior to their disappearance?" DCI Beaumont asked evenly.

Ishaan shrugged, slumping deeper into an ornate side chair. "As I already told you, we'd chat here and there. I was helping Esme study history once. She clearly fancied me." He shot his father a smirk. "Not that I'd muck about with her. She's white."

Sadiq kept his face impassive while irritation flared. Ishaan knew perfectly well that fraternisation with a white girl was unacceptable. Still, Sadiq couldn't prevent an uneasy pang at this new information on Esme's apparent attachment to his cocky son.

DC Nichols leaned forward intently, observing Ishaan. "In what way was Esme's interest evident?"

"Oh, you know, getting all tongue-tied when I looked at her a certain way, finding excuses to hang about and talk." Ishaan stretched leisurely. "Poor girl was lovesick if you ask me. But like I said, I don't date."

Beaumont and Nichols shared a subtle look that Sadiq interpreted immediately—they found Ishaan's claims highly dubious.

"Regardless, focusing on Esme specifically could provide insight," Beaumont said carefully. "Anything she might have confided about troubles or plans for the future?"

Ishaan's smug expression flickered briefly. "Well, she was chafing a bit under her mum's thumb, from what I gathered. Wanted to cut loose and have fun sometimes." He shot Sadiq an insolent glance. "We all feel that at seventeen, right Father?"

"And you claim ignorance regarding any specific intentions to wander off that night?" Nichols pressed.

Ishaan huffed impatiently. "Look, the last I saw them, Ashley was whispering about meeting some mates—probably lads she fancied. Esme seemed keen for adventure, and off they went. Now you lot are here, asking ridiculous questions when it's likely just drunk teen girls embarrassing important dads by acting stupid."

Sadiq tensed, staring unseeing into the stormy night. Ishaan clearly aimed that barb at his turned back, resenting the perceived overreaction. Sadiq yearned to reprimand his son for rudeness, which hindered the investigation. But he remained rigidly silent.

Beaumont's clipped tone cut through the tension. "I believe that's enough for now, Mr Sadiq."

Taking his cue, Sadiq faced the room, features schooled despite churning emotions. "If you'll excuse us, George, I shall escort my son to his room."

He kept his hand firmly gripping Ishaan's shoulder as they left, feeling the slender muscles braced for rebellion. In the hall, Sadiq halted, turning his son to face him eye to eye, searching the beloved visage so like his late wife's. There he glimpsed the truth—for all Ishaan's cocky bluster, he was deeply unsettled by events.

Sadiq's expression softened. "We will speak soon, just us. For now, get some rest, son."

Dismissing Ishaan's sullen nod, Sadiq watched his retreating figure sadly. However aligned their motivations appeared, clearly, the gulf between father and son had widened. Perhaps beyond repair if Sadiq couldn't re-establish the bonds of trust now strained to breaking. He only prayed their fragmentation didn't shatter young lives in the process. Esme and Ashley deserved far better from them both.

* * *

Standing amidst Brandling House's labyrinth of echoing stone corridors, George conferred with DCS Sadiq and PC Ella Nightingale regarding strategy.

George said, "Our immediate focus remains comprehensively interviewing all present parties while meticulously gathering potential evidence from rooms and grounds without contamination. Once initial data analysis and suspect profiling are complete, we'll expand physical search parameters guided by forensic findings."

Sadiq gave a terse nod of approval. "Sounds like solid procedure. What specialised resources have been tapped so far?"

Before George could respond, his mobile rang. Detective Constable Blackburn's deep baritone emanated from his mobile. "Apologies, urgent development, sir."

Sadiq waved for George to take the call while Ella swiftly updated the HMET Commander on forensic assets and search dogs en route.

"What's up, Tashan," George answered.

"Cross-referencing the offender registry, I've identified twenty individuals currently residing within three miles of Brandling House whose prior records strongly align with our working behavioural profile regarding Esme and Ashley's disappearance," Tashan reported.

George clutched his mobile tighter, pulse quickening. This narrowed suspect pool represented their first tangible leads.

"Nice work. What details stand out?"

"Histories of violence or manipulation targeting vulnerable females, with seven serving time for abduction charges specifically," Tashan answered grimly.

George met Ella's and Sadiq's intent gazes. "Get Alexis and Jay to help canvas their last known addresses straight away. We'll rendezvous within the hour."

Ending the call, George addressed Sadiq urgently with the new information as Ella fired off directives over her radio.

Once George had finished, Sadiq crossed his arms. "Let us hope your team isolates any promising connections." He paused. "What specifically is the working theory regarding events that night?"

George waved them down a darkened corridor away from lingering teachers, where their voices echoed ominously. "Leading hypothesis suggests Ashley Cowgill, a behaviourally troubled teen craving autonomy, instigated this escape, likely luring eager but academically focused Esme Bushfield. We suspect illicit substances or company may have influenced their departure. I'm leaning towards the latter, sir, but it may be a mix of the two."

Sadiq nodded.

George continued. "Crucially, I want to know why here and why now, sir? Specifically, what made two very different teenagers suddenly leave the house? And why?"

Sadiq studied George intently whilst lightly shaking his head. "These girls hoped to escape their parents' hold. Yet found themselves more caged than ever before."

The Sadiq's knowing words resonated through George with chilling premonition.

Why on earth would they go into Middleton Woods late at

CHAPTER SIX

night?

Chapter Seven

Detective Chief Inspector George Beaumont followed Head Lecturer Wayne Wardman and Detective Constable Candy Nichols up the grand staircase of Brandling House. Their footsteps echoed in the cavernous stone foyer below as they climbed to the second-level students' quarters. Wayne carried an impressive old keyring laden with ornate skeleton keys, which jingled as he walked.

Approaching a polished oak door, Wayne selected an antique iron key and unlocked it with a heavy clunk. The door creaked open reluctantly as if the dark room beyond resisted exposing its secrets.

Stepping inside, George was met with an oppressive stillness. The floral duvet on the four-poster bed lay undisturbed, and decorative throw pillows were perfectly arranged. Books were neatly shelved alongside academic trophies and ribbons. A riding jacket hung tidily in the open armoire. Esme's absence permeated the orderly space like a phantom ache.

George made a non-committal sound, moving farther into the room. His eyes landed on the antique wardrobe; doors flung open to reveal neatly hanging school uniforms and sensible casual attire—modest dresses, sensible shoes. Quite a contrast from the daring red mini dress and strappy heels she had worn to sneak out that fateful night, according to witness statements.

What had inspired the studious girl's dramatic change of style? A desire to reinvent herself away from parental expectations? Or perhaps pressure from her more rebellious friend?

George's gaze moved on to the elaborate vanity set, surface cluttered with cosmetics. He noted the extensive eye makeup palette with smoky shadows and dramatic liner shades.

"We'll need to photograph and document everything in situ initially," George instructed Candy, who had already begun making meticulous notes on her tablet. He crossed to the desk, gloved hands hovering over a leather-bound journal and uncapped fountain pen as if physical contact might dissolve the lingering vestiges of Esme's presence.

"What sort of personal effects are you looking for?" Wayne asked gently.

"Mobile, bank cards, jewellery. That sort of thing," said George. "If her bank cards and mobile are missing, then we can put an alert out." He scrutinised the room, alert for any signs of struggle or hastily gathered items. But nothing appeared disturbed.

George turned to Wayne, disappointed at finding nothing. "We'll get a SOC team over."

Wayne nodded mutely.

"We'll need access to Ashley Cowgill's room next."

Again, Wayne nodded mutely, leading them two doors down the hallway. As the heavy lock disengaged, George steeled himself.

Where Esme's room was pristine, Ashley's appeared chaotically disordered, with strewn clothing and possessions reflecting her turbulent state of mind.

"Ashley always was one to make a mess and ignore tidying up," remarked Wayne Wardman from the doorway, frowning in disapproval. "It was the same last year, you see."

George cocked a brow at the criticism but remained focused on gleaning insights into the brooding teen's state of mind.

Rifling through the cluttered desk, he found a crumpled pack of cigarettes and a broken lighter amidst scribbled lyrics and edgy sketches. The haze of stale smoke and perfume hung heavy in the enclosed space.

They finished documenting Ashley's possessions in tense silence. George better understood the brooding girl's simmering frustration and impulsivity. But the catalyst that drove both teens out into the darkness, likely never to return, remained frustratingly obscured.

Wayne hovered in the hallway as George finished the inspection. Finding no concrete evidence, he stepped out.

"Find anything?"

George shook his head. Eventually, he said, "We'll need to interview her friends urgently regarding any risky behaviours or connections."

Wayne nodded. "I'll ensure access to any students that could provide relevant background." He hesitated. "For all her faults, Ashley deserves to be known wholly, not just the broken parts."

"Don't you worry about that," George said.

* * *

DCI George Beaumont stood gazing out the mullioned windows of Brandling House's library, watching the relentless rain lash the empty gardens. He pondered Constable Candy Nichols' suggestion to commence a physical search for the missing girls immediately despite the inclement conditions.

On the one hand, swift action was sensible with the trail growing colder and parents desperate for answers. Every passing hour heightened the risks, especially given the witness statement placing Esme and Ashley wandering towards the sprawling woods that stormy night. Delay bred danger.

Yet the elements presented daunting obstacles. Evidence preservation alone would prove challenging with the deluge compromising potential crime scenes. Any minute traces or fibres left behind were likely washed away or rendered useless. And the swollen, muddy terrain would slow searchers while heightening hazards like hypothermia or injury traversing the dense, slippery woods. Adding haste risked mistakes or exhaustion oversights that could mean the difference between success or tragedy.

George exhaled heavily, the enormity of the decisions weighing upon him. Two young lives hung in the balance, their survival potentially determined by this judgment call. He knew the window for locating missing persons alive narrowed exponentially as time stretched on. But was rushing in blindly better than careful planning and provisioning?

Just then, Candy approached, following his gaze into the churning grey. "It's shocking out there, sir," she remarked solemnly. "But the girls have been out there far too long."

George turned to her, seeing his own restless urgency reflected in her eyes. But Candy's youthful features also held a faith and optimism untarnished by bitter experience.

George set his jaw firmly and gave a single decisive nod. "What's the situation?"

"The latest canvassing of Middleton has turned up nothing useful. There's nothing at all to suggest Esme and Ashley headed that direction."

George grimaced.

"And then there's the parents," Candy added pointedly. "They're frustrated by the lack of progress."

George scrubbed both hands down his face. She was right. The pressure cooker of emotions barely contained so far would soon erupt without concrete developments.

Leaning forward intently, Candy continued, "Which is why I suggest assigning family liaison officers immediately, sir. To provide empathy and communication channels amid the chaos."

George considered for a moment, then nodded. "Good idea."

He flipped through personnel files thoughtfully. "Let's tap Cathy Hoskins. Level-headed and compassionate. Should mesh well with the parents."

"Good call, sir," Candy said. "And for Ashley's volatile situation, I'd suggest DS Elaine Brewer, sir. She faced similar family dynamics as a teen herself."

George raised his brows, intrigued. He knew DS Elaine Brewer to be a competent and insightful detective prior to transferring to liaison work. But hadn't realised she potentially identified with missing teen Ashley Cowgill's struggles.

"Explain Elaine's background and how it suits this role," George requested.

Candy leaned forward eagerly. "Well, Elaine grew up in a rather broken home herself. Her mother left abruptly when she was nine, leaving her confused and hurt. The abandonment trauma haunted her for years." Candy's voice gentled with empathy. "I think that personal experience uniquely equips Elaine to relate to what Ashley is going through. Her own struggles could forge connection and trust with Sandra Cowgill especially."

George nodded slowly. "Impressive, Candy. Well done."

Candy flushed slightly at the praise. "Thank you, sir. I try to understand what drives people, their hidden wounds and all. Figured you'd appreciate that perspective in reviewing candidates."

"Absolutely." George gave her an approving look. "I'll let you manage the liaisons, then."

"Thank you, sir."

George watched as Candy briskly drafted a request for Hoskins and Brewer's assignment, feeling the first spark of hope in hours. Perhaps they could maintain the crucial parental alliances necessary to keep the investigation progressing if Elaine and Cathy proved to be perfectly matched to the role, as Candy believed.

Alone again, George glanced at the storm lashing the windows. Every minute that passed made preserving fragile clues less likely, especially with the parents' cooperation rapidly eroding. But he refused to lose faith. Somewhere beneath the downpour, traces of Esme and Ashley's path remained.

* * *

Steeling herself as she stepped across the threshold into chaotic gloom, DS Elaine Brewer crossed the worn living room carpet towards Sandra Cowgill's slumped form. Approaching slowly, she touched the distraught mother's shoulder.

"Mrs Cowgill? I'm Detective Sergeant Elaine Brewer, the

family liaison officer assigned to you by DCI Beaumont."

Sandra turned blank, bloodshot eyes up at her numbly. Elaine's heart ached for the pain radiating off this fragile woman. She knew that haunted look all too well.

Settling on the sagging sofa, Elaine spoke gently. "I'm here to offer support navigating this tough time and serve as your direct contact with the investigative team. Please reach out to me day or night if you need anything at all."

Sandra just stared at the crumpled photo of her daughter clenched in white-knuckled hands.

"You must feel so very helpless right now," Elaine ventured softly. "But I promise every effort is underway to find Ashley. We will bring your girl home."

At that, Sandra finally reacted, face contorting as she turned on Elaine fiercely.

"Don't patronise me! You lot don't actually care about some delinquent teen causing problems!"

Sandra's bitterness erupted, pent-up emotions overflowing. "Now she's finally pushed it too far to handle the scandal!"

Though the insult stung, Elaine understood lashing out from profound fear. Placing a gentle hand on Sandra's trembling arm, she replied earnestly, "You're so right; I can't understand your pain as her mother. But please believe me when I say that no child is considered beyond hope or less deserving of urgent care. Especially not Ashley."

Sandra searched Elaine's face intently as if parsing truth from empty platitudes. Elaine bore the scrutiny openly, willing this suffering mother to recognize her sincerity.

Finally, Sandra's taut posture slackened as she crumpled into Elaine's sturdy embrace. Heart-wrenching sobs tore from her throat as she clutched Elaine like a lifeline. Gently stroking Sandra's dishevelled hair, Elaine let her cry until spent.

When Sandra finally pulled back, wiping her eyes self-consciously, Elaine gave an encouraging smile. "Why don't we make some tea while you tell me about your sweet girl? Her hopes, talents, favourite things. I'd love to know Ashley beyond just photos."

Sandra managed a watery but grateful smile. "I think I'd like that. To have someone really see and care about my beautiful daughter."

Settling into the cosy kitchen nook over steaming mugs, Elaine listened intently to Sandra describe Ashley's passion for photography, her talent for capturing authentic moments, and the joy she felt being creative.

As Sandra recalled happy memories, the colour seemed to return to her wan cheeks. Elaine was heartened to finally glimpse the devoted mother still shining beneath the defeat and fear. That persistent love would be their lantern guiding lost Ashley back to a safe harbour. Elaine only prayed it proved bright enough against gathering storms. Whatever darkness had swallowed the girl, Elaine was determined to illuminate the way home. She owed that much to both these hurting souls grasping for light amid the chaos.

* * *

Meanwhile, the grand foyer of Brandling House teemed with distraught parents demanding answers about their missing daughters. Their anxious voices echoed off the stately wood-panelled walls and high moulded ceilings as they pressed for information from the stoic officers.

DCI George Beaumont observed the tense scene from the grand staircase, with constables positioned strategically around the ornate hall should emotions spill over. Many parents had arrived hastily, still in office attire or casual wear. Everyone's eyes ringed with fatigue and worry after two endless nights of a lack of answers.

A smartly dressed man in pressed slacks accosted a uniform officer, jabbing his finger at her. "This is outrageous! We should be free to take our children home for their safety, not held prisoner by incompetent police!"

The officer kept her tone calmly authoritative. "Sir, I understand your concern, but we must follow protocol to aid the search efforts."

Nearby, a mother clutched her teen daughter, voice shrill. "Do you expect us to just sit idly by while our children's friends are missing? We demand action!"

At the hall's centre stood Head Lecturer Wayne Wardman, his typically polished appearance dishevelled as he attempted to mollify the distraught parents single-handedly, the task clearly overwhelming.

Catching George's eye, he hurried over, looking harried. "Detective, might I suggest allowing the students to return home with their families? Tempers are reaching a boiling point, as you can see."

George frowned, sympathy warring with reason. "No," was all he initially said. But after a tense moment, he added, "Allowing the students home is going to impede our investigation. I need to interview them ASAP."

Descending the stairs, George moved through the hall, projecting calm authority. The uniformed officers seemed to relax slightly at his presence. He couldn't blame them—

the swirling currents of emotion here could overwhelm the steeliest constitution.

Chapter Eight

Head Lecturer Wayne Wardman glanced down at his tablet, scrolling. "Right, I've scheduled Willa Montrose first in the green parlour. One of our most promising teachers."

DC Candy Nichols shook her head briskly, ponytail swishing. "Actually, I think we need to speak with Pamela Cliff immediately."

Wardman's polite smile faltered. "I'm not sure that's prudent. Miss Cliff can be rather... dramatic in her responses."

"Regardless, we're told Pamela knew Ashley and Esme better than anybody else," Candy countered evenly.

Sensing Wardman's reservations, George interjected, "I trust Detective Constable Nichols' judgement. We'll interview Miss Cliff first."

Looking perturbed, Wardman nevertheless led them to the blue parlour where a waifish blonde girl awaited, nervously pleating her skirt. Candy gave George a discreet nod before entering briskly.

After entering himself, George studied timid student Pamela Cliff intently as she perched on the edge of the velvet settee. Her pale eyes flitted around nervously beneath a wispy blonde fringe.

"Miss Cliff, I'm Detective Constable Nichols. Let's chat

about the night your classmates went missing, shall we?"

Pamela's pale eyes widened anxiously. "Is this an interrogation? I already told the other officer everything!"

Candy softened her tone. "Not at all. I just want your honest impressions of that night. Any observations about Esme and Ashley's behaviour could be very helpful."

Pamela worried her hands but nodded timidly. As Candy gently probed, the girl gradually opened up about perceived slights from Esme and perceived wildness from Ashley. George noted telltale signs of superficial hearsay and conjecture rather than first-hand accounts.

"Were you close with either girl personally?" Candy asked.

"Not really," Pamela admitted. "They kept to themselves mostly. But I overheard things and saw how they acted at school in the dinner hall. I was friends with both girls in year 7, but I don't think they became friends until year 11."

"I see." Candy kept her face neutral, though George could tell she found the uncharitable gossip superficial like he did. "So why did you tell one of my colleagues you were 'fast friends' with both of them?

"Because I wanted to be, I suppose. I wanted us to be a trio rather than them just being a duo. You know?"

Candy nodded. She turned to her boss and narrowed her eyes. She was sat in an armchair, leather notebook open. She asked, "How did Esme and Ashley fit into the social dynamics here?"

The girl hesitated. "Well, Esme focused more on her studies than socialising. We were friendly but not particularly close."

"And Ashley Cowgill?" Candy asked. "Did you interact with her much?"

Pamela bit her lip. "No, she thought I was too geeky and

mousy. Ashley hung around older blokes mostly. She was boy crazy."

George's gaze sharpened, catching the faint disdain in Pamela's tone. "These were fellow students? Or other affiliations?"

Pamela looked down, pleating faster. "I shouldn't gossip. But she was always sneaking off to meet some townie she was infatuated with. 'Bad boy' types old enough to drive and buy them alcohol and things."

"I see." George studied the girl's averted eyes intently, sensing nervousness around the topic. "And did Ashley seem more preoccupied than usual that night, perhaps referencing meeting someone?"

Pamela shook her head jerkily. "No idea. Like I said, we didn't talk."

George shared a subtle look with Candy. The girl clearly knew more but resisted divulging for some reason—time to apply pressure delicately.

"We understand you want to avoid speculation," Candy said gently. "But if Ashley confided anything that could explain her disappearance, it's vital you inform us. Anything at all."

Pamela squirmed under their intent gazes. Just as George opened his mouth to prod further, she burst out—"I did hear Ashley mention the caretaker was sweet on her! But it was just a silly rumour, probably."

Candy quickly noted this down with a significant look at George. His pulse quickened. The reclusive caretaker had motive and opportunity if an illicit dynamic existed with the troubled teen.

"When precisely did you hear this regarding the caretaker?" George asked.

CHAPTER EIGHT

"Well, as you know, we were dropped off last Friday after school, and Ashley was bragging to some girls about him giving her special attention on Saturday morning that Friday night," Pamela admitted miserably. "But she was prone to exaggeration for attention; it may have meant nothing!"

George leaned forward intently. "What exactly was said about this attention?"

As Pamela haltingly revealed the graphic gossip she overheard, George exchanged a look with Candy, seeing his own resolve reflected back. They would need to scrutinise the caretaker immediately.

When Pamela provided no further insights, George wrapped up the interview genteelly. But his mind churned with urgent deductions. If the brooding caretaker had an inappropriate fixation on Ashley, her disappearance may have stemmed from violent rejection when fantasy met reality.

Outside, after the interview, Candy stood with George and Wardman.

"I must say, Constable, I fail to see how that was productive," Wardman commented stiffly. "Miss Cliff clearly craves drama and attention. I suggest redirecting efforts to more credible witnesses."

Candy lifted her chin. "With respect, sir, eliminating less fruitful avenues is also productive." She paused. "My instincts say we dig deeper, even if it means tolerating 'theatricality'."

George grinned at Candy's use of air quotes. "It also means we can speak with the caretaker and see what he said to Ashley on Friday night. If anything."

"Exactly, if anything," said Wardman. "Everything Miss Cliff says is a lie."

"Even so, we must look into it," said George.

Before Wardman could argue, jangling keys signalled the approach of Eugene Garforth climbing the staircase. He paused, seeing the detectives.

"Still badgering the poor students, I see," Garforth said irritably. "Has it not occurred to you they've simply run off for a tryst? Youths rebelling to spite their stodgy elders?"

George frowned at his dismissive tone. "Our duty is examining all possibilities thoroughly, Mr Garforth. Two lives hang in the balance."

Garforth waved a hand airily. "Highly dramatic assessment. They'll turn up once they've had their fun. Mark my words."

"Your lack of concern about students supposedly in your care is duly noted," Candy said bitingly.

Garforth scowled. "My dear, I agreed to rent accommodations, not play warden! Wardman handles the brats." He shot an impatient look at the head lecturer, who averted his eyes uncomfortably. "And I get paid." He paused before saying, "Though evidently not paid enough."

George's jaw tightened. "We deal with facts, Mr Garforth, not assumptions. Now, if you'll excuse us..."

George ushered Candy down the hall before she could retort, Wardman trailing behind. Garforth's apathetic attitude grated on George, but he'd keep his mouth shut. The two girls were more important than arguing, even if Garforth was a prick.

Candy shook her head angrily as they walked. "What an arsehole! Those girls are missing from his house and possibly in danger!"

"I know. But we must stay focused on facts, not emotions," George reminded her gently.

Candy took a deep breath. "You're right, of course, sir. My

feelings got the better of me. I apologise, sir." She squared her shoulders determinedly. "On to the next interview?"

George squeezed her shoulder. Candy's passion could be channelled productively if tempered by reason. With her insights and his experience, they would find the girls.

* * *

The heavy oak doors of Brandling House's library flew open as a powerfully built, grey-haired man stormed in, features etched with fury.

"What in blazes is going on here, Wardman?" he thundered. "Why haven't you found my daughter yet?"

DCI George Beaumont observed Head Lecturer Wayne Wardman visibly shrink before the imposing figure's onslaught. This must be Esme Bushfield's father.

"Mr Bushfield, please, let's discuss this calmly," Wardman implored, hands raised placatingly.

But Bushfield was not to be appeased. "Do not attempt appeasing me!" He advanced on Wardman, jabbing an accusatory finger into his chest. "You were entrusted with my girl's safety and well-being. Now Esme has inexplicably vanished on your watch!"

Wardman looked helplessly at George. Stepping forward, he interjected in a firm yet diplomatic tone, "Mr Bushfield, I'm Detective Chief Inspector Beaumont leading the investigation into Esme and Ashley's disappearance. Believe me, we are exploring every avenue to find answers."

Stanley transferred his smouldering glare to George. "Yes, well, forgive my doubt in your competency after two full days without progress. Esme would never stay out willingly this long!" His face contorted in anguish. "She's in danger; I just know it!"

George's expression softened with empathy. "You have every right to be distraught, Mr Bushfield. Rest assured, we are utilising substantial resources to locate Esme. But avoiding undue panic is sensible. OK?"

Bushfield seemed to wrestle internally before giving a terse nod. But tension still simmered beneath the surface. George tread delicately.

"Do you mind if we have a chat in private?" George asked. "Learning more about Esme could aid the search."

Still glowering, Bushfield allowed George to steer him to a quiet corner while Wardman slumped at his desk in relief. Constable Candy Nichols approached George discreetly as he left, her expression full of questions. He gave a subtle head shake—not now. Finding rapport took precedence.

Settling into a leather armchair, Bushfield seemed to deflate, anger giving way to profound weariness and worry. George adopted a compassionate yet authoritative tone.

"I understand your concern, given Esme's responsible nature. We will uncover why she acted out of character."

After a thirty-minute conversation, where George learnt all about Esme and the future her mother and father wanted for her, George decided it was time to speak to somebody else.

The father managed a stern nod, jaw twitching with emotion. After a heavy silence, he met George's eye. "Question those around her, especially the owner. Men like Eugene Garforth always have secrets..." He left the ominous implication hanging.

Making a mental note, George firmly clasped Bushfield's shoulder. "Every detail aids our progress. Stay strong for

CHAPTER EIGHT

Esme."

George felt cautiously hopeful parting ways with the distraught father. Securing Bushfield's cooperation was critical, regardless of his volatile moods. They were united by devotion to the missing girl, depending on their alliance.

Rejoining Candy, George noticed her keen interest. "You picked up on the reference to Garforth?"

"Quite intriguing," she confirmed. "Perhaps some history exists between these elite men?"

"My thoughts exactly, Candy." George stroked his beard thoughtfully. "Have Alexis discreetly look into any financial ties or bad blood." George thought about his father. "Powerful figures often guard strategic secrets."

Candy nodded, ponytail bobbing. "I'm on it, sir." She hurried off, steps energised by this promising new angle.

Alone again, George gazed out at the now-clearing sky. Stanley Bushfield's dramatic appearance felt like a storm passing, the air clearer somehow. One father's impassioned pleas resonated with George's own gut instincts—something sinister was afoot in this historic house of privilege and secrets. Too many things remained unsaid.

* * *

At Elland Road station, DC Jay Scott slid into a seat across from his colleague DC Tashan Blackburn in the bustling bullpen.

"Talk to me, Tash—where are we at with alibis for those released sex offenders in the vicinity?" Jay asked without preamble, leather folio open and ready.

Tashan straightened, folding his muscular arms across his broad chest. "DI Mason's team conducted thorough interviews. Three individuals lack solid confirmation of their whereabouts the night of the disappearance."

Jay's pen paused over his notebook. "Right, mate, lay it out for me. Who are they, and what's suspicious?"

Consulting his tablet, Tashan recited details methodically. "Timothy Rhodes served eight years for sexual assault of a minor before getting paroled last April. He claims he was home that night, but no witnesses confirm. Known for targeting vulnerable teens."

Jay's jaw tightened, but he remained professional. "OK, that's one. Next?"

"Deshawn Miller, multiple past charges of child enticement and abuse. Released two months ago, also lacks verifiable alibi that night."

Tapping his pen angrily, Jay muttered, "Too bad vermin like Miller keep slipping free to hunt more victims." He exhaled, getting his emotions under control. "Final one?"

Tashan glanced up, assessing Jay's tense expression before continuing. "Last is Derek Layfield. Did fifteen years for child trafficking. Alibi is just his drunk mate, hardly reliable."

Slapping his notebook closed decisively, Jay met Tashan's eyes. "Right then. We need all three hauled in promptly for intense questioning. The longer those rats roam free, the colder the trail gets."

Tashan nodded. "Agreed. DI Mason already issued summons demanding their appearance today or immediate arrest warrants. He's taking the lead on interrogations given his experience extracting the truth from slippery offenders."

Jay smiled grimly. "Too right. We'll have DI Mason ferret out any holes in their stories while you and I observe their reactions closely." He stood abruptly, too restless to keep sitting with his blood boiling, imagining the vulnerable girls at the mercy of such monsters.

Tashan studied him with concern. "How's your mum?" he asked gently.

Jay turned away, jaw twitching. "She has her good days and her bad days. Today is a good day."

"Good," said Tashan. And then he added, "Just remember we're in this together. Rely on us when things get heavy personally. That's what friends do."

Jay managed a tight smile, grateful for his friend's steadiness. With Tashan's calm logic balancing Jay's passionate nature, they made an effective team. He needed that brotherly support now during his mum's terminal cancer battle, though he struggled accepting vulnerability.

Shaking off gloomy thoughts, Jay checked his watch. "Let's grab DI Mason and get set up in the interview rooms. We've got three creeps to break before dusk."

Striding down the hallway beside Tashan, Jay mentally steeled himself.

Chapter Nine

Two hours later, Jay stepped out of the observation room, sickened after watching Derek Layfield smugly recount his twisted fantasies under DI Mason's masterful interrogation.

The man displayed no remorse, merely annoyance at the inconvenience of being hauled in. Though none of the three convicted offenders had cracked yet, their slimy delight reminiscing about past victims turned Jay's stomach.

Leaning against the concrete wall, Jay closed his eyes and forced his breathing to slow. He couldn't afford to be consumed by helpless rage, or darkness would win. Light still remained if he dared keep faith.

His vibrating mobile offered a welcome distraction. Glancing at the screen, Jay noted DCI George Beaumont was calling. He quickly collected himself and answered.

"DC Scott here, boss. Everything OK?"

George's commanding voice instantly focused Jay's thoughts. "Status on interviewing those recently released sex offenders?"

Jay quickly summarised the lack of alibis and hostile attitudes but no admissions yet.

"Hmmm, we'll have Mason keep at them. But stay vigilant for other angles, too." George hesitated, then said, "Focus

CHAPTER NINE

discreet inquiries on Wardman, the instructors, the caretaker, and Garforth. I sense uneasy secrets there. Can I count on you, Jay?"

Gratified by George's trust in him, Jay stood taller. "Absolutely, boss. I'm on it."

After finalising the details, Jay hung up feeling re-energised.

* * *

DC Jay Scott leaned back in his desk chair, lacing his fingers behind his head as he processed his latest directives from DCI George Beaumont regarding the missing girls' case.

Beaumont wanted Jay to take point discretely, looking into Head Lecturer Wayne Wardman's professional background and connections tied to Brandling House and also probing into the on-site teachers, staff, and instructors.

And especially significant—investigating shady rumours swirling around the estate's owner, Eugene Garforth. Jay sat up straighter, gears already turning. He lived for unravelling complex puzzles like Garforth's shadowy depths.

Grabbing a fresh notebook, Jay began jotting down preliminary notes and actions. First step, comprehensive records search on all three primary targets, cross-referencing for any shared ties or red flags. He'd dive deep into Wayne Wardman's company first, scrutinising financials and affiliations.

For the teachers and housing staff, especially the caretaker, Jay figured probing their digital lives would prove insightful. People got sloppy about security online, often revealing too much. He'd have their electronics seized for forensic extraction of messages and activity. Should uncover misconduct if present.

But Eugene Garforth posed the biggest question mark. The cagey aristocrat clearly had wealth and connections enabling secrecy. Simply searching his official records wouldn't cut it. This called for old-fashioned, boots-on-the-ground investigating.

Jay's mobile rang just as he started compiling a list of Garforth's known associates to interview. Seeing Beaumont's name, he answered promptly. "Now then, boss. I'm just getting started on those background investigations you requested."

"Good lad," Beaumont replied. "One other point on Garforth to aid your enquiries-" He lowered his voice conspiratorially. "I've heard whispered rumours among community members that he rather fancies young women as companions if you catch my drift."

Jay sat up straighter, pulse quickening. "Seriously? He's one of those, is he?"

"Nothing substantiated," Beaumont cautioned. "But where there's smoke..."

"There's likely fire smouldering," Jay finished grimly. "I'll make discreet inquiries, boss. Wealth like Garforth's lets certain appetites run wild, if you know what I mean."

"Precisely." Jay could envision Beaumont's sharp nod. "Get a sense of his networks and where he spends time off-estate. Could illuminate patterns."

"Consider it done, boss," Jay assured. They exchanged a few more details and then signed off.

Leaning back again, Jay tapped his pen thoughtfully against pursed lips. He needed to dissect this mosaic of clues to build a picture of Garforth's true persona. The stately estate owner projected charm and class. But Jay's instincts smelled

CHAPTER NINE

something rotten festering underneath.

Snapping his fingers, Jay sat forward and added local gyms to his list where Garforth might prowl for eye candy. Also, nightclubs and lounges. Places where pretty young things gathered and boundaries got blurry late at night.

Cracking Eugene Garforth's facade wide open could be the breakthrough they needed. Jay felt energised, sinking his teeth into a meaty challenge like this. The truth was in there somewhere. He just had to find the loose thread to unravel Garforth's web of lies.

Jay's computer chimed with an incoming message from Constable Alexis Mercer requesting assistance canvassing Garforth's social contacts. Grinning, Jay fired back an enthusiastic reply. He and Alexis made a killer team, her methodical diligence and people smarts perfectly complementing Jay's big-picture creativity. Together, they'd smoke out whatever skeletons Garforth had stashed away, no matter how deep the rich bastard had buried them.

Rubbing his hands together, Jay got to work compiling a database on Garforth's properties, known associates, family ties, and business interests. He wanted to map the man's whole sphere of influence before hitting the streets.

The clock ticked towards nightfall as Jay lost himself in the flow of research. He finally leaned back, rolling his stiff shoulders as his computer screen blurred. There was still more digging to do, but he had laid a damned solid foundation tonight. Garforth's house of cards would soon collapse.

Shutting his laptop, Jay stood and stretched. Time to meet Alexis at the first nightspot on their list. A small jazz lounge popular with older gentlemen and aspiring performers. The kind of discreet venue ideal for indulging certain proclivities.

Fetching his leather jacket, Jay felt energised for the hunt ahead. They might not find answers immediately, but he and Alexis would keep chipping away at Garforth's facade. Late nights and legwork didn't intimidate Jay—not when young lives depended on unearthing the truth.

* * *

Detective Chief Inspector George Beaumont strode into the library, his hawkish gaze sweeping the room. Outside, the relentless downpour continued unabated, representing another obstacle in the arduous search for missing teens Esme Bushfield and Ashley Cowgill.

But George refused to let challenges impede progress.

The sound of approaching footsteps drew his gaze as Constable Candy Nichols entered briskly, leather folio tucked under her arm. He gave her a weary nod.

"Any developments I should know before we speak with the Medley lad?" he asked.

Candy shook her head, ponytail swishing. "Afraid not yet, sir. Forensics is still processing fibres and boot imprints found near the dormitory wing exterior. And Technical is working round the clock to crack encryption on the girls' mobile data and social media."

George grimaced, scrubbing a hand down his face. "We're losing precious time waiting for those results when the parents are ready to storm the bloody place."

Squaring his shoulders, George met Candy's eye with renewed conviction. "Right then, let's have a chat with young Master Medley and see what secrets we can reveal."

Candy gave him an encouraging smile, falling smoothly into

step behind him as they navigated the labyrinthine corridors. But George sensed the underlying strain in her taut posture. This case taxed them all.

Pausing outside the blue parlour where Gregory awaited, George hesitated, wheels turning rapidly. Perhaps a hard-facts approach wasn't prudent with an adolescent. Building rapport could prove more productive.

He turned to Candy. "I'll take the lead with Medley, given the family dynamics at play. Focus on observing his mannerisms and flagging anything questionable."

Candy nodded obediently, but George glimpsed a shadow of disappointment flit across her youthful features at being relegated to backup again. His expression softened.

George entered the parlour where a lanky blond youth slouched in an armchair, picking at his cuticles. Gregory glanced up sullenly as they approached.

"Let's just get this over with," he grumbled.

George settled on the antique sofa across from the boy and adopted a casual tone. "I appreciate you speaking with us, Gregory. We're just trying to understand your schoolmates' mindsets before they disappeared that night."

"Don't really know them," Gregory muttered with a shrug.

George leaned forward. "Still, you may have picked up on things from a peer's perspective that we adults overlook. Any observations at all could help us locate Esme and Ashley."

Gregory grimaced, looking distinctly uncomfortable. George glanced at Candy, who gave an almost imperceptible nod signalling the boy's evasive body language.

"We know adolescents have secrets," George continued gently. "I used to be one, believe it or not." The DCI grinned. "But this is the time to share anything you know to aid our efforts without fear of consequences. I promise."

Gregory shifted, glancing between them warily. George held his breath, sensing the boy wrestling with indecision. Finally, he sighed, shoulders slumping.

"Look, Ashley seemed pretty on edge at the weekend," he admitted sullenly. "We were... friendly a while back before it ended. She was always intense and dramatic, but this felt darker. Reckless. Like she wanted to just burn it all down, you know?"

Gregory fidgeted with his watch and avoided their eyes. George remained motionless, letting the silence compel Gregory onward.

"Anyway, the other night, she came by my room after everyone was asleep," Gregory continued haltingly. "Said she was finally getting out of this hellhole for good. Her words, not mine."

He flushed. "I figured it was just Ash being dramatic again. Said she'd message me from wherever she ended up." He met George's intent gaze pleadingly. "I swear I didn't think she'd actually run off into the night or I'd have warned someone!"

George kept his expression neutral, processing this new information. "Did she mention anything else? Any plans or someone picking her up?"

Gregory shook his head jerkily. "No. Just ranted about being done with the prison that was life and all the pathetic sheep. Didn't even say goodbye before storming out." He looked down, picking at a fraying hole in his trousers.

George studied the boy's hunched posture, seeing shame mingled with grief now the shock had worn off. Ashley's scornful bravado hid deep wounds Gregory clearly understood too well.

CHAPTER NINE

After gently prodding the sullen teen for any other relevant details, George wrapped up the interview, shaken by the revelations. That burst of fiery defiance was likely Ashley Cowgill's final cry before disappearing into the night's perilous unknown. Would it prove a permanent farewell? The thought spurred him on with blazing urgency.

Out in the wood-panelled hallway, Candy turned to George, eyes bright with conviction. "This confirms premeditation. Ashley meant to run away that very night and took Esme with her. But to where?"

George gripped her shoulder tightly. "I'm not sure, but I promise you I'll find out."

* * *

Before heading home for the night, George decided to emphasise the urgency of a search of the staff's rooms to Head Lecturer Wardman, hoping it would encourage full cooperation in facilitating access. But approaching Wardman's office, he overheard the head lecturer arguing with a tall, imposing figure George recognised as the reclusive estate owner, Eugene Garforth.

"For the last time, the family quarters are off-limits!" Garforth was bellowing. "I'll not have your lot tromping about invading my privacy!"

Wardman attempted to placate the furious man. "Mr Garforth, please lower your voice. The detective is only trying to be thorough…"

Garforth jabbed an accusatory finger into Wardman's chest. "Don't indulge him! I agreed to a search of the public areas, not personal rooms!"

Sensing the situation escalating, George stepped forward authoritatively. "Mr Garforth, might I have a quick word?"

Garforth whirled angrily. "Come to strong-arm me, Detective? I know my rights!"

George kept his tone even and reasonable. "I understand your reluctance, but excluding any areas could undermine the investigation and extend this undesirable process."

Garforth's eyes flashed dangerously. "Don't try swaying me with manipulative arguments! I won't have strangers digging through my private affairs!"

George crossed his arms. "I see. Are there specific reasons for your opposition, Mr Garforth? Anything you wish to avoid us uncovering, perhaps?"

Garforth advanced until they were nearly nose-to-nose, his impressive height bearing down on George's sturdy frame. But George didn't flinch from the intimidation tactic.

Garforth jabbed a finger at George's chest. "Now you listen here! I'm a respectable gentleman of means. Don't you dare insinuate otherwise with your paranoid inferences!"

Sensing Garforth's volatility, George switched tack, adopting a more conciliatory tone. "I'm sorry if I offended you. I'm simply attempting to be thorough, for the girls' sake. But I understand your position."

Garforth continued glaring suspiciously, but George stood calmly, unfazed. After a tense beat, Garforth huffed. "Yes, well...I'm sure you meant no real harm." He adjusted his collar, regaining some composure.

George gave a polite smile that didn't reach his eyes. "I assure you I did not, Mr Garforth. Every clue could be critical."

With a final terse nod, Garforth strode off. George watched him thoughtfully before turning to Wardman. "Your cooperation in providing access would be greatly appreciated."

Wardman swallowed. "Of course, Detective. I'll speak with Mr Garforth again. Discretion is our highest priority."

Chapter Ten

DCI George Beaumont stood pensively beneath the elaborate stone archway leading into Brandling House's cavernous library. His sharp gaze swept over the distraught parents, tense students, and watchful officers gathered uneasily amidst the rows of leather-bound books and carved mahogany furnishings.

George noted the strained atmosphere enveloping the ornate room like an invisible fog. Parents huddled in tense knots, tear-streaked faces etched with fear and rising anger after another fruitless night lacking answers. Across the room, students spoke in hushed murmurs, darting glances around nervously as if suspects themselves.

His scrutiny paused on waifish blonde student Pamela Cliff standing slightly apart from her peers, pale eyes fixed intently across the room. Following her gaze, George spotted cocky Ishaan Sadiq casually draped in an armchair entertaining his friends with some lively tale, seemingly oblivious to the surrounding anguish.

George's eyes narrowed thoughtfully, reading clues in body language and rapport. While other students projected wariness towards the imposing figure of DCS Sadiq's son, timid Pamela watched Ishaan's antics with undisguised yearn-

CHAPTER TEN

ing. Smitten, despite his arrogant nature, or envious of the attention he commanded? George filed away the observation for later consideration. The social hierarchies at play among these elite youths likely shaped perspectives and motives around Esme and Ashley's disappearance.

His scrutiny was passed on to Head Lecturer Wayne Wardman, who attempted to field anxious parental questions while maintaining a professional facade of control. But his jaw muscle occasionally ticked in visible agitation as he repeated vague assurances and deflected more pointed inquiries.

Eugene Garforth was nowhere to be found.

A tap on George's shoulder made him turn. Gregory Medley. "I've been thinking, Detective, and there's something I need to tell you about. Something I didn't tell you earlier."

* * *

DCI Beaumont stared intently at Gregory Medley's nervous figure. As much as he wanted to believe this was just another case of reckless teen experimentation gone wrong, his instincts sensed ominous undercurrents swirling beneath the surface, slowly dragging Esme and Ashley into perilous depths.

"You're absolutely certain Esme was involved in this illicit activity?" Beaumont asked, a deep furrow between his brows.

Gregory squirmed under the detective's piercing gaze. "Yeah, I mean, I saw her myself that night, out on the grounds getting high with Ashley."

"But that seems out of character for an educated girl like Esme. Help me understand what happened," Beaumont prodded gently.

Sighing, Gregory leaned back into the antique armchair,

clearly reluctant to elaborate. But Beaumont waited patiently, allowing the heavy silence to work its magic.

Finally, the boy capitulated. "Fine. It was late Monday night, around 10 pm. I was headed to the kitchen for a snack when I saw them through the window, over by the gazebo. At first, I thought they were just chatting. But then Ashley lit up a joint and passed it to Esme."

Gregory shook his head. "I was shocked. I always pegged Esme as a total teacher's pet. But she barely even coughed after taking a long drag. They were giggling about something, and then Ashley pulled a little plastic bag out of her pocket."

"You're certain the bag contained cannabis products?" Candy interjected.

"Looked like it to me. She popped a few gummy candies in her mouth and gave some to Esme, too. Didn't seem like Esme's first time either, the way she tossed them back." Gregory flushed.

"Did they mention where the drugs came from?" Beaumont asked.

Gregory hesitated before mumbling, "Sounded like maybe Ishaan scored them stuff. Heard Ashley say his name at one point."

Beaumont and Candy exchanged a loaded glance. The cocky lad was looking more suspicious by the minute.

"Why didn't you inform someone immediately about this, Gregory?" George questioned intently.

Gregory squirmed again. "I dunno, it's not like teachers actually care what we get up to. They just punish anyone who talks." He looked down, picking at a loose thread on his trousers. "I figured Ashley was always messed up these days anyway, and it was none of my business."

CHAPTER TEN

George studied the boy's hunched posture. He recognised shame and grief now that the shock had faded. Ashley's scornful bravado clearly masked deep wounds this boy understood all too well.

"Did you witness anyone else around them that night?" Candy gently prompted.

Gregory thought for a moment. "Now that I think about it, Noah Wilman was nearby on a balcony. Couldn't see if he was also smoking, but I know those three have smoked together before."

Candy made a quick note.

George leaned forward intently. "Gregory, I understand your reluctance, but holding anything back could severely undermine the investigation. Is there anything else relevant you can recall from that night?"

The boy hesitated, leg bouncing nervously. Finally, he sighed. "It's probably nothing... But at one point, I heard Ashley telling Esme she wanted to show her somewhere in Middleton Woods. Said they could hang out there, and no one would find them."

Candy's pen scratched rapidly across her notepad.

"Where?" asked DCI Beaumont.

Gregory shrugged. "Ask Noah."

George continued probing gently for a few more minutes. But Gregory claimed that was everything he knew. After wrapping up the interview, Beaumont stood in the hallway with Candy, mulling it all over.

"This sheds new light on the girls' state of mind and activities leading up to vanishing," Candy said, fidgeting with her pen. "But also expands our suspect pool. Perhaps a dealer got confrontational if they owed money?"

DCI Beaumont nodded grimly, arms crossed. "We'll need to investigate these other teenagers linked to drug use on-site—Noah Wilman and Ishaan Sadiq especially."

He shook his head in dismay. "And inform the parents. They deserve honesty, even if painful. No more assumptions Esme was simply a studious victim."

Candy nodded. "Of course, sir." But he could tell she dreaded that conversation as much as he did.

* * *

DCI George Beaumont stood outside the imposing oak door of Pamela Cliff's room, steeling himself before entering the private space of one of the missing girls' peers. He had obtained the proper permissions from Wayne Wardman to conduct full room searches after emphasising their necessity in locating Esme and Ashley. Still, crossing this threshold to sift through a young girl's belongings felt daunting.

Taking a deep breath, George turned the ornate iron handle and pushed inside. His sharp gaze swept the feminine space. Pale pink bed linens and printed throw pillows contrasted the heavy antique furnishings of Brandling House.

George moved farther into the room, alert for anything amiss. His eyes landed on the ornate oak wardrobe; doors left gaping open to reveal school uniforms and casual attire—modest dresses, cardigans, nothing provocative.

He scanned the cluttered desk, noting a closed laptop and notebooks with looping handwriting. George opened drawers, finding pens, trinkets, sweet wrappers—mundane items. As he shifted aside papers, his gloved hand brushed something solid buried beneath a jumper. Heart quickening, the detective carefully unveiled a mobile phone concealed amongst the clutter.

Why hide a mobile? George bagged the mobile as potential evidence and made notes on its concealed location. This could prove a promising lead if the tech team could access its messages and activity. Clearly, timid Pamela had secrets to protect.

A soft creak outside the room made George pause, senses prickling. But only silence followed. Shaking off unease; he continued documenting his search results thoroughly, ensuring chain of custody for anything removed.

Suddenly, a loud thump echoed from the hallway, followed by muffled giggling. George spun, adrenaline spiking until he realised it was just students messing about. With a rueful sigh, he turned back to his task. Still, something about this ancient house set his nerves on edge.

Finishing up, George stepped into the hallway, feeling watched. His eyes traced the dark oak wainscoting and arched ceilings, imagining generations of elite inhabitants passing through these ornate halls, their whispered secrets soaked into ancient walls along with the elaborate carvings.

A draft ruffled George's hair, carrying a faint dripping noise. Condensation, likely, but it unsettled him. Turning down the corridor, flickering sconces cast dancing shadows, conjuring spectral movements at the edge of vision. George shivered.

The atmosphere evoked reading Harry Potter as a teen, imagining concealed dangers lurking in secret chambers and petrifying-monsters. But here, no clever wand work would defend against hidden threats: only dogged professionalism and sharp instincts.

An icy trickle of foreboding slithered down George's neck.

Were less fanciful monsters stalking these halls, cloaked in respectable facades? He quickened his pace as eerie whispers seemed to echo all around.

Shaking off irrational dread, George headed towards Gregory Medley's room next.

Turning the handle, George stepped inside the rumpled room. Posters of musicians and footballers covered the walls in chaotic collages. Textbooks spilt haphazardly across the unmade bed, which was strewn with crisp packets and trainers.

Moving farther in, George noted the cluttered wooden desk. Amidst pens, sweets wrappers, and crumpled energy drink cans, a laptop sat open, displaying a paused football video.

Rifling through the drawers, George found magazines featuring scantily clad women tucked between school notes. His brow furrowed. It seemed even quiet Gregory was not immune to peer pressure and pubescent curiosity. But did it extend beyond fantasies?

George searched carefully through stacks of video games and sports gear, uncovering nothing suspicious. He shifted a pile of dirty laundry, nose wrinkling at the musty aromas. Teenage boys evidently had much to learn about hygiene.

Straightening, George surveyed the room thoughtfully. Gregory seemed a typical teenage lad overall, if messier than average. Nothing so far suggested direct involvement in the girls' disappearance. No signs of any drugs, either. But the careless clutter provided fertile ground for overlooked clues.

He shone a torch beam over the rumpled duvet and underneath the bed frame, seeking any small details the careless teen may have missed. Balling socks, forgotten crisps, and dust bunnies abounded, but nothing remarkable.

CHAPTER TEN

George paused, peering closer at the far wall. Were those tiny scrapes in the ornate wood panelling? Kneeling awkwardly, he examined the marks, heart quickening.

"Bring the camera over here, will you, Candy?" George requested. As she complied, he indicated the scratches, which appeared consistent with prying something up from the floor. Candy diligently photographed the marks from all angles.

George's fingers traced the grooves thoughtfully. "Reckon something was regularly moved aside here, likely this loose floorboard." He nodded at a warped plank beneath the scratches. "Help me lift this, will you?"

Together, they carefully pried up the board, revealing a dusty cavity. George's pulse leapt when he spied what appeared to be small plastic bags and packets concealed inside.

"Bingo," Candy murmured. Pulling on gloves, George retrieved several small bags containing dried leaves and white pills. His expression darkened as implications sank in.

Candy turned the items over carefully as George shone the torch beam. "Cannabis, by the looks of it. And quite a lot..." She met George's gaze grimly.

"So timid Gregory was dealing, it seems," George surmised, jaw tight. This changed the game substantially. Gregory could be directly entangled with Ashley and Esme's disappearance if drugs connected the dots.

George instructed Candy to get the contraband logged and rushed to forensics immediately. Then he stood swiftly, joints protesting the awkward position as urgency coursed through him.

They needed to bring Gregory back in straight away. Hopefully, the threat of charges would finally compel complete honesty regarding his drug connections with the missing girls.

George mentally tallied follow-up actions needed, energised by this break in the case.

With a last cursory sweep of the room, George headed out with Candy on his heels. "Good eye spotting those scratches, sir," she praised as they marched downstairs. "We might not have looked twice otherwise in all that clutter."

George nodded, gratified. His meticulousness had unveiled a pivotal development. "Let's keep sharp. I want Gregory and his parents confronted with these findings before he has a chance to destroy other contraband or," he said, thinking of Ishaan, "align alibis with any partners in crime."

* * *

After, George descended to the library, where Wardman awaited an update. George maintained neutrality, relaying the mobile phone discovery and planned tech analysis. But internally, questions swirled. What was timid Pamela hiding? And what other darkness festered inside these walls?

Wardman fidgeted upon hearing of the phone but merely advised total discretion, clearly uneasy at scrutiny extended towards his students. George made non-committal sounds but stood firm on pursuing all leads thoroughly, in a professional manner, belying mounting unease.

He didn't share what they'd found in Gregory's room. Instead, George decided to make himself busy whilst waiting for Gregory's parents to be placed somewhere private so they could be there when George interviewed their son.

Excusing himself briskly, George headed down a passage towards the deserted wing housing staff quarters. The utilitarian decor contrasted the opulent finery of the main house.

CHAPTER TEN

In the spartan bedroom assigned to the live-in caretaker, George's searching gaze inventoried worn clothing and dog-eared paperbacks stacked haphazardly. He riffled through crumpled crisp packets and betting slips littering the rickety night stand.

Kneeling stiffly, George shone his torch beneath the creaking bed, illuminating dust bunnies and a battered magazine featuring scantily clad women. His lip curled in distaste. Clearly, the caretaker possessed baser appetites despite Wardman's assurances of his reliability. George bagged the magazine as potential evidence of fixation on young women.

His mobile rang, jolting George from his contemplation. Constable Nichols summarised forensics' initial findings, but no major breakthroughs yet on physical evidence from the rooms. George acknowledged the update grimly. He had hoped for revelations by now after upending these private spaces. But their secrets lingered just out of reach, shrouded in ancient shadows.

Straightening slowly, George surveyed the barren room; jaw set stubbornly. The truth was out there somewhere. And he would not rest until all was brought to light.

Chapter Eleven

DCI George Beaumont sat in the stately dining hall of Brandling House awaiting Gregory Medley's arrival, DC Candy Nichols beside him. The damning contraband they had discovered in Gregory's dorm room was now undergoing urgent forensic analysis. Once they had solid evidence, confronting the deceitful boy with his deeds was crucial. Hopefully, the seriousness of potential charges would finally compel complete honesty from timid Gregory regarding his connections to the missing girls and any drug suppliers.

The heavy door opened, and Head Lecturer Wayne Wardman entered briskly, followed by a nervous-looking Gregory and his parents. Mr and Mrs Medley's tense expressions upon seeing the detective and constable did not bode well for cooperation. But George squared his shoulders, undeterred. Too much was at stake to tiptoe around the truth any longer.

"Mr and Mrs Medley, please have a seat. We need to discuss some concerns around your son's activities here," George began gravely. The couple exchanged an uneasy glance but sat silently beside Gregory at the long table.

George slid the evidence photograph of the drugs across to Gregory. "Would you care to explain this contraband we found concealed in your room earlier today, Gregory?"

The boy went deathly pale, staring at the image. But after a quick sideways look at his stone-faced parents, he set his jaw mutinously.

"What's contraband?" asked Gregory, which resulted in a smack across the back of his head from his father.

"Drugs, you stupid boy!"

"I have no idea what any of that stuff is or how it got there," Gregory claimed sullenly.

George leaned forward, gaze intense. "Let's not play games here, Gregory. The drugs were hidden beneath your floorboard. So, either you stashed them there, or you're covering for someone else who did. Which is it?"

Gregory slumped down, avoiding George's eyes. "I already told you everything I know. Those aren't mine."

Mr Medley spoke up sharply. "Now you listen here, Detective Chief Inspector. You've no proof those... those items belong to my son." He grasped Gregory's shoulder almost painfully. "He says they're not his, and I believe him. So unless you can prove otherwise..."

George kept his expression neutral. "The contraband is undergoing forensic analysis as we speak. Fingerprints and DNA don't lie." He let that hang pointedly.

Gregory squirmed under the heavy silence. George leaned forward. "Now is your chance to get ahead of this. Tell us the truth about where the drugs came from, who supplied them, and whether this is linked to Esme and Ashley's disappearance."

Looking cornered, Gregory turned beseeching eyes on his mother, who sat tensely wringing her hands.

"Please, darling, just tell the detectives what you know," Mrs Medley implored gently. "We only want to help you."

Lip quivering, Gregory seemed about to speak but then shook his head vehemently. "You won't believe me anyway! You've already decided I'm guilty." He glared around at the adults defiantly.

George kept his tone calm and reasonable. "I'm simply following the evidence, Gregory. If you're being truthful that the drugs were planted, tell me who you believe is actually responsible."

The boy hesitated, a war of emotions playing across his face. Finally, he burst out angrily, "It was Ishaan and Noah! They're always bragging about scoring drugs and trying to seem cooler than me." He shrugged. "They've been in and out of my room all weekend." He looked between his parents pleadingly. "I'll bet anything they hid it there to get me in trouble as payback for... something. When I went to the toilet, etc. Plenty of time to hide them. But you have to believe me – I don't do drugs!"

Mr Medley seemed swayed by this passionate denial, but George remained outwardly sceptical. "That's quite an accusation. Do you have any proof those other boys planted evidence? Any past conflicts that could motivate such actions?" He wondered what the Detective Chief Superintendent would say about the accusations.

Looking offended, Gregory drew breath for another denial but was interrupted by Candy interjecting gently, "We understand why you're scared. But this is your chance to tell us everything relevant so that we can help you." She shot his parents an appealing look. "That's all any of us want – to understand the full truth."

The boy looked between the adults' intent faces and seemed to deflate, anger melting into shame and fear. "I... I don't have proof. But Ishaan is always causing trouble and trying to drag me into things," he confessed unhappily.

George nodded, keeping any reaction muted for now. He made eye contact with Candy, signalling time to turn the screw.

She flipped open her folio. "In the meantime, we'll need your fingerprints and DNA sample for comparison once forensic results are in. Standard procedure."

At this, Gregory blanched, looking younger than his seventeen years. Before he could protest, George stood swiftly.

"This way, please, Gregory. The sooner we eliminate you as a suspect, the sooner we can move forward." He kept his tone kind but firm. Gregory had one last chance to come clean before evidence boxed him in.

The Medleys followed George and Candy to a small room down the hall where a Tyvek-cladded Scene of Crime Officer awaited to process Gregory. Young Medley baulked at the sterile swabbing and printing tools, but his father kept a firm hand on his shoulder, resignation on his weary face.

Watching Gregory's frightened eyes as his fingerprints were inked, George leaned down gently. "Last chance to get ahead of this. Speak now, or the evidence will do the talking for you."

But Gregory just shook his head frantically, lips sealed. With a regretful sigh, George straightened and nodded at the waiting officer to proceed with documenting the sullen teenager's biometrics. He hoped for Gregory's sake the test results exonerated the boy, but his gut said this ran deeper than schoolboy spats.

After ushering the Medleys out, George turned to Candy in the hall. "Have the drug samples rush analysed. We need those results ASAP."

Candy nodded, already contacting the forensic lab. As much

as George preferred patient legwork, this case demanded quick resolution with young lives at stake. Sometimes, justice required calculated risks.

* * *

After leaving Gregory with Candy, George spotted Head Lecturer Wayne Wardman speaking in hushed tones with the caretaker. George slowed his pace, picking up on the tail end of their conversation.

"...told you, the pipes in the old wing cause those dripping noises, nothing sinister." Wardman clasped the caretaker's shoulder reassuringly. "I know the ghost stories can prey on the imagination."

George's ears pricked up. "Sorry to interrupt. What ghost stories are those?"

Wardman flushed. "Oh, just idle ramblings to spook the students, Detective. I'm sure a practical man like yourself pays them no mind."

"I don't dismiss things lightly when investigating a disappearance," George said carefully. "What have you heard?"

The caretaker spoke up nervously. "Some say they've heard whispering echoes in the deserted east wing attics. And cold spots or odd shadows if you're up there at night." He shivered. "Gives me the chills just thinking about it!"

Wardman gave an indulgent smile. "Yes, well, adolescent imagination coupled with draughty old infrastructure can conjure all sorts of illusions."

George cleared his throat pointedly. "Even so, insight into local legends and folklore often provides clues. Please, tell me more."

CHAPTER ELEVEN

Sighing, Wardman gestured for George to follow him into the library. Settling into a leather armchair, the head lecturer explained the lore around Brandling House's ghosts.

"There are two common tales passed down," Wardman began. "One claims a jilted 18th century bride named Eliza still stalks these halls mourning her lost love, occasionally heard weeping or whispering names. Hence the whispering some students report hearing."

George nodded thoughtfully. "And the other spirit?"

"Ah yes, a more ominous figure known as the Caretaker," Wardman said. "Legend claims a former caretaker went mad here a century ago and lured young maids to their deaths before hanging himself. His evil spirit purportedly stalks the attics still."

Wardman gave a delicate shudder before continuing. "Some believe ill fortune befalls any who hear his ghostly whispers. Which explains the caretaker's unease just now."

George frowned. The dripping noises and odd whispers he'd experienced certainly aligned with the caretaker legend. A chilling coincidence, perhaps, but George knew better than to dismiss such things during an investigation.

"Thank you for the insightful background," he told Wardman sincerely. "I'll factor the local lore into our ongoing inquiry."

Wardman looked mildly discomforted by this but simply nodded. "My priority remains cooperating fully to aid your efforts, however unorthodox," he said diplomatically.

George stood. "Speaking of which, I'll need to begin searching the boys' rooms upstairs without further delay. Starting with rooms on the top floor."

Wardman's eyebrows shot up. "All the rooms? Is that

entirely necessary?"

"I'm afraid so," George said firmly. "The contraband found in Gregory's room means no student can be above suspicion now."

Seeing Wardman's continued reluctance, George crossed his arms. "Mr Wardman, two girls are missing. Fears of reputation must not impede this investigation. You do want them found, don't you?"

Wardman looked affronted. "Of course! Very well, do what you must upstairs." He sighed. "I suppose parents should be informed of the room searches as well?"

"Indeed. Full transparency is key."

Wardman grimaced but led George upstairs without further objection. As the head lecturer informed the students about impending room searches, George noted the ripple of unease passing through the ornate dormitories. These elite youths were unaccustomed to such invasions of privacy.

Wardman collected search permissions from anxious parents, placating them with assurances of discretion. But Stanley Bushfield refused to coddle sensitivities.

"Spare nothing in your search!" he demanded, face ruddy. "Whatever embarrassment might occur pales next to finding Esme. Leave no mattress unturned if need be!"

Wardman paled but didn't argue. George felt cautiously hopeful having an ally unafraid to ruffle feathers. The truth mattered more than decorum with lives at stake.

With paperwork and permissions handled, George prepared to commence searching the male students' dorms, starting with the third-floor rooms. Positioning his team there made strategic sense. The upper rooms provided alternative access points for illicit activities, be it sneaking out or allowing

CHAPTER ELEVEN

dishonest persons entry.

If someone aided the girls' disappearance, areas lacking oversight deserved scrutiny first. And based on Gregory Medley's accusations, George felt particular suspicion around cocky Ishaan Sadiq's third-floor room. The arrogant little shit hardly seemed above framing another student to protect himself.

Shaking off grim speculation, George focused on the task at hand—meticulously searching the upper rooms for any clues illuminating motive or opportunity. The burdensome responsibility of two young lives relied solely on him maintaining steely professionalism and seeing the truth hidden in the darkness.

* * *

DCI George Beaumont stood in the elegant hallway outside Noah Wilman's room, steeling himself before crossing the threshold to search the space. Out of all the male students, Noah's potential connection to the missing girls felt most promising and ominous.

Gregory Medley's revelations hinted at Noah's involvement in smoking cannabis with Ashley and Esme shortly before their disappearance. And the boy's sullen disposition and friendship with troubled Ashley suggested a brooding figure easily swayed towards riskier behaviours.

Making the decision to prioritise scrutinising Noah felt prudent. If illicit drugs tied into the girls' fateful choices that night, Noah likely held pieces to the puzzle. George only hoped tangible evidence waited to be uncovered within the boy's inner sanctum.

Nodding at the officer accompanying him, George turned the ornate handle and entered Noah Wilman's dorm room. His piercing gaze swept over rumpled bedsheets and askew piles of clothes and sports equipment. Textbooks lay strewn atop a desk littered with food wrappers and headphones—typical teen disarray.

Meticulously, George searched each area, alert for any notable items. He shifted aside sweatshirts and video games, finding nothing remarkable. Kneeling stiffly, he shone a torch beneath the sagging bed frame. More cast-off junk food and a notable odour, but no hidden contraband leapt out.

Straightening with a sigh, George moved to examine the desk. Shuffling textbooks and notepads revealed nothing suspicious. He sat in the swivel chair, gloved hands hovering over the closed laptop, unsure if he had clearance to access its contents.

That's when a zippered leather case tucked behind the chair caught George's eye. Heart quickening, he retrieved the case and carefully unzipped it. Nestled inside were several small plastic bags filled with dried plant matter—cannabis, without a doubt.

"Bag these," George instructed the accompanying officer grimly. This could confirm Noah likely supplied the drugs to Ashley and maybe Esme, too. A critical lead, but circumstantial without proof, he was with the girls that fateful night.

Continuing his meticulous sweep, George eyed the rumpled bedding again thoughtfully. He knelt and gingerly lifted the thin mattress. And there it was—a freshly rolled joint resting atop the box spring. Heart racing, George quickly bagged the crucial evidence. This spliff placed Noah not only in recent proximity of cannabis but actively consuming it in this very room.

He locked eyes with the gaping officer. "Have this rush analysed for..." George trailed off as loud voices echoed from the hallway outside.

A moment later, the door flung open, and an imposing couple in business attire swept in, features etched with fury. The insignia on the man's bespoke suit marked him as high-powered. Noah Wilman's parents, without a doubt.

The man fixed George with an imperious glare. "Just what do you think you're doing ransacking my son's room?"

George straightened calmly. "Mr and Mrs Wilman, I presume. I'm Detective Chief Inspector Beaumont, heading the investigation into two students' troubling disappearance from these premises." He gestured at the evidence bags. "During our search, these illegal substances were uncovered in plain sight."

Mrs Wilman gasped sharply. But her husband continued glaring. "On whose authority? I was not informed of any search, Detective." He practically spat George's title. "I'll be speaking to my legal counsel about this outrageous invasion of privacy."

"The appropriate permissions were obtained, I assure you," George replied evenly, refusing to be intimated. "However, consulting your solicitor is certainly your right."

He stepped forward intently. "Right now, our priority must be locating Esme and Ashley. Any information Noah can provide is crucial, especially relating to any drug-related activities or associates."

At the mention of drugs, Mrs Wilman turned ghostly pale. But Mr Wilman bristled, stepping between George and his wife. "You have no grounds to harass my son with baseless accusations, Detective. And we will not speak with you again without legal representation."

With that, he grasped his wife's elbow and steered her forcibly from the room. George watched them go, lips pressed into a grim line. He'd hoped Noah's parents would press the boy to cooperate fully. But blind loyalty bred obstruction.

Turning back to the remaining officer, George requested Noah's laptop and mobile be seized for urgent analysis—any communication regarding drugs or plans that night could prove invaluable.

Chapter Twelve

Noah Wilman sat hunched in the leather library chair, shame-facedly avoiding his parents' stunned expressions as he confessed to dealing drugs at Brandling House.

DCI George Beaumont kept his tone gentle but firm. "I know this is difficult, but we need the full truth regarding the missing girls. Did Ashley or Esme purchase cannabis from you that night?"

Noah shook his head jerkily. "No, I never sold to them. I only ever used weed for myself... it helps me relax and study." He glanced at his parents timidly. "With all the pressure to get top marks to get into a top university, sometimes I just needed an escape, you know?"

Mrs Wilman pressed a hand to her mouth, eyes glistening, while her husband's face reddened with anger.

Seeing Noah's discomfort, George probed delicately, "When did you start using cannabis, and what drew you to it?" Giving space for Noah's perspective could reveal deeper pressures influencing his risky choices.

Noah's shoulders hunched further. "I guess... last spring when I was studying. Everyone talked about weed helping you focus and de-stress. Sounded loads better than taking the sleep meds and antidepressants the doctor gave me." He hesitated before adding softly, "It made me feel more normal to fit in for once."

His parents exchanged an uneasy look at this candour.

"At first, it was just on weekends, recreational," Noah continued haltingly. "But then I brought some back here because classes and exams this term are brutal. The high took the pressure off and helped me power through long study sessions." He flushed, avoiding the detectives' eyes. "Never dreamed I'd get in so deep selling it to mates too. I'm sorry."

George nodded thoughtfully, seeing beyond the sullen teen to the overlooked vulnerability within. "Thank you for explaining, Noah. It's clear you were self-medicating undue burdens. But together, we can get you proper help moving forward." He then eyed Noah intently. "Now then, I need the full truth regarding the drugs found hidden in Gregory Medley's room. Did you plant them there to frame him?"

Noah shifted in his chair, glancing nervously at his stone-faced parents before responding. "No. I mean, Greg's my mate. I wouldn't stitch him up like that."

George leaned forward, gaze piercing. "Yet Gregory insists you and Ishaan Sadiq conspired to hide drugs in his room as payback for some conflict. Care to explain?"

Looking cornered, Noah shook his head vehemently. "That's not what happened! OK, maybe I complained to Ishaan about Greg being short on cash he owed me. But we didn't actually plant anything, I swear."

Seeing George's scepticism, he insisted desperately, "You have to believe me! Ishaan joked about hiding drugs just to scare Greg into paying up quicker, but I told him to leave it alone. I never wanted Greg to get in real trouble."

Noah turned pleadingly to his parents. "Tell the detective

I'm telling the truth. Ishaan's the shifty one you should be questioning, not me!"

Mr and Mrs Wilman exchanged an uneasy glance, seeming swayed by their son's impassioned denial despite the evidence against him.

Watching Noah intently, George remained outwardly non-committal. But internally, he questioned the boy's honesty. Given the cannabis stash and drug-related communications found in Noah's possession, this felt like another layer of deception to obscure his central role. George would keep digging for the truth, however deep the troubled boy had buried it.

"Thank you, Noah."

"I'm really sorry, Detective." Noah offered a faint, grateful smile. "Truly."

But his father slapped a hand on the table sharply. "Enough apologising! George, you can see my son simply made a foolish mistake. This nonsense ends now." He glared meaningfully. "Surely we can come to an understanding as reasonable men."

With the way Mr Wilman had just addressed George, the DCI desperately wanted to correct the man. But instead, he said nothing, inviting somebody else to speak.

Mrs Wilman grasped her husband's arm pleadingly. "Darling, let's just take Noah home. He knows now drugs were not the answer." Her tone turned beseeching as she faced George. "We'll get him counselling straight away. But please, don't let this ruin his future prospects over some youthful poor judgment."

George's expression remained resolutely impartial. "With respect, the law does not allow me to simply overlook confessed distribution of narcotics, regardless of circumstances." He kept his voice firm but not unkind. "Actions have consequences."

Mr Wilman surged to his feet, face thunderous. "Now you listen here! I'll ruin you if you dare charge my son over some misguided rebellion! I have powerful connections." He jabbed a finger at George's chest. "You'll regret this, I swear it."

George calmly stood his ground. "Are you threatening an officer of the law conducting an investigation, Mr Wilman?" His steely tone left no room for bluster.

The older man glared venomously. "Mark my words, if you pursue this, I'll make certain Detective Chief Superintendent Sadiq's arrogant son sees consequences for his disgusting misconduct with those girls!"

George's expression remained impassive, but inwardly, he sighed. Wealth and influence complicated matters exponentially, as always. But he refused to compromise ethics or the case.

"Your son made his choices," George replied evenly. "My duty is uncovering the facts without bias, regardless of pressure or threats." George held Wilman's furious gaze unflinchingly. "Now, shall we continue this discussion productively, or do you require your solicitor?"

Wilman seethed but finally threw up his hands. "Bah, do what you will! The smug police protect each other against respectable citizens." He speared George with one last venomous glare. "You'll get what's coming to you soon enough."

With that, he stormed out, his wife scurrying worriedly behind. George watched them go, lips pressed into a thin line. Wilman's obstructionism was predictable. But threatening the DCS's son and George himself was foolish. Justice would

CHAPTER TWELVE

be served impartially, whatever the cost.

Later, George sat alone in the library, methodically compiling his official report on events thus far. His pen paused over Noah Wilman's admitted drug infractions.

Weighing Wilman's threats, George was tempted to omit minor details to avoid complications. But he knew any omissions, however well-intentioned, could undermine trust in the investigation's integrity.

Squaring his shoulders resolutely, George added the drug evidence to the report without dilution. He refused to compromise ethics or Candy's thorough documentation, no matter the fallout.

Shutting the file firmly, George gathered his notes. He would ensure Noah and the missing girls all received justice fairly, even if powerful forces conspired otherwise.

* * *

DCI George Beaumont stepped out of the library at Brandling House, rubbing his tired eyes. The revelations unearthed from Noah Wilman still swirled in his mind like the relentless rain lashing the windows. He felt they were progressing, yet answers dangled agonisingly out of reach.

His mobile rang, jolting him alert. Seeing it was Superintendent Jim Smith, George answered briskly, "DCI Beaumont."

"George, listen carefully," Smith said without preamble. "I've learned DCS Sadiq is en route back to Brandling House to meet with you."

George's brow furrowed. "Did he say why? I already updated him on developments earlier."

"No details given. But this feels irregular, him taking such a personal interest," Smith said uneasily. "Thought you should have fair warning."

George's jaw tightened, disliking surprises. "Right. I'll handle the boss appropriately. Thanks for the heads up."

After ringing off, George stood pensively in the corridor. Sadiq's intense oversight undoubtedly complicated matters, but speculating was unproductive. George would proceed as planned and deal with whatever arose.

Spotting DC Candy Nichols down the hall, George waved her over. "DCS Sadiq is returning imminently to meet with me," he informed her. "So you'll oversee continuing the dormitory searches in my absence."

Candy's eyes widened. "Of course, sir. Did he say what he needs?"

"Unspecified, but likely an update on Noah's drug revelations and the father's threats," George deduced. He grasped her shoulder. "I know I'm leaving the operation in good hands. Carry on meticulously, and alert me to any developments."

Candy nodded staunchly, ponytail bobbing. "You can count on me, sir. We'll keep digging and documenting everything relevant." She offered an encouraging smile before hurrying off.

George watched her go with a surge of paternal pride at how much the vibrant young detective had grown under his wing. Despite the chaos, they would uncover the truth together, one intricate fragment at a time.

Glancing at his watch, George headed downstairs to wait for Sadiq's arrival. He stood beneath the elaborate stone archway leading into the library, listening to the unrelenting downpour outside. It reminded him of last week's snow, the grounds picturesque under a blanket of white. Now, the flurries had given way to dreary rain, meteorological metaphors for the unpredictable twists and turns of this complex investigation.

The ominous echo of approaching footsteps in the corridor signalled Sadiq's impending presence. George straightened, adjusting his tie and smoothing any tension from his features. He would handle this latest variable with pragmatic professionalism however it impacted the winds already buffeting their course.

Moments later, Detective Chief Superintendent Mohammed Sadiq swept into the library, expensive Italian loafers clicking sharply on the marble tile. His piercing gaze instantly locked onto George with laser focus.

"DCI Beaumont. Let's discuss this case frankly," Sadiq pronounced without preamble, sinking into a leather wingback chair by the carved hearth and steepling his long fingers.

George sat across from him, expression neutral. "Of course, sir. What specifically did you want to address?"

Sadiq's dark eyes bored into him. "The illicit substances uncovered trouble me greatly, Beaumont," Sadiq said gravely, steepling his long fingers. "We must discern if recreational use influenced events that night or if darker forces are at play."

George nodded thoughtfully. "Agreed, sir. The drugs introduce complex angles."

He hesitated, choosing his words with care. "The cannabis stash in Gregory Medley's room especially muddies the waters. I'm unsure whether it connects directly to the girls' disappearance or is an unrelated infraction."

Sadiq's dark eyes sharpened with interest. "Explain your reasoning. Leave no possibilities unexplored."

George considered how to convey his carefully weighed perspectives. "On one hand, the drugs could suggest the teens were embroiled in risky recreation that turned sinister. Perhaps stolen stashes or debts owed to dangerous dealers?"

He shook his head grimly. "But the cannabis could also be a peripheral issue. Noah denies selling to Ashley or Esme specifically. And while suspicious, mere possession alone doesn't prove his involvement that night."

George met Sadiq's gaze evenly. "In essence, I don't want to assume connections prematurely when coincidences happen. But neither do I dismiss potentially crucial evidence. It's a delicate balance, sir."

Sadiq nodded slowly, brooding gaze distant as he contemplated George's measured words. After a pensive moment, he refocused on George with fresh resolve.

"Your caution shows wisdom and integrity. Assumptions erode both," Sadiq acknowledged. "Still, we cannot ignore troubling instincts. Your balanced approach provides a diplomatic model, Beaumont."

George dipped his head slightly at the rare praise from his stoic superior. "My job is to figure out the truth, sir."

The conversation lulled as the downpour intensified outside the mullioned windows. George waited attentively for the DCS to steer the discussion.

Finally, Sadiq sighed heavily, weariness creeping into his tone. "The pitfalls of youth confound me. How to guide them wisely..." He trailed off, eyes clouded with pain.

George remained tactfully silent, sensing profound revelations lay beneath the surface.

Sadiq focused on George again, gaze uncharacteristically vulnerable. "Since losing my dear wife two years ago, raising our son Ishaan alone has proven... challenging. Her gentle wisdom balanced my harsh edges. Without it, the boy grows wild."

He passed a weary hand over his eyes. "Don't mistake me—Ishaan is a good child at heart if misguided. But the temptations of youth coupled with my distractedness..." Sadiq shook his head, shamefaced. "Well, you see the consequences manifesting now."

George nodded slowly, glimpsing the heavy toll of buried trauma and impossible expectations upon this imposing yet grieving figure. His brusque exterior clearly concealed inner turmoil.

"I understand the struggles, sir," George offered gently. "But at least you're there for him, sir." He thought of his own strained relationship with his father.

Sadiq's mouth quirked with sad irony. "Yet when they stray off course, the world blames lacking parents, not those who steered the ship awry." He exhaled sharply. "But dwelling in past failures aids no one. We must focus on bringing this case safely to harbour. However, that may require navigating the hazardous waters ahead."

"Well said, sir," George concurred respectfully. "Rest assured, the investigation remains locked on truth above all else. If your son is involved in any way, he will face fair and impartial handling; you have my word."

Sadiq studied George closely as if discerning his sincerity before nodding curtly and rising to take his leave.

But he paused at the tall doors, half-turning back with uncharacteristic hesitance. "The matters discussed here..."

"Remain in utmost confidence," George finished gently.

Sadiq managed a brief smile that conveyed immense gratitude.

He held Sadiq's gaze evenly. "Noah, in particular, may hold

vital clues to their disappearance despite initially obscuring his involvement."

Sadiq absorbed this silently before speaking. "And the boy's parents? How have they responded to your inquiries?"

"As anticipated, with hostility and denial," George replied. Seeing Sadiq's eyes narrow, he continued delicately, "But we are focused only on facts, not opinions. The truth remains our sole aim." George explained about Mr Wilman's threats.

Sadiq nodded slowly, tension easing somewhat. "This case requires utmost discretion regarding youthful misjudgements. Crucial reputations are at stake on all sides." His piercing look made the layered implication clear.

"Naturally, sir," George concurred. "We pursue justice for the victims, not petty grudges or gossip."

Seemingly satisfied by this tactful assurance, Sadiq checked his gleaming Rolex and said, "Keep me apprised of developments. I want a swift resolution, Beaumont."

"Of course, sir," George acknowledged formally as Sadiq swept from the library in a swirl of designer coat.

Alone again, George crossed to the window, watching the detective chief superintendent's powerful form growing smaller as he exited the grounds, trailed by two officers holding umbrellas aloft.

Sadiq's intense interest in the case hinted at personal stakes. But George knew speculating was futile. He would simply navigate the layered currents as steadfastly as possible, wherever they led.

Right now, he needed to confer with Candy and the forensics team for updates. George headed determinedly into the corridor, leather shoes squeaking on the polished floors.

Chapter Thirteen

George was seated, listening to the rain tapping the dark panes as he reflected on the revealing glimpse behind Sadiq's staunch facade. They both contended with complex familial bonds amplified now by the missing girls' case. But George took solace in their united dedication to truth above all else. Whatever storms raged outside, within these walls they strove towards justice.

Rising slowly, George headed upstairs towards Candy's temporary command post, organising the room search efforts. But approaching the second floor, raised voices within gave him pause.

"This is outrageous!" Stanley Bushfield's enraged tone echoed down the hall. "I won't have my daughter's reputation smeared by scandalous accusations!"

Exchanging a loaded glance with the accompanying uniformed officer, George quickened his pace and entered the room.

Inside, Candy stood calmly facing down the irate father while a distressed Dorothy Bushfield dabbed at tears with a monogrammed handkerchief.

Seeing George, Candy addressed him evenly. "Mr Bushfield is upset regarding revelations around Esme's secret drug use, sir. I was explaining processes to validate accounts without assumptions."

"Validating slander more like it!" Bushfield blustered, face reddening. "I refuse to endure impious character assassinations against my daughter!"

George stepped forward diplomatically. "Mr Bushfield, believe me, we aim only to assemble an accurate sequence of events that night. No judgments are being made around Esme's personal choices." He smiled. "Trust me."

Bushfield seemed slightly mollified by George's reasonable tone. Dorothy grasped her husband's arm pleadingly. "Perhaps we are overreacting, darling. This likely means nothing." Though her anxious eyes betrayed deeper concerns.

"We must prepare for scrutiny when word spreads," Bushfield muttered darkly before collecting himself. He met George's gaze squarely. "Detective, I apologise for my outburst. Stress can... amplify emotions."

"It's not me you need to apologise to," George said, arms folded.

Stanley inclined his head towards Candy. "I'm very sorry, young lady."

Candy nodded. "It's understandable, but believe us when we say Esme's good name won't be disparaged without cause. OK?"

Dorothy flashed Candy a grateful smile through her tears.

After the subdued parents took their leave, Candy turned to George, looking rattled. "I should have relayed the drug angle more delicately, sir. Dorothy was so distraught..."

But George squeezed her shoulder reassuringly. "You showed composure despite the tension. Well done, DC Nichols."

CHAPTER THIRTEEN

Candy nodded, buoyed by his staunch confidence in her. She quickly updated George on the latest search developments: nothing substantial yet, but steadfast progress cataloguing rooms.

George listened attentively, proud of Candy rising to lead the team through chaotic waters. He knew the answers they sought lurked just out of sight in this labyrinth of stone. Together, they would drag them into the light.

* * *

Having a cup of tea, George thought about his boss, Detective Chief Superintendent Mohammed Sadiq, and his son, Ishaan. George understood that anxiety on a fundamental level as a father himself. But Sadiq also represented an authority figure with influence over the investigation's trajectory. Balancing empathy with unflinching objectivity proved challenging when wary souls depended on George's skills of discerning truth from shadows.

Rising slowly, George crossed to stare out at the rain-lashed night, mind-churning. He started slightly when approaching footsteps heralded Sadiq's abrupt return.

Turning quickly, George met the DCS's piercing gaze. "Sir? Did you need something more?"

Sadiq waved a dismissive hand. "Forgot my mobile. But since I'm here..." He studied George intently. "Your handling of this case and team has been commendable so far. You have a bright future ahead." He paused to offer his hand, which George took. "I'm glad Jim put you forward for your promotion. You deserve it."

George blinked, surprised by the spontaneously offered

praise. "I... appreciate that endorsement, sir."

Sadiq gave a brusque nod. "Don't take it lightly. I don't waste words. A good head on your shoulders, Beaumont. Sharp instincts." His mouth quirked wryly. "Remind me of myself before this grey crept in."

George smiled slightly, unsure how to respond. But Sadiq's expression quickly sobered again. "Regarding my Ishaan... I know you'll handle him objectively as circumstances require." Sadiq exhaled heavily. "The boy is a bit mischievous at times but harmless overall. Just youth acting out, seeking attention from a distracted father." He met George's eyes. "Surely you understand such antics?"

George inclined his head non-committally. "Boys will be boys, as they say." He kept his tone neutral.

Sadiq seemed to wrestle with himself before adding gruffly, "Just ensure fairness and discretion with Ishaan's role. He's influenced easily by peers down questionable paths."

Though professionally phrased as a request, George detected the layered expectation beneath the words. He chose his response carefully.

"Of course, sir. As I said before, we pursue truth, not petty grudges or gossip. No special treatment, for good or ill." George met Sadiq's searching look steadily. "Your son will be handled the same as any other witness involved. That I can promise you."

Sadiq absorbed this solemn vow stoically before giving a brusque nod of acceptance. But as he turned to go, the DCS glanced back with an unreadable expression.

"You show wisdom beyond your years, Beaumont. A rarer quality than one might hope." His piercing eyes seemed to convey a deeper meaning. "Don't lose sight of that moral

CHAPTER THIRTEEN

compass. Not all share its steadfastness when the waters grow choppy."

With that cryptic remark hanging ominously, Sadiq departed into the stormy night once more.

Alone again, George stood very still, parsing the nuanced conversation. The rare praise indicated Sadiq's grudging respect for his principled professionalism. But references to George's bright future also carried an implied warning—that crashing waves lay ahead should this investigation steer in the wrong direction against prevailing winds and powers.

Sadiq clearly pushed for fairness regarding his son. But George sensed that if Ishaan's role deepened beyond juvenile mischief, the DCS would close ranks to protect his own rather than the case's abstract integrity. Familial bonds ran bone-deep and irrational.

George moved slowly back to the tall windows, shoulders heavy with burden. Moral steadfastness sounded noble, but came at a cost. Outright threats were one thing. But underlying subtle threats, like the one his boss had just aimed at him, were far more dangerous.

* * *

After Detective Chief Superintendent Sadiq's departure, George remained in the library pondering his cryptic parting words. The entire conversation left an unsettled feeling in George's gut.

Shaking off the gloom, he decided to seek out the caretaker, Bradley Welburn. Perhaps that reclusive figure had overheard or witnessed something useful if George could coax it out of him.

Exiting the library, George headed downstairs towards the utilitarian wing housing the caretaker's cramped quarters. The decor here lacked the rich wood panelling and wainscoting of the main house, hinting at the social divide between owner and staff.

Rounding a corner, George nearly collided with a shaggy tan and white Springer Spaniel who gave a delighted "Woof!" at seeing him.

Kneeling, George ruffled the dog's velvety ears affectionately. "Well, hello there! Aren't you friendly?"

The ageing dog's plumed tail whipped eagerly at the attention. Just then, a gruff voice called out. "Jessie! Get back here now."

Straightening, George saw a burly, bearded man holding a broom and dustpan, watching them sternly. He wore faded coveralls with a name patch reading 'Bradley'.

George cleared his throat. "Apologies. I didn't mean to distract your dog from duties."

The man just grunted ambiguously before turning back down the hall. George followed his brisk stride. "Actually hoping I might have a quick word, Mr Welburn? About the missing students."

Pausing outside a door bearing a plaque reading 'Caretaker', the man eyed George warily. "Not much I can tell you. I stay to the staff quarters, away from the school hubbub." His tone held an aloof finality.

But George remained politely persistent. "Even so, you may have overheard or noticed something useful. Any unusual comings and goings lately? Anything about the girls' behaviours or routines?"

Bradley shook his head, thumbing his bushy beard distractedly. "Don't pay the students much mind beyond cleaning up their messes." He whistled for the dog. "Come along, Jessie!"

She gave George a longing backwards glance before trotting to her master, who disappeared inside, shutting the door firmly. George stood pensively for a moment before turning away. Bradley's standoffishness confirmed he was the secretive type who required finesse to open up.

Rounding the corner, George stopped short at the sight of Eugene Garforth descending the staircase, looking around shiftily before disappearing down the hall.

George's eyes narrowed thoughtfully. What business did the elite owner have sneaking about the staff quarters unannounced? His idle dismissal of student affairs apparently had limits where his own eccentric purposes necessitated oversight.

George vowed to keep an attentive eye on Garforth's comings and goings. The man clearly hid shifty agendas under his posh veneer. He only hoped Jay and Tashan could find something on the man before it was too late.

* * *

Deciding he was too restless to head home just yet, George headed outside and towards the groundskeeper's shed. Knocking briskly, he heard shuffling movement within, followed by the door cracking open guardedly. A grizzled, overall-clad man peered out, posture visibly relaxing at seeing George's police ID.

"Ah, Detective! How can I help?" The man pulled the door fully open now.

George glanced around the tidy workspace. "Just following

up on any observations you might have made recently. Understand you're often out on the grounds, even at odd hours."

"That's right," the man nodded. "Grounds don't tend themselves, do they? I'm Harold, by the way. Been working this land fifteen years now."

"Pleased to meet you, Harold," George said sincerely. "I expect you know the property like the back of your hand by now. Makes you uniquely positioned to aid our investigation."

Harold looked thoughtful. "Suppose that's so. Never saw much, truth be told. But things do happen under the cover of darkness sometimes." He hesitated before adding with a shrewd look, "Rumours abound about the owner, Mr Garforth, despite being married and associating with certain... unsavoury women from town late nights when he thinks no one is about. If you catch my drift." He shrugged. "Not that I should be telling you that, should I? He pays my way, after all."

George frowned. Stanley Bushfield had hinted at Garforth's shady proclivities as well. This aligned all too well.

"Well, I appreciate the truth," George said. "Anything else to add?"

"Nope, sorry."

Thanking the candid groundskeeper for his time, George made mental notes summarising the intriguing leads and conversations.

But the caretaker, Bradley Welburn, remained an enigma. His aloofness hinted at deeper awareness, yet fear or loyalty controlled his tongue. Was there true sinister intent beneath the surface? George's instincts said no, though personal pains clouded objectivity at times. Perhaps Welburn wished to remain separate, no easy feat amidst close quarters and gossip.

Re-entering Brandling House, George wound his way upstairs slowly. He knew Candy remained immersed in coordinating room searches, but was currently on a break.

So, there, alone in an empty parlour, George sank into a leather armchair and closed his eyes, massaging his temples.

Esme and Ashley were counting on George to continue working towards justice. To continue looking for them. This serious goal kept him steady despite growing troubles. But the many secrets and evasions of those around him required careful judgment. Not all problems were equally dangerous.

Rousing himself with effort, George headed towards the foyer where the muted echo of Candy's voice directing officers signalled progress cataloguing rooms.

"DCI Beaumont!" George heard Candy shout.

"What is it?" George asked tersely, mentally preparing for the worst.

Rounding the corner, he spotted her standing outside the front parlour, features taut.

Candy gripped his arm, eyes bright. "It's Ashley, sir. She's been found—alive!"

Chapter Fourteen

George froze, shock hitting him like cold water. "What? When? Where?"

"Just a few minutes ago, sir, disoriented in the foyer," Candy explained breathlessly. "Covered in mud, clothes soaked... seems completely traumatised."

"Where is she?"

"The library."

George was already striding swiftly towards the library. "Notify emergency services immediately to have her evaluated. And contact her parents—discretely for now. This will be an emotional mess."

He entered the library, where faint whimpers and incoherent mumbling sounded from a hunched figure wrapped in a blanket before the fireplace. Kneeling slowly, George cautiously approached the dazed teen.

"Ashley? I'm Detective Chief Inspector Beaumont. You're safe now; we're getting you help."

Her glazed eyes stared right through him, body shuddering violently. Mud and debris clung to her matted hair, and her jeans and jumper were soaked through. She looked utterly spent and shattered.

Just then, her breathing accelerated into panicked gasps.

George quickly shifted back, giving her space, as Candy rushed over.

"She's hyperventilating, poor thing. We need emergency services here now," Candy said urgently into her radio.

Kneeling a cautious distance away, Candy spoke gently. "Try taking slow, deep breaths, Ashley. Focus on my voice; you're safe."

But the traumatised girl remained curled inwards, lost in her own hellish reality. Candy kept murmuring soothing phrases while George looked on helplessly. Wherever Ashley had been, she emerged bearing wounds no blanket or softly spoken comfort could mend.

The wail of approaching sirens pierced the heavy silence. Shortly after, paramedics hurried in to assess the nearly catatonic teen. George provided details quietly as they checked vitals and respiration.

"Definitely showing signs of severe shock and panic attack," the senior paramedic noted, shining a penlight at her dilated pupils. "We'll need to sedate and warm her at the Hazlehurst Centre until she's stabilised enough to interview."

They prepared to move Ashley onto a gurney as George and Candy looked on grimly. But the girl suddenly sprang up with a guttural cry. "Where the fuck are you taking me?"

"To a specialist centre in Morley, love," the senior paramedic said. "It's a medical centre."

"No! No, please, I can't..."

She crumpled back down, ragged sobs tearing from her throat. The paramedics exchanged an uneasy glance.

Candy stepped closer; hands raised soothingly. "I know you're frightened, Ashley. But we need to make certain you're OK. The doctors will help you."

At this, the distraught teen only wailed louder, fists clenching her soaked hair. The professionals moved to intervene, but George halted them with a raised hand.

"Wait. She's been through trauma and needs to feel in control." He crouched slowly so his face was level with Ashley's downcast eyes. "You decide what happens next. We're right here with you, no matter what you choose. You're safe."

George kept his tone low and calm. And finally, it seemed to penetrate her panicked haze. Ashley's breathing slowed slightly as she peered up at him with a spark of awareness.

"Want... my mum," she rasped painfully.

George nodded. "Of course. We'll bring her straight away."

The paramedics looked doubtful but didn't argue. Candy squeezed Ashley's hand reassuringly. "You're so brave. And so strong. Your mum will be here soon."

Ashley clutched Candy's hand like a lifeline, drawing comfort from her steadfast presence. George observed the teen's returning lucidity with cautious relief. Whatever horrors she had faced, Ashley was fighting back bravely.

While Candy kept the girl calm, George stepped out to update Sandra Cowgill himself. Her guttural cry upon hearing the news pierced his heart. But she quickly pulled herself together.

"I'm coming. Don't let them take her away!"

George assured Sandra they would await her arrival before disconnecting. No parent should endure such agony. But thankfully, this family's wounds could start healing now.

Returning to the parlour, George crouched beside the huddled teen again. "Your mum will be here soon, Ashley. You're being so very brave."

She managed a faint nod, eyes clearer but haunted.

CHAPTER FOURTEEN

* * *

The heavy oak doors of Brandling House's stately library were thrown open as Sandra and Johnny Cowgill burst in, faces etched with equal parts desperation and fury.

"Where is she?" Sandra cried, eyes wild as she scanned the room. "You said you found our Ashley!"

DCI George Beaumont quickly stepped forward; hands raised placatingly. "Mrs Cowgill, please try to stay calm. Ashley is safe now. She's just through there with Constable Nichols."

He gently guided the distraught parents farther into the library's cavernous interior. In an armchair by the carved marble hearth, a shock blanket-wrapped figure sat hunched and trembling despite Constable Candy Nichols' soft murmurs of comfort.

Sandra froze, clasping a hand over her mouth at the sight of her dishevelled daughter. Then, a guttural sob tore from her throat as she rushed forward.

"Oh, my baby! My precious girl!"

Kneeling, Sandra enveloped Ashley in a fierce embrace. The girl remained stiff and unresponsive, eyes glazed. Johnny hovered behind his wife uncertainly, face etched with relief and concern.

"Give her space to adjust, Mrs Cowgill," the senior paramedic urged gently. "Ashley is very overwhelmed right now."

But Sandra refused to relinquish her traumatised daughter. Rocking gently, she smoothed back Ashley's mud-matted hair, tears flowing freely.

"You're safe now, darling. Mummy's here. I won't let you

go, I promise."

Johnny rested a broad hand on Sandra's slender shoulder. "Come now, love. Let the girl breathe a bit." Though his gruff tone held a telltale quaver.

At her father's familiar voice, Ashley seemed to emerge slightly from her thousand-yard stare. She peered up at him blankly. "Dad?" she rasped.

Johnny's breath hitched as he dropped to his knees before her. He grasped her mud-caked hands tightly in his calloused ones.

"There's my brave girl," he said hoarsely. "We've been so worried, Ash. You're home now where you belong."

Fresh tears shone in his eyes at the miraculous reunion with the defiant daughter whose antics so often frustrated him. At this moment, her precious presence was all that mattered.

Observing the emotional family reconnection, DCI George Beaumont discretely motioned Candy towards the corridor. There would be difficult questions soon enough. But right now, these scarred souls deserved privacy to heal.

Once in the hallway, George turned to Candy grimly. "Have emergency services bring a female counsellor experienced with trauma victims. No uniformed officers—they'll only distress Ashley further."

Candy nodded, already relaying orders into her radio. Muted agony echoed from the library, hinting at the gruelling road ahead. But George clung to fragile hope. Ashley was alive and safe. For now, that glimmer through the darkness must sustain them.

Soon after, the requested counsellor arrived to gently evaluate Ashley's mental state. Sandra refused to leave her daughter's side, staring challengingly at the willowy brunette.

CHAPTER FOURTEEN

"I'm Judith," the counsellor said soothingly. "I want to help Ashley feel calm and secure. Is it all right if I sit with you both?"

Sandra searched the woman's compassionate green eyes before giving a terse nod. She smoothed Ashley's lank hair protectively as Judith settled nearby.

"Hello, Ashley. You've been so very brave getting through something terribly frightening." Judith kept her tone low and warm. "I can only imagine how exhausted you must feel now. It's safe to rest—your family is right here."

Ashley's eyes flickered briefly to the counsellor's kind face at the gentle words. Her shallow breathing slowed slightly as some tension ebbed from her hunched shoulders.

Judith smiled encouragingly. "There now, just keep taking nice deep breaths. No need to speak until you're ready."

She continued guiding Ashley through grounding visualization exercises until the girl's rigid posture finally slackened fully, her head drooping. Sandra ran her fingers through Ashley's hair as she drifted into an exhausted sleep, her first taste of peace in days.

Rising quietly, Judith joined George and the Cowgills in the hallway. "The shock has her completely shut down for now. But rest and time will help tremendously." She hesitated. "Has she said anything about... any events?"

George shook his head grimly. "Nothing coherent yet. We're operating blind regarding what transpired after she and Esme Bushfield disappeared from the grounds late Monday night." He scrubbed a hand down his bearded face. "One girl found, at least. But there's still another out there depending on our efforts."

Sandra clasped her husband's hand tightly, expression

distraught. "How can Ashley have made it back alone if Esme is still missing?" She blinked back fresh tears. "Those poor girls must have endured unthinkable horrors out there!"

Johnny enveloped his wife in a steadying embrace as she dissolved into muffled sobs, the euphoria of reunion giving way to haunting unknowns and the lingering spectre of danger.

Judith spoke up gently. "Let Ashley wake naturally and feel in control. Pressuring details risks re-traumatising her." She handed Sandra a card. "Call anytime. I'll check on her tomorrow once she's home and settled."

Walking Judith out, George felt immense gratitude for her compassionate insight. Navigating the delicate emotional dynamics around the investigation would require a keen understanding of both parents and victims.

Returning to the library, George stationed an officer outside and notified headquarters Ashley was found but had not yet been interviewed. Until they could glean clues from the still-incoherent girl, all he could do was vigilantly oversee her protection and care.

* * *

George slipped out quietly, leaving the reunited family to cling to each other. There would be difficult questions to ask in time. But this precious moment of miraculous reunion was theirs alone. He stood gazing out at the moonlit grounds, heart heavy but full. One life saved amidst the darkness. It rekindled flickering faith when so much remained uncertain.

The parlour doors opened behind him, and Candy slipped out, looking drained. George turned to her.

"Ashley finally agreed to go to the SARC centre, though only

CHAPTER FOURTEEN

if her mum stays right by her side," Candy reported wearily. "Poor girl is completely traumatised. No details yet on what happened. Whenever I tried broaching the subject, she just screamed."

"Screamed?"

Candy nodded. "Like a wild animal."

George nodded grimly. "Poor thing."

"How do you want to proceed, sir?"

"We'll need to approach interviews gently when the time comes. For now, helping Ashley feel secure takes priority."

Candy smiled faintly. "You showed real empathy with her, sir. Well done."

George shrugged. "You were the superstar, Candy, not me." But her praise warmed him nonetheless.

They stood in silence for a moment before Candy spoke hesitantly. "Do you think Ashley escaping means... there's hope for Esme, too?"

George chose his words carefully. "I hope so. But until we have answers, all we can do is persist in the search." He gripped her shoulder bracingly. "Go home, get some rest. It's been a long day for everyone."

Candy bit her lip but complied, wisps escaping her trademark ponytail as she trudged off.

Alone again, George rubbed tired eyes. One girl found, but at what cost? And young Esme still lost out in the darkness. This case remained far from closed.

***

Half an hour later, Mrs Cowgill called George through. Apparently, Ashley had managed to sit up, and the brief rest seemed to have settled her disoriented thoughts, her gaze clearer and more present.

But spying a uniformed officer in the corridor, her breath quickened into frightened gasps.

Sandra grasped her hands, speaking urgently. "It's OK, darling! They're here to keep us safe." But Ashley only whimpered, pulling away from her mother's touch.

Exchanging a worried look with Sandra, George said, "I want to give Ashley space. She's been through trauma we can't comprehend." He stepped out to redirect officers away from sight. Ashley's comfort took priority over standard procedures now.

When he returned, Ashley's panicked hyperventilating had slowed under her mother's gentle reassurances. Johnny stood behind Sandra, uncertainty and pain etched on his weathered features. However imperfectly, it was clear the Cowgills loved their broken daughter fiercely.

Kneeling slowly where Ashley could see him, George kept his voice low and calm. "I know you've been very scared, Ashley. We only want to help you feel safe now. What do you need?"

The girl hesitated before rasping hoarsely, "I... want... my room."

Sandra clasped Ashley's hand. "Of course, sweetheart. Let's get you home." Rising unsteadily, Ashley clung to her mother, avoiding the men's eyes.

As Johnny moved to support his disoriented daughter, she flinched away sharply with a faint whimper. Hurt flashed across his face, but he backed off.

"I'll fetch the car round," he muttered gruffly, ducking out before emotions could further overwhelm the fragile reunion.

As Sandra guided a shuffling Ashley towards the doors,

CHAPTER FOURTEEN

George stepped forward urgently. "Mrs Cowgill, we need to get her to the SARC centre in Morley before she goes home. We talked about it earlier, if you remember?"

Sandra's face hardened, clutching Ashley tighter. But George met her eyes. "Please. It's crucial we preserve all possible clues to find Esme and identify those responsible."

The fight seemed to drain from Sandra's body. She swallowed painfully. "If we 'ave to... but quickly. She needs care, not more trauma."

George observed the huddled form of traumatised teenager Ashley Cowgill clinging to her mother. The girl's thousand-yard stare pierced George's heart, hinting at unimaginable horrors endured since her disappearance with Esme two hellish nights prior. Now, mercifully found, but at what cost?

George mentally steeled himself for the invasive procedures ahead that logic deemed necessary, though compassion recoiled at further violating her fragile psyche. Meticulously gathering evidence took priority with a brutal offender potentially still stalking vulnerable Esme. Instead, George simply wanted to wrap the shattered girl in a blanket of safety and tell her everything was going to be OK.

Yet emotion must not sway dutiful professionalism now, however it shredded his soul.

An officer approached cautiously. "We're ready to escort Miss Cowgill to the SARC centre in Morley, sir."

George nodded heavily. "Thank you, Constable. Discretion remains paramount."

The man's eyes softened with understanding. "Of course, sir." George knew he could trust this team to handle Ashley with utmost care. But still, his heart clenched as the constable returned to the huddled pair.

Sandra tensed instinctively at his presence, clutching her daughter tighter. The officer kept his voice low and soothing. "Ma'am, the medical team needs to proceed with examining Ashley now. We'll drive you there together."

At this, the dazed teen began trembling violently, pressing closer against her mother and squeezing her eyes shut. Sandra turned, blazing eyes on the hapless constable. "Can't you see you're frightening her? She needs rest, not more trauma!"

But Constable Amy Hughes interjected gently. "Mrs Cowgill, I know this is so difficult. But legally, we must gather any potential evidence immediately." Her compassionate gaze never wavered. "You'll be right by her side the whole time, I promise."

Sandra searched the officer's face intently. At her slight nod, the man stepped forward again respectfully. "Is it alright if I escort you to the vehicle, Ashley? Nice and easy, no need to rush."

The girl flinched at his outstretched hand but allowed Sandra to guide her waveringly towards the doors. George observed her hunched posture and shuffling gait, so unlike the spirited teen he'd heard stories of. What twisted evils had occurred? And why?

At the doors, Sandra suddenly baulked. "Her clothes—she can't wear these stained things any more!" She made to remove Ashley's soiled jumper.

"No, don't!" George interjected sharply. At their startled looks, he softened his tone. "I'm sorry. But her clothes may hold crucial trace evidence we can't risk losing." He met Sandra's distraught eyes pleadingly. "I understand wanting her comfortable. But those clothes could provide links to what happened and who's responsible. I'm sure you understand."

CHAPTER FOURTEEN

Sandra wavered, tears pooling as Ashley shuddered softly beside her. But finally, she exhaled shakily. "Of course, I just want her safe and warm." She touched Ashley's lank hair tenderly.

"If you need me, call me," George said to Ashley, handing over his card.

Wrapped in a blanket, Ashley managed a whispery, "Thanks," before allowing Sandra to guide her haltingly outside. But as the heavy doors closed after them, she paused, turning back to meet George's eyes for the first time.

"Find her," Ashley rasped fiercely before her mother bundled her into the waiting car.

George stood silently on the steps, watching the vehicle disappear up a rainy Town Street, shoulders weighed down by the burden of promise. One girl was beyond his protection now. But by some miracle, Ashley had survived hell's crucible and emerged with the fire still yet in her eyes. Now, he must honour that tenacious spark. He dared not fail young Esme while wisps of hope yet lingered in the engulfing darkness.

Chapter Fifteen

DCI George Beaumont nodded soberly as forensic scientist Maya Chen clinically detailed the invasive examination process required to gather potential DNA evidence from sexual assault victims like traumatised teenager Ashley Cowgill. They stood just outside the private room where Ashley was resting after enduring the harrowing evidence collection at the Hazlehurst Centre in Morley, a Sexual Assault Referral Centre, SARC for short.

"First, the victim agrees to be examined by forensically trained nurses," Maya explained softly, her naturally composed demeanour subtly radiating compassion. "We have to recognise that this is a profoundly traumatic incident for the victim. But we need to meticulously gather as much evidence as possible to identify the perpetrator."

George sighed heavily, the weight of responsibility feeling crushing. "I know how critically important the work is, Maya. But hearing how we force victims to relive horror for the sake of justice... it never gets easier."

Maya's dark eyes glinted with empathy. "We must continue gently. If we secure DNA evidence, the offender may already be in the system. Or we can definitively implicate a suspect through forensic match."

CHAPTER FIFTEEN

She crossed her arms pensively. "Our 'crime scene' is Ashley's own body. Biological evidence naturally decays over time. The longer the delay collecting samples, the lower our recovery chances."

George nodded grimly. "We're in a constant race against the fading evidence trails. Hopefully, there's enough to get what we need."

"The specialist examiners are highly skilled at extracting even trace amounts," Maya assured him. "First, we photograph documented injuries, which will corroborate the victim's account of events. Then we strategically sample areas likely to retrieve DNA based on her story."

She hesitated delicately. "Of course, swabbing such intimate violation sites could be re-traumatising despite consent. We must proceed with utmost care and empathy."

"Absolutely," George agreed vehemently. "Physical recovery means nothing without psychological healing, too. We want justice, not hollow victories leaving more scars."

Maya gave a faint smile. "Well said. The team strives to make the process feel empowering, not exploitative. It's a delicate balance."

Just then, PC Georgina Waldron approached, holding an evidence collection kit. "The exam is complete; we have samples ready for transit to the lab." Her expression was grave. "Poor girl endured it all bravely, but she's in a bad way now. We should let her rest before questioning."

George thanked Georgina sombrely, then turned back to Maya as she prepared to leave with the samples. "What's our analysis timeline for results?"

"If testing isolates DNA, we'll urgently cross-reference it against criminal databases," Maya replied briskly. "But full processing could take up to 72 hours."

Seeing George's discouraged face, she added, "Try not to fret over delays. The samples should be robust. Focus efforts identifying persons of interest to interview based on her accounts in the meantime."

George nodded, shoulders straightening. "Too right."

Maya gave an approving look before departing to begin evidence testing. Alone in the hallway, George took a steadying breath. However agonising this process proved for victims, it brought hope of finally exposing the guilty. Once DNA spoke its damning truth, the perpetrator's days in sinister shadows were numbered.

Striding from the SARC Centre, George called DI Alexis Mercer.

* * *

Alexis Mercer's figure was focused on her laptop in the office. Her cascade of golden hair was pulled back in a practical ponytail, and though faint shadows ringed her striking azure eyes, her jaw was set with steady determination.

It was Alexis' first day back after being held captive by former DCI Alistair Atkinson during that horrific case last month. By all rights, the trauma should have broken her. But if anything, surviving that crucible had only honed Alexis' formidable resolve to see justice done.

Right now, her formidable focus was directed on comprehensive background research regarding the key figures tied to Brandling House and the missing girls. They needed to uncover any telling threads hinting at secrets that could unravel this mystery.

CHAPTER FIFTEEN

Hearing George's voice on the other end of the phone, Alexis straightened briskly, all business. "Making progress collating financials and records on our primary persons of interest, sir. Several promising angles already unfolding."

George said, "Let's hear it then."

Consulting her notes, Alexis began outlining her findings. "Regarding estate owner Eugene Garforth, there are indications of substantial debts and transactions suggesting attempts to access additional capital against property holdings."

"OK."

"Loans potentially sought out of growing desperation. His lavish lifestyle far exceeded viable income as holdings declined. A powerful motive for cutting corners."

"Interesting," George remarked. "Anything more concrete we can pin down?"

Alexis allowed herself a small smile. "As a matter of fact, yes. I've also unearthed records of an ugly divorce five years back. Garforth left his wife of 20 years for a woman nearly half his age—Eleanor Ward, aged only 22 and evidently his mistress for some time."

She quirked an eyebrow. "Safe to say the scandal would have undermined Garforth's elite social standing. And despite his roving eye, the settlement left a considerable financial impact as well."

George's lips twisted wryly as he listened. Pompous Garforth's taste for young women echoed unpleasantly given the missing teens.

Scanning her notes again, Alexis frowned. "There are also whispers of further affairs beyond his secretary mistress, sir. Rumours of Garforth keeping company with impressionable women aged sixteen to eighteen, too." She paused. "If true, that preference for young women... Well, I don't want to finish the sentence, sir."

Jaw tightening, George murmured, "Let's hope it's only gossip, but have Jay discreetly corroborate where Garforth spends time and with who. His affairs clearly show a willingness to exploit power dynamics with vulnerable younger women."

"Already on it, sir," Alexis confirmed. "I've passed the names of usual haunts for Garforth along. Jay and Tashan will canvass patrons tonight regarding any dodgy interactions."

George nodded approvingly. Thorough as always. He knew Alexis' insights would be pivotal, mainly because of her methodical diligence. The woman's grit and resilience inspired him. If anyone could take trauma and transform it into a moral purpose, it was Alexis.

"What else is on your radar?" George prompted.

Alexis took a bracing breath. "The records search on caretaker Bradley Welburn revealed an arrest nineteen years ago at age twenty-five on charges of rape of a minor under sixteen."

George's expression darkened. "Go on."

"The case never made it to trial—was dismissed on technicalities," Alexis elaborated. "But clearly markings of deeply concerning behaviour, even if never convicted." She hesitated. "I don't like to make assumptions about guilt. But given his access, we should investigate whether Welburn has displayed any inappropriate conduct or relationships with students that staff might have suppressed."

"Agreed," George said. His skin crawled picturing timid girls at the mercy of a predator in a place supposedly safe.

CHAPTER FIFTEEN

"We'll bring Welburn in for thorough questioning straight away regarding any fraternisation. Discreetly for now, though, to avoid tipping him off."

"I'll coordinate with uniforms to have him intercepted quietly when off duty. We need to handle this delicately but urgently."

"Thanks. And excellent work today, Alexis," George said sincerely. "We're making progress unearthing ugly truths thanks to your diligence. Stay strong."

Alexis blushed at the rare praise from her boss. It was the beginning of an infatuation, most likely one-sided with Isabella Wood in the picture. Then again, obstructions were usually easy to get rid of, especially when you were Alexis Mercer. "Thank you, sir. I'm just doing my part for those who don't yet have a voice."

Her words resonated with George's own moral purpose. It was appreciated considering that right now young lives depended on their focus and fortitude.

* * *

After finishing the call, a uniformed officer rushed over to George.

"Sir, we've spotted possible trace evidence still adhered to Ashley Cowgill's jeans. Appears to be algae and sediments consistent with freshwater ponds."

George's pulse quickened. "Any ponds in the vicinity she could have encountered?"

The constable nodded eagerly. "Yes, sir—Top Hall Pond lies within reasonable range of Brandling House. It's known as Merryvale locally."

At George's confused look, he elaborated. "After some drunkard called Merryvale supposedly got rolled down the hill and into the pond years back. The muddy shallows are rife with algae and weeds."

The DCI grinned. He knew of the pond, of course, because he had once tried fishing in the bloody thing like an idiot and ended up losing a brand-new float and hook he'd bought from Eddie Coots.

George gripped his shoulder approvingly. "Good work. Get a dive team dispatched to that location immediately. Any remnants or trail there could prove vital."

As the officer hurried off to mobilise search efforts, George stared into the distance, unseeing. Something told him the innocuous pond concealed sinister secrets. Its placid surface reflected the tranquil pastoral surroundings of Brandling House's sprawling estate. But George knew better. Where better for evil to lurk than camouflaged by nature's beauty?

* * *

The harsh fluorescent lighting of the Sexual Assault Referral Centre exam room accentuated Ashley Cowgill's wan complexion as DCI George Beaumont gently attempted to interview the traumatised girl. The sterile environment, with its clinical furnishings, only seemed to amplify Ashley's distress as she huddled on the exam table beside her mother.

Sandra Cowgill kept a protective arm wrapped around her daughter's shuddering frame, eyeing George warily as he approached. He kept his posture non-threatening and his voice soothing.

"I know this is difficult, Ashley. But anything you can

remember from that night could help immensely in finding Esme," George coaxed. "Even the smallest detail."

At the mention of her missing friend, Ashley flinched as if struck, eyes squeezing shut. Sandra smoothed the girl's lank hair, glaring at George.

"She's been through an ordeal, Detective!" Sandra admonished sharply. "Interrogating her right now will only make things worse."

"I'm sorry, Mrs Cowgill," George said gently, "but time is of the essence. Please, Ashley, try to think back carefully. Do you recall leaving Brandling House with Esme?"

Rocking slightly, Ashley shook her head jerkily without lifting her eyes. "Don't remember... everything's blurry..." she rasped.

Frustration flared in George's chest. He knew better than to pressure the clearly traumatised girl. But young Esme remained out there depending on any shred of insight Ashley could provide.

Crouching to meet Ashley's downcast eyes, he kept his tone calm and coaxing. "It's normal for trauma to affect memory. But I know you're trying very hard, Ashley. Let's start simple—what's the first thing you can recall after being at Brandling House?"

Ashley's breath hitched as she struggled to form fractured recollections into coherence. When she finally spoke, her voice was barely audible. "Cold... so cold. And dark. I couldn't see anything." She began trembling harder, fisting her hospital gown.

Exchanging a worried look with Sandra, George continued delicately. "Was Esme there with you? Did you hear her voice or sense her nearby?"

But Ashley only moaned, pulling her knees to her chest. "Can't remember! There was yelling, and I was scared. Why can't I remember?" She dissolved into guttural sobs.

Sandra cradled her, anguish etched on her drawn face. She speared George with a reproachful look. "This was clearly a mistake. Ashley needs care, not more stress!"

Shame heated George's face. In his urgency, he had pushed too hard, reopening fresh wounds. Esme deserved justice, but not at such a cruel cost.

"You're absolutely right, Mrs Cowgill," George conceded humbly. "Ashley has been remarkably strong just enduring what she has."

He stepped back, giving the distraught girl space. Perhaps in calmer moments, fragments would resurface naturally. But right now, compassion took precedence over procedure.

After Ashley's distress finally eased somewhat, George attempted a gentler approach, keeping his voice low and even.

"I understand if specifics feel too overwhelming presently," he said. "But sometimes focusing on sensory details can help jog memories without triggering emotions as sharply. So, let's just take it bit by bit. Are there any particular scents or sounds you recall standing out?"

Ashley took a few gulping breaths, considering the question carefully. "An earthy, muddy smell, I think. Damp and... rotten, like mould or compost." She tensed again. "It scares me for some reason."

"You're doing really well," George encouraged. "No need to force more. What you've shared already provides real progress."

Sandra clutched her daughter's hand, fresh tears trailing her cheeks. "My brave, strong girl," she murmured.

Just then, a soft knock preceded Dr Miriam Kowalski's entrance. The willowy clinician gave George a pointed look. "Detective, might I suggest we conclude this discussion for now? Ashley needs rest and care."

Chastened by his prior missteps, George acquiesced readily. "Of course, Doctor. Thank you again for your compassionate diligence with Ashley. Please let me know if we can support her recovery in any way."

Dr Kowalski gave an approving nod before turning her kind eyes to Ashley. "Why don't we relocate you to a more comfortable room so you can get some sleep?"

At this, some alertness seemed to return to Ashley's haunted eyes. She grabbed her mother's hand desperately. "Home. I want to go home, Mum. Please!"

Sandra gathered her daughter close, rocking gently. "Soon, sweetheart, I promise. We just need the doctors to make sure you're not badly hurt first. Then we'll be home in your own safe, warm bed."

But Ashley only wailed inconsolably about wanting her room. Sandra turned pleading eyes on Kowalski, at a loss. With a sympathetic look, the doctor intervened.

"Alright, I think Ashley has endured enough upheaval for today. As long as she rests and you monitor for any worrying symptoms, home may be best."

Sandra exhaled in tearful relief. "Oh, thank you, Doctor!" She lifted her daughter's ravaged face tenderly. "You hear that, darling? We're going home now."

Ashley managed a faint, flickering smile at those words before allowing her mother to guide her haltingly from the room. Watching them go, George scrubbed a hand down his face, feeling drained himself.

Chapter Sixteen

It was midnight, and Detective Chief Inspector George Beaumont stood in the Incident Room at Elland Road police station, surveying the large map pinned to the wall cluttered with sticky notes marking search areas and clues. Despite exhaustive efforts, Esme's whereabouts remained a mystery.

George's sharp gaze traced the web of multi-coloured threads linking persons of interest and locations. But the frustrating lack of actionable leads leapt out like a glaring void. Witness accounts were scant and inconsistent. Digital forensics had yet to crack encrypted data. And the trails across sprawling Middleton Woods were long and cold, washed away by unrelenting rain.

Squaring his broad shoulders, George mentally steeled himself against gathering doubt. He refused to lose faith that they would uncover answers.

Just then, Detective Sergeant Yolanda Williams approached, her graceful movements belying strength and intellect. "Sir, the latest canvassing reports just arrived. I'm afraid they offer very little."

George waved her over impatiently. "Let's have it then."

Yolanda nodded briskly, consulting her notes. "Officers conducted door-to-door inquiries for five miles in every direction from Brandling House's main gate. Most residents had nothing useful to share. However..." She skimmed further down the page. "An elderly woman in her eighties, Mrs Partridge, claims she saw two figures enter a blue transit van parked on Gipsy Lane late Monday night. Possibly relevant?"

George stroked his beard pensively. "Definitely." He thought about his first murder case as a DI, the so-called Miss Murderer. He pondered a moment longer. "Send officers back to re-interview Mrs Partridge in the morning for any additional details she can recall on the van's appearance or occupants. Go with them. Take Tashan and canvas the area for CCTV, etc."

Yolanda hesitated delicately. "Regarding Mrs Partridge's statement, there may be context worth considering."

George's eyes narrowed. "Go on."

"Well, sir, Mr Partridge passed five years back, but by all accounts, Constance Partridge's mental faculties have steadily declined since losing her longtime partner," Yolanda said gently, not dismissively. "I only mention this as it could explain inconsistencies in her statement without unreliable intent."

George pinched the bridge of his nose. "You make an excellent point, Yolanda. Ensure you get on that CCTV search tomorrow morning, ASAP."

"Right away, sir," Yolanda acknowledged. "But before I go, I've been reviewing CCTV footage secured from nearby petrol stations, shops, and residential areas, and unfortunately, there are no sightings of Esme or Ashley identified positively so far."

George's face fell. He had pinned high hopes on camera footage capturing the girls' movements after leaving Brandling House. "Right. Keep analysing and widening the search radius. They must show up somewhere."

Striding from the Incident Room, George nearly collided with DC Elaine Brewer. Her haggard expression struck George, so at odds with her typically polished appearance.

"I'm so sorry, DS Brewer," George said. "You look dead on your feet. Are you OK?"

Elaine waved off the collision wearily. "No harm done, sir. And you're right; it's been round-the-clock strain. But that's the job." She attempted to muster her usual brisk demeanour but faltered.

Noting her uncharacteristic vulnerability, George gently guided Elaine down the hall to an empty office. Once seated, he leaned forward attentively. "Talk to me. What's weighing on you?"

Elaine fiddled with her mug, gathering composure. Finally, she admitted softly, "It's Ashley's mum, Sandra. We've forged a close bond, given my own... experiences growing up. I know how much she needs support now." Elaine hesitated, shamefaced. "But honestly, it's growing beyond my professional capabilities alone."

"How so?" George asked kindly, sensing the depth of Elaine's empathy for Sandra's plight.

Elaine sighed heavily, shoulders slumping. "Sandra leans on me at all hours for emotional support. But it's... it's gotten unhealthy, truth be told. Co-dependent even. She begged me to come stay the night to 'keep the monsters away'."

George nodded slowly, understanding blooming. "The trauma has left her clinging to whatever security she can find in you. But that had definitely crossed professional boundaries, I agree." He pondered carefully. "Could referring

CHAPTER SIXTEEN

Sandra to a crisis counsellor alleviate this co-dependency while preserving your valuable connection?"

Elaine's eyes lit up. "Yes, that's perfect! I should have realised sooner. Thank you, sir." She stood, re-energised. "I'll call a referral line straight away and set up an immediate consult. You're quite astute about emotional dynamics."

George waved off the compliment, though privately pleased he could offer some reassurance. "I try to understand the psychology tangled up in cases. Helps avoid missteps."

He walked Elaine out, feeling lighter. They were making progress, however, incrementally. As a father himself, George understood the unbearable pain of powerlessness to aid your child. If he could alleviate even one frightened parent's anguish, it counted as progress while pursuing broader justice.

* * *

DCI George Beaumont exited the police station, shoulders slumping with bone-deep weariness as he made his way to the Merc. The case had carved out an emptiness in George's own chest. The anguish mirrored the gnawing helplessness churning within him.

He was starting to doubt himself.

Were they chasing dead ends? Had the trail gone cold too soon? Shaking his head sharply, George shrugged off creeping defeatism. He refused to lose faith when young lives depended on perseverance, piercing the opaque darkness shrouding this case.

Turning onto the Ring Road towards home at last, George's thoughts drifted to his loving fiancée Isabella waiting there. She should be in bed asleep, but likely she'd have a hot meal on the table and a welcome embrace to revive his flagging spirit. Not to mention a cold nose and wagging tail from loyal terrier Rex. At times like these, simple comforts provided a lifeline.

Pulling into the drive of the brick house he and Isabella had recently made their home, George drank in the cheery glow of lamplight within. The ink-dark sky whispered of gathering winter, but George hoped the snow would hold off.

It would add nothing to their search for Esme Bushfield.

Stepping inside, Rex immediately scampered over, stumpy tail whipping excitedly. George couldn't help but smile as he knelt to give the shaggy dog's ears an affectionate ruffle. Rex's uncomplicated joy acted as a balm to his soul.

"There's a good lad George murmured. "Have you been guarding the house from squirrels today, hmm?"

Rex just panted up at him adoringly before trotting off towards the kitchen, where tempting aromas emanated. Straightening with a wince at his creaking knees, George followed at a slower pace.

In the kitchen, Isabella stood at the cooker, stirring a pot of rich beef stew. George came up behind her, wrapping his arms around her curvy waist and nuzzling her fragrant dark hair.

"Something smells divine, my love," he rumbled. "But shouldn't you be in bed?"

Isabella twisted in his embrace, hazel eyes gleaming playfully. "Well, it's not me – I proper stink!" She gestured at her casual attire splattered from cooking. But to George, she looked radiant.

"I don't care one bit," he said. "In fact, I prefer it when you stink." He drew back to gaze at her tenderly. "Happy Valentine's Day," he said, pulling a small gift box artfully

CHAPTER SIXTEEN

wrapped in shimmering paper and tied with a crimson ribbon from his inside jacket pocket.

"George! We agreed, no presents this year," she admonished, even as her fingers eagerly untied the bow.

George chuckled, drinking in her unconcealed delight. "What can I say? The thought of seeing your beautiful smile when you opened it made my willpower crumble."

Lifting the hinged lid, Isabella caught her breath seeing the delicate silver locket nestled inside. "Oh, it's absolutely lovely," she breathed, gingerly lifting the pendant and watching the delicate chain slither over her fingers.

"Here, let me." George moved behind Isabella, gently brushing back her long chestnut hair to clasp the gleaming chain around her graceful neck. His rough fingers lingered, tracing across her bare shoulders. Isabella shivered at his tender touch.

Turning to face him again, Isabella reverently brushed her thumb over the locket's engraved letters—Isabella. "The engraving is lovely."

George rubbed his neck self-consciously. "That it is," he said. "I may have called in a favour with a certain jewellery-smithing mate to have it commissioned specially for you."

"George Beaumont, you are utterly impossible!" Isabella swatted his arm playfully before leaning up on her toes to kiss him soundly. "But incredibly sweet, too," she conceded softly.

Resting his forehead against hers, George said earnestly, "You deserve this and more, my love."

Isabella gripped his shoulders almost fiercely, her eyes suddenly misty. "You and Olivia are my entire world." Drawing back, she fixed him with a mock stern look. "So no more lavishing me with luxuries, you hear? Your love is the only gift I'll ever need."

George scrunched his nose. "No promises!" He grinned.

"What are you smiling at?"

"You just look so beautiful, Izzy. This, right here—it's what makes the long days bearable."

Isabella's expression softened as she reached up to caress his bearded cheek. "Go wash up, and I'll plate everything up for you."

Over hearty helpings of stew and crusty bread, George unburdened the case troubles weighing on his mind while Isabella listened attentively, absently stroking Rex curled at her feet. Her thoughtful questions and unwavering confidence in him never failed to provide clarity. With Isabella's compassion illuminating his perspective, the path forward emerged from the haze—keep pushing the team unflinchingly towards justice and answers.

Later, George sank back against the plush pillows with a contented sigh, strong arms wrapped around Isabella as she curled into his side. Her thick dark hair was tousled charmingly across the crisp white sheets. George gently smoothed a strand behind her ear, heart swelling as she nuzzled into his palm.

"I've missed this," Isabella murmured, tracing mindless patterns on his bare chest.

George hummed in agreement, the comforting weight of her body against his, chasing away lingering remnants of tension from the day as he ran his fingers through Isabella's silky tresses. "I know, Izzy," George murmured. "I've missed having you all to myself. No distractions or demands on our time except being together." He placed a tender kiss on her temple, breathing in the sweet floral scent of her shampoo.

CHAPTER SIXTEEN

Isabella smiled against his shoulder, fingers trailing lazily down his side. "Mm, just wait until Livvy's a bit older, and we'll have to barricade the door to keep her from interrupting. This is heaven by comparison."

George chuckled and envisions their bright-eyed toddler's uncanny knack for barging in at the most inopportune moments. "Too right. We should treasure the quiet moments while we have them."

Propping herself up on one elbow, Isabella regarded him earnestly, mischief dancing in her hazel eyes. "Exactly. So, however, will we pass the time, Detective Chief Inspector?"

George arched a teasing brow. "I'm sure a clever detective sergeant like yourself can devise a few... creative investigative techniques."

Isabella bit her lip to suppress a grin and trailed a finger down his torso. "Hmm, I may have one or two ideas."

Their lips met in a slow, passionate kiss, the rest of the world fading away.

With tantalising slowness, wearing only the silver locket, she shifted atop him, fingertips tracing each contour of muscle honed from years of physical training. George skimmed his palms reverently down her sides, eliciting a delightful shiver when he reached her hips.

Like choreographed dance partners, they moved together flawlessly, each caress and kiss intimately familiar yet still exhilarating. George cherished these stolen interludes when he could appreciate every nuance of Isabella's expressions, the melodic sounds of her pleasure, the sensual slide of skin on skin.

They stayed wrapped up in each other as their breathing slowed, trading lazy kisses and caresses. George marvelled anew at the contradiction of the formidable investigator who could stare down stone-cold killers and the tender lover currently doing her best to melt him into a puddle with her affections.

Isabella snuggled into his side again with a contented noise. "Happy Valentine's Day."

* * *

George and Isabella, whilst lost in their world of tender intimacy, were oblivious to the fact that their curtains remained ajar, a sliver of vulnerability in their otherwise guarded lives. They were a picture of love and trust, a stark contrast to the lurking darkness outside.

As, in the shadows of the night, a figure sat in a car, their breath fogging up the window, a voyeuristic photographer, their lens a silent intruder into the private world of George and Isabella. With each click of the camera, they captured moments not meant for any eyes but those of the lovers themselves. A perverse excitement surged through them, a twisted joy in invading the sanctity of another's most intimate moments.

They chuckled softly, the sound barely audible over the hum of the car's engine. They were exhilarated by their own daring, the thrill of the forbidden act feeding their dark desires. It was a dangerous game they played, one that could unravel at any moment, yet the risk only heightened their excitement.

As George and Isabella lay entwined, their camera continued its silent assault. Each photo was a stolen piece of a puzzle, a puzzle that, once completed, would reveal the depths of their depravity. Their laughter grew louder, a chilling soundtrack to the unfolding scene.

But this was more than just a perverted thrill for them. This act of voyeurism was a carefully calculated move in a much larger scheme. They were gathering information, piecing together the lives of George and Isabella for reasons known only to them. Each photo was a clue, a tool to be used in a game of chess where the stakes were dangerously high.

Their motivations were as mysterious as their identity, a shadow lurking in the night, watching, waiting. They were a puppet master, pulling the strings in a twisted performance where the unwitting actors played their parts.

As the night wore on, their collection grew, each photo a testament to their skill and cunning. They were a hunter, and George and Isabella were their unwitting prey. But the true nature of their game remained hidden, a secret as dark as the night itself.

Finally, as the couple fell asleep, they retreated into the shadows, their mission accomplished.

George and Isabella, now alone, were unaware of the eyes that had watched them, the lens that had captured their most private moments. They were blissfully ignorant of the danger that lurked just beyond their view, a threat that was now one step closer to revealing itself.

Chapter Seventeen

The following day, DC Candy Nichols pulled up outside the quaint brick facade of Coward's Cafe in the sleepy village of Middleton. Her pulse quickened as she stepped out of the car into the blustery morning. The owner, Justin Coward, had called that morning about potentially critical CCTV footage related to missing teen Esme Bushfield's disappearance. Candy tried to temper rising hope with professional caution, but the prospect of finally a solid lead after days of fruitless searching made her eager.

Entering the cosy cafe, Candy was greeted by savoury aromas and welcoming warmth that belied the grim reason for her visit. Justin hurried over; concern etched on his boyish face.

"Thanks for coming so quickly, Officer. Let me show you the footage straight away."

He led Candy to a cramped back office lined with monitors displaying grainy feeds from both inside the cafe and the exterior street. Taking a seat, Candy focused intently as Justin queued up video from the prior Monday evening.

"I was reviewing old tapes per your department's request when I spotted something odd," Justin explained, queueing grainy footage showing the darkened street. A petite blonde

CHAPTER SEVENTEEN

figure appeared in the circle of light beneath a streetlamp. Candy leaned forward—the girl's hesitant posture, even in pixelation, was instantly recognisable as Esme.

"There she is, the missing girl your team asked us to look out for," Justin confirmed needlessly. Candy catalogued details as Esme paced nervously, appearing to await someone's arrival. Moments later, a male figure approached from the shadows. Esme seemed to relax at his presence, embracing him warmly.

Candy's pulse kicked up a notch. "Can we get a clear view of this man's face?"

Justin shook his head apologetically. "He's quite careful to keep angled away. Believe me, I've analysed it frame by frame, looking for identifying features. But the footage quality is too poor." Justin shrugged. "All I can tell is that he's a black man. Maybe mixed race?"

Candy bit her lip in frustration as the mysterious figure guided Esme inside the cafe entrance below the camera's limited range. "But Esme seems comfortable with him?"

"Very much so," Justin confirmed. "I pulled the interior footage as well once I realised it was her."

He brought up a second video showing Esme and the man seated at a corner table, leaning in close with clasped hands. Though the man's face remained obscured, Esme's smile and frequent laughter spoke of deep familiarity.

Candy jotted notes rapidly, pulse elevating again. This had to be a boyfriend Esme's parents knew nothing about. While concerning, given her age, it also supplied a pivotal lead if they could identify him.

"They were here for two hours until closing," Justin supplied. "Seemed very intimate and affectionate. Paid cash too, unfortunately, so no card trail."

Candy chewed her pen thoughtfully as Esme and the mystery man exited hand in hand once more into the night. A secret relationship could explain much about the normally responsible girl's uncharacteristic behaviour lately.

Back at her car, Candy quickly dialled DCI Beaumont to update him on developments. She could hear the excitement in her superior's voice as he issued rapid directives.

"Excellent work, Candy. This may prove the breakthrough we've desperately needed," George praised enthusiastically. "We'll need to discreetly show Mr and Mrs Bushfield the footage straight away to see if they recognise the individual."

Candy flushed with pleasure at impressing her astute mentor as she signed off. Starting the engine, she headed straight for the Bushfield's apartment in the city centre, mind racing. Surely Esme's meticulous mother at least would know if her studious daughter had a boyfriend, let alone one intimate enough to inspire rebellion.

Unless this relationship was more forbidden than typical youthful rebellion...

* * *

Meanwhile, George hastily prepared the Bushfields to view the mystery footage, underscoring the discretion required to avoid public speculation jeopardising the investigation.

"We must keep this development strictly confidential for now," George emphasised gravely. "No one outside this room can know Esme was spotted with an unidentified male that night."

The Bushfields nodded solemnly, clasping hands tightly. Dorothy pressed a monogrammed handkerchief to her mouth, steeling herself visibly. Stanley' stern expression could not fully disguise the quiver in his voice.

"Just tell us what you've found, Detective Chief Inspector. We simply want our darling girl back home safely."

George's chest tightened at their palpable yearning. "Of course. Detective Constable Nichols is bringing the footage now."

When Candy arrived, she exchanged an anxious look with George before cueing the video. They both braced for intense reactions once the Bushfields saw their daughter in a deceitful context.

But as the CCTV images flickered across the laptop screen, Dorothy gasped loudly, going deathly pale. She grasped Stanley' arm with white-knuckled urgency.

"No, it... it can't be! That's... that's absurd and false!"

Candy paused the footage, alarmed. "You recognise him, ma'am?"

"I... I..." Dorothy faltered, clearly wrestling some internal battle.

Stanley interjected sternly, "This proves nothing. Some hoodlum clearly coerced our daughter into this scandalous facade." His tone brooked no argument.

Candy and George exchanged an uneasy glance at this baffling denial. What were the Bushfields hiding?

"Please, you must identify this man if you're able," George implored gravely. "We only want the truth to bring Esme home safely."

Dorothy dabbed at fresh tears, avoiding their eyes. "The truth? The truth is our darling would never willingly fraternise with such objectionable company!"

"I know the footage is an enormous shock."

Dorothy made a strangled sound. "Shock is hardly the word! To see our innocent angel sneaking about with some rogue nearly twice her age..." She pressed the handkerchief to her trembling lips. "It's positively criminal!"

Stanley gripped his wife's shoulder, glowering fiercely. "Some predator clearly coerced our girl into that deceitful scenario. Mark my words!" His knuckles whitened. "When I discover his identity, he'll curse the day!"

Candy leaned forward earnestly. "We understand your distress, Mr Bushfield. But speculation only hampers our investigation." She hesitated delicately. "Are you certain you don't recognise the man at all?"

"Absolutely not!" Stanley thundered, surging to his feet. "Esme is a proper young lady, not some trollop cavorting with strange men!"

Seeing Candy's startled look, George interceded calmly. "No one believes Esme behaved improperly. But she kept this relationship secret, so identifying the gentleman is imperative."

He met Stanley' stormy gaze unflinchingly. "Whoever this man is, he holds answers. You want to find Esme, right?"

Stanley wavered, the fight seeming to drain from him. He sank down beside Dorothy, head in her hands. "Forgive my outrage. When it's your child lost out there..." His voice cracked unexpectedly.

Dorothy clasped his trembling hands in hers. "We know you're doing everything possible. But our minds torment us with all the horrors she could be facing with some wicked stranger!" Fresh tears coursed down her wan cheeks.

Heart aching for their pain, George moved to kneel comfortingly before the distraught parents.

"We will not stop searching for your daughter," George said.

CHAPTER SEVENTEEN

Dorothy dissolved into muffled sobs, clinging fiercely to her husband now. Stanley lifted reddened eyes over her bent head, managing a faint nod of gratitude at George's sincere promise.

After giving the rattled parents a few moments to compose themselves, George gently redirected the conversation. "Now then, can you recall Esme mentioning recently that could explain these secretive actions? Any peculiar absences or interests?"

Dorothy dabbed her eyes, sitting up slightly. "She was a touch moodier than normal lately... But I assumed adolescent growing pains." She looked imploringly at George. "Teenage rebellion doesn't mean she'd turn to some wicked man, does it?"

"Of course not," Candy assured her softly. "But even small conflicts at home can make girls vulnerable to manipulation." Seeing their stricken looks, she added, "Nothing you did caused this. Predators are master deceivers."

Stanley passed a shaking hand over his ashen face. "We should have been more vigilant for problems... My demanding career kept me away frequently." His voice caught roughly. "But never did I dream my absence could lead to such disaster."

"You shouldn't blame yourselves," George insisted gently. "The fault lies with whoever lured Esme into danger." He leaned forward intently. "Which is why we need to figure out who this man is. Any small detail could prove vital."

The tormented parents wracked their minds but could produce no concrete suspicions around Esme's mystery acquaintance.

"And you're sure you don't know this man?" George asked again.

"For the last time, we do not!" Mrs Bushfield drew herself up defiantly. "Now I really must ask you to leave unless you've actual productive updates."

Recognising adamant denial cemented by fear, George had no choice but to reluctantly withdraw without answers. But the Bushfields' explosive reaction only deepened his suspicion they hid sinister secrets beneath their polished veneer. Whatever Esme had become entangled in, her parents feared the shameful truth emerging, even at the cost of her life.

Exiting the opulent apartment, Candy turned to George with frustration. "They're hiding something! Why can't they see we only want to help Esme?"

George squeezed her shoulder bracingly. "Fear blinds people to the truth, Candy. And reputation means everything in their circles." His mouth twisted bitterly. "But we know Esme met that man in secret the evening she disappeared. Finding his identity remains critical, with or without her parents' help."

Candy took a steadying breath and nodded. "You're absolutely right, sir. We'll uncover the truth ourselves." Her jaw took on a stubborn angle. "And maybe then they'll admit what they're hiding to protect Esme instead of their facade."

George managed a faint grin at his protégé's fervour despite pressures. Her passion lifted his spirits, reminding him why seeking justice mattered.

"Too right. Now let's get back and formally document the footage so we can circulate screen grabs discreetly to potential witnesses." He started briskly towards the car with Candy on his heels.

"This case never gets easier, does it?" Candy remarked

CHAPTER SEVENTEEN

sadly, following his gaze. "No matter how many we work."

George gave a heavy sigh, the weight of urgency bowing his shoulders. "That's why we can't ever give up."

Sliding into the driver's seat with a weary sigh, George pulled out his mobile to update the team on his discouraging visit with the Bushfields. Scrolling to DI Luke Mason's number, he typed out a quick summary:

"Bushfields failed to ID mystery man despite clear familiarity on CCTV. I suspect they know more than admitting—shockingly unhelpful. Priority remains determining bloke's identity through forensic analysis on our end. Hopefully, your interrogations today prove more fruitful, mate."

Next, George shot off a text to eager young DC Jay Scott: "No revelations from the Bushfields yet regarding Esme's mystery man. But there's unease there—keep discreet background checks going on both parents' circles and communications. Paper trail likely buried deep."

Setting his mobile down, George pinched the bridge of his nose against an impending headache. He set off to the station. The Bushfield apartment already seemed like a distant memory swallowed again by the busy city centre rolling past his car windows.

Chapter Eighteen

DCI George Beaumont pulled up at the kerb outside the imposing Brandling House, engine idling as his tired, piercing green eyes scrutinised the stillness shrouding the architecture. Only the faintest light edged the peaked gables and mullioned windows. No signs of life stirred within the grounds.

George leaned back in the seat, groaning as his stiff shoulders protested the long hours hunched in futile study. An unnerving silence engulfed his vehicle, perforated only by the steady patter of rain. He wondered what secrets whispered within the walls of Brandling House about events tied to this place's dark legends.

The ceaseless downpour reflected the bleak hollowness churning inside George lately. Endless, fruitless searches while each minute heightened danger for missing teen Esme Bushfield.

George gritted his teeth, the familiar rush of frustrated impotence threatening to overwhelm professional reason again. Shadows encroached like grasping claws if he dwelled on helplessness. Better to focus on tasks at hand, however futile they felt.

Checking his watch, George noted the dive team was still en route to begin meticulously searching the ponds based on debris found on Ashley Cowgill's clothes. Time they should be utilising already while fragile evidence washed away...

George inhaled deeply, halting his restless fidgeting. A sharp mind, not frayed nerves, must guide actions now. He needed to prepare his team, not dwell on the uncontrollable elements conspiring against them. There was still hope if they persisted.

With a determined nod, George exited the car into the frigid downpour. The icy droplets needling his neck and matting his hair focused his thoughts forward as he splashed towards the front door. Nursing frustrations wasted precious time that young Esme did not have to spare.

George's shoes clacked loudly in the cavernous stone foyer, echoing his grim isolation. Usually a hive of police activity this early, today, an eerie emptiness reigned.

George paused beneath the curved oak staircase, brows furrowing. Where was everyone? He specifically instructed key personnel to arrive promptly today for an urgent briefing.

Shaking his head, George continued towards the back parlour, which served as their makeshift headquarters. Perhaps the team was already gathering there and preparing. Though the absolute silence fostered unease in George's stomach.

Striding down the wood-panelled corridor bordering the gardens, George suddenly froze. Mere steps from the closed parlour doors, the fine hairs on his neck prickled. His senses came alive, honed from years of detecting something amiss and out of place.

Pulse elevating, he crept forward soundlessly, ears straining. Was that faint whispering beyond the polished oak doors?

Poised to kick them open in confrontation, George hesitated. Perhaps weariness bred paranoia? Shaking his head sharply, he was reaching again for the handle when a chill draft stirred the curtains, carrying a faint metallic jangling. George tensed, senses prickling. Likely just old pipes clanging, he told himself firmly, refusing to be unnerved by imaginings. He had no time for distraction by eerie noises that fed superstitious dread. Esme was relying on him keeping a clear head.

The faint sound came again—a distant ringing clatter almost like chains being dragged across the stone. George hesitated, then shook his head sharply. He would not go chasing spectral goose chases conjured by an exhausted mind to avoid facing harsh realities. Real dangers hid not in imaginary haunts but in the murkier recesses of human souls, where evil masked itself in familiar facades. If George succumbed to chasing phantoms rather than braving the tangible darkness right in front of his eyes that had destroyed one young life and possibly another, then he truly failed in his sworn duty to uphold justice.

But another sound disturbed George, and the heavy oak door creaked open, stirring the dust motes swirling in the meagre light. George looked up sharply, half-expecting a spectral visitor based on the eerie atmosphere. But the bulky, bearded figure silhouetted in the doorway was only the caretaker, Bradley Welburn, doing his rounds.

Seeing George, Welburn shuffled in, thumbs tucked into the straps of his denim coveralls. "Now then, Detective. I trust you're doing OK, eh?" His gruff tone held a note of grudging respect. "Nasty business, young ones running off into the night. Especially with the wretched spirits roaming these parts."

George's gaze sharpened. "What spirits are those?"

"Well, you've heard the local legends, surely." Welburn

glanced around nervously, even in the light. "These old grounds have their fair share of ghosts wandering."

Leaning forward intently, George fixed Welburn with his piercing stare. "Tell me."

The caretaker shrunk back but mumbled, "Right, well, folks round here whisper of a pale lady seen drifting about the Drift late at night, clad in grey with long silver hair. Those passing her say a bone chill worse than the cold night air grips their hearts. My own uncle swore he saw her himself!"

Welburn visibly shivered before continuing. "Then there's talk of a young blonde girl playing hide and seek 'round the trees, giggling like it's all a game. But her face... it doesn't seem of this world, glowing too bright and terrible." He made a warding gesture. "Harbingers of doom if you cross their path after dark, or so the old-timers say."

George listened intently, features schooled into scepticism to avoid encouraging superstitious folly. But inwardly, he filed away the intriguing details. Local lore often held seeds of truth, however distorted into legend.

"Hmph, ghost stories," George scoffed aloud. "More superstitious nonsense. Though I admit, ladies matching those descriptions on the grounds late at night could prove important." His tone made clear chasing shadows was futile compared to real evidence.

Welburn shot him a sour look. "Suit yourself, Detective, but some things can't be explained away so easily." He whistled softly for his dog Jessie, lingering near the door before departing without another word, shoulders hunched self-consciously under George's scrutiny.

"No such thing as ghosts," George said as he rubbed his eyes. They hadn't gone to bed until three that morning. George was exhausted, especially as Isabella had woken him up in the throes of thrashing, apparently having been screaming about witches at about six am.

A heavy weariness seeped into George's bones as he placed his hand on the cold brass doorknob; a chilling draft stirred the curtains behind him. He froze, skin prickling as the cloying scent of damp earth and metal assaulted his senses.

There came a noise then like iron chains dragged across stone. George whirled, heart in his throat. But only the empty room met his wild eyes.

Shaking his head sharply, George wrenched open the heavy door, eager to escape the oppressive atmosphere. His nerves were simply frayed from fatigue and frustration.

* * *

Stepping outside into the bracing morning air helped dispel the last clinging unease from George's mind. The world felt newly washed, full of hope and possibility after the night's purging rain. He strode briskly down the gravel drive to where vehicles were pulling up on Town Street, ready to greet the search teams and provide direction. Thermal drones were already buzzing overhead, operators calibrating sophisticated instruments. No shadows would escape their scrutiny.

Seeing George approach, the lead coordinator gave him a brisk nod. "Morning, sir! The lads are just gearing up to begin a sweep of the pond perimeter. We'll be as thorough as humanly possible."

George clapped the man's shoulder approvingly. "That's exactly what I need to hear. We have a missing girl out there. I know your team won't stop until we find them."

CHAPTER EIGHTEEN

The coordinator straightened, looking gratified by George's faith in their capabilities. "Too right, sir! My men understand how precious little clues can make all the difference." He turned to muster his team. "You heard the detective—by the book and leave no stones unturned, lads!"

George observed the ripple of determination passing through the searchers at their leader's rallying call. They looked up for it. Good.

"Right then, we have a long day ahead," George declared crisply. "So let's get to it!"

* * *

A chill winter breeze rustled the fallen leaves scattered across the damp grass as DCI George Beaumont strode purposefully towards Top Hill Pond. Beside him, eager young DC Jay Scott scrambled to match the detective's brisk stride, nearly tripping over an exposed tree root in his haste.

Approaching the pond's muddy bank, George noted the search team technicians already unpacking equipment and speaking in low, serious tones. He felt cautiously hopeful at this tangible progress after days of opaque dead ends. Surely the pond's secrets would unveil clues to finding missing student Esme Bushfield if explored meticulously.

The stocky, balding coordinator straightened at George's arrival. "Ah, Detective Chief Inspector. We're just finalising calibration of sonar and underwater drones for an exhaustive sweep of the pond and connected drainage pipes." He gestured at the assembled equipment. "My most experienced technicians will thoroughly scan and document any subsurface anomalies."

George nodded approvingly. "Sonar imaging should help identify any submerged items or disturbances. But we'll also need divers prepared for close visual inspection."

"Of course, sir," the coordinator affirmed. "My most experienced pair will enter after the bots map terrain and potential snags. These waters can be treacherous if careless." He lowered his voice grimly. "Mud's been known to swallow a man halfway to hell if not cautious."

Suppressing a shiver at the ominous reference, George replied briskly, "I trust your team's expertise to handle the conditions safely. Just ensure every inch is scrutinised, OK?"

The coordinator slapped a gloved hand on the equipment case. "Don't you worry, sir. My lads know how to succeed. Trust us to do our jobs."

Leaving the man to oversee preparations, George stepped back, exhaling heavily. At least dredging through murky depths did not require grappling with the entitled aristocrats concealing secrets. And George much preferred that.

Noticing Jay hovering awkwardly, George gestured him over. "Remember, our role is calm oversight. Don't distract the specialists."

"Got it, boss," Jay responded eagerly. "But this is dead exciting. I've never been involved in anything like this before!" His bright grin dimmed slightly at George's stern expression. "But there's a girl's life at stake. Point taken. Sorry, boss."

Suppressing a fond smile at the lad's irrepressible spirit despite the bleak task, George clapped Jay's shoulder lightly. "Keep up the positive energy, Jay, but be respectful, OK?"

"OK, boss," Jay said, practically glowing under the gruff praise as they moved to the water's edge. George knew the vibrant young detective's innate cheer often lifted flagging morale during these grinding investigations. He would do well nurturing that gift along with Jay's analytical diligence. But he needed to be more respectful.

Consulting his tablet, Jay remarked, "The smaller Top Hill Pond makes more sense for initial searching over the sprawling pond in the park, right boss? Less surface area to cover before moving onto bigger waters."

George nodded approvingly. "Logical. And according to the architectural plans, this pond's drainage connects to the larger pond in the park, anyway, so we'll need to inspect that at some point." His mouth thinned grimly.

Chapter Nineteen

As the tedious dredging commenced under Jay's attentive supervision, George did a circuit of the perimeter barriers, noting with frustration the crowds of curious onlookers lingering nearby. Despite police tape and warnings, these sensation seekers still flocked like moths to a flame, hindering access and progress.

Spotting a boisterous group of teens jostling recklessly at the tape's edge, George strode over sternly. "You! Step back! This is a restricted area, not a spectacle."

The youths glanced over sullenly before continuing their antics. "Piss off, pig," one jeered. "Reckon we've a right to see our mates get dragged from the pond."

George's eyes blazed at the disrespect. "I suggest you do one before I get mad!" He stepped closer menacingly. "Now!"

Grumbling bitterly but cowed by George's formidable presence, the teens dispersed from the increasingly tense scene. George shook his head grimly before moving to address the hovering press corps.

"Detective Chief Inspector!" one pushy journalist called out while her colleagues snapped photos. "Why the pond search now? Is it a body recovery?"

Raising a hand to block their invasive lenses, George declared sternly, "This is a highly sensitive ongoing investigation. No further comment."

But the tabloid vultures continued hurling invasive questions to goad any reaction as George turned his back on them. He understood public interest but despised impulsive speculation fuelling misinformation and circus sideshow appetites.

Returning to Jay, who was noting the interactions, George remarked irritably, "I wish we could rope off the whole bloody area to keep distractions away. This obsessive gawking only hampers our work."

Jay nodded sympathetically. "Vultures the lot of 'em, boss."

They watched in pensive silence as the divers ventured deeper, trailing safety lines behind them. The pond's calm surface revealed nothing of the hidden depths below where dangers might lurk. But George remained confident in the seasoned team's ability.

After an hour of meticulous searching, however, the pond seemed to be relinquishing nothing but algae and minnows. George noted the divers surfacing to confer with the frowning coordinator. Striding closer, he overheard their frustrated discussion.

"It's no use fumbling about in this muck," the stocky lead diver declared, ripping off his mask irritably. "Zero visibility past two feet with all the stirred-up silt." He shot his partner an accusing look. "I told you not to go barging about stomping like a bull!"

The other diver bristled. "Sorry, but it's hopeless now. No way to spot anything in this swampy shit." He winced when he saw the DCI watching him. "Please excuse my French, sir."

Sensing escalating tensions, the coordinator intervened

diplomatically. "Easy, lad, we're all feeling the pressure here. Take five to clear your head while I update the detectives?"

The team complied grudgingly, sloshing their way to shore with frustrated energy. George frowned, impatience simmering beneath his calm facade.

Approaching the coordinator questioningly, George asked in a low tone, "What's your next strategy if they can't get visual confirmation?"

The man grimaced apologetically. "I reckon dredging is our sole option left, sir. We'd need to systematically scoop sections, sift through contents above water." He gestured at the churned-up pond. "Not a pretty solution, but we can't grope about blindly down there forever."

George nodded sharply. "Understood. Just get it done quickly and thoroughly." He turned his piercing gaze on the restless divers. "Are they OK?"

"A young girl is missing, sir. They're all a bit tetchy and on edge. I think that's natural." He clapped his gloved hands briskly. "Right, lads, back to work!"

In short order, they had recalibrated their strategy to systematically dredge sections in a rational grid.

A heavy melancholy settled upon DCI George Beaumont as he stood alone near the roped-off Hill Top Pond, observing. His sharp eyes followed the divers' slow, carefully controlled movements in the gloom beneath the surface, knowing their diligent commitment was likely the best chance at uncovering solid leads. Yet the lack of definitive breakthroughs so far still gnawed at George.

Glancing at his watch, George noted the late hour. As much as it pained him to leave the site, he knew he could be utilising time productively by following up on other personal leads

CHAPTER NINETEEN

while the divers continued their tedious hunt. Specifically, George aimed to track down the elusive caretaker, Bradley Welburn, who had been suspiciously slippery regarding his activities and whereabouts when last questioned. Perhaps away from the intimidating pressure of formal inquiry, George could coax greater honesty from the gruff man if he caught him unawares.

With the decision made, George called Jay over to apprise him of taking temporary leave. "I'm going to follow up on a few promising threads back at Brandling House. Maintain coordinated efforts here and alert me straight away if anything of note arises."

Jay nodded crisply, his youthful features set with solemn purpose. "You can count on me, boss." He offered an encouraging grin.

Clasping Jay's shoulder gratefully, George replied, "We'll get there, Jay. We always do."

Departing the bustling pond site, George experienced an almost surreal hush enveloping his senses as he navigated the ascending path alone. With only the crunch of gravel beneath his boots perforating the silence, memories and unease he had kept carefully compartmentalised during the urgent investigation came seeping back through mental cracks.

Pausing midway along the deserted path known eerily as The Drift, George gazed warily between the thick trunks crowding claustrophobically on either side. As a young teen, he had breathlessly pedalled this route, adrenaline spiking when shadows seemed to lunge from the blackness. The chilling local legend of a witch's ghost cursing any who dared trespass near her house had lurked in young George's imagination then like the creeping fog tendrils now curling between the trees.

Shaking his head sharply, George shrugged off irrational tension. He refused to be unnerved by superstitious folly; however, this winding forest passage and its phantoms had pried open a vulnerable sliver of his hardened psyche. The missing girls depended on his unflappable professionalism, not flights of fancy.

Nevertheless, George felt profoundly grateful when the stark facade of Brandling House finally emerged from the swirling mists. Striding swiftly towards it, George was struck by how the imposing architecture appeared almost like a stern sentinel keeping vigil over Middleton Park.

Entering the cavernous main hall, George was greeted only by echoing silence, the space devoid of its usual officers. Checking his watch, he surmised the hour had drawn them to the kitchen for a meal before resuming duties. But the emptiness fostered unease after his unsettling walk. George tried shrugging off irrational tension, reminding himself that dangers often hid behind familiar facades, not in spectral imaginings. The true monsters were of the human variety.

There was no such thing as phantoms or witches.

Detective Chief Inspector George Beaumont strode briskly inside Brandling House, keen eyes scanning for signs of new developments in the urgent search for missing student Esme Bushfield. Detective Constable Jay Scott scrambled to match George's swift, determined pace towards the back parlour serving as their makeshift headquarters.

Reaching the polished oak doors, George paused, intrigued to hear multiple agitated voices filtering out to the hall. Hand on the brass knob, he said aloud, "Sounds like something's brewed since I've left."

CHAPTER NINETEEN

Entering the room, George's gaze landed first on Ashley Cowgill's distraught mother, Sandra, arguing fiercely with a uniformed officer. Her husband Johnny stood close behind, features thunderous.

"This is fucking ridiculous!" Sandra was declaring hotly. "Our daughter has endured severe trauma and needs rest, not to be dragged back to this dreadful place!"

Approaching briskly, George interjected in a firm but soothing tone, "Let's all take a deep breath and explain what's happened." He turned calmly to the flustered officer. "SITREP?"

The man glanced down to consult his notes. "Right, well, apparently, Ashley Cowgill demanded to be brought back to Brandling House just an hour ago, sir. Wanted to aid the search for Esme Bushfield personally despite still recovering from her ordeal."

"This is fucking bullshit!" Johnny exploded before George could respond. "Our girl's in no fit state to be traipsing about outside a clinical setting." He jabbed an angry finger at the officer. "You should have refused and contacted us first!"

Holding up a placating hand, George said gently, "I understand your concern completely. But Ashley is of age to make her own choices. Our priority is supporting her during this unstable time, not exerting control."

He turned back to the officer evenly. "What is Miss Cowgill's current condition? Does the consultant therapist deem her mentally competent?"

The man glanced at his notes again. "Dr Miriam Kowalski medically cleared Ms Cowgill before releasing her into police custody for transit here from her home. Notes indicate she's quite adamant and lucid regarding aiding the search despite ongoing trauma symptoms."

George nodded. "OK. Thanks for the update."

Sandra's anger crumbled into tears. "It's our job to keep our baby safe! Why can't she see that?"

George chose his next words carefully. "Because Ashley probably feels she failed someone who depended on her. That guilt is a powerful motivator now, however misplaced."

At George's approach, Candy looked up, features tight with concern. In an undertone, she murmured, "Ashley's quite determined, sir. But I worry she's on the knife's edge still."

George nodded, studying the high-strung girl thoughtfully.

Taking a seat across from Ashley, George kept his posture open and non-threatening. "Ashley, I understand you asked to return to aid the search efforts for Esme. We appreciate you braving this difficult step." He held her darting eyes. "Now, what do you remember of your reasons for originally coming here that night?"

Ashley bit her lip, leg jiggling restlessly. In a rasping voice, she replied haltingly, "It was my idea to sneak out. Wanted adventure and figured Esme needed fun too." Her eyes squeezed shut. "But it all went so wrong!"

Candy squeezed Ashley's shoulder reassuringly as sobs overtook her. Once she had regained shaky composure, George probed delicately, "What fun activities did you have in mind originally?"

Ashley shrugged jerkily, shame clouding her drawn features. "Just walk through the woods at night, maybe have a smoke or a drink. Break the rules together." She twisted the end of her braid, addled gaze distant. "I thought Esme wanted that too. But she got upset, we fought..."

"You had an argument?" George pressed carefully. "What did you fight about? Even fragments help establish events."

CHAPTER NINETEEN

"It's blurry..." Ashley's breathing quickened, hands clenching. Sensing rising panic, Candy shot George a warning look.

Softening his tone further, George redirected gently, "It's alright, no need to force anything. You're very brave coming back here at all. But is there any specific spot in the area that feels significant to focus on?"

Ashley's eyes cleared marginally. Brow furrowing, she replied haltingly, "The stage by the pond... we went there... Esme was scared, but I laughed it off..." Her breaths accelerated again into gasps.

Candy intervened smoothly, steering the crumbling girl away for a quick break. Watching them go, George mentally reviewed this new information. The stage was a solid lead at last. If forensics could uncover trace evidence of events there, significant breakthroughs were possible.

Snagging his radio, George requested an immediate priority search of the stage near the pond in Middleton Park. Any biological traces or signs of disturbance could prove critical, though degradation from the elements remained a challenge. Then again, the stage had a roof over it. But that could cause problems of its own, especially if people spent time under the stage to get out of the weather.

Shit.

Ending the transmission, George took a steadying breath. They were finally closing in. One piece led to another if you just traced the chain. Now, he needed to gently press Ashley for any other glimmers buried in her shattered mind. Psychological recovery took time, but they were racing fate to find Esme.

Chapter Twenty

George lingered outside the room, observing through the narrow pane of glass as DC Candy Nichols spoke in low, soothing tones with the hunched figure of traumatised teen Ashley Cowgill. Though Ashley had bravely insisted on returning to Brandling House to aid the search for missing friend Esme Bushfield, the endeavour was clearly taxing her fragile psyche to its limits.

George wrestled internally, jaw tightening. Every instinct screamed to intervene and cease questioning that risked further psychological damage. But the clock ticked mercilessly as the hope of finding Esme alive dwindled with each fruitless hour. George desperately needed Ashley to dig up any fragment of memories from that ominous night, no matter how traumatic it was before the cold darkness swallowed more innocent lives.

Scrubbing a hand down his face, George forcibly steadied his whirling thoughts. He must temper empathy with reason. Ashley was barely holding together, but she had come willingly, determined to help find Esme despite the costs. He owed it to both girls to gently coax out resonances from Ashley's shattered psyche that could illuminate answers. There was no neat, painless path ahead.

CHAPTER TWENTY

Squaring his shoulders, George entered quietly. Ashley was curled into herself on the leather sofa, arms wrapped tightly around her knees. Seeing George, Candy shot him a worried glance even as she continued speaking reassuringly to the trembling girl.

Kneeling slowly to meet Ashley's downcast eyes, George kept his voice infinitely gentle. "Why don't we start simple? What were you and Esme planning to do last Monday night when you left the house?"

Ashley bit her lip, leg jiggling faster. "I don't really remember..." she mumbled vaguely, still not looking up. "Just wanted to get out for a bit, I guess."

Nodding patiently, George tried again. "Understandable after feeling cooped up. Did Esme seem bothered by anything that day? Upset or nervous at all?"

At this, Ashley finally glanced up, brow furrowing. "She was quieter than usual in lessons. And she got snippy when I kept peeking at her notes." Ashley shrugged weakly. "Figured she was just stressed about exams, though."

George leaned forward slightly, intrigued by this new information. "How unusual was it for Esme to be distracted during class?"

Ashley picked at a loose thread on her sleeve. "Pretty weird for her. Esme was normally little miss perfect student." Her eyes took on a faraway sheen. "Always had her nose in some giant textbook and highlighters all colour-coded."

She flushed slightly. "Drove me mental how easily good grades came to her. Me, I could barely focus long enough to..." Ashley trailed off, paling as she seemed to remember it was her idea to sneak out that fateful night.

Seeing her withdraw again, George redirected the conversation. "This boyfriend we saw Esme with. Did she mention him at all to you?"

Wrapping her arms around herself protectively, Ashley shook her head jerkily. "What boyfriend?"

George showed her a picture of Esme and the man in Coward's Café.

"She never said anything about some mystery fella. Esme wasn't like that." Ashley blinked hard. "Was she?"

"You tell us," said George.

"She wasn't interested in boys. Not really. Not if you discount Ishaan," Ashley said.

"She liked Ishaan?"

Ashley shrugged. "Who didn't."

Gently, George said, "You're being so brave, Ashley. I know how difficult this is. We just need you to think carefully back to when you last saw Esme that night. Can you provide any other details after your argument at the stage?"

Ashley shuddered violently, rocking harder. Candy squeezed her shoulder supportively. "It's alright, just take your time. You're safe here."

After a long moment, Ashley finally whispered in a ragged, near-inaudible rasp, "We argued. Esme got mad about... about something I said..." Her breaths accelerated dangerously.

Exchanging another tense look with Candy, George cautiously prompted, "What did you argue about, Ashley? We need the full truth to find Esme."

But Ashley only released a strangled groan, fists clenching white-knuckled. Sobs threatening to erupt into hysteria. Signalling George discreetly, Candy intervened with calming phrases about breathing deeply and regaining control.

Watching the girl's distress escalate sharply, self-recrimination threatened to drown George. He never should have allowed this confrontation so soon against all instincts. But the deed was done now; he could only forge ahead with utmost care and patience.

When Ashley's hyperventilating finally eased somewhat, Candy caught George's eye again and gestured subtly at her watch. Time was slipping away, but they had pushed this poor girl to her very limits for now. Wordlessly, George nodded and withdrew, shoulders slumping with shame at causing such anguish.

In the quiet hallway, George noticed Ashley's parents approaching briskly, clearly having heard their daughter's distress. He moved swiftly to intercept them, raising placating hands.

"Mr and Mrs Cowgill, please-"

Sandra spoke, voice jagged. "Just answer me this—will raking through painful memories actually help locate that other missing girl?" Her eyes probed George's beseechingly.

George chose his next words exceedingly carefully. "I cannot guarantee that, but any details could prove the critical missing piece. Our intentions are solely to gently recover those lost memories, not cause further harm." He held Sandra's uncertain gaze. "Please trust that I only want what is best for both girls, however difficult the way forward appears."

As the Cowgills digested this in uneasy silence, the parlour doors opened, and Candy exited discreetly. Approaching swiftly, her expression conveyed deep foreboding. George's pulse elevated in instinctive dread.

"Sir, a word, please," Candy murmured tersely. Her stark tone brooked no delay. Excusing himself hurriedly from the Cowgills, George followed Candy down the shadowy corridor until they were out of earshot.

Halting beneath a curtained alcove, Candy faced George grimly. "I think Ashley's on the brink of complete psychological breakdown, sir." Her frown deepened. "She needs help, not questioning."

George scrubbed a hand down his face, guilt and frustration churning within him. "You're right. I'm sorry."

"No need, sir. You haven't done anything wrong. If anything, you're more respectful than anybody in your position needs to be." She smiled and nodded at her boss. "I think, though, sir, she's given all she safely can for now." Her piercing eyes flashed. "Is that OK?"

"I should inform her parents that we will cease questioning for now and arrange a safe transport to the hospital for supervised recovery," he said quietly. "I'm going to arrest Garforth and take him away for questioning."

Candy nodded. "A wise call, sir." She touched his arm gently. "Do you want me to go with Ashley?"

Bolstered slightly by her compassionate strength, George nodded. "Please." He hesitated. "And keep me informed."

* * *

Alone again, George sank back into the leather armchair, scrubbing a hand down his face wearily. The tense encounter had illuminated little definitively, though Ashley's fractured recollections at least hinted that Esme's atypical behaviour may have preceded her disappearance, not been spurred by it—a subtle yet potentially telling thread.

But heavier on George's mind was Ashley's acute distress and whatever psychological wounds festered. He could not in good conscience subject her to further interrogation until she had recovered. But by doing so, he was failing Esme.

Straightening slowly, George tucked away his notebook. The truth waited silently to be uncovered, but it could not come at an innocent girl's expense. Ashley had endured unspeakable darkness; she deserved every care now, not further harm. Esme would surely want it that way.

Exiting the parlour, George headed upstairs to resume coordinating search efforts, the image of Ashley's haunted eyes lingering hauntingly.

"Oh! Apologies, sir, I was coming to update you on developments."

George's pulse quickened instinctively. "Go on, then."

"Sergeant Greenwood has Eugene Garforth in custody as requested, sir."

After thanking the officer, George headed downstairs towards the more humble staff quarters housed in the west wing. He kept alert for any signs of the caretaker, hoping to intercept Welburn going about his routine duties. A casual conversation might reveal clues spoken in confidence that were impossible to extract via formal interrogation.

Descending the narrow staircase, George quietly navigated the starkly utilitarian lower hall towards the caretaker's cramped residence. Hearing shuffling movement within, George paused, listening intently. The cadence and footfalls matched his recollection of Welburn's lumbering gait rather than any furtive intruder.

Raising his fist, George knocked briskly, calling out, "Bradley Welburn, It's DCI Beaumont. Are you in?"

* * *

DC Alexis Mercer steadied her nerves with a slow exhale before approaching the imposing oak door of the duplex apartment. She had an appointment to interview Lori Marie Garforth, the ex-wife of elusive estate owner Eugene Garforth, who was a person of intense interest in the disappearance of teenager Esme Bushfield from his property Brandling House.

Alexis knew any insights into Eugene's character could prove critical, but something about this unknown woman unsettled her. The aura of faded wealth clinging to this neighbourhood contrasted ominously with the reputation for volatility Alexis had heard whispers of regarding Ms Garforth. Intimidating socialite versus seasoned detective—Alexis steeled her resolve before knocking firmly.

The door swung open abruptly, revealing a tall, imposing woman with dramatically coiffed platinum blonde hair. Icy blue eyes raked over Alexis contemptuously.

"You must be the constable. Well, you'd better come in then." The woman turned and strode inside without waiting for a response.

Smoothing her surprise at the brusque greeting, Alexis followed the woman into a dated sitting room cluttered with antique furnishings. Vivid oil paintings crowded the walls, and ornate mirrors reflected Alexis's own tense expression.

Turning sharply, the woman fixed Alexis with an imperious stare. "I'm Lori Garforth. What exactly do you want?"

Alexis opened her notebook calmly despite her inward fluster. "Thank you for agreeing to speak with me, Ms Garforth. As you know, we're seeking information on Eugene Garforth regarding an active investigation."

Lori waved a hand brusquely. "Yes, yes, that whole sordid business with the school girls at his precious Brandling

House." She raised one sharply sculpted eyebrow. "I kept the name for appearances after the divorce. But make no mistake, I'm done with that snake."

Intrigued by this venomous tone, Alexis asked conversationally, "How long were you and Eugene married, if you don't mind me asking?"

Lori shrugged elegantly. "Nearly ten years, unfortunately. The last few were utterly wretched." She shook her head resentfully. "But one must keep up appearances."

Sensing an opening to press for more, Alexis remarked, "The divorce seemed quite sudden two years ago. Was the split rather...contentious?"

Snorting derisively, Lori sneered, "That's putting it mildly. But one must be pragmatic in maintaining social circles." Her glare turned icy. "Not that the details are any business of yours."

Chastened, Alexis backtracked diplomatically. "My apologies, I didn't mean to pry. I only wished to determine if Eugene confided any unusual personal... predilections to you that could prove relevant to our investigation."

Lori's haughty expression shifted briefly to unease. She turned away under the pretence of adjusting an ornate vase. "I make it a policy not to speak ill of exes. But Eugene did have unsavoury appetites, even then." She hesitated before continuing bitterly, "I saw how he leered at schoolgirls when he thought I didn't notice. And don't get me started on the filth he called 'art photography' on his phone."

Lori's lip curled with disgust before she seemed to remember herself. "But I shouldn't speak on it. The man has powerful allies to protect his reputation."

Alexis' pulse quickened, glimpsing the hidden ugliness Lori

hinted at beneath Eugene's polished veneer. But clearly, the socialite had shared all she dared. Coaxing more required delicacy and discretion.

Closing her notebook, Alexis adopted a casual tone. "You've given me helpful background context, thank you. My apologies again for the intrusion."

As Lori walked her briskly to the ornate front doors, Alexis turned to her with an encouraging smile. "If you recall anything further related to Eugene's behaviours or relationships with young women, please call me directly any time. Your insights could prove invaluable."

Handing Lori her card, Alexis firmly met the tall woman's uncertain ice-blue eyes.

"I understand your predicament regarding reputation and connections. Anything you share will be handled with utmost sensitivity. You have my word."

Lori searched Alexis' earnest expression before giving a brief, tight nod as she closed the door firmly.

Striding down the marble steps back to her car, Alexis exhaled unsteadily. The interview had yielded unsettling hints aligning with broader suspicions about depraved appetites hidden beneath Garforth's respectable veneer. Her very skin crawled recalling Lori's oblique references to schoolgirls and pornography.

Settling in the driver's seat, Alexis firmly shoved down disgust and outrage to mentally review the situation objectively. However disturbing, she lacked solid evidence yet to justify confronting the influential man outright. That would take meticulous research and analysis of records to uncover irrefutable truth.

Starting the engine decisively, Alexis was about to pull away when she received a knock on the window. A tall, beautiful woman with dramatically coiffed platinum blonde hair and Icy blue eyes stared at Alexis. Lori Garforth. Alexis wound down the window. "Everything OK, Ms Garforth?"

Lori dropped a USB drive through the window into Alexis' open hand. She said, "You'll find some very interesting emails on that." Then Lori walked away.

As Alexis navigated the winding streets back towards the station, her unease transformed into burning determination.

Chapter Twenty-one

The sounds of rummaging abruptly ceased, followed by a weighty silence. George was about to knock again more firmly when the scarred wooden door reluctantly creaked open a crack. Bloodshot eyes beneath bushy brows peered out warily.

Seeing George standing expectantly, the door opened wider, revealing Welburn's hulking figure in grease-stained coveralls. "Evening, Detective. I was just tidying up." Despite the casual words, his shifting eyes betrayed unease.

Keeping his tone friendly, George replied, "Mind if I come in for a chat?"

Welburn hesitated, gaze flickering down the empty hall, before stepping reluctantly aside. "Aye, suppose there's no harm in a chat."

Ducking into the cramped, dusty area, George let his observant gaze sweep over the surroundings, searching for any illuminating details. The worn wooden desk was littered with crumpled takeaway wrappers, stained mugs, and dog-eared racing forms. An ashtray overflowing with cigarette butts sat among scattered tools. The fragrant aroma of fresh tobacco smoke lingered in the air. Along the far wall, sagging shelves held paint cans, boxes of lightbulbs, and assorted clutter. A rickety bed with a lumpy mattress took up much of the

CHAPTER TWENTY-ONE

remaining floor space.

Overall, the disorder did not surprise George given the nature of Welburn's work. But something about the dingy space kindled his intuition. What was it exactly?

Turning casually to Welburn lingering by the doorway as if ready to bolt, George gestured at the chaotic desk. "Apologies for interrupting your work. I can't imagine working in this creaky, old house is restful."

Welburn simply grunted, avoiding direct eye contact. "Managing well enough. She still stands steady, Brandling House does." He scooped some wrappers into the rubbish bin, adding gruffly, "Keeping after the kids leaves little time for sitting about."

George nodded. "About that—I wanted to ask if you'd had any issues with unruly students lately? Any concerning behaviours or individuals come to your attention?" He kept his tone conversational.

Welburn scratched at his beard, still not meeting George's eyes fully. "They're all a wildly boisterous lot, Detective. But the missing girls were no worse than the rest as far as I ever saw." His tone held a note of wariness.

"I see," George replied neutrally. "And you've had no notable incidents with any particular students then?" He glanced deliberately around. "No signs certain individuals have been spending time here with you?"

At this, Welburn finally lifted his head, features tightening. "Not sure I take your meaning, Detective."

George crossed his arms. "It's just you have quite the little den for off-limits entertainment here if you wished." He gestured at the dingy bed. "And yet I notice no touches making it feel like home…"

He trailed off as Welburn shifted his bulky frame, clearly discomfited. "My private affairs are none of your concern, Detective," he grumbled evasively.

"They are if they involve minors under your care and this roof," George countered gravely. "I know items were removed following our initial search. What might forensic analysis of those reveal about your..."

George said nothing more, inviting Welburn to speak. But instead of speaking, Welburn's ruddy features paled at the implied threat. He attempted no blustering denial, just kept his eyes on George.

The silence between George and Welburn stretched taut as a garotte. George kept his gaze fixed intently on the hulking caretaker, radiating stern expectation. He would not allow Welburn's evasive silence to obscure the grim truth hinted at in his file.

Finally, George bit out coldly, "Enough dancing around it. Let's discuss the police report from nineteen years back alleging your sexual misconduct with a fifteen-year-old girl under your supervision."

Welburn flinched violently, face draining of colour. "I- I don't know what you mean," he stammered weakly, not meeting George's eyes. "I were barely more than a lad myself nineteen years ago!"

"You were twenty-five years old, Mr Welburn," George corrected crisply. "Considered a full-grown adult despite the shamefully lax law at the time." He speared Welburn with an icy glare. "We take a very stern view of adults exploiting minors now. The welfare of vulnerable youths in your care is my priority."

Sweat now beaded Welburn's brow under George's unrelenting scrutiny. He twisted his grimy cap in meaty hands. "It were all just a big misunderstanding, I swear it! The girl got disciplined and told wild tales for revenge."

He finally lifted pleading eyes to George. "You have to believe me, Detective—I never touched her! Those charges destroyed my good name over nothing!" Welburn waved his arms about. "Just look where I fucking live now! And what I fucking do for a job! All because of that-that stupid fucking girl and her lies!"

George's expression remained grimly impassive. "So you say. But there's no smoke without a fire." He tilted his head. "What reason would a young girl have to falsely implicate you? Eh?"

Welburn's mouth opened and closed helplessly. Seeing he had no credible response, George pressed the offensive.

"Just admit it to me now! You're the one who kidnapped and raped Ashley Cowgill, and you still have Esme Bushfield!"

When George did not relent, Welburn switched to blustering defiance. "I won't be badgered to prove my innocence against some teenage delinquent's attention-seeking lies years ago! Surely you have more pressing current matters to investigate? Such as finding Esme Bushfield!" Sweat now dripped down Welburn's ruddy features as he desperately sought any escape. But George had backed him into an inescapable corner.

"Tell me the truth, Welburn."

Shoulders slumping in defeat, Welburn rasped reluctantly, "I am telling you the truth."

On his way out, what drew George's gaze was a single framed photograph on the dresser of a smiling young brunette girl, no more than eight years old. Studying it, George decided against retreating and inquired conversationally, "Who's the little one? Your niece?"

Welburn shuffled his feet, avoiding George's eyes. "My daughter, Claire. It were taken before..." He trailed off raggedly before clearing his throat. "Well, she must be nearly twenty now." He lapsed into pained silence.

George's eyes traced the girl's vibrant smile, contrasting her father's current defeated aura. "You two were close then?" he asked gently.

Welburn sat heavily on the creaking cot. "Aye, thick as thieves once upon a time." He stared down at his scuffed boots. "Her mum took off when she were just seven. But we managed alright, me and Claire." His gaze took on a faraway sheen. "I'd sing her silly songs while cooking supper, and we'd stay up late just giggling over nothing." A faint smile ghosted his bearded face before fading. "Happy days... seem a lifetime ago now."

Seeing an opening in the man's unexpected candour, George pulled over a rickety chair. "What changed?" he probed, keeping his tone neutral.

The smile slid off Welburn's face. "Claire's mum came back after five years. Filled the girl's head with poisonous lies about me." His fists clenched. "Took my daughter away for good, just like that."

"I'm sorry," George said sincerely. "Losing those you love leaves a wound nothing can heal." George thought about Mia and her threats. So far, she'd done nothing to take his rights away as Jack's father, but the woman didn't usually make threats without following them through.

Welburn grunted ambiguously before visibly recoiling back behind his fortress of gruffness. "We all have our burdens to bear alone. Anyhow, my life's not your concern." He stood

CHAPTER TWENTY-ONE

abruptly, nodding at the door. "I'm sure you've important police work awaiting, Detective."

Sensing the man's walls slamming back up, George internally debated his next move. Having glimpsed the deep hurts Welburn suppressed, he felt reluctant to resume aggressive interrogation just yet. The caretaker was prickly as a porcupine, but George's instincts said probing gently might yet reveal crucial insights if he built some rapport first.

Rising slowly, George adopted a casual tone. "Actually, I've hit a wall on this blasted case and could use a fresh perspective." He paused. "It's why I was so hard on you. No hard feelings?"

"Aye, whatever," Bradley replied.

"Why don't we head upstairs to the library and have a chat, see if your knowledge can complement my own?"

He could see the temptation to unburden himself warring with reluctance in the caretaker's cagy eyes. After a moment, Welburn gave a terse nod and gruffly replied, "Suppose I can spare a few minutes glancing things over."

* * *

Sat nursing a cup of coffee in the canteen, Alexis considered Lori's biting characterisation of Eugene as possessing unsavoury appetites for schoolgirls even years ago during their sham marriage. The socialite's disgust impugning his cache of photography was clearly no baseless rumour. While lacking solid proof yet, Alexis' intuition insisted Lori's vague disgust hinted at depravity still shielded beneath Garforth's upstanding veneer. She resolved to dig much deeper into his digital history as the investigation's next urgent priority.

Back upstairs in the Incident Room on the Homicide and Major Enquiry Team floor, Alexis briefed an attentive DCI George Beaumont on Lori's interview. His jaw visibly tightened hearing aspersions of paedophilia and pornography related to Garforth.

"This aligns with wider rumours we've heard from multiple sources now that Garforth has... unorthodox proclivities involving students," George noted grimly, scrubbing a hand down his face. "God knows the sort of secrets he could be hiding behind that distinguished image."

Alexis nodded gravely. "Which is why we must include digital forensics' capabilities immediately searching his devices, accounts, the works." At George's pensive look, she pressed on. "I know Garforth has powerful allies, but surely the risk merits aggressively pursuing this lead?"

"You're absolutely right; the girls' safety is paramount over politics," George affirmed. He glanced sideways at her knowingly. "Which is why I want our best digital bloodhound, Detective Sergeant Josh Fry, working closely with you on this sensitive angle. Both stealth and urgency are vital."

Bolstered by George's staunch support pursuing Garforth, Alexis spoke with DS Fry, who swiftly delegated background analysts to collate the man's phone records, bank statements, and travel history for anomalies.

As they worked, Alexis briefed DS Fry on Lori's disturbing disclosures meriting deeper digital forensic investigation of Garforth's online activity and devices. Lean and bespectacled, Josh listened intently, eyes glinting.

"So we might be looking at networks of exploitation if the creep's been trading illegal photos or videos," Josh clarified. At Alexis' nod, he cracked his knuckles decisively. "Well, we won't leave a single digital stone unturned until the truth comes out and those girls are located safely."

In the cyber lab glowing with neon computer towers and equipment, Josh demonstrated astonishing technical capabilities, teasing out layers of hidden user activity across the deep web and encrypted apps.

Face grim, he waved Alexis over to view the uncovered material on his monitors.

"Garforth was pretty sloppy covering his digital tracks with this burner phone and hidden cloud storage," Josh reported, a hard glint in his eyes behind the spectacles. "I found encrypted image files buried in spoofed cloud accounts..."

He trailed off as Alexis gasped audibly, hand flying to her mouth at the sight of the first few photos displaying provocatively posed girls who appeared under legal age.

"Dear God, how long has this monster been collecting such stomach-churning material?" Alexis choked out in her horror. She could scarcely fathom such blithe exploitation of children.

Josh just shook his head, equal parts enraged and revolted. "Files date back five-plus years. I'll run some programmes and see whether I can identify the girls in the photos." Josh winced when he clarified, "The girls may not have been underage in these photos, so we need to be sure before accusing him."

Chapter Twenty-two

In the library, Welburn perched uncomfortably on the edge of a leather chair by the cold hearth while George sat across from him. He could feel the man's restless energy churning behind his outward lethargy. George knew he must tread delicately to earn trust, not demand it.

Settling across from Welburn, George inquired about Bradley's past, and how long he'd been working at Brandling House.

The caretaker looked taken aback at George's polite interest. He scratched at his bushy beard before responding gruffly, "Going on twelve years now. Managed the grounds under Mr Garforth before Wardman took over lately."

George nodded. "And lived on the premises all that time?" He smiled ruefully. "I could never manage time away from my little girl so regularly."

At this, Welburn's eyes flickered with a hint of wistfulness. "Just me and my loyal old dog Jessie these days."

"Jessie keeps you company on the long nights, then?" George probed gently, sensing a softening in the man's rough exterior. "I know my Rex is always eager to greet me after a long shift."

Welburn's shoulders relaxed a fraction as he replied, "Aye,

my good girl's still got some spunk left. Don't know what I'd do without her friendly face waiting after dealing with this lot." He shook his head, but his mouth twitched into a ghost of a fond smile rather than its usual scowl when speaking of the students.

George smiled sympathetically. "I can only handle so much time away from my boy before missing him fiercely, too. Weekends together make up for the long work days apart." He chuckled self-consciously. "Probably share more over the phone with him than in person, truth be told."

A faraway look entered Welburn's eyes. "It were like that with my Claire bear growing up. She'd jabber my ear off through supper about schoolyard tales." His gaze took on a sheen. "Tea parties with her dolls, dancing about to the radio... Silly memories stick with you."

Seeing an opening, George probed gently, "You two were close then?"

Welburn grunted, the vulnerable moment shuttering again. "A long time ago, in another life, seems like."

Suppressing his investigative instincts, George, hoping to rekindle the rapport, simply replied, "Change is never easy on the young ones especially."

The caretaker slumped deeper into the leather chair, looking oddly small and diminished surrounded by the opulent furnishings. "We were a right pair, Claire Bear and me. Thick as thieves once upon a time." His stare took on a faraway sheen. "I'd come home knackered, but then her giggles and smiles lit up my world."

He shook his head ruefully before his expression clouded again. "But it all went to shite too soon. Her mum came back after five years and filled Claire's head with poisonous lies."

Welburn's fists clenched, knuckles whitening. "And took away my little girl for good, just like that."

"I'm very sorry," George said sincerely, memories of his own splintered relationship with Jack's mother churning up complex emotions. "When a child gets caught in the middle, it cuts deepest. But you clearly loved her. She'll remember that."

Welburn searched George's face intently before giving a gruff nod of acknowledgement. Some tension seemed to leave his hunched frame. After another weighted beat, he stuttered. "I still dream of her sometimes... see that seven-year-old face smiling up at me, trusting and loving. Then I wake to this empty house." His throat bobbed with emotion. "All I'd give to see my Claire bear safe and well. A parent will walk through fire for their child. Surely you understand, Detective?"

He met George's eyes; all pretences stripped away to reveal raw pain. George felt an unexpected swell of empathy for this gruff man consumed by inner torment. But he also remained clear-eyed when assessing the facts. Protecting innocents now took priority over past wounds, however deep.

Choosing his following words delicately, George replied, "Children are the most precious gifts we're granted. When I look at my baby daughter, I'm filled with awe and purpose again." He caught and held Welburn's gaze steadily. "But right now, young lives need our protection. So I'm asking you plainly once more: do you know anything that could help find Esme Bushfield?"

Welburn's eyes shuttered again behind his defensive mask. Heavily, he rose from the creaking leather chair. "Wish I could offer more than thoughts and prayers, sir. But..."

Frustration flared in George's chest, but he kept his tone

CHAPTER TWENTY-TWO

neutral, not revealing the suspicions still churning despite the glimpse of paternal devotion. "Tell me, Bradley." George nodded encouragingly. "Any gossip or odd behaviours stand out before the disappearance? Even minor details might prove useful."

Welburn frowned pensively, tugging his bushy beard. "Students chatter constantly, and it is hard to keep track. Though…" He hesitated, glancing uneasily at George. "There were whispers about Miss Cowgill keeping late hours with Eugene Garforth. But just foolish gossip, surely."

George tensed, thoughts racing. "Go on."

"Well, Ashley were known to be… overly friendly with menfolk. And Garforth has certain tendencies–" Welburn broke off awkwardly. "It's all nonsense, no doubt. Shouldn't have mentioned it."

"I determine what proves useful, not you," George countered firmly, thinking about the groundsman who said something very similar. "Now explain exactly what you overheard and observed regarding Garforth and Ashley."

Sweat beaded Welburn's brow as he revealed snippets of gossip about Ashley supposedly visiting Garforth's quarters after hours on multiple occasions the weekend before going missing while emphasising ignorance of any certifiable misconduct.

George listened intently, expression inscrutable. If true, this confirmed the profoundly disturbing exploitation of a vulnerable girl under the roof she should have felt safest.

After extracting every last shred Welburn could recall, George stood abruptly, gathering the files. On edge after questioning, Welburn blurted out, "Do you really think young Esme could be lying out there murdered somewhere?"

George paused, taken aback by the outburst. The caretaker looked stricken, all gruffness stripped away. "Poor lamb. It's all just so evil and senseless, innit?"

Seeing only raw pain in the man's eyes now, George felt his suspicions momentarily abate. Perhaps there was still hope of redemption for broken souls if truth prevailed. He clapped Welburn's shoulder gently. "We'll find out what happened to her, Bradley."

Welburn searched George's face intently before giving a short nod, some tension leaving his hunched frame. George couldn't justify further interrogation without corroborating evidence. Whatever happened in his past shouldn't dictate his future, but there was still no smoke without a fire. But George sensed a door had cracked open to rapport if nurtured cautiously.

DCI Beaumont gathered the heavy files under his arm before sitting and turning to Welburn once more. "Thank you for speaking plainly today—it aids the investigation more than you know." He paused. "And I'm sorry I went so hard on you."

Bradley got up. But pausing at the doorway, some inner debate played across Welburn's bearded face. He half turned back, mouth opening as if to speak before closing it tightly again, jaw flexing. With a dismissive grunt, he disappeared into the hallway's shadows without another word.

Was the man innocent?

No.

Lingering facts left Welburn on George's suspect list. The isolated lifestyle. Shifty responses to alibi questions. And most tellingly, the caretaker's evasive gaze, as if concealing deeper shame. George's instincts screamed that the man harboured sinister secrets, but whether they were related to

CHAPTER TWENTY-TWO

Esme and Ashley was another question entirely.

For now, George had grounds to bring Garforth in for intense questioning. His slippery facade would finally crack under sustained pressure.

* * *

Alexis couldn't keep still, her mind swirling with questions after the disturbing discoveries unearthed about Eugene Garforth. As she headed down the hall, her mobile rang. Glancing at the screen, she saw it was Josh Fry and quickly answered.

"Please tell me you found something more concrete to use against Garforth, Sarge," she said without preamble.

Josh's frustrated sigh greeted her. "I wish I had better news. I finished facial recognition analysis on all the girls in those recovered image files." He hesitated before continuing heavily. "They check out as adults according to our databases—all over eighteen when the photos were taken."

Alexis closed her eyes as her hopes sank. "Damn. So the slimy eel was careful staying just inside legal bounds."

"It seems that way outwardly," Josh agreed grimly. "But I'm still digging deeper into encrypted partitions and metadata trails across his devices and cloud accounts. If there's anything dodgy or deletions of more incriminating evidence, I'll uncover it."

Alexis could hear the clacking of Josh's keyboard through the phone. "You're a genius, Josh, thank you," she encouraged. "If anyone can find hidden skeletons or evidence tampering, it's you."

"Too right," Josh affirmed. "I won't quit digging until the full ugly truth comes out about Garforth and what happened to those girls. It just might take longer to unearth well-buried secrets. But the creep can't hide behind his flashy image forever. I'll keep you updated on progress."

Heart buoyed by Josh's unrelenting commitment, even facing initial setbacks, Alexis thanked him sincerely before hanging up. She stewed over this new hurdle but took comfort in knowing her tireless partner on the digital front would uncover whatever damning trails Garforth tried concealing through the ether.

Squaring her shoulders, Alexis swiped to her contacts, her intention to update George Beaumont on the momentary investigative stall but assure him ethical lines would yet be exposed.

* * *

Back at the pond, George monitored their progress attentively but without micro-managing. Regular check-ins with Jay whilst George had been up at the house had confirmed the exhaustive search was progressing steadily without shortcuts.

By late afternoon, however, the dredging yielded little but sludge and detritus. George's jaw tightened, but he maintained calm optimism.

Nodding determinedly, the divers soldiered on through the frigid grey afternoon. As dusk's shadows stretched across the rippling water, the stocky coordinator trudged wearily over to George.

"We've dredged every square inch, sir. All bagged and catalogued for analysis as instructed." He grimaced. "But so far, our eyes have spotted nothing remarkable or human-related." He closed his eyes. "Sorry, sir."

CHAPTER TWENTY-TWO

George remained stoic, giving a curt nod. "Thank you for your diligent efforts. We'll take a one-hour tea break. Then we'll commence searching the larger park pond through the night." He met the tired man's gaze steadily. "The darkness changes nothing, I presume?"

"It's all darkness below the surface, sir," the man said, straightening his sagging shoulders. George knew these men would keep fighting however bleak the outlook grew. Their tireless commitment shored up his fraying perseverance.

While the team took a short meal break, George checked in with Jay. "Any word yet from Constable Nichols regarding Ashley Cowgill's condition?"

Jay shook his head, swallowing a hasty bite of protein bar. "Afraid not, boss. Last update an hour ago said Ashley was barely speaking even to her family liaison officer Elaine Brewer. Trauma's really done a number on her."

George's jaw tightened. "We can't force communication before she's ready. But time is against us." He took a deep, calming breath. "We need something, Jay. Anything."

"Too right, boss," Jay agreed. "Thing is-" He paused as George's mobile rang loudly.

George checked the screen and answered swiftly when he saw it was Constable Nichols. "What's the latest with Ashley, Candy?"

Candy's breathless voice spilled through the line. "Sir, she finally opened up to me about some hazy memories from that night! I know it's not much, but Ashley says she recalls a screaming argument with Esme by the smaller pond shortly before everything goes black."

George gripped the phone tighter, pulse elevating. "That's the first concrete details we've gotten. Well done! Did she specify the disagreement topic or Esme's emotional state?"

"Unfortunately, not yet," Candy admitted regretfully. "Getting even that much was like drawing blood from a stone. But hopefully, now the seal is broken, Ashley will keep voluntarily providing bits and pieces."

"We can hope," George agreed neutrally, tempering swelling anticipation. "For now, this gives reason to keep searching the pond. And keep coaxing gently for anything more Ashley can recall. We're making real progress."

Chapter Twenty-three

George thought it would be best to let Eugene Garforth stew and refocus efforts on interviewing the remaining students who had been enrolled in the exclusive academic retreat programme at Brandling House. They urgently needed fresh angles of inquiry after hitting dead ends with the staff's financial and PNC records, CCTV analysis, and canvassing local areas.

One student in particular, Gregory Medley, leapt to George's mind. The introspective lad had seemed eager to assist during initial questioning after the disappearance. But there were puzzling discrepancies in his statement. George had made a note of that needing clarification.

He vividly recalled Gregory's interview. The boy presented a composed front, responding clearly in his cultured accent. But undercurrents of unease radiated from Gregory's awkward posture and evasive eyes, hinting at deeper anxiety or secrecy barely concealed beneath his courtesy.

Specifically, the way Gregory minimised his familiarity with Ashley and Esme had struck George as curiously evasive and dismissive.

Yet George's sharp observational skills had catalogued subtle tells muddying this polite indifference—the way Gregory's eyes flickered downwards at the mention of the girls, feigning absorption in straightening papers. Or how he adjusted his shirt collar repeatedly when asked about interactions with them at Brandling House.

Something about their relationships provoked discomfort in the self-conscious teen despite the façade he attempted. George's instincts prickled at that, and scrutiny into these dynamics could help solve the case.

* * *

The rain had finally ceased its relentless deluge as DCI George Beaumont navigated the winding country lanes toward the quaint village of Bramhope. Beside him, DI Luke Mason studied notes on the Medley family.

They were en route to conduct a more intensive follow-up interview with Gregory Medley, a student present at Brandling House during the disappearance of teens Esme Bushfield and Ashley Cowgill.

"The lad seemed genuinely eager to assist the investigation during our initial questioning," George remarked, eyes fixed on the slick road ahead. "But my observations noted discrepancies in his account."

Luke grunted ambiguously without looking up from the file. "And the parents consented to further interrogation at home?"

"With reluctance," George confirmed wryly. "And insistence they are present, of course." He cast Luke a sideways glance. "The Medleys are an influential family accustomed to caution in legal matters."

Luke harrumphed at that. "Let's hope Mum and Dad don't obstruct the truth with misguided interference then." He

CHAPTER TWENTY-THREE

turned another page in the notes. "Just hope he's honest with us when his mum and dad are about."

George's mouth quirked up briefly. Luke's flair for piercing pretence would serve them well if the Medleys proved less than forthcoming. "Too right. We press for genuine answers despite their stonewalling."

Ten minutes later, they pulled up the long gravel drive to the imposing stone manor house set amid meticulously manicured grounds. The ornate facade evoked old moneyed heritage and privilege.

A uniformed housekeeper showed them to an elegant sitting room where Mr and Mrs Medley awaited, tight-lipped. Gregory sat hunched on a gilt-edged love seat, posture oozing discomfort.

Following stiff introductions, the Medleys settled onto an antique couch in clear proximity to their son, telegraphing their protective presence. George repressed a twinge of annoyance at this transparent intimidation tactic.

Adopting a pleasant tone, he began. "Thank you again for allowing this follow-up. Gregory's insights have proved quite helpful regarding interpersonal dynamics at Brandling House."

He noted Gregory flush and study his shoes at the implied mention of his relationship with Ashley.

Turning his full attention to the boy, George asked kindly, "How have you been holding up since we last spoke, Gregory? I know the situation has been distressing for everyone."

Gregory shot an uncertain glance at his silently watching parents. "I am... managing adequately enough," he muttered awkwardly.

George leaned forward. "Managing suggests a struggle.

Speak freely, Gregory. Have you been sleeping alright? Eating normally?"

Looking mildly surprised by the solicitous questions, Gregory admitted, "Truthfully, rest has eluded me since Esme's continued disappearance. I cannot silence troubling thoughts." He flushed again, clearly self-conscious, revealing vulnerability before his stoic parents.

Nodding sympathetically, George pressed gently, "Regarding Esme's disappearance, what's troubling you?" Prompting the boy to unburden his conscience could lead to unplanned revelations.

Gregory's eyes glinted with emotion behind his spectacles. "Esme was always kind despite my social awkwardness. That her vibrant spirit might be extinguished forever..." He broke off hoarsely before continuing, "Forgive my gloomy musings. I know you remain hopeful of her return."

"Very much so," George assured him. "Which is why I wanted to discuss your thoughts regarding Esme. Did you notice any changes concerning you?" He kept his tone open, inviting reflection. Probing too forcefully could make the sensitive teen withdraw, but patience might coax hidden insights to surface.

Gregory looked introspective. "Esme did appear more on edge and withdrawn on Monday compared to Friday, for instance. She wasn't that typically bubbly self." He hesitated. "I didn't pry, given it's not my place to meddle. But I hoped the malaise might pass naturally."

George digested this quietly. So Gregory had noted concerning shifts in Esme's demeanour but avoided deeper involvement. Why was that? There seemed no overt malice in the socially awkward boy but rather a tendency for passive observation instead of action.

Remembering Gregory's favourite subject from previous small talk, George changed tack. He asked conversationally, "Has your aptitude for reading subtle behaviours aided your studies in psychology?"

Gregory brightened, sitting straighter. He looked at his parents and grinned. "The detective understands." He turned to George. "Very much so, Detective. I've always enjoyed watching and interpreting people's complex interactions." He smiled self-consciously. "Few notice me, allowing me to study their authentic selves, not public facades."

George smiled encouragingly. "A valuable gift!" He took a deep breath and said, "Ever thought about becoming a detective?"

The young man beamed. "No, but perhaps I should." Growing animated, Gregory revealed examples of decrypting classmates' non-verbal cues during debates to correctly predict outcomes. And discerning romantic connections through discreet but telling social behaviours before they became public.

"Keen observation unveils many secrets hidden in plain sight," Gregory concluded enthusiastically before blanching at his own candour.

But George only chuckled. It was that or cringe at the young lad. "Like I said, we could use such perceptiveness on the force."

Gregory practically glowed under the appraisal once more before his mother interjected severely, "I hardly think that is an appropriate career path for someone of Gregory's pedigree." Her disapproving look dimmed the boy's smile.

"Of course, you know best, Mother," he replied quietly,

posture shrinking.

Annoyance flared in George briefly before Luke redirected the conversation. "We appreciate your time today, Gregory. Is there anything else you can think of?"

"Speak with Ishaan Sadiq. He knows more than he's letting on," was all Gregory said.

George took the cue and stood as well, shaking Gregory's hand warmly. "Please don't hesitate to call if you have any further recollections that may aid the investigation. Your input is invaluable."

Gregory nodded, appearing heartened by the assurance he could still help. As George and Luke made their farewells to the Medleys, he felt cautiously optimistic the boy would open up further given patience and encouragement. Seeds were planted, and in time, greater understanding could bear fruit.

Or so he hoped.

Back in the car, George mused aloud, "The lad has a keen eye but is so bloody dramatic."

Luke laughed. "My thoughts exactly, son."

A knock on the passenger window of the Mercedes stopped George and Luke talking.

It was Gregory Medley.

Luke pressed the button, and the window wound down. "OK, Gregory?" Luke asked.

"Apologies for intruding," Gregory began, voice slightly wavering. "Might I have a brief word? Without my parents."

George glanced at Luke before nodding. "Of course." George gestured to his phone. "Because you're alone, I'll need to record this."

"Fine with me," he said. "I have things I don't want my parents to know."

CHAPTER TWENTY-THREE

George unlocked the doors, and Gregory got in the back before perching nervously on the edge of the seat.

The DCI started the recording and introduced himself and DI Luke Mason before asking Gregory to introduce himself and confirm he was giving a statement voluntarily.

"Now, tell me what's on your mind," George prompted, keeping his tone open. Gregory seemed to wrestle internally before taking a bracing breath.

"Well, I happened to overhear a rather concerning exchange between Ashley Cowgill and Esme Bushfield this past Sunday evening..." He trailed off uncertainly.

George leaned forward. "Go on."

"While passing by Ashley's room, I heard her bragging quite loudly to Esme about... having just left fellow student Ishaan Sadiq's bedroom quite late at night." Gregory flushed scarlet. "This is why I told you to speak with him earlier."

George nodded. This contradicted Ishaan's claims of barely knowing the girls. "Did she mention anything specific about the nature of this secretive visit?"

Gregory squirmed. "The colourful implications she made left little doubt it was an... intimate encounter, Detective." He studied his shoes, clearly mortified.

Stroking his beard thoughtfully, George turned this new information over. If truthful, it suggested Ishaan exercised more influence over the girls than his dismissive account implied.

"And did Esme give you the impression such behaviour from Ashley was expected or out of character?" George asked.

Gregory considered this. "She did not seem shocked per se, but I sensed discomfort at the topic. Esme urged Ashley to be more discreet in sharing private affairs." He shrugged helplessly. "Beyond that, I cannot speculate too far, sir."

George nodded reassuringly. "You've given us an important new lead. Ishaan may have concealed key details if he and Ashley were indeed intimate." Already deep suspicion of the arrogant lad stirred anew. Ishaan would face intense new questioning soon. But that meant speaking with the Detective Chief Superintendent Mohammed Sadiq for permission.

Seeming to steel himself again, Gregory continued hesitantly, "One other small detail also struck me as concerning, though it could just be idle gossip..."

George refocused intently. "Go on."

"Well, on Monday, I happened to overhear Ashley complaining to Esme about old men's proclivities, specifically Mr Eugene Garforth..." Gregory flushed again deeply. "She, well, implied he had inappropriate predilections regarding female... undergarments."

Seeing George's eyes narrow, Gregory rushed to add, "But it was likely just vulgar slander, sir! Mr Garforth has a respectable reputation to uphold. I thought you should know in case it proves relevant, but please don't launch any formal accusations on my account!"

George held up a hand. "You've done exactly right informing us, son. We need every clue, however inappropriate. I appreciate your discretion."

Gregory looked mildly relieved, though still ill at ease.

Gregory left the car, appearing newly bolstered.

George said, "Please call on me day or night if you think of anything, OK?"

"Will do, sir."

* * *

CHAPTER TWENTY-THREE

DCI George Beaumont sat at the desk in his office; fingers steepled thoughtfully as he mentally sifted through the new information provided by shy student Gregory Medley. The revelations about Ashley Cowgill's secretive visit to fellow pupil Ishaan Sadiq's bedroom and possible inappropriate behaviour by owner Eugene Garforth were certainly shocking if true. But George knew he must tread with utmost care.

Despite that, he wanted to know about the potential selling of underwear straight from the horse's mouth, so he called Sandra Cowgill.

After picking up, George said, "It's DCI Beaumont. May I ask Ashley a few questions?"

"Please only ask one or two, Detective," Sandra said. "She's very tired."

"Understandable."

Ashley's timid voice answered. "H-hello?"

"Ashley, this is DCI Beaumont. I'm so sorry to trouble you, but some new information has surfaced I hoped you could clarify," George began gently.

"Oh. OK." Wariness suffused her tone.

Adopting a casual air, George continued. "Now, I understand you paid a secret late-night visit to fellow student Ishaan Sadiq's bedroom quite recently. Can you tell me about that?"

Stunned silence met this provocation. Finally, Ashley stammered uncertainly. "I don't know what you mean. Why would I go to Ishaan's room?"

"You tell me?" George asked. At the silence, he asked, "Perhaps you boasted of an intimate encounter to impress Esme?"

"I-no-I never..." Ashley trailed off, flustered. After a tense beat, she finally admitted in a small voice. "I may have... embellished events to Esme. But I swear nothing improper occurred with Ishaan!"

George noted her evasive verbal tells with interest but kept his tone friendly. "No judgment here; I just need the truth." Using her own words, he asked, "May I ask why you embellished events?"

Ashley hesitated before confessing, "Esme thought Ishaan was quite fit but was too timid to flirt with him. So I might have... exaggerated my own familiarity a bit out of jealousy." She groaned softly. "Pretty daft trying to compete with her."

Nodding thoughtfully, George changed tack. "Speaking of jealousy, we have reason to believe Mr Eugene Garforth had inappropriate relations with students. Specifically coercing certain girls to sell him used undergarments."

He paused, hearing Ashley's breathing quicken anxiously. "Can you elaborate at all on these rumours?"

"That's surely just malicious gossip!" Ashley shrilled before mastering herself. "Mr Garforth always behaved properly, far as I saw."

George noted her obvious nerves at the topic but merely said pleasantly, "I appreciate your honesty debunking that ugly rumour. We just have to fully investigate all angles, you understand."

"Y-yes, of course," Ashley replied, voice wavering slightly.

"Now then, I know recalling traumatic events is difficult," George continued delicately. "But can you reflect back to Monday evening at all? Even small details could prove critical."

Tension rippled through the lengthening silence until Ashley whispered almost inaudibly, "I've told you everything I can, Detective." Panicked breathing echoed through the line.

CHAPTER TWENTY-THREE

"It's all just... blank after leaving the stage." Ashley's voice climbed towards hysteria.

George frowned, scanning his notes.

"I know this is hard," he persisted gently. "But could-"

"That's enough for now, Detective," Sandra Cowgill interrupted.

Cursing himself, George quickly apologised. "I apologise for upsetting Ashley. Tell her to focus on her recovery, and I'll call you soon.

Ending the call, George leaned back heavily. Ashley's extreme reaction to probing her lost memories solidified his suspicions that psychological blocks concealed pivotal truths. But forcing the matter risked irreparable damage. For now, he would need to delicately unravel events through external evidence.

Chapter Twenty-four

The crowd of reporters and cameramen jostled eagerly as DCI George Beaumont stepped up to the podium outside Elland Road police station, their shouting voices clamouring for his attention. George waited stoically for the din to die down before speaking into the microphones.

"Thank you all for coming. I will provide a brief update on the investigation into the disappearances of Esme Bushfield and Ashley Cowgill from Brandling House that occurred on the evening of Monday, February 12th. After this statement, I will not be taking questions."

The press erupted again, voices overlapping.

"Is it true one girl has been found?"

"Were they abducted?"

"Is there a suspect?"

George held up a hand for silence. When the commotion finally eased, he continued firmly.

"The investigation is active and ongoing. All resources are being utilised to locate both missing teenagers. Last Monday evening, the girls inexplicably left Brandling House grounds past curfew and have not been seen since. One has been located alive but is in delicate condition. The other, Esme Bushfield, remains missing."

CHAPTER TWENTY-FOUR

The reporters again shouted over each other, demanding details. George stood unfazed, waiting for them to exhaust themselves.

"While unable to disclose specifics compromising the investigation, I assure you that we are diligently pursuing all credible leads and evidence. Several persons of interest have been interviewed extensively."

At this, the press questions amplified tenfold as journalists shoved microphones forward insistently, clamouring for more information. Flashes from cameras nearly blinded George, but he remained steadfastly composed.

"Please, I must ask that there be no further outbursts." George waited as the angry buzz gradually settled. "As I stated, no details about specific investigative actions or suspects can be shared at this stage. However, I am appealing today for any member of the public who saw suspicious activity in the vicinity of Brandling House or Middleton Woods on the evening of Monday, February 12th, to urgently come forward."

He made direct eye contact with the broadcast cameras. "Even the smallest fragment of information could prove critical. If you noticed any unfamiliar persons or vehicles near the grounds that night, alert us immediately. Esme's survival depends on community vigilance."

The reporters again surged forward, pelting George with invasive questions which he stoically ignored.

"Is it true the missing girls were trafficking drugs?" one tabloid journalist yelled out.

Another speculative voice shouted, "Sources say this was a cult ritual killing—can you confirm?"

The increasingly wild theories and accusations being hurled underscored the need for measured information control,

George knew. Unrestrained media speculation risked compromising the investigation and public response.

Raising his hands for order, George stated calmly, "There will be no further comments at this time. My sole aim today is urging anyone with credible information related to Esme and Ashley's disappearance to step forward now. Thank you."

He stepped back from the podium as the incensed press mob shouted after him angrily, demanding answers. Microphones and cameras jostled aggressively as they surged forward, but uniformed constables moved quickly to form a barrier, allowing George's retreat to the station doors.

Inside the organised chaos of the bustling station, George breathed out slowly before turning to DC Alexis Mercer, who had watched the media scrum by the doors. "Well, that was a bloody circus," he remarked wryly, scrubbing a hand down his face. "But hopefully we shook something loose from the public."

Alexis gave a grim nod of agreement. "Let's hope so, sir. Though headline sensationalism often brings more misleading tips than truth." She hesitated before adding delicately, "Some are already suggesting you reveal more details to sate the frenzy and prevent damaging speculation."

George's mouth thinned as he shook his head sharply. "True, but even that one in-a-thousand tip-off might solve the case." He paused. "And I will not risk the investigation's integrity or victims' dignity to appease publicity demands." His tone brooked no debate. The ruthless media would spin any crumbs he threw them anyway.

Checking his watch, George headed towards his office, the dutiful Alexis trailing close behind. "Now we redouble efforts on verified leads before the trail gets muddied by publicity

CHAPTER TWENTY-FOUR

tips. You coordinate with forensic accounting on Garforth's finances. I want rock-solid evidence we can leverage hard."

"On it, sir," Alexis affirmed, already pulling out her phone. Her pragmatic swiftness to implement orders without fuss reminded George of her invaluable capability. With Alexis driving one angle relentlessly and his own intensity on the other, the truth could not evade them for long, whatever powers tried obscuring it.

Settling wearily into his chair in the Incident Room, George contemplated the sparse Big Board grimly. He wished fervently to give the ravenous press concrete facts that would spur real progress.

Instead, he could only make vague appeals while keeping cards close to his chest for the investigation's integrity. Only the truth mattered to George, not polls or politics.

Rubbing the exhaustion from his eyes, George leaned forward. There was no time for self-doubt with young lives hanging in the balance and a possible pervert in custody.

Picking up a thick folder prepared by his team for an interview with Eugene Garforth, George went to find Luke Mason. Out there, lost in the shadows, Esme still clung to fragile hope. And he would not fail her, whatever obstacles he came across.

* * *

The air in the interview room was thick with tension as DCI George Beaumont and DI Luke Mason sat across the scarred wooden table from a reticent Eugene Garforth. The middle-aged owner of Brandling House had a pinched, haughty expression barely concealing his apparent unease at being asked to answer further questions regarding the disappearances of students Ashley Cowgill and Esme Bushfield.

George opened the file folder on the table before him, perusing the pages intently, aware of Garforth shifting impatiently. Finally looking up, George kept his tone polite but firm.

"Thank you for coming in again today, Mr Garforth. Just some routine follow-ups as the investigation progresses."

Garforth gave a thin smile. "Of course, though, I already told the other officers everything I know, which is precious little." His tone dripped condescension. "I don't involve myself in the day-to-day trivialities of how Wayne manages his business."

"We appreciate your cooperation," Luke assured smoothly, though his eyes remained steely. "Still, we must be extremely thorough in following up on every lead. A young life hangs in the balance."

Garforth sighed affectedly. "Yes, yes, tragic business that. But you're wasting time interrogating me when the real scoundrels are out there free."

Ignoring this, George asked, "Let's start with your relationship with student Ashley Cowgill."

Garforth looked at his solicitor, who nodded. "What relationship?"

"These surveillance images clearly show you interacting in a familiar manner," said George, sliding across a file of images.

Garforth glanced at the photos casually before adopting a look of offended indignation.

"I've no improper relations with students if that's your implication," he huffed. He again looked at his solicitor, who nodded. "What you see here is chit-chat. I was doing inspections as is my right, and this student here begged my help moving some heavy furniture so it would better fit their room. I politely obliged and then sent her on her way. Nothing untoward transpired."

Luke leaned forward intimidatingly. "Are you certain, Mr Garforth? Because witnesses allege Ashley boasted of rather intimate encounters with you. Coerced ones."

Sweat beaded Garforth's brow as he vehemently protested. "Outrageous lies! I have a sterling reputation in this community." He stabbed a ringed finger at the pictures. "These prove nothing except your own grubbiness for conjuring sordid motives from innocent interactions."

Unruffled, George placed several printed emails on the table that after they'd verified were genuine, they had printed off from Lori Garforth's USB stick. "Actually, this correspondence with your mistress tells quite a different story. Many references to your appetite for 'younger company'. Would you agree that Ashley was younger 'company'?"

Garforth went red as he spluttered incoherently. Finally, he exclaimed heatedly, "You've no right ransacking my private affairs, no matter who put you up to it! Those emails are clearly fabrications planted to smear me."

Luke snorted derisively. "Come off it, man. The jig is up. We have enough evidence to bury you unless you start talking." He leaned in menacingly. "What really happened with those girls?"

"Absolutely nothing."

Garforth looked at his solicitor, who said, "My client will no longer answer any questions relating to the emails or the photos." The solicitor looked between Luke and George. "Do you have any other relevant questions for my client?"

Sweating, Garforth seemed to deflate slightly in his chair. He passed a hand over his face, composure cracking.

George eyed Eugene Garforth sternly across the interrogation room table. "Let's discuss some other deeply troubling allegations regarding your conduct with female students, Mr Garforth."

Garforth scowled. "More outrageous slander, no doubt." He straightened his tie irritably. "Honestly, I've had enough of you dragging my good name through the mud chasing schoolyard gossip."

When Garforth just scowled silently, George continued mildly, "How do you explain the fact that we have statements alleging she left your room boasting of rather intimate encounters with an elderly gentleman matching your description."

At this, Garforth slammed his fist on the table angrily. "Enough! I won't sit here as you spout filthy lies told by some attention-seeking trollop!" His face turned puce with fury. "How dare you take the word of a delinquent child over an upstanding gentleman like me!"

Still irritatingly calm, George pressed on. "This same student claims Ashley mentioned you soliciting... used intimate apparel from her." He raised an eyebrow. "Care to explain that?"

At this, Garforth shot to his feet, chair crashing backwards. "Why you devious, muckraking bastard! I'll see you sacked for this smear campaign!" he roared.

"Mr Garforth, control yourself," Luke ordered sharply. But the man was beyond reason.

Eugene looked at his solicitor. "I want to leave, Geoffrey! I'm done with their disgusting insinuations!" Garforth continued bellowing whilst looking at the detectives. "Not another word will you twist against me, you snakes!"

CHAPTER TWENTY-FOUR

As Luke stood up, Garforth suddenly clutched his chest, face draining of colour. He staggered unsteadily, wheezing alarmingly. "Sit down and catch your breath!" Luke ordered.

The solicitor quickly guided the man back into his seat. "Try to take slow, deep breaths," he advised calmly before looking at George. "We need medical assistance immediately."

As George swiftly exited to call emergency services, he heard Garforth whimper weakly, "Please, I feel so strange... there's been a mistake..."

Returning to the interview room, George kept his distance as Luke monitored the distressed man. But his piercing gaze remained fixed intently on Garforth. The violent outburst had only elevated his suspicions—clearly, they had hit a raw nerve.

Once the man was stable, George would resume the relentless interrogation until the truth was finally dragged from the shadows. They were so close to unravelling ugly secrets festering behind Garforth's distinguished veneer.

Chapter Twenty-five

George turned down a side hall in Elland Road police station to the media room where Press Manager Juliette Thompson directed operations. Raising her eyes from two computer monitors streaming the news conference coverage, Juliette gave George a polite nod.

"That was some intense spotlight out there, George. What can I do for you now that the dust is settling?"

George crossed his arms, features set gravely. "I need to formally request circulating the Cowards Café CCTV images of Esme across all media and social channels. I'm hoping somebody recognises her mystery male companion.

Juliette pursed her lips uncertainly. "Releasing intrusive images risks backlash given the family's visibility and major donor connections. Are you sure about this, George?"

Scrubbing a hand down his face, George nodded heavily. "I didn't take the decision lightly. But that footage captures Esme's last confirmed sighting before vanishing. We're grasping at straws here."

He held Juliette's hesitant gaze. "I know it's an intrusion the parents would prefer avoiding. In fact, they pretty much kicked off when I showed them the images. But time is running out to generate leads. We have to try everything."

CHAPTER TWENTY-FIVE

Juliette considered a moment before conceding with a slow exhale. "Very well, George; I'll finalise the media package and utilise targeted social ads. Hopefully, the public comes through."

George managed a weary smile. "I appreciate you dealing with the PR fallout. My priority is sparking key evidence to find Esme."

Afterwards, George headed upstairs towards his office with long, determined strides. Esme's window of survival was rapidly shrinking. He desperately hoped exposing her image widely would generate pivotal leads without damaging rapport with influential family allies. A deeply uneasy compromise—but lives outweighed etiquette.

Settling heavily behind his desk, George studied Eugene Garforth's phone records. Alexis had handily highlighted each differing phone number a different colour as well as providing an extensive key he could follow. She was good like that, and George appreciated it.

It appeared Eugene was in regular contact with his caretaker. But why? Was it only for maintenance? Or other reasons?

Needing to take a break, he looked at the CCTV images once more. Out there, lost in the shadows, Esme still clung to fragile hope as each hour slipped away. Dark water churning with obstacles on all sides, yet George pushed steadily onward. The currents could not claim innocent lives—not if every ounce of tenacity and grit remained.

His decisions today might disrupt reputations and ruffle the feathers of the well-connected. But so what? Esme Bushfield deserved every chance, and George would do whatever he could to find her.

A call on his mobile interrupted George from his thoughts.

"DCI Beaumont."

"Sir, the full sweep of Garforth's Brandling House office is finally complete," DC Alexis Mercer reported.

George felt a prickle of anticipation. "Very good. Did the search turn up anything useful related to our missing persons or his suspicious relationships?"

Hesitating, Alexis chose her following words carefully. "There are some documents regarding scholarships for female students." She paused before continuing delicately, "And we've found a lot of printed images of naked young girls."

George grimaced, equal parts disgusted and galvanized by the mounting circumstantial evidence supporting their worst suspicions about Garforth's character. "Girls?"

"Yes, sir, the same ones we found on his phone."

Legal images then, thought George. Shit.

"Right then, we need access to that office computer straight away to dig into his digital footprint for more evidence. Maybe the crafty bastard slipped up."

He could practically hear Alexis wincing through the phone at his enthusiasm. "That may prove challenging, sir. We learned Garforth's solicitor has him refusing access so far due to the ongoing health issues."

George's jaw clenched at the blatant obstruction. But it only strengthened his resolve to uncover the truth. "Health issues or not, the law provides leeway to securing critical evidence. I'll handle the weasel and his solicitor myself."

After hanging up, George briefed DI Luke Mason on the updates. He assigned Alexis to coordinate with Detective Sergeant Josh Fry, preparing warrants and systems access in anticipation of seizing Garforth's electronics.

Then he squared his shoulders and stalked towards the

station medical wing where Garforth was recovering under guard—time to flex legal prerogatives whilst wearing the man's resistance down.

Striding into the room, George took in Garforth's pathetic form propped up in bed looking smaller somehow without his expensive suits. A solicitous man in a tailored navy suit, Solicitor Geoffrey rose from Garforth's bedside, buttoned coat brushing papers spread on the movable table.

"Ah, Detective, I trust you remember me. Geoffrey Campbell." The man smiled blandly, offering a smooth, manicured hand. "I understand you have some additional questions for my client, Mr Garforth. Perhaps matters could wait until he's recovered fuller faculties-"

"My questions can't wait," George interjected crisply, ignoring the extended hand. He speared the sweating Garforth with an uncompromising look. "We need immediate access to your Brandling House office computer regarding the ongoing case into the disappearances of Ashley Cowgill and Esme Bushfield."

Garforth rallied some of his familiar pomposity, blustering, "Now see here, I've been more than cooperative despite outrageous allegations against my good name! Can't a man even convalesce in peace without harassment?" He appealed piteously to his lawyer. "Tell them, Geoffrey! Without proper warrants, they've no right invading my private affairs trawling for salacious gossip."

The oily solicitor raised a diplomatically pacifying hand. "Detective, perhaps in exchange for this access you seek, the pornography allegations could be... quietly re-evaluated, eh?" His smile didn't reach his eyes. "No harm revisiting divergent recollections. And all the women were of age."

George crossed his bulky arms, unmoved by the bribe. "No, We've too much evidence to re-evaluate anything..." He paused. "Unless your client wishes to confess right now."

Sweating nervously, Garforth wavered under George's uncompromising posture before finally acquiescing resentfully. "Oh, I suppose take the blasted computer then! Not that you'll find anything remotely improper beyond an accidental malware download last month." He glanced shiftily between George and his lawyer. "I had everything scrubbed, of course, by tech consultants. Stupid bloody viruses and the lark. But still, fine. Rather you waste time on pointless searches than keep harassing my good name!"

George narrowed his eyes, assessing the too-emphatic malware explanation. Or a potential cover story for scrubbing evidence...

"We appreciate your cooperation, Mr Garforth," George acknowledged briskly. "And my team has strong capabilities resuscitating digital artefacts your... consultants may have overlooked." Garforth blanched slightly at the implied threat. George pressed his momentary advantage.

"Now then, while my officers collect the computer, perhaps you could try recalling additional details about Esme Bushfield's last known communications or plans that night?"

Garforth squirmed anxiously. "For the hundredth time, I've shared everything of use! Direct your invasive scrabbling elsewhere."

As the man sullenly crossed his arms like a reprimanded child, George observed his micro-expressions closely—the nervous ticks, averted glances, the sheen of sweat despite the room's chill. Every non-verbal cue screamed concealment. Garforth surely hid crucial information about the missing girl,

CHAPTER TWENTY-FIVE

perhaps believing corrupt allies could shield his misdeeds indefinitely.

As George moved to exit the hospital room, Garforth suddenly blurted out, "If you insist on harassing innocent men, why not interrogate that caretaker, Bradley? He has a dodgy history, I recall."

Pausing, George turned back with a piercing look. "You refer to Bradley Welburn, I assume? The man you personally vetted and hired?" He arched an eyebrow. "Seems to me like you're trying to throw other people under the bus."

Garforth waved a hand dismissively, but his eyes were shifty. "Well, he came highly recommended by an old school chum, and I believe in second chances." His expression turned sly. "But the old adage stands—fool me twice and all. Perhaps Bradley merits... fresher scrutiny."

George stroked his beard thoughtfully. "It's interesting you mention Bradley, as I've recently had a little look through your phone records which show you called Mr Welburn quite regularly, including the night of the girls' disappearance." He narrowed his eyes but said nothing more, inviting Eugene to condemn himself.

Sweating under George's knowing scrutiny, Garforth crossed his arms defensively. "See here, a man naturally chats more with staff to provide extra guidance acclimating them." He forced an oily smile. "My dedication to nurturing employees often goes overlooked unjustly. And after recent turmoil, one-second guesses things..." He paused. "And plus, if I remember correctly, I needed him to maintain something within the house, though don't ask me what as I forget."

His façade cracked slightly with irrational bursts of emotion. "I remind you, those girls brought chaos and scandal on themselves! Your aggression is aimed quite incorrectly, Detective." Garforth fumed, face mottling. "Bradley always disrupted order at Brandling House. Are multiple offences required before you lot take action?"

As the man worked himself into greater agitation, and his composure slipped, George watched him shrewdly. What workplace disruption did Garforth accuse Bradley of previously? And why protect him until now? Perhaps this caretaker knew too much... fear of exposure seemed to waiver Garforth's habitual underlings loyalty.

George filed away the details for further scrutiny later. But Garforth was overplaying his hand, transparently grasping at straws, trying to cast off blame. Time to let the man's uncontrolled emotions further betray his deepening legal quagmire.

"We appreciate you updating us on relevant background, Mr Garforth." George smiled thinly. "My team will revisit Mr Welburn and all personnel comprehensively; rest assured. Every stone shall be overturned."

George stepped closer and relished the visible panic creeping across Garforth's face at the prospect.

"And I mean every stone. Every. Single. One."

Nodding briskly to the apoplectic man and his anxious solicitor, George strode from the room quite satisfied at expertly planting seeds of paranoia. Soon, Garforth would desperately incriminate anyone to divert suspicion—the perfect environment for truth to emerge.

* * *

DCI George Beaumont gazed out the window of the Mercedes,

CHAPTER TWENTY-FIVE

watching the rain-slick streets of Leeds roll past through the rhythmic sway of the windscreen wipers, shifting gears smoothly as he navigated the slippery roads winding towards Brandling House. Beside him, DI Luke Mason sat in silence.

George's thoughts churned with their recent intense interrogation of elusive estate owner Eugene Garforth. The man's arrogant denials and violent outbursts at direct allegations confirmed George's suspicions—Garforth was hiding sinister secrets behind his distinguished facade.

But without concrete evidence, they couldn't hold him indefinitely. George's jaw tightened with frustration. Garforth remained a slippery fish, wriggling free of the hook each time they got close to reeling him in.

"That smug bastard knows more than he's saying," Luke remarked, reading George's pensive expression. "He'll slip up eventually if we keep the pressure on."

George nodded grimly. "Too right. That reaction wasn't feigned—we struck a nerve mentioning his tastes for 'younger company'." His mouth twisted in disgust. "Hard to believe the influential circles are shielding that perverted animal."

Luke grunted in agreement, expertly navigating a curve one-handed. "Money and connections bury a multitude of sins. But we'll keep digging, son. His sort always slips up when complacent."

George scrubbed a hand over his face wearily. "If only we had solid evidence now, we could hold Garforth while forensics search his property top to bottom."

"Agreed, but we've no grounds for a magistrate to issue a warrant based on suspicion alone," Luke countered pragmatically. "Have to play this carefully, son."

George nodded reluctantly. He knew Luke was right—they

had to build an airtight case before confronting Garforth again, despite the urgency gnawing at George's mind.

They were running out of time to find the missing girl alive if trapped somewhere by her abductor. But there was nothing to be gained racing ahead recklessly either.

Clenching his fists, George forcibly focused his circling thoughts. He couldn't afford distraction dwelling on the unknown. All he could control was meticulously gathering evidence and applying pressure to those withholding the truth. The rest he must leave in fate's hands.

Chapter Twenty-six

The familiar outline of Brandling House emerged from billowing mist, the imposing architecture radiating centuries of secrets and lies shrouded beneath elegant facades. George hoped sincerely that whatever answers lay hidden in the house's depths, they could unearth them in time to save fragile young lives from further harm.

Exiting the car, George turned his face up to the weeping grey sky in resignation. "Always making our job harder, eh?" He shook his head grimly. "Fucking pathetic fallacy." But there was no point complaining about the uncontrollable elements—he had to play the hand he was dealt. And right now, time was his most precious and swiftly draining asset.

George strode briskly up the path towards Brandling House, the rain-soaked gravel crunching under his boots. The imposing edifice loomed closer through the sweeping curtains of rainfall; details obscured behind the watery veil.

With Luke a steady, solid presence just behind him, George crossed the covered portico to the front doors. He couldn't suppress a faint shudder in the shadowy alcove, memories of a pale face glaring from an upper window in his youth swirling to the surface. But he shook off irrational unease—they had no time for chasing phantoms. Real dangers lurked, not ghosts.

Stepping into the dim foyer accompanied by the echo of the heavy doors, George was greeted only by empty silence. The cavernous space felt hollow, devoid of the usual police and civilian bustle during the active investigation. Their soggy footfalls seemed oddly muffled by the shadows looming overhead.

"Odd," Luke said. "Too quiet in here. Feels like a bleedin' tomb." He cast his gaze around the shadowy corners warily.

Just then, the heavy click of approaching footsteps echoed down the corridor. George tensed instinctively before forcing himself to relax as DC Candy Nichols emerged briskly around the corner. He shouldn't be letting eerie atmospherics unsettle his composure.

"There you are, sir," Candy greeted crisply, her keen gaze missing nothing. "Alexis is upstairs in Garforth's office."

Scrubbing a hand down his face, George said, "We're here to check on the diving team before calling it a night. Have you heard anything?"

"Nothing, sir, sorry."

With a terse nod, George turned and pushed open the doors leading outside, Luke following closely behind.

Squaring his shoulders against the wind, George turned his collar up and ventured into the grey damp, Luke matching his purposeful stride.

The icy rain needled George's neck and matted his blond hair as they headed down The Drift towards Top Hill Pond. Intermittent thunder rumbled ominously overhead. But George quickened his pace, refusing to be deterred by physical discomforts. Every delay or distraction stole precious time that young Esme did not have to spare.

As the murky pond came into view through the trees, George

frowned to find the place eerily deserted. Stopping short, he quickly pulled out his mobile to ring the search coordinator. Shielding the phone from the weather, George demanded tersely, "Where's the dive team? The pond's empty."

The coordinator's tinny voice crackled through broken reception. "Apologies, sir, I thought we had updated you. Sonar scans were inconclusive, so we commenced work at the larger pond in Middleton Park an hour ago."

Cursing under his breath, George scrubbed rain from his eyes. "Fine, we're on our way there now. Tell your men to keep combing methodically—our best hope of a break is underwater." He couldn't keep the edge of desperation from his tone.

Ending the futile call, George swung towards Luke. "Why does critical information constantly fall through bloody cracks?" he burst out angrily.

Luke simply shrugged, unruffled by George's rare outburst. "Never a tidy business, investigations. You know that well as any, son." His steady expression reminded George that predictability or fairness had no place here—the guilty did not politely announce themselves. They could only persist unrelentingly.

George took a deep, bracing breath, the chill air clearing his mind. Luke was right—delays and disappointments were inevitable facing an impossible, high-stakes task. All George controlled was maintaining focus despite the suffering and not losing faith when exhausted hope faltered.

On the blustery walk down The Drift and into Middleton Park, the two detectives discussed their lives rather than the case.

"How's our Isabella doing?" Luke asked kindly, reading

George's pensive expression. "Handful enough managing a new babe without your chaotic hours thrown in the mix."

George's mouth quirked up, thinking of his warm, patient fiancée who somehow kept their little family thriving despite his demanding, unpredictable career. "A goddess, that one. Don't know how she manages it." His voice softened. "But I'm trying to do better being present when I'm home. Both my girls need that."

Luke nodded approvingly. "As long as you're doing your best, that's all anyone can ask." He shot George a knowing look. "You've shouldered heavy burdens alone before. But you're not that young detective starting out now." Luke's stern visage creased into a fond smile. "You've people who care to share the load, mate."

George blinked quickly against the stinging in his eyes, grateful for his mentor's steadfast faith and wisdom. Knowing he had loyal friends and a loving family awaiting him helped George confront the darkness without losing himself. He would make it through this like all the other impossible trials — side-by-side with those who gave his life meaning.

Clearing his tight throat gruffly, George steered the conversation to safer ground. "Enough brooding – how's the wife?"

Luke's smile faded, his usual lively eyes clouding with uncharacteristic pain. He cleared his throat roughly before answering.

"Sheila's been having a difficult time lately. Her memory problems are worsening more rapidly than expected." He traced a gloved finger idly along the foggy passenger window. "Early-onset Alzheimer's, the specialists say now, though she's barely sixty."

CHAPTER TWENTY-SIX

Luke shook his head, grief etched across his worn face. "My vibrant girl fading before my eyes, forgetting cherished moments and people." His voice caught slightly. "Our golden years vanishing like smoke."

He turned to George with a sad smile. "Can't deny it's tearing me apart, son. I've managed a brave face on the job, but going home to see my wife so confused and frightened…" Luke's stoic facade cracked. "Christ George, we were going to travel Europe. I'll soon be a full-time caregiver, watching her disappear completely. And that'll mean I'll have to leave the team."

George gripped Luke's slumped shoulder firmly.

"You listen to me—you won't be alone, understand?" George held his mentor's grieved eyes unflinchingly. "You're family to me, Luke. Whatever you and Sheila need, I'll make sure you have support." George offered a sad but encouraging smile. "I'll speak with DSU Smith so you can have some paid leave so you can still make some memories together before…" He trailed off heavily.

Luke blinked quickly, gratitude shining through his haggard expression. He clasped George's hand resting on his shoulder. "You're a good man, George Beaumont. Always have been." His smile trembled slightly. "Don't know what I'd do without you in my corner."

"Right then, the first step is having you both over for dinner as soon as possible. Isabella would love fussing over Sheila, and I know how much she loves little Liv."

Luke gave a watery chuckle. "That all sounds brilliant, actually. Thanks, son." He shot George a pointed look. "I mean it."

The leafless trees stood like sombre sentinels guarding time-worn secrets and listening to sacred promises.

Rounding a bend, George spotted the police vehicles clustered ahead near the pond's grassy bank. The stocky search coordinator lumbered over, an apprehensive look on his weathered face. George's stomach tightened.

"Evening, gentlemen," the man greeted soberly. "Afraid there's been no progress in our scans so far." He hesitated, not meeting their eyes. "Truth is, conditions underwater are nigh impossible. I can't see a bloody thing down there; we're just feeling about blindly. It's a proper death trap."

George's jaw clenched. He glanced at the pond's deceptively calm surface. "No way to improve visibility at all?"

The coordinator shook his head wearily, rain dripping from the brim of his cap. "We've tried every trick imaginable, believe me. But silt keeps churning up when anyone sets foot down there. It's pitch blackness until you suffocate." He shuddered lightly before continuing gruffly, "Begging your pardon, sir, but my lads are at their limits. I can't in good conscience keep endangering-"

George lifted a hand, expression taut but resigned. "You don't need to explain. I understand fully." He clasped the man's shoulder. "Your team has gone well above and beyond. I couldn't ask for more. Thank you."

The coordinator looked immensely relieved by George's measured reaction. "I take no pleasure in conceding defeat, sir. My men would dredge that wretched pond until judgement day if it'd bring your missing girl home safe." His craggy features creased with sorrow. "But we've tried absolutely everything physically possible now. Maybe tomorrow we can continue. Let the pond settle overnight?"

"OK," George acknowledged simply. Allowing the weary

searchers a break from repeated risk felt right. "I'll be here in the morning, 7 am sharp." He offered the coordinator a tight smile and nod of gratitude before turning away; shoulders bowed under the bitter weight of failure.

Luke lingered a moment longer, clapping the coordinator bracingly on the back and murmuring his thanks before joining George, where he stood staring across the pond's muddy banks. Neither spoke for a long moment, the bleakness bearing down upon them. Finally, George scrubbed a hand down his face, accepting reality with resignation.

"Guess she's not down there then," he acknowledged heavily. "But if she's not there, where is she?" He looked at the woods. If she were in there, they'd have no chance of finding her.

But Luke's shrewd eyes had already narrowed thoughtfully. "That's the stage, right?" He pointed towards the roofed stage on the other side of the pond. "That suggests they'd already managed to navigate the pond towards wherever they were going."

"Right."

He glanced meaningfully at George and then back at the stage. "Forensics found nothing, right?"

"Right."

George followed Luke's assessing gaze. "What am I missing?" George asked.

"First thing tomorrow, we're going to speak with the Cowgills. I've heard hypnotising works well. Ashley'll tell us where they headed after arguing. I promise."

Clapping Luke's shoulder, George said with gruff appreciation, "Thanks, Luke. I didn't even think of that."

Luke nodded, falling into step as George strode towards the

stage with blazing purpose.

"And you know how good I am at organising search parties," Luke said, referring to a case of a missing child two years ago in Cross Flatts Park in Beeston. "I'll lead it whilst you do your thing. That way, we'll find her, OK?"

"OK."

Chapter Twenty-seven

DCI George Beaumont steered the Mercedes down the familiar streets towards home, the rhythmic swish of the windscreen wipers gradually lulling his scattered thoughts. Rain pelted the glass as dusk's shadows stretched through the city, reflecting his own bleak mood. Another long and ultimately fruitless day searching for missing teen Esme Bushfield without definitive breakthroughs was finally drawing to a weary close.

At this stage of an intensive investigation, the gruelling hours and relentless pressure took an exhausting toll even on George's formidable stamina. But there was no time for rest yet. Not with a young girl lost out there relying on him for justice and rescue.

Rubbing gritty eyes as he waited at a light, George forcibly dragged his flagging mind back to analysing their lack of progress. The treacherous terrain of Middleton Woods posed immense challenges for search teams. While public willingness to provide intelligence on the case was encouraging, verifying and following up the deluge of tips drained resources from more concrete leads.

George sighed, watching the drenched streets roll past. Every new fragment of information felt loaded with possibility, yet still, the opaque truth eluded his grasp. He only hoped Detective Superintendent Smith's decision to extend the custody period for slippery suspect Eugene Garforth would finally allow George to expose the man's secrets through sustained interrogation.

Just then, his mobile rang, the shrill tone piercing the brooding silence. Keeping one hand on the wheel, George, without checking the caller ID, pressed the answer button on the dashboard.

"DCI Beaumont," he responded crisply, turning right.

"Evening, George," came Detective Superintendent Smith's Geordie baritone through the tinny speaker. "Two quick items to update you on."

George felt his weariness abate slightly, thoughts sharpening with professional alertness. "Go ahead, sir."

"Right. Well, first, I've authorised the custody sergeant to extend Mr Garforth's detention period up to 36 hours. CPS agrees your team has reasonable grounds to continue holding him for further questioning. We want to keep up the pressure on the man."

George nodded approvingly, even though Smith couldn't see the gesture over the phone. "Excellent call. We're not letting that eel slip free until he cracks."

"Too right," Smith agreed. "Secondly, just letting you know we've had CID staff from other teams agree to handle the tip line and initial intelligence filtering overnight. Frees your team to focus on priority leads."

George exhaled in muted relief. The endless task of responding to each public call drained resources from the investigation's pivotal angles. "Much appreciated, sir. Thank the HMET leaders for me. Any word yet if forensics cracked into them?"

"Afraid no update yet on that front," Smith replied apologetically. "But hopefully by morning. Oh, and CID did say the hotline has fielded over two hundred tips already, FYI. Most still require a follow-up so far, but you know the odds of a diamond among the gravel."

George stifled a groan at the number. He was immensely grateful for the public's willingness to come forward but recognised the difficulties created for investigation teams by the flood. Every piece of intelligence had to be properly serviced, no matter how useless it seemed. One careless oversight could undermine the entire case later.

"At least the media coverage is generating leads, even if it makes our lives more chaotic," George acknowledged pragmatically. "Please relay my sincere thanks to the CID staff handling the thankless chore of call filtering and intelligence management tonight. It's one less burden on our plates."

"Will do," Smith assured him. "We're all rowing together on this one to get results. I know you'll steer us straight, George."

Signing off with renewed motivation from his supervisor's steadfast confidence, George was about three minutes from home when his mobile rang again. Expecting Smith with another update, he answered on the hands-free system without checking the screen.

"DCI Beaumont," he responded briskly, indicating right towards his neighbourhood.

"Evening, George," came DI Luke Mason's gravel tones through the car speakers. "Got an organisational check-in for you on the expanded search deploying at first light tomorrow."

George instantly shifted mental gears to the new topic, fatigue receding again. "Go ahead, Luke."

"Right. Well, from a personnel standpoint, we're stretched a bit thin," Luke reported bluntly. "Between forensics, canvassing, and now search teams, it's all hands on deck. But the volunteer emergency groups bolster numbers at least."

George's mouth twisted ruefully. Relying on well-meaning civilians always added unpredictability. "We take what we can get. Now, what's your take on terrain factors tomorrow?"

Luke grunted. "That's the other glaring issue—expansive woods and multiple ponds are less than ideal search conditions at the best of times. But with recent heavy rain..." He trailed off pointedly.

George grimaced, envisioning muddy quagmires and swollen, murky waters. "You're absolutely right. We'll need to equip team leaders accordingly for the hazards." He drummed his fingers on the wheel pensively. "At least the public appeals should keep tip-offs flowing. Any promising ones yet?"

Luke huffed in frustration. "More nonsense than useful nibbles so far. Which reminds me, the bloody media will be circling more ravenously after that press conference. What joy." George could envision Luke's scowl at the unwelcome complication.

"Don't I know it," George commiserated ruefully. "Let's discuss media management strategy at tomorrow's briefing. Naturally, the girls' ages attracted press coverage across the board. But servicing those vultures distracts from the investigation." The words came out more bitterly than intended, hinting at George's bone-deep weariness.

Luke seemed to pick up on George's fading reserves. "No

worries, son. One day at a time, and we'll get there." His stalwart faith lifted George's spirits slightly. They would claw their way through this mess somehow, together.

Pulling into his driveway, George quickly confirmed briefing logistics with Luke before hanging up gratefully. As he gathered his things, George glanced up at the comforting glow in the windows of home. Somewhere waiting inside, his loving family carried on, a refuge from the stormy darkness George faced professionally every day. Just picturing his girls' smiling faces fortified his weary mind to fight on.

Shutting off the ignition, George sat for a long moment, breathing slowly, letting the day's tensions seep away. He refused to carry the bleakness and despair in with him if he could help it. His family deserved the best of him in whatever stolen moments they shared, not the shell-shocked ghost haunted by horrors witnessed. He'd put them through enough last year when chasing the Ripper's spawn.

With a determined nod, George exited the car and hurried through the rain towards the welcoming lights. His solace awaited within.

* * *

The evening sky over Leeds was painted in moody shades of grey and violet as DCI George Beaumont walked his energetic Jack Russell terrier, Rex, through the familiar paths of Middleton Park. Despite the late hour, George needed to clear his head after another intensely frustrating day of hitting dead ends in the search for missing teen Esme Bushfield.

Leaving Rex to sniff eagerly at a tree, George paused to gaze across the rippling pond waters as dusk gathered. He vividly recalled playing here as a boy, pretending to solve imaginary crimes with his friends. How simple the world had seemed then compared to the murky realities he now confronted daily.

With a weary sigh, George moved on, his feet finding the overgrown trail winding up the wooded hill almost unconsciously. As a daring teen, he had often slipped over the wall, due to the locked park gates, after dark to wander these paths, adrenaline pumping at the illicit freedom. The moonless shadows had seemed alive with unseen threats back then.

Reaching the crest, George turned downhill, following the curve of the road through the car park towards the pond. A damp breeze stirred the leaves around him, carrying whispered echoes of long-ago laughter. Rex trotted happily at his heels, sniffing and exploring the night scents.

The sound of George's mobile ringing sharply broke the muffled stillness. Rex's ears pricked up as George fished the device from his coat pocket quickly. Glancing at the screen, he saw it was Jay Scott and answered briskly.

"DC Scott, what's going on?"

Jay's eager voice responded. "Evening, boss. I know it's late, but I wanted to give you a quick heads up on a promising lead that just came in."

George felt his fatigue abate slightly, professional instincts sharpening. "Go on, then."

"Right, so I was sifting through the latest intelligence reports and noticed a caller who identified Esme's mystery companion from the cafe footage as potentially Ashley's uncle."

George's pulse quickened. "Ashley's uncle? Any confirmation on that?"

"I am just cross-referencing now, but the initial background check suggests it could be Craig Bell—her dad's brother-in-law. Basically, Ashley's dad's sister's husband, I'm digging deeper into Bell's history and connections as we speak."

"Good work catching that, Jay," George said, pleased by his protégé's initiative pursuing the lead after hours. "Keep me informed if you unearth any concrete ties between this Bell fellow and Esme. Could be a critical breakthrough." He paused. "And send me some images of him."

"You got it, boss," Jay assured him eagerly before ringing off.

Pocketing his mobile, George felt cautiously hopeful as he watched Rex darting after a stick along the water's edge. The uncle angle warranted close scrutiny for sure. But why would Esme be hanging out with Ashley's uncle? It didn't make much sense.

Continuing along the winding wood-lined trail as darkness fell, George was reminded vividly of his boyhood fascination with local ghost stories. He and his friends had dared each other to pass this way after nightfall, often sprinting home in imagined terror. The woods' shadows had indeed seemed full of lurking horrors then.

Even now, mentions of young ladies waving back on foggy days; the blue lady; a phantom horse and cart; the headless horseman; a white wolf that would get you if you left the path; the ghostly woman scattering ashes; the ghost of Lady Maude; and the headless dog, scared George shitless.

George paused, peering over the edge into the inky water of the pond. He recalled the legend of a pale, vengeful spirit who haunted the pond, but he'd always dismissed it. It was the two witches that apparently lived in Brandling House, two spinsters who had been wrongfully executed as witches centuries ago, that terrified George more.

Tearing his gaze from the still blackness, George shook himself sharply. He refused to indulge in eerie imaginings fuelled by exhaustion and nostalgia. No good came from chasing shadows conjured by an overwrought mind. Right now, facts required clear focus.

With a determined breath, George moved briskly onward towards the narrow, hilly path known eerily as The Drift, the familiar trees seeming to lean closer overhead. He kept alert for anything unusual, but no shapes stirred in the tangled brush lining the secluded path. Rex trotted alongside happily, undisturbed by ominous atmospherics.

A faint metallic jangling suddenly carried on the breeze, too clear to dismiss as branches clattering. George halted, skin prickling warily as his hand drifted to his belt. Peering ahead into veiling shadows, he again shook off creeping unease. Likely just his tired mind playing tricks, or perhaps the caretaker making late rounds.

But when an indistinct scuffling echoed from up ahead, George hesitated, senses tingling. There it was again—a muffled crackling in the underbrush like something moving stealthily just off the path. This time, Rex also froze, hackles rising as he emitted a low warning growl.

Pulse elevating, George crept forward silently, one hand resting near his concealed weapon. "This is the police!" he called firmly into the void of wind-stirred leaves. "Make yourself known, now!"

Only ominous silence answered his demand. George continued forward cautiously until the woods opened up at the crest of the hill next to Top Hall Pond. Scanning the area intently, he again called out, "I know you're there! Come out where I can see you, hands up!"

Rex suddenly erupted into ferocious barking, fixing at one shadowy spot near the pond's edge. George tensed, gripping his weapon. At that instant, a figure exploded from the bushes, sprinting frantically for the tree line.

"Stop right there!" George bellowed, giving chase. But the suspect had already vanished into the woods' depths. Winded, George could only follow helplessly for a few paces before losing the trail completely amidst the identical trees.

Fists clenched in frustration; he swung back towards the pond, mind racing. Had they just missed capturing a pivotal suspect thanks to the bloody poor lighting? Heart pounding, George fished out his mobile to call Jay. He instructed his protégé to get forensics and an underwater search team to Top Hall Pond immediately while the scene was fresh.

Striding to the disturbed section of the bank, George scrutinised the trampled grass and broken branches left in the suspect's wake. Obscured as it was, this felt like the first solid break in days. Whoever lurked here had secrets to hide, and George would uncover them whatever it took. No one escaped him for long once in his crosshairs.

Mind already analysing the implications, George hurried back up towards Brandling House to help coordinate the impending search efforts. Adrenaline flooded his system, resurrecting his usual laser focus. They might finally have reached a pivotal junction that could crack this case wide open.

But George also felt the heavy weight of responsibility settling upon him. He had witnessed their shadowy suspect first-hand, come face to face with the possible monster who snatched Esme's life. And somehow, the villain had slipped through his fingers into the night because George lacked quickness or skill. His jaw tightened. That failure cut deepest of all, more than the fatigue or frustrations.

Chapter Twenty-eight

Shrill sirens pierced the night's stillness as police vehicles converged on Top Hall Pond, red and blue lights strobing through the misty darkness. Forensics teams poured from the cars, unloading an array of specialised equipment with practised efficiency. Within minutes, the serene park transformed into a hive of urgent activity.

DCI George Beaumont paced restlessly at the edge where the shadowy suspect had fled, fists clenching and unclenching at his sides. Frustration simmered beneath his tightly controlled exterior. He had been so close to apprehending the figure—potentially the key to finding Esme Bushfield. Yet, the perpetrator slipped through George's fingers like water, disappearing into the night's depths while precious time ticked away for the missing girl. The failure sat heavy in George's gut.

Nearby, DC Candy Nichols knelt to comfort a still agitated Rex, murmuring soothingly into the dog's fur. Her vibrant blue eyes met George's tense gaze over Rex's head.

"We'll find them, sir," Candy reassured quietly, conviction burning bright. "This is the break we've been desperately needing."

George managed a terse nod, bolstered slightly by his protégé's unwavering faith. He turned to survey the expanding crime scene, where white-clad forensic analysts meticulously combed every inch of the muddy ground.

Some crawled on hands and knees, noses nearly brushing the earth as they scoured for minuscule fibres or impressions. Others wielded high-powered metal detectors and ground-penetrating radar, seeking anomalies beneath the surface. Above, drones buzzed methodically back and forth, thermal cameras probing the darkness for hidden heat signatures.

No stone would remain unturned tonight.

Striding over to Stuart Kent, George demanded brusquely, "What have you found so far?"

Kent looked up from his crouched position and photographed a shoe print. "It's still early, but there are definite signs of recent human traffic in the area." Stuart gestured at the trampled underbrush and snapped twigs. "We'll analyse these tracks to determine what we can about the suspect's physical profile."

George nodded curtly. "Good. Anything else of note?"

"Actually, yes." Kent reached into a clear evidence bag and withdrew a small, dark object. "We found this snagged on a branch near where the suspect emerged."

George's pulse quickened as he leaned closer to examine the item. It was a scrap of red fabric, torn and smeared with mud. The frayed edges suggested it had been ripped free during a struggle or hasty flight.

But what made George's breath catch was the embroidered design peeking through the grime—a distinctive swirling he recognised instantly. According to witnesses, it matched the mini dress Esme Bushfield had been wearing when she disappeared.

CHAPTER TWENTY-EIGHT

"Tag it and get it to the lab for testing immediately," George instructed hoarsely, hope warring with dread in his chest. This could be the crucial link placing Esme at the scene. But under what circumstances?

George turned to find DC Jay Scott approaching swiftly, phone in hand and expression grave. "Boss, I just received word from the station. The press has been tipped off about tonight's developments and are already speculating wildly."

George exhaled sharply. "Bloody vultures." He scrubbed a hand over his face. "We need to get ahead of this narrative before it spirals out of control."

Jay nodded, already moving to relay instructions to the team. They couldn't afford sensationalism derailing the investigation now, not when they were finally gaining traction.

Candy appeared at George's elbow, ponytail bobbing with her characteristic energy. "Sir, what's our next move? How can this new evidence guide the search?"

George met her eager gaze, resolve crystallising. "We regroup and redirect all efforts to this area. Esme was here recently, likely against her will." His eyes blazed with determination. "We comb these woods and hills until we find her or a body. There's no in-between now."

Candy swallowed hard but nodded staunchly. "Understood, sir." She hurried off to coordinate the expanded search parameters, leaving George staring into the pond's black depths.

Somewhere out there, a monster lurked who preyed on young girls. But now, the playing field had shifted. This scrap of clothing was the first tangible link between predator and prey. And George would follow that thread relentlessly into whatever darkness it led until Esme was found and the guilty faced justice.

* * *

By the time weak sunlight began filtering through the misty treetops, the area surrounding Top Hall Pond had transformed into a hive of activity. Uniformed officers and trained civilian volunteers fanned out in meticulous grids, carefully probing every inch of the muddy banks and dense underbrush for further clues to Esme Bushfield's whereabouts.

DCI George Beaumont stood at the centre of the organised chaos, issuing directives and fielding a constant barrage of questions and theories from his team. Though his eyes were shadowed from a sleepless night, a feverish intensity burned within their green depths. The discovery of Esme's torn clothing fragment had galvanized him, renewing hope that had started to wane.

Nearby, DC Alexis Mercer pored over a detailed map of the search area, her golden head bent in concentration as she marked off sectors already cleared. Methodical and thorough, as always, Alexis insisted on personally checking each team's progress to ensure no avenues were overlooked. Her meticulous nature provided a vital counterbalance to the investigation's sometimes frantic pace.

A few feet away, DCs Jay Scott and Candy Nichols conferred quietly, blue and green eyes serious as they analysed the implications of this new evidence. The usually exuberant pair was uncharacteristically subdued, the gravity of what Esme's torn mini dress could represent weighing heavily.

"This confirms she was taken against her will, likely by the suspect George spotted," Jay murmured, running a hand through his artfully mussed hair. "Poor lass must have been terrified."

Candy bit her lip, fingers toying with the end of her fiery ponytail. "I just keep picturing her struggling, maybe trying to break free..." She trailed off, blinking rapidly. Though hardened by the job, cases with kids always hit Candy hardest.

Jay reached out to squeeze her shoulder bracingly. "We'll find her, Candy. The boss won't rest until we do, and neither will we." His ordinarily playful face was set with grim resolve. The easy camaraderie between the two friends now carried an undercurrent of shared purpose.

Glancing at the junior officers, George felt a swell of fierce pride at their dedication. His team was the best for a reason—they poured heart and soul into every case, especially when young lives hung in the balance.

Just then, DI Luke Mason approached phone in hand and brow furrowed. George tensed instinctively. The senior detective's body language telegraphed trouble.

"Son, we have a... situation developing," Luke said in an undertone, angling the phone screen so only George could see. "The media vultures have descended en masse outside the police barricades, clamouring for a statement on this 'pivotal breakthrough' in the case."

George's jaw clenched as he scanned Luke's live news feed, which showed a sea of jostling reporters and flashing cameras vying for the most shocking angle. He could practically hear the salacious speculation and wild theorising already.

"We need to contain this before it explodes into a full-blown media circus," George bit out tersely. The last thing they needed was the press whipping the public into a frenzy and hindering the investigation with false leads.

Luke nodded grimly. "I'll have our media liaison issue a statement emphasising that the investigation is still ongoing and urging the public not to jump to conclusions or interfere."

"Good," George approved. "Let's keep this as controlled as possible. The focus must stay on finding Esme, not chasing headlines."

As Luke moved off to coordinate the media response, DC Tashan Blackburn strode up purposefully, a tablet clutched in one large hand. The tall detective's usually impassive face was etched with urgency.

"Sir, forensics just sent over their initial analysis of the mud and pollen traces found on Esme's mini dress scrap," Tashan reported, deep voice edged with barely restrained excitement. "The composition matches samples taken from a marshy area on the far north side of these woods."

George's pulse leapt as he quickly processed the implications. "Indicating that's the direction she was most likely taken after the suspect fled the pond?" He paused. "That matches what Ashley told us, too."

Tashan nodded sharply. "I've pulled up satellite imagery of that sector. There are several abandoned mineshafts scattered deep within the densest parts of the forest." His dark eyes met George's meaningfully. "Ideal spots to hide someone."

George felt adrenaline surge through his exhausted limbs, the primal thrill of closing in on their quarry. This could be the pivotal lead that unravelled the entire mystery.

"Redirect all search efforts to the north woods," George commanded crisply. "I want every inch of that area scoured for any signs of Esme or our suspect. Derelict structures are a top priority."

As Tashan relayed the new directives to the team leaders,

CHAPTER TWENTY-EIGHT

George turned to stare into the thick tangle of trees stretching ominously ahead. Somewhere within that shadowy labyrinth, a young girl fought for survival, utterly alone. And a predator lurked, guarding dark secrets.

But the balance of power had just shifted. Armed with new clues and an iron determination, George would lead his team fearlessly. They would comb every inch of this isolated forest and bring the truth to light, whatever the cost.

Scanning his colleagues' faces, each lined with fatigue but blazing with resolve, George felt a fierce swell of pride. Together, they were an unstoppable force for justice, uniquely equipped to unravel this sinister mystery.

"Right then," George declared into the buzzing radio. "Let's move out and bring Esme home."

"Speaking of Esme, boss, I think you need to see this," said Jay.

* * *

The pale winter sunlight struggled to penetrate the low cloud cover as DCI George Beaumont pulled up outside the quaint facade of Coward's Cafe early Friday morning. The sleepy village of Middleton was just stirring to life, a light dusting of frost glittering on the cobbled streets. But rest had eluded George all night following the dramatic encounter at Top Hall Pond. He was eager to chase down any leads that could identify the shadowy figure who had fled into the woods.

Stepping briskly from the car, George crossed to the cheerfully painted cafe, hoping owner Justin Coward could finally shed light on the mystery man accompanying missing teen Esme Bushfield on that pivotal CCTV footage. The unknown figure's identity felt like a lynchpin that could unravel this entire confounding case.

The bell above the door announced George's arrival. Glancing up from wiping down the counter, Justin Coward straightened quickly, surprise flitting across his boyish features. Dark smudges under his eyes spoke of many sleepless nights since Esme's disappearance.

"Detective Chief Inspector Beaumont," George said, producing his warrant card."

"Morning, sir," Justin greeted courteously, setting aside his dish rag. "How can I help this early?"

George replied, "Apologies for the abrupt visit. I was hoping you might have time for some follow-up questions regarding the CCTV images from Monday night."

Justin nodded readily. "Of course, anything that could help find Esme." He bustled behind the counter. "Let me get you a coffee. The pot's fresh."

Settling into a corner booth with hot mugs, George withdrew a folder from his briefcase. "I understand you weren't able to identify Esme's companion in the footage previously. But we're exploring some new possibilities, and I was hoping you could look again carefully at a few photos."

He slid several glossy headshots across the table. Justin leaned forward intently, brow creased in concentration as he slowly examined each one. At the photo of Eugene Garforth, he glanced up and shook his head.

"That's the manor house owner, correct? He's not the gentleman with Esme that night."

George nodded, unsurprised. If Garforth were foolish enough to flaunt his deviance so publicly, they would have uncovered it. He was too sly.

CHAPTER TWENTY-EIGHT

The next picture was Programme Head Lecturer Wayne Wardman in a pressed suit and tie, smiling with polished charm for the camera. Again, Justin shook his head apologetically. "Only seen him in passing. Wasn't the one."

George felt a prickle of unease at Justin's instinctive adverse reaction upon glimpsing the third photo of Brandling House caretaker Bradley Welburn glowering under bushy brows.

"No, not him either, though he looks familiar..." Justin studied the stern image thoughtfully before shrugging. "Sorry, just a passing resemblance to someone, but not your man."

Nodding casually, George made a mental note to subtly verify Welburn's alibi again. Something about the caretaker's evasive manner still struck him as suspect.

But all other thoughts evaporated when Justin Coward visibly startled at the final headshot, leaning closer as if struggling to believe his eyes.

"Wait a moment. This fellow does look extremely familiar." He tapped the photo intently. Yes, I'm almost certain he was the one dining with Esme that night!" Justin met George's intent gaze. The hair, eyes, bone structure... it must be him!"

George managed to conceal his shock, mind racing. "You're quite sure? This specific man with Esme that evening?" He slid the photo back across.

Justin studied it again and nodded firmly. "I'm almost positive, Detective Chief Inspector. Now that I've seen him clearly, his image is jogging my memory of mannerisms as well. He and Esme certainly seemed... very close and familiar."

Taking a bracing sip of coffee to steady his thoughts, George asked neutrally, "And can you describe how they were interacting?"

"Well, they sat very near each other and were rather tactile—

hands clasped, leaning in to talk." Justin flushed slightly. They were laughing and just seeming very cosy, like a new couple mooning over each other, honestly."

He met George's eyes almost apologetically. "I know it seems wrong given her age and this fellow clearly being older. But they genuinely appeared romantically entangled based on body language. And to be honest, she looks much older than her age. Much, much older."

George carefully kept his expression neutral despite reeling internally. "And no signs she was distressed or coerced at all?"

Justin shook his head decisively. "Not in the slightest. If this is the man, Esme seemed perfectly smitten being close to him." He frowned pensively. "Does that help identify him for?"

Examining the photo closely, George replied vaguely, "It's a possibility we'll need to verify." He tucked the headshot away before Justin could glimpse the name printed at the bottom—Craig Bell.

Mind whirling, George clasped Justin's hand warmly. "You've been very helpful. Please call if you think of other details. Even small things could prove vital." He handed over a business card.

Back in the warmth of the idling vehicle, George withdrew the crumpled photo again, studying Craig Bell's handsome yet awkward features. Nothing in the unassuming man's sheepish smile suggested a capacity for manipulating vulnerable young girls, but George knew too well how often evil hid behind unassuming masks.

Arriving at the bustling station, George headed straight for the Incident Room. Striding through the organised chaos, he spotted DC Jay Scott glancing up from his computer. Beckoning Jay over briskly, George handed him the photo.

"Good work tracing the tip on Ashley's uncle. Get me everything on this Craig Bell ASAP—background, connections, the works. Discreetly."

Jay's forehead creased slightly as he studied the unremarkable features. "Her uncle, boss? I'd only just started background checks..."

George waved a hand impatiently. "Doesn't matter—you unlocked a strong lead. Now we need to know who this man really is and how entangled with Esme."

Looking pleased by the praise despite his confusion, Jay nodded. "You got it, boss. I'll dig into this Bell fellow straight away."

Clapping Jay's shoulder approvingly, George headed to update DSU Smith on these promising but explosive new developments. They would have to strategise handling sensitive family connections moving forward. But finally, daylight was piercing the shadows surrounding Esme Bushfield's disappearance.

Chapter Twenty-nine

DCI George Beaumont's jaw clenched as he studied the file on Craig Bell, eyes narrowed in laser focus. Ashley's uncle had a face you wanted to trust—open, friendly, harmless. But George knew all too well how evil often cloaked itself in the most innocuous disguises.

"Talk to me, team," he said brusquely, glancing up at the tense faces gathered in the incident room. "What have we uncovered on Bell so far?"

DC Alexis Mercer straightened, tawny hair glinting under the fluorescents. "Plenty to raise red flags, sir." Her usually serene features were etched with disgust. "Multiple sealed juvenile records, a mysteriously withdrawn complaint from a 14-year-old neighbour, whispers of inappropriate conduct at his teaching post that were quickly hushed..."

George rubbed his beard grimly, a sick feeling settling in his gut. Another bloody predator slipping through cracks, leaving shattered lives in his wake.

"Keep digging," he ordered. "I want every rock overturned, every skeleton dragged out of the closet. No way this guy snatches another innocent girl on my watch."

His team nodded grimly and dispersed purposefully, the hum of activity amplified. They would leave no thread un-

CHAPTER TWENTY-NINE

pulled until the full ugly truth saw daylight.

Turning to DI Luke Mason, George lowered his voice. "Thoughts on Bell being involved in something even darker? This feels bigger than one vile man's sick proclivities."

Luke's grizzled face deepened into a scowl. "The reach is troubling. Far as Manchester, possibly. And the type of victim he targets…" He swallowed hard. "Prime hunting for human trafficking rings."

Ice slid down George's spine at the loathsome prospect, fists clenching white-knuckled. If they were dealing with organised crime systematically destroying children…

"We'll burn it to bloody ash," George ground out, green eyes blazing. "Every last twisted one of them. Those kids deserve nothing less."

Luke's jaw tightened as he gave a sharp nod. "With pleasure, son."

George turned back to the Big Board, gaze boring into Craig Bell's smiling mugshot. The pieces were coalescing like a noose, trapping the vile snake in his own poisonous coils. Soon, there would be no shadows left for him to slither away—and George would relish snapping the cuffs himself, looking the monster dead in the eyes as he dragged him into the searing light.

Pouring himself yet another coffee from the stained carafe, George rolled his tight shoulders and tuned back into the bustle of his team, tirelessly mining data. Alexis pored over digital records with meticulous zeal, teasing out elusive connections. Tashan interviewed former associates with stern focus, dark eyes unflinching as he probed hidden corners. Jay fielded tip lines with dogged determination, voice rough from hours of coaxing every scrap from hesitant witnesses.

But it was Candy who erupted from her cubicle with wide eyes, ponytail whipping urgently. "Sir, you need to see this now!"

George surged to her side in two long strides, pulse kicking up. On Candy's screen, grainy CCTV footage showed Craig Bell meeting furtively with a slight blonde figure; heads bent close together.

"That's Esme," George said hoarsely, recognising her instantly, even in low resolution. "When was this taken?"

"Two days before she went missing," Candy replied, toggling through timestamps efficiently. "And it's not the only meeting." More clips flashed by in rapid succession—Bell and Esme conferring in shadowy alleys, exchanging small packages, the man's hand lingering too long on her arm...

George's blood boiled, a red mist descending. That lecherous slug grooming an innocent girl, twisting her trust until she delivered herself into his fetid clutches. The betrayal cut deep, imagining Esme's dawning terror when the friendly mask contorted into a leering gargoyle.

"We've got the bastard now," George bit out, voice shaking with barely leashed fury. "Haul him in for questioning straight away. Let's see how much he smirks when faced with his own damning actions in living colour."

As Candy relayed the directive, setting the machine in full motion, George paced like a caged lion, mind churning. Every fibre of his being yearned to confront Craig Bell immediately, to slam his reptilian skull against the wall until he spilt Esme's location through broken teeth.

But the procedure must be followed carefully. George knew too well how easily righteous rage could derail an airtight case, how monsters like Bell slithered free on technicalities when the letter of the law bent under emotional strain.

No, this required icy, meticulous precision to trap the snake with his own venom—and George would conduct the concerto flawlessly.

* * *

Esme's parents arrived at the station, red-eyed and frantic. George led them to a private room, heart aching at their barely tempered hysteria.

"Please, what's happening?" Dorothy Bushfield begged, hands twisting a monogrammed handkerchief into shreds. "Have you found our Esme?"

George took a steadying breath before gently urging the troubled couple to sit. "We've uncovered troubling evidence implicating Ashley's uncle, Craig Bell, in Esme's disappearance."

Stanley Bushfield jolted as if electrocuted, his face mottled with puce. "What? Ashley's uncle is involved? How? Why?" He narrowed his eyes. "Craig was a teacher—a greatly respected teacher. We trusted him..."

"I'm afraid we have surveillance footage showing him meeting inappropriately with Esme on several occasions before she vanished," George continued carefully. "As well as a highly concerning history of misconduct with underage girls."

Dorothy let out a choked sob, swaying dangerously. "No! Not Craig! He seemed so kind, so interested in Esme's ballet..." Her eyes widened with dawning horror. "Oh God, the special tutoring sessions he insisted on..."

George met the stricken parents' gazes steadily, voice

gentle but resolute. "I promise you, we will pursue this lead relentlessly until we find Esme and ensure any who harmed her face the full consequences."

"Please, just bring our baby home," Stanley pleaded brokenly, all bluster drained away. "She's our entire world."

Heart twisting, George clasped the devastated father's shoulder. "I swear to you, I will not rest until Esme is safe. You have my word."

As the Bushfields shook with silent anguish, George emerged into the chaotic shared office to find Ashley being comforted by Elaine Brewer. The girl's knuckles were white, clenched in her lap.

Elaine rubbed soothing circles on her bent back, murmuring reassurances as George approached slowly.

"I know you're struggling at the moment, Ashley," he said quietly. "But we need to have a private chat, just you, me, and DI Mason."

She looked up at him, face a mask of devastation. "What? Why?" Her breath hitched on a sob. "I haven't done anything w—" She broke off, retching violently.

As Elaine held her heaving shoulders, George crouched to meet Ashley's tortured eyes. "Listen to me carefully, Ashley. You are not to blame for any of this. We know you haven't done anything wrong, but we need you to be honest about what happened. We need you to be honest about Craig Bell. Predators like Bell are master manipulators. They exploit trust and innocence." His jaw hardened. "But we will ensure he and anyone else involved faces justice. You're not alone any more."

As Ashley dissolved into racking sobs, burrowing into Elaine's soothing embrace, George quietly backed out of the room, giving them privacy. Anger simmered in his chest. How many more young lives would evil men like Bell steal before the suffering ended?

George exhaled slowly, features hardening into a mask of determined calm. This was what he had trained for, the sacred duty he had sworn himself to uphold through any storm. Esme was still out there, a young soul battered but unbroken, clinging to hope. George would be her beacon home.

Squaring his shoulders, George turned the handle and entered the interrogation room, eyes blazing with grim purpose.

The hunt was on.

And Craig Bell's time had run out.

Chapter Thirty

The interview room's stark fluorescent glare bounced off grey cinder block walls, casting harsh shadows across Ashley Cowgill's pale, pinched face. She huddled deeper into her oversized jumper, fingers twisting into knots on the scarred metal table.

DCI George Beaumont, face carefully neutral, sat across from the trembling teenager, DI Luke Mason, a looming presence at his side. The relentless ticking of the wall clock punctured the thick, expectant silence.

George leaned forward, hands clasped. "Ashley, I know this is difficult. But anything you can tell us about the night you two disappeared is critical. Even the smallest detail could be the key to bringing her home safely."

Ashley's shoulders hunched higher, gaze fixed stubbornly on her bitten nails. "I've already told you everything," she mumbled. "That's all I know."

Luke's jaw tightened, his patience fraying. "Come off it, lass. There's no evidence you've lost your memory." His voice sharpened. "Holding back only puts your friend at greater risk."

"I swear, I don't—" Ashley's voice cracked, her eyes welling. She swiped at her tears angrily. Why won't anyone believe

CHAPTER THIRTY

me?"

George held up a placating hand, shooting Luke a warning glance. They needed to build trust, not bulldoze the fragile girl. He gentled his tone. "We do believe you want what's best for Esme. That's why it's so important you tell us the full truth, no matter how painful."

Meeting Ashley's wounded eyes steadily, George continued. "We have evidence your uncle Craig Bell met inappropriately with Esme before she vanished. Hours of them interacting."

Ashley stiffened, face draining of colour.

"Now, that alone is damning," George said evenly. "But what concerns me more is the pattern emerging of Bell pursuing vulnerable young girls. His teaching records are littered with hushed complaints and sealed files. Always targeting the isolated ones hungry for approval." George's eyes flickered briefly to the two-way mirror, behind which he knew Ashley's anxious parents watched.

Leaning back, George kept his gaze trained on Ashley's every micro-expression. "I think Bell used his charm to manipulate Esme, filling her head with pretty lies. And I suspect you carry guilt fearing you delivered your friend into a predator's hands." He paused. "I also suspect your uncle did things to you that you didn't agree to."

At that, Ashley crumpled like a marionette with cut strings, violent sobs wracking her thin frame. It was like the floodgates had opened.

"It's my fault," she choked out. "I'm the reason Uncle Craig noticed Esme at all! I'm the one who introduced them at my dance competition."

George and Luke exchanged a loaded glance as Ashley continued in a torrent of anguished words. "He was so excited to meet my 'lovely friend'. He kept going on about her poise and potential. He promised to help launch her ballet career in London..." She shuddered, face twisting. "He was a PE teacher, a dance expert. I thought he was being supportive. But the way he looked at her..." Ashley gulped. I made Esme a target. It's all my fault!"

"No," George countered firmly, gripping Ashley's shoulders. "The only one at fault is the man who exploited a child's trust. You did nothing wrong."

Through hitching breaths, Ashley divulged how Bell showered Esme with special attention and gifts over the following months. "She started having all these private lessons with him on weekends. He'd pick her up in his posh car for London outings to meet industry people."

Ashley looked down. "At first, Esme seemed to love the big city buzz. But then she grew distant, cancelling our plans at the last minute. Jumping anytime her phone chimed." Her voice dropped. "Almost like she was scared of disappointing him."

George's stomach knotted at the classic grooming signs, rage simmering under his calm facade. "Did Esme confide any concerns about your uncle's intentions?" he probed gently.

Eyes haunted, Ashley nodded jerkily. "She tried brushing it off as silly, but I could tell something was eating her." Worrying her sleeve, she continued haltingly. "Esme said Craig was getting too intense. His touches lingered, and he flew into rages if she missed his calls—like a proper controlling boyfriend, not a mentor."

Ashley squeezed her eyes shut. "I told her to stay away from him, that he was bad news. But she insisted I misunderstood." Her voice cracked. "Uncle Craig was her ticket out of this

CHAPTER THIRTY

claustrophobic city, her only chance to be somebody."

She began to sob. "And you know what's worse?"

"What?" asked George, gently.

"He was saying all of the same things to Esme as he'd said to me."

Rubbing his beard tensely, George said, "And what happened the night you both disappeared? What were your plans?"

Bottom lip trembling, Ashley whispered, "Apparently, Craig told Esme he had a private place in the woods where they could party without anybody noticing. A leaving party before she left for London." Tears streamed freely down her blotchy cheeks. "I begged her not to go, that we could get help, but she was frantic. Kept repeating Craig would fix everything. That he loved her and would protect her in London."

"London?" Luke pressed. "Bell was taking her there that night?"

Ashley shook her head. "The next morning." She brushed away a tear. "Esme swore me to secrecy. That morning, they were going to leave the woods together and were driving straight through to his London flat. A fresh start, he'd apparently called it." Her breath hitched. "I tried to reason with her, make her see how dodgy it all sounded, but she wouldn't hear it. She accused me of jealousy, of holding her back like everyone else." Her sobbing became hysterical. "I— I said I'd go with her to the party in the woods. I thought I could change her mind. That's why we argued by Miggy Pond. Because I tried to get her to stop."

"Why didn't you tell us this earlier?" Luke asked.

George snapped his head towards the DI, eyes narrowed.

Wiping her nose on her sleeve, she continued, voice rising.

"Like I said, we had a huge row out by the pond. I called her naive, a fool blinded by shallow flattery. Esme screamed that she didn't need me and that Craig was the only one who believed in her dreams. Then she took off into the night." Ashley lifted red-rimmed eyes. "So I followed her. I had to. She wouldn't last one minute on her own because I'd been to one of Uncle Craig's parties before. I knew what happened there."

George nodded but said nothing, inviting her to speak.

"I feel so guilty about it. My best friend. Delivering herself to a monster, and I couldn't stop her." She dissolved into broken sobs, folding in on herself.

Aching for the destroyed girl, George squeezed her shoulder. "You did everything you could, Ashley. This is not your blame to carry."

As Luke slid a box of tissues across the table, George stood abruptly, a muscle ticking in his clenched jaw. He needed to hit something. Preferably Craig Bell's smug face.

Leaving the interview room, George turned to Luke, eyes blazing. He said, "We're bringing Bell in for formal questioning straight away. I want his every device seized and records scoured for London property holdings or associates."

Upstairs on the HMET floor, George strode towards the Incident Room, barking orders as he went: "I also want an urgent CCTV review of all motorways between Leeds and London—motorway cameras, petrol stations, the works."

Officers scurried to comply, the station erupting into action. They'd give Bell one chance to come willingly. After that, George would greatly enjoy introducing the bastard to the bonnet of his car.

CHAPTER THIRTY

* * *

A breathless urgency crackled through the air as George and his team prepared for the simultaneous raids on Craig Bell's properties. The Incident Room buzzed with activity—bulletproof vests clipped on, static hissed from radios, and booted feet thumped concrete.

George surveyed the assembled officers, eyes fierce with resolve. "Ashley's intel has given us our best chance to find Esme alive. Every second counts now." His voice rang with conviction. "We move hard, we move fast. Flush Bell out and lock down the entire street."

Fervent nods rippled through the crowd. Every cop here understood the life-and-death stakes, the knife's edge they balanced on.

In the corner, DC Alexis Mercer pored over property schematics, her blonde brow furrowed in concentration. "We've got three confirmed locations—Bell's London flat, a warehouse by Canary Wharf, and a country cottage outside Leeds." She paused. The Met are on comms."

George nodded sharply, pulse quickening. The noose was tightening.

"Right, Alpha team takes the flat. Bravo, the warehouse. Charlie with me to the cottage," George instructed brusquely. "DI Mason will coordinate. Questions?"

Determined head shakes and steely expressions met his gaze. They were lean, hungry wolves ready to run their quarry to ground.

"Good luck," George said, tugging a black ski cap over his blond hair. Then, they were mobilising, a well-oiled machine of controlled chaos. Adrenaline replaced fatigue, the primal thrill of finally taking action electrifying exhausted limbs.

In the car speeding north, Luke was a grim, silent presence at the wheel, and George mentally war-gamed every possible scenario awaiting them. Every minute carried Esme further from reach—they must strike surgically, allowing no avenue for escape.

"Nearly there," Luke murmured as neat hedgerows flashed past, giving way to tangled woods. George checked his mobile—Alpha and Bravo teams were in position, awaiting his signal.

Rounding a bend, their target came into view—a white-washed cottage nestled amid towering oaks, quaintly charming in the insipid late afternoon sun. Appearances truly fucking deceived.

"Go," George hissed into the radio. Car doors opened in unison, disgorging black-clad figures who ghosted across the overgrown garden on cat-feet, encircling the cottage.

Heart pounding, George crouched by the front door, Luke flanking him with a baton. At George's curt nod, Luke swung hard, splintering wood with an almighty crack. "Police! Craig Bell, show yourself!" George roared, surging inside.

Adrenaline narrowed the world to snapshots—a chintz sofa knocked askew, shattered china crunching underfoot, photographs swaying on the wall. Cleared room by room, the cottage was deserted.

George was disappointed. There was no Esme, no Bell. But a notebook abandoned on the kitchen table snagged his eye. Flipping it open, his breath caught at the meticulous records of names, ages, locations, and prices.

"George..." Luke's tight voice cut through the red haze. He held up a scrap of red fabric – the rest of Esme's mini dress

CHAPTER THIRTY

carelessly consigned to the rubbish bin.

Before George could process the reality of precious seconds slipping away, his radio crackled. "Flat's a negative on Bell and the girl. Over." Another burst of static followed. Ditto warehouse. But you've got to see this, boss…"

Forty minutes later, George stood in a cavernous room that could've passed for a photographer's studio if not for the stomach-churning subject matter. Images of teenage girls in various states of undress and distress papered the walls, a grotesque collage of suffering. In the centre, an old military cot stained with unmentionable fluids turned George's stomach.

"That utter fucking monster," Alexis spat, features twisted with revulsion. "There's got to be dozens of victims here." Her manicured hands shook slightly as she bagged reams of damning correspondence for evidence.

George's jaw ached from clenching, a sick fury roiling in his gut. How many stolen childhoods, how many walking ghosts, while Bell and his cronies profited? The notebook in George's coat pocket took on a new, insidious weight.

At the warehouse's far end, Tashan and Jay perused a cork board. Their faces were ashen, lips pressed into thin lines. George didn't have to look to know what they'd found. Esme smiled out from the mosaic of horrors, a delicate butterfly pinned for perverse consumption.

George reached down with a gloved hand, gently unpinning Esme's photo, bile scalding his throat. He would not leave her among this filth a second longer.

Just then, his mobile trilled, DI Mason's number flashing. "The Met's got Bell," Luke reported, voice thrumming with grim elation. "Picked him up at King's Cross trying to board a train to Paris. The Met's bringing him up to Leeds as we speak."

They had him! At last!

His heart pounding, George strode purposefully outside. The first raindrops were speckling the pavement.

No more running now, you pathetic coward, he thought savagely. George would ensure Craig Bell rotted in a cell for every day remaining in his miserable life. Retribution had finally arrived.

Chapter Thirty-one

Six hours later, the interview room crackled with barely restrained tension as George faced the unassuming man responsible for shattering countless lives. Unshaven and rumpled from the rough arrest, Bell still managed a veneer of affronted indignation.

"I've done nothing wrong," he blustered, ratty eyes darting. "This is outrageous harassment by you lot!"

"Then answer the question," said George. "Why where you in London?"

"Because it's half-term, you idiot! I'm entitled to a break!"

"Fine." DCI George Beaumont fixed Craig Bell with an intense stare. "Let's stop dancing around this, Mr Bell. Were you and Esme involved romantically?"

Craig visibly recoiled, his ruddy features draining of colour. "Absolutely not!" he exclaimed, voice pitched high with offence. "I care for Esme, yes, but strictly familial, nothing sordid!"

George tilted his head, unconvinced. "The intimate way you interacted at the cafe indicates more than friendly concern."

When Craig just spluttered incoherently, George pressed on. "You must admit, a middle-aged man meeting his teenage niece's friend at night, plying her with wine and whispering affections does imply inappropriate relations."

"How dare you!" Craig erupted, face mottled with fury. "I was supporting a vulnerable girl, not mucking about! She's nearly eighteen and sought my counsel, which I provided in good faith." He jabbed a finger at George accusingly, spittle flying. "I've done nothing illegal, so stop these vile insinuations! I'm a teacher, remember!"

Leaning back calmly, George let the incensed man vent until he was spent. As Craig slumped back, chest heaving, George remarked conversationally, "The age of consent being sixteen does mean relations between you wouldn't necessarily be criminal."

He held Craig's uncertain gaze. "But the perceived impropriety could still create motives if exposed. Reputations and families were at stake."

As Craig paled, Luke interjected sternly, "Too right. Well-respected teachers tend not to risk scandal over schoolgirl dalliances without good cause." He narrowed his eyes menacingly. "So what was she really to you, Bell? A secret bit on the side?"

"How many times must I say it—there was no affair!" Craig shouted, face purpling again. "Your wicked insinuations are utterly false!"

But George glimpsed the naked fear in the man's frantic denials. They had struck painfully close to the nerve. It was time to rip off the bandages concealing fetid secrets.

Leaning forward intently, George pinned Craig with his piercing green eyes. "If you've any speck of decency, you'll admit the truth now. Because if you're lying to conceal involvement in Esme's fate, I will see you rot in prison for it."

CHAPTER THIRTY-ONE

Craig's bluster melted away, leaving him deflated against the cushions. "Please," he rasped, eyes imploring. "I've done nothing to harm that girl; you must believe me. I could never!"

When George remained stoically silent, Craig leaned forward, wringing his hands desperately. "All I'm guilty of is caring too much! I listened when Esme was unhappy and met her for confidential talks. Nothing untoward transpired, I swear it!"

Seeing he remained unmoved, Craig changed tack, stuttering nervously, "Now see here, I'm no violent man! I have never been in a fight in my life. What possible motive could I have to harm Esme?" He gave an unhinged bark of laughter. "It's madness to accuse me of foul play!"

Luke harrumphed derisively. "What better motive than hiding your sordid affair? Maybe the girl threatened to expose your perversions?" He smirked coldly at Craig's stunned expression. "Seems you had plenty to lose if this naughty secret got out, eh?"

"No, you've got this all wrong!" Craig exclaimed, chest heaving again. "I want Esme found safe, I swear it! I've been worried sick searching myself since she disappeared." His voice cracked with emotion. "Please, you must believe me!"

George merely commented mildly, "Interesting you never mentioned those extensive private searches when initially denying any relationship." He cocked his head. "Why so eager to conceal your connection and movements if innocent?"

Craig did not argue, sinking his head into trembling hands with a choked groan. The truth he had fought so hard to bury now encircled him inescapably.

In the taut silence, George decided to prod the most painful bruise not yet acknowledged: "Ashley mentioned Esme had been acting moody and ill before vanishing. Are there any complications related to your intimacy that might have caused friction?"

He let the inference hang pointedly. Craig lifted his head slowly, eyes widening in shocked comprehension. "No!" He recoiled violently as if gut-punched. "You think... dear God, never!" He shook his head, gagging reflexively. "I couldn't possibly... and she never said..."

Overwhelmed, Craig lurched up, wheezing. He turned to his solicitor. "I need your help, useless prick! This has gone too far!" He glared wildly at the two detectives and his solicitor. "Let me leave now unless you're charging me!"

Seeing they had pushed Craig to the brink, George smiled, gathering his thoughts. Their suspicions had been confirmed; the rest depended on evidence. He got up and nodded at Luke. The interview was over for now.

"We'll be back with further evidence," George said. He eyed Craig. "I suggest you speak with your solicitor and tell us what you're hiding."

Pausing at the door, he said calmly, "Interfering with our investigation will only raise deeper concerns. I trust we can count on your full cooperation from here on?"

When Craig nodded rigidly, trembling, George took his leave, his mind churning over the confrontation's dark implications.

* * *

A damp chill permeated the air as DCI George Beaumont stood on the slippery, wooden bank of Top Hill Pond, watching the police divers surface one by one with their finds. The team had spent hours meticulously dredging the pond's murky depths since George's dramatic encounter there last night.

Now, under the gloomy grey sky, George scrutinised each sodden piece of newly recovered evidence laid out on the tarp—torn cardboard box remnants, several cheap flash drives caked in sludge, a laptop warped by water damage. It all pointed to someone hastily disposing of items they clearly did not want to be found intact.

George's pulse quickened as he turned over the possibilities. What secrets did this electronic trove contain that justified dumping it rather than properly destroying such damning information? Who was the one lurking here trying to spirit away the incriminating technology? And what role might the contents play in solving the disappearances of Esme Bushfield and Ashley Cowgill?

Mind racing, George watched as Stuart Kent carefully bagged each item, dictating descriptions and logistics to accompanying SOCO Hayden Wyatt. The electronic devices could hold immense significance, though filth and corrosion rendered accessing their data a challenge.

Glancing over as the divers climbed wearily from the pond, George called out, "Excellent work securing these, lads. We'll get them to our tech experts straight away and keep searching based on what surfaces."

The men nodded, looking gratified that their dangerous, tedious efforts had finally borne fruit. As they peeled off their wetsuits, George saw DI Luke Mason approaching purposefully from where he had been coordinating more exhaustive search efforts.

Luke cocked one bushy grey brow sardonically as he eyed the sodden recovered items. "Well, now, it looks like our nighttime visitor did chuck some interesting rubbish in that pond." He fixed George with a piercing look. "Has to be connected to our slithery friend Garforth, eh?"

George replied grimly, "It seems likely. Though whether the arrogant bastard acted alone dumping it or had his shady solicitor do the chore is debatable."

He pictured the elegant, silver-tongued lawyer who clung to Garforth constantly, shielding his influential client from consequences. The man gave George an uneasy feeling, like a predatory shark circling relentlessly.

George scrubbed a hand down his face wearily. "Best not to speculate yet. Once we figure out what's been hauled up, we can strategise how to leverage it if it proves relevant."

Luke grunted ambiguously, shrewd eyes still assessing the pond. "Still irks that the snake who dropped this is slithering about free while we muck around in the mire." He shrugged his broad shoulders. "But you're right; there is no sense in getting ahead of facts. Not when we've got Bell in custody."

Falling into step with George, heading back towards their vehicles, Luke asked conversationally, "How are we handling the chain of analysis on those gadgets? I assume we want our best tech bloodhound digging into them?"

George nodded decisively as he opened the car door. "Straight to Josh Fry in Digital Forensics. Whatever's on there, Josh will sniff it out." Starting the ignition, he added tightly, "And then we squeeze Garforth and his scheming solicitor for answers."

Luke smirked coldly at the prospect as they navigated the winding country lanes back towards Leeds. "It should be fun taking Garforth and his solicitor down a peg or two. They are always strutting about imperious in their fancy suits like judge and jury."

CHAPTER THIRTY-ONE

His craggy features creased into a scowl. "Acting so high and mighty defending scum like Garforth. When really, he's just another greedy bastard happy to profit off others' misery." Luke spat out the window in disgust.

"Too right," George agreed grimly, hands tightening on the wheel. He loathed defence solicitors who helped guilty men like Garforth evade justice through legal technicalities. The morally bankrupt would rationalize any behaviour for the right price.

Exhaling heavily as the urban sprawl came into view, George added pragmatically, "Still, the likes of Hayes do serve an important purpose in our justice system, ensuring lawful process and such." His mouth twisted ruefully. "Can't fault them for doing their jobs, much as I may despise the types they represent."

Luke grunted, only partially mollified by this rational perspective. They rode in thoughtful silence the rest of the way back to the bustling police headquarters, both eager to unearth whatever revelations lay buried in the recovered electronic files.

Inside the Digital Forensics lab, George quickly briefed DS Josh Fry on the delicate assignment of analysing devices dredged up from the suspect pond dump site. Josh absorbed the context, eyes glinting behind his glasses.

"You think this is tied to our pal Garforth then?" he clarified, keen gaze darting between the electronics laid out on his worktable. At George's terse nod, Josh cracked his knuckles decisively. "Leave it to me, sir. I'll tease out every last megabyte if it helps bring evidence to light." His expression hardened. "Monsters who hide crimes through technology never realise it's a double-edged sword. Their digital footprints lead right to the truth if you know where to look."

Clapping Josh's shoulder gratefully, George said, "No one I trust more to trace those steps than you, Detective Sergeant. Let me know the instant you find anything to leverage."

Chapter Thirty-two

DCI George Beaumont sat in his office, sifting intently through a stack of financial reports related to key persons of interest in the investigation. A sharp rap at the door drew his gaze up to see DS Josh Fry's lanky frame silhouetted in the doorway, an eager glint in his bespectacled eyes.

"Sorry to interrupt, sir, but I have some initial analysis ready on those devices we fished out of the pond," he reported briskly, wheeling a television mounted on a mobile stand into George's office. "I think you'll find the contents rather... illuminating."

George felt his fatigue abate as he sat up sharply, waving Josh in. "Go on, then. What have you uncovered so far?"

Plugging cables deftly into the back of the flat-screen, Josh responded over his shoulder, "Right, so most of the hardware was badly water-damaged, but I managed to extract data from two of the DVDs so far."

He finished setting up and pressed play before continuing. "Brace yourself, sir—it's rather unsettling footage, apparently filmed in secret."

George's gut tightened as hazy footage filled the screen, showing a nondescript office. "Where is this exactly?" he asked tersely, scrutinising cluttered shelves and ornate wallpaper visible in the background.

"It's hard to confirm definitively without broader context," Josh cautioned. But the decor does resemble your man Garforth's personal quarters in Brandling House from what I gathered."

George felt his pulse elevate in anticipation as Josh elaborated. "Now watch the foreground subject..."

Peering closer, George realised with a jolt that a young female student occupied the leather couch; half turned away from the concealed camera. She appeared to be reading a book in the elegant, unfamiliar space.

"It's innocent enough so far," Josh remarked. But watch what happens when the girl gets up to leave."

George watched closely as the student gathered her school bag before standing and stretching. As she raised her arms overhead, her loose top rode up, fully exposing her midriff and bra momentarily. She adjusted her clothing and exited through a rear door. She was completely unaware of the illicit filming.

Sitting back heavily as the first video ended, George rubbed his jaw. "The girl seems of age, but it is still an unacceptable invasion of privacy. What's on the other disc?"

Josh exchanged the discs, answering tightly, "Same location, different subject. Equally unsettling behaviour."

The second scene showed a pretty brunette perched on the leather couch, brow furrowed over a complex textbook. Sunlight glared in from an unseen window, illuminating her smooth, bare legs as she twirled a strand of hair absently.

After several minutes, the girl set her book aside and stood, revealing her casually provocative outfit of cropped tank and mini skirt. George noted she appeared college-aged as the

CHAPTER THIRTY-TWO

camera lingered lewdly on her curves as she bent to retrieve a fallen notepad. Straightening up, the student gathered her things obliviously before exiting.

Ending the footage there, Josh grimaced distastefully at George. "Certainly seems our suspect filmed these scenes covertly without consent. But both girls read as legal adults, sir." He hesitated delicately. I'll keep analysing for any more conclusive evidence."

Just then, a knock preceded DI Luke Mason poking his head in curiously. "Got an update on the pond findings, George?"

Noting their grim expressions, Luke stepped fully inside, scowling. "That bad, eh?"

After viewing the recordings in tense silence, Luke spat in disgust, "Devious bastard! Luring girls into his lair to leer at them secretly." He cracked his knuckles menacingly. "Can't wait to bash his smarmy face in."

"Easy now," George warned pragmatically. This supports suspicions of Mr Garforth's voyeuristic tendencies but proves nothing conclusively criminal." At Luke's outraged spluttering, he raised a placating hand. I agree it's repulsive, but we must be cautious in building an airtight case."

Turning to Josh, he directed, "Have our techs conduct forensic photography of Garforth's Brandling House office space immediately. We'll do visual match analysis to confirm location."

Josh nodded, already jotting notes. "Will do, sir. I'm still restoring damaged files on the laptop and flash drives. Hoping for more conclusive evidence once recovered."

After Josh departed swiftly, George scrubbed both hands down his face as if to scour away the lingering vileness. "We need something irrefutable to finally expose Garforth's guilty conscience, not just immorality."

Luke still bristled like a bulldog straining at its leash. "I say we drag the slimy weasel in right now and crack him open!" Slamming his meaty fist on George's desk, he exclaimed hotly, "String him up by his bollocks until he squeals the truth!"

"Enough!" George ordered sharply. "I know your outrage, believe me. But we do this the right way, lawfully, or the guilty go free." He held Luke's burning gaze steadily. "I refuse to allow that, no matter how it tests my restraint. Now, you must trust our process, however maddeningly slow it seems."

Gradually, Luke's flaring nostrils stopped heaving. He gave a gruff nod, jaw flexing. "Aye, you're right, as always. My temper outpaces reason sometimes." Shooting George a grudging look of respect, he added bluntly, "That's why you're the boss, son. Cool head prevails."

* * *

DCI George Beaumont was reviewing witness statements in his office when a sharp rap at his door made him glance up.

A uniformed officer stepped in, features grim. "Sorry to interrupt, sir, but we've just gotten word of a death that may be tied to your missing girl's case."

George sat up sharply, instantly on alert. "Go on then, what's happened?"

"17-year-old male, Noah Wilman, was just found deceased in his home from an apparent overdose," the officer reported sombrely.

George's pulse quickened. The name Wilman stirred faint recognition. "Believe it's a suicide then?"

The officer nodded. "We recovered a note at the scene

expressing extreme guilt over 'ruining innocent lives.' The family confirmed he attended school with both Esme Bushfield and Ashley Cowgill."

George leaned back heavily, scrubbing a hand down his face. His instincts screamed that this tragic event and the missing teens were connected by more than coincidence.

"Any known relationship between our victims and this Wilman lad?" he asked tersely.

"Still piecing together background, sir, but initial indications suggest possible romantic ties and jealousies involved." The officer flipped pages in his notes. "Wilman also had a minor drug possession charge recently, which could explain the overdose method."

George waved a hand sharply. "I want the full post-mortem and tox report the instant they're available. Priority one." He fixed the officer with a piercing look. "If this poor boy was involved somehow and opted out due to guilt..."

The implications hung heavily. George refused to dismiss any thread that could finally unravel the dark events surrounding Esme and Ashley's fateful disappearance. One more innocent life lost compelled him to breach the shadows at any cost.

After the officer departed, George stood and paced his office, thoughts churning. He grieved another promising young life cut short, but also recognised the potential break Wilman's death represented. Guilt was a powerful motivator, and teenage passions bred rash decisions.

* * *

DCI George Beaumont sat at his desk scrutinising financial

records, searching for irregularities tied to key persons of interest. A sharp rap at his door drew his gaze up to see Detective Chief Superintendent Mohammed Sadiq's imposing frame filling the doorway.

"Got a minute, Beaumont?" Sadiq asked without preamble, his usual air of sophisticated confidence somewhat diminished. Before waiting for a response, he entered and took a seat, leather satchel in hand.

"Of course, sir." George quickly closed the file, giving his superior his full attention. Sadiq's strained expression and visit sans entourage raised his instincts that this involved more than routine case direction.

Clearing his throat gruffly, Sadiq withdrew a bundle of papers from his bag. "Found these amongst Ishaan's belongings and thought you should see them." He passed the rumpled letters to George like discarding something distasteful. "Seems the boy's become rather fixated on this missing girl, Ashley."

George accepted the letters cautiously, seeing Ishaan Sadiq's angular script, addressing them passionately to Ashley Cowgill. His pulse quickened. "And Ishaan volunteered these correspondences?"

Sadiq shook his head bitterly. "Hardly. I confronted him after a teacher reported odd behaviour and was forced to search his room." His shoulders slumped wearily. "Never anticipated needing to invade my son's privacy, but drastic times call for drastic measures."

George sorted through the letters, keeping his expression carefully neutral. But the overly familiar terms and clinging tone unanimously struck an uneasy note. "This does seem to indicate a strong infatuation, sir," he said delicately. "Beyond

CHAPTER THIRTY-TWO

typical youthful interest."

Sadiq scrubbed a hand down his face, looking suddenly aged. "From snippets I overheard, I knew the boy had become obsessed with a girl, but I never imagined it could be tangled up in your investigation."

George chose his following words with care. "We cannot fully dismiss the potential significance, however coincidental the connection may seem." He met Sadiq's fierce gaze. "Your son inserted himself into events by lying about the victims' departure that night. His fixation demands scrutiny."

Sadiq looked aggrieved but nodded reluctantly. "I understand your obligation to follow the trail wherever it leads." He hesitated before adding heavily, "Ishaan is still just a misguided boy. But if he has strayed into darkness, the fault is mine." Sadiq seemed to crumble under the weight of paternal responsibility.

Seeing genuine remorse in the man's anguished eyes, George's tone gentled. "You've done nothing wrong, sir. Teenage passions burn hotly out of our control at times."

Sadiq's mouth quirked slightly. "I was rather consumed by my university sweetheart once upon a time." He exhaled heavily. "I pray my faith in Ishaan's core goodness proves justified, however misguided his actions of late."

George nodded, wanting to believe the best of the arrogant but impressionable teen. He shuffled the unsettling letters together. "We will proceed objectively, sir. But also empathetically, remembering our own youthful recklessness." He met Sadiq's eyes with compassionate assurance. "Young hearts and minds yet have room to grow."

Sadiq seemed to relax slightly, comforted by George's non judgmental approach. But George remained guarded internally until facts bore out impressions. With lives at stake, he could not afford emotional subjectivity. His duty compelled maintaining clinical distance.

After another strained conversation that teetered between parental devotion and professional neutrality, George politely walked Sadiq out. Alone again, George sat heavily at his desk, scrutinising Ishaan's scrawled words. The language trod the line between genuine infatuation and something more sinister.

Phrases leapt out, unnerving in their intensity: My heart only beats for you... You consume my thoughts... Anything for your affection...

George's pulse quickened reading a particularly explicit passage. Ishaan's graphic description of winning Ashley's intimacy through aggressive pursuit sent chills down George's spine. Was this harmless dramatic prose or something more ominous?

The unhealthy attachment Ishaan fostered towards Ashley could not be ignored, given his established dishonesty about her disappearance. George would need to bring the boy back in for intense re-questioning regarding his relationships with both missing girls. Even if Ishaan's only crimes were deception and lust, he still held answers that could potentially unlock deeper truths.

A knock at his door interrupted George's brooding thoughts. DI Luke Mason entered, keen gaze landing immediately on the letters scattered across George's desk. "What've we got here then?"

Quickly updating his partner on the unexpected development, George handed over the unsettling bundle. Luke's shrewd eyes narrowed as he read, craggy features etching into deeper lines.

"Well, now, this paints things in a decidedly dodgy light," Luke muttered darkly. He stabbed a finger at Ishaan's salacious imagery.

Looking up grimly, Luke declared, "We need to lean hard on this moody pup, son."

George tilted his head non-committally. "Perhaps. Or Ishaan could just be an overheated, infatuated, arrogant teen." At Luke's sceptical grunt, he conceded. "I think it's a good idea to bring Ishaan back in for intense re-questioning."

Chapter Thirty-three

DCI George Beaumont stood in the Incident Room, scanning the latest forensic analysis reports with laser focus. His sharp green eyes widened as he reached the section detailing photographic match results between the illicit video footage and Eugene Garforth's private Brandling House office.

According to the forensic technicians' conclusions, the decor visible in the videos conclusively identified the filming location as Garforth's quarters in the manor. This damning evidence shattered the pompous man's claims that the vulgar recordings were misrepresented fiction.

Pulse elevating, George quickly pulled DI Luke Mason aside to update him on the breakthrough findings.

"It's concrete now—Garforth secretly filmed those girls in his personal spaces," George confirmed grimly, jaw tight with contained fury. "The fucking snake's been harbouring depraved deeds behind closed doors this whole time."

Luke's craggy features creased in matching disgust. "Devious bastard! This ought to nail his smarmy hide to the wall for good." He cracked his knuckles menacingly.

"Steady on," George cautioned. "This proves his voyeuristic tendencies beyond doubt but not necessarily criminality regarding Esme and Ashley." At Luke's incredulous snort,

CHAPTER THIRTY-THREE

he conceded, "Granted, the evidence paints an increasingly damning portrait of the man's morality and relationships with students."

Scrubbing a hand down his face, George continued solemnly. "Either way, we finally have concrete justification for holding Garforth on obscenity charges once he's medically fit."

He met Luke's steely eyes. "Have uniforms posted outside his hospital room day and night. No more slippery escapes for that snake before he faces the music."

Luke smacked a meaty fist into his palm with vicious satisfaction. "With pleasure, boss. I'll handle the arrangements myself." His scowling features made clear the guards would have orders to use any necessary force, preventing Garforth from absconding from justice's grasp at this time.

As Luke strode off to coordinate the suspect's protective watch, George felt himself breathe easier for the first time in days. The noose had finally closed around Eugene Garforth, however hard his high-priced lawyers fought the charges.

No more shielding behind silk ties and status.

* * *

The mood was tense as DCI George Beaumont stood surveying Eugene Garforth's stately office in Brandling House, watching SOCOs combing meticulously for evidence. After the damning forensic confirmation that Garforth had secretly filmed girls here, George ordered the manor declared an urgent crime scene. Whatever dark secrets hid in its depths must finally be exposed to harsh scrutiny.

Stepping aside as an officer carefully shifted Garforth's imposing antique desk, George fought to keep his expression dispassionately professional. But the sight of unmarked cardboard boxes stacked in the carved recess made his pulse spike with vindicated fury.

The tech's gloved hands visibly trembled as he opened the flaps to reveal contents—dozens of plastic bags containing female undergarments. Faded Polaroids showed teenage girls posing self-consciously alongside handwritten notes on appearance and measurements.

The officer gagged, face paling with horror. "Bloody hell..." He looked to George for direction, features hardening. "The beast's been collecting trophies of his victims."

Jaw clenching, George managed tightly, "Bag and document it all. We'll cross-reference for possible matches to known associates or prior complaints." He had promised himself to remain detached. But these obscene reliquaries of stolen innocence tested even his steely composure.

This long-overdue vindication was sour consolation for the trauma Garforth had secretly inflicted, smugly untouchable until now. How many silenced girls had suffered his predation, believing none would dare stand against a man of wealth and privilege?

Continuing his measured circle of the shadowy study, George scrutinised each crevice like an archaeological dig unveiling society's shameful secrets. On the surface, only distinguished furnishings worthy of Garforth's sterling reputation. But peel away genteel pretences, and sickness festered just beneath.

Eugene Garforth put on an air of upstanding nobility, but behind closed doors, he was a monster thriving on exploitation, his status weaponised to grant access to vulnerable prey. How many bright souls had he snuffed out behind that jovial smile?

Pausing before an oil portrait of Garforth, George studied the refined image intently. In the painting, Garforth exuded wisdom and dignity, surrounded by icons of knowledge and antiquity. Captured for posterity as the consummate gentleman guiding future generations.

George's lip curled derisively. The only knowledge Garforth imparted was depravity masquerading as care, his hands defiling rather than nurturing. No fine trappings or credentials softened that ugly truth now exposed for all to see.

Turning sharply from the mocking portrait, George swore to himself Garforth's sins would be punished to the fullest extent, no matter how deep the rot permeated. Brandling House's foundations had been built on lies that must be torn out root and stem before healing could begin.

Striding from the oppressive study into the hall's relatively bracing air, George spotted DI Luke Mason observing the methodical search efforts, craggy features etched with disgust. At George's approach, Luke turned, granite eyes smouldering with outrage barely contained.

"Well, how's our mate Garforth looking now?" Luke bit out caustically, already reading George's dark expression. At the confirmation, Luke shook his head furiously. "Deserves to hang for this, slow and painful. The bloody animal."

"Steady on," George reproached sharply, grasping Luke's rigid shoulder. As much as he shared the gut-level revulsion, they must stay disciplined. "We go by the book so the fiend has no loopholes to wriggle through when this reaches court. OK?"

He held Luke's burning gaze intently. "Garforth will pay, Luke. Trust me."

The taut muscles under George's hand gradually unclenched as Luke processed his rational words. Finally, he exhaled gruffly and nodded. "Aye, OK, son."

Back in the office, they continued observing SOCOs diligently dismantling Garforth's shrine of lies. Piece by piece, his facade crumbled under the weight of conscience ignored for decades. But it was only a start scraping pus from the festering sore. More darkness surely waited in unseen corners.

* * *

DCI George Beaumont observed Sergeant Josh Fry meticulously reviewing data salvaged from the water-damaged electronics recently dredged up from the suspect pond dumping site. The entire team recognised these damaged devices potentially held the evidence needed to finally expose Eugene Garforth's hidden sins.

Leaning over Josh's shoulder, George scrutinised the cryptic fragments rapidly populating the multiple computer monitors. "What have we got so far, Detective Sergeant?" he asked briskly. "Any substantial data sets recovered yet?"

"Making steady progress, sir," Josh reported, fingers flying adeptly across the keyboard. The drive platters were badly corroded, but I'm extracting snippets here and there. I just need to reassemble them into coherence."

He tapped a few final keys decisively before sitting back and meeting George's gaze. "In fact, I've managed to decrypt a partitioned section of the laptop's hard drive containing some alarming content."

Seeing he had George's full attention, Josh elaborated gravely, "It appears to be an extensive digital archive of

CHAPTER THIRTY-THREE

explicit photos and communications implicating Mr Garforth in an exploitative underage sex ring."

George's pulse spiked, but he kept his tone carefully neutral. "Do we have irrefutable proof on identities and ages at this stage?"

"Still confirming details, but evidence points strongly to girls under the UK's age of consent," Josh reported. He pulled up a file, pointing at time stamps. "And see how it spans decades? This was no isolated lapse in judgement, sir."

Studying the nauseating material clinically, George noted the elaborate encrypted security measures taken to guard the hidden archive. This was no careless collection of pornography but rather meticulous documentation of organised abuse.

"We'll need to thoroughly trace and verify each victim," George directed tightly. "Leave no slimy stone unturned bringing all Garforth's sins into the light. What about the other devices?"

"Just finished restoring key data sets on two of the flash drives," Josh confirmed, fingers flying again. "Equally damning records implicating Garforth and other powerful figures in events at Brandling House."

He brought up photos dated the night Esme and Ashley disappeared. Young girls mingling with distinguished older gentlemen at a decadent party, liquor flowing freely. In several images, Garforth had an arm possessively around giggling teen girls, their smiles betraying intoxication.

"Bastard was parading his conquests right under everyone's noses," Alexis Mercer growled from over George's shoulder, fists clenching.

"It's concrete now—Garforth exploited his position to manipulate vulnerable girls like Esme," George acknowledged grimly. His eyes blazed with icy fury at seeing proof of the corruption he long suspected was rotting Brandling House's foundations.

After further tense study of the appalling archive, George straightened, jaw set with determination. "Have our child crimes specialists thoroughly analyse and document every shred of recovered data," he directed Josh crisply. "No victim forgotten. I want an airtight case ready when we crucify Mr Garforth and his enablers publicly."

Josh nodded sharply, already preparing drives of evidence for transport and encryption.

George watched Josh pause. "Wait a moment, sir. What are these?"

Josh pulled up more images, including semi-nude shots of Ashley Cowgill. "It looks like Ashley features in the recent content."

Alexis reeled at this confirmation of their worst suspicions—that Garforth harboured desires for underage girls and hadn't limited himself to just looking. Wrenching her eyes from the screen displaying Ashley's vulnerability, Alexis speared Josh with a searching look.

"Please tell me this is sufficient evidence to charge the bastard now rather than waste another minute."

Josh smiled mirthlessly. "Yes, sir—timestamps, metadata trails, the works leading straight back to that predator." His smile faded. "With this, we can charge Garforth for sure."

Fifteen minutes later, Josh queued up the most damning proof of Garforth's child exploitation in front of assembled appalled detectives. Jaws clenched, George surveyed Ashley's haunting image before spearing Josh and Alexis with a grateful look.

CHAPTER THIRTY-THREE

"Great work. We arrest Garforth today and put the pressure on." George was already striding purposefully towards the Incident Room's exit.

Chapter Thirty-four

"What now?" Craig Bell asked. He was looking worse than he was earlier. Clearly being in a cell didn't suit the man.

George smiled thinly, a predator scenting blood. "We've already compiled quite the damning file on you, Mr Bell." He splayed crime scene photos across the scarred table. "Stalking vulnerable teenagers, plying them with false promises of fame and fortune, then traffic—"

"Youthful dalliances," Bell interrupted, pale face hardening. "You can't prove anything improper. My solicitor—"

"Will have a devil of a time explaining this," George cut in, voice deadly soft. He laid the notebook in front of Bell. "Meticulous records of your sordid enterprise."

Cornered, Craig Bell changed tact with the panicked cunning of a lesser predator. "Look... hypothetically... if I had some valuable information to trade, there could be a deal struck, immunity offered..." He grinned. "Right?"

White-hot rage seared through George's veins, blistering away his practised calm. You bastard! "You're in no position to bargain!" he snarled, slamming a fist on the table. Bell flinched satisfyingly.

"Her life is on your worthless head. So you'd better start singing like a fucking canary," George ground out, looming

CHAPTER THIRTY-FOUR

into Bell's space until only inches separated them. "Last. Chance."

Sweat prickled Bell's upper lip as the gravity of his predicament settled. His eyes took on a feverish sheen. "Fine," he muttered, tongue darting out to wet cracked lips. "But this stays between us. They'll kill me..."

George raised an expectant brow, face an unyielding mask. 'They'? Who were 'they'?

Bell sagged, defeated. "I work for someone else. It was his idea to procure Esme." He paused, gathering nerve. "Eugene Garforth. He runs the whole show. Well, he's second in command, and don't ask me who's in charge because I don't know, alright?"

A jagged laugh ripped from Bell. "That posh fucker bankrolls the operation, hand-picking the cream of the crop to 'foster', if you catch my meaning." He sneered. "High-class clientele expect pristine goods reared to their exacting tastes."

The DCI Thought about what DS Josh Fry had told him: "It appears to be an extensive digital archive of explicit photos and communications implicating Mr Garforth in an exploitative underage sex ring." Air evacuated George's lungs, leaving him reeling. Was the aristocratic Garforth the shadowy kingpin behind this vile empire? Or was there, like Bell said, somebody even higher?

But even as the pieces rearranged into a sickening new pattern, a chilling clarity emerged. Garforth's dismissive uncooperativeness, the layers of security, the remote country estate. All smoke and mirrors for grooming victims right under their averted eyes.

Craig Bell still prattled desperately, growing more confident of his toehold. "I've given you the big fish! Surely that merits consideration..."

But George scarcely heard the weak appeals, mind racing ahead. He grabbed his mobile, punching a familiar extension. "DC Blackburn. I want an arrest warrant for Eugene Garforth immediately. Apparently, he's involved up to his eyeballs."

Hanging up decisively, George turned to the two-way mirror and addressed the grim faces he knew gathered. "Search every inch of that bastard's estate. If he's laid one tainted finger on Esme..."

The threat hung, a silent promise in the humming air.

George rounded on Craig Bell, eyes frigid. "Get this vile creature out of my sight. His part is done." He clenched his fists. "For now, anyway!"

As Bell was dragged spluttering away, George sank onto a metal chair, adrenaline finally seeping out, leaving him spent. The depravity at play here beggared belief. A human trafficking ring operating with impunity, masterminded by a supposed pillar of the community.

His fists clenched until nails bit flesh. He had allowed Garforth's affluent charm to misdirect him, blinding him to the calculated predator crouched beneath the bespoke suit.

And Esme paid the price for that grievous oversight. Every violated child wore her face.

But wallowing in guilt helped no one now, George told himself firmly. Esme still drew breath, still dreamt of rescue. And come hell or high water, he would find her.

And God help Garforth when George did.

* * *

CHAPTER THIRTY-FOUR

The police convoy sped through the misty evening, a dark serpent winding along city roads. In the lead car, DCI George Beaumont gripped the steering wheel, knuckles white, jaw set. Beside him, DI Luke Mason studied the warrant papers in grim silence.

Every mile marker brought them closer to the hospital where that snake was because Eugene Garforth wasn't merely a dismissive toff with airs of impunity. Behind the bespoke veneer lurked a predator of the foulest order, trafficking innocence with blood-chilling calculation.

A trafficking kingpin hiding in plain sight, cloaked in aristocratic respectability. It beggared belief. But the damning paper trail didn't lie: Sordid transactions with Craig Bell's pimping syndicate. Gloating exchanges of exploited flesh. Smoking guns illuminating Garforth's diabolical appetites.

And Esme was the final grotesquerie plucked for his tainted palace. The threads had led here from the start, but George had allowed the beast's polish to misdirect him. His jaw ached from clenching. Never again.

"Nearly there," Luke remarked quietly, steely eyes noting the familiar landmarks. George merely nodded, pulse thudding against his constricted throat.

All those days of circling, of polite masks and furtive whispers, had boiled down to this final, brutal confrontation. Today, Eugene Garforth's darkest secrets would be dragged screaming into the light—and God help the bastard when they were.

As the private hospital emerged from the ghostly veil of fog, looming and sepulchral against the bleak sky, George willed his hammering heart to steadiness. The monstrosity had fooled them all, a bloated carcass of respectability concealing a nest of perversions within.

George would pry open the rotten cavity and rescue the lost souls trapped inside if it was the last thing he did.

Car tyres squealed on the tarmac, shattering the pregnant hush as the police contingent disembarked, fanning out in practised formation. They made their way up to Eugene's room.

George strode towards those doors, Luke flanking him, warrant clutched like an amulet against evil. The detectives exchanged a charged look, a thousand silent understandings passing between them. Then George raised a fist and pounded on ancient oak, the impact reverberating through his bones.

A beat passed—then two. The detectives waited, their coiled energy held in check. Then came the clicking of expensive shoes on marble, and the door swung open to reveal Eugene Garforth's greasy solicitor, Campbell, and his patrician sneer.

"Ah, detectives. To what do I owe the pleasure at this ungodly hour?" His eyes flicked contemptuously over the assembled police presence. "Mr Garforth is currently asleep in his room." He narrowed his eyes. "Is there something I can assist you with?"

The casual arrogance, the unruffled poise of a man convinced of his untouchability, ignited a fury in George's belly.

"We have a warrant for Eugene Garforth's arrest on suspicion of human trafficking and sexual exploitation of minors," George declared with icy control, the damning paper thrust forward like a shield.

"This way," said Campbell, and George followed.

When they reached another oak door, the DCI pushed his way through, seeing Garforth propped up in bed.

"What is all this?" Garforth asked.

CHAPTER THIRTY-FOUR

"Eugene Garforth, I'm arresting you on suspicion of human trafficking and sexual exploitation of minors. You do not have to say anything. But it may harm your defence if you do not mention when questioned something which you later rely on in court. Anything you do say may be given in evidence."

"What?"

"You will accompany us to the station for questioning."

For a fleeting instant, something ugly writhed across Garforth's distinguished features, a glimpse of the monster beneath. But then the patrician mask clicked smoothly back into place, and he waved them inside with mocking cordiality.

"My, such dramatic accusations." Garforth led them into the opulent library, sinking into a chair with languid grace. His tone remained infuriatingly patronising. "I'm sure this unpleasantness can be cleared up swiftly."

George loomed over the seated man, his bulk dwarfing the fine-boned aristocrat. "Unpleasantness?" he ground out through clenched teeth.

"You sexually abused and trafficked multiple underage victims, you sick fuck!" George hissed, fists clenching and unclenching at his sides. "We have all the evidence needed to bury you."

Garforth merely looked up at him, unimpressed. "Language, Detective Chief Inspector. Such baseless slander ill-befits an officer of the law." His lips thinned. "My solicitors will soon put paid to these scurrilous allegations."

George leaned in closer, holding the man's reptilian gaze. "No solicitor will save you now, Garforth. We have reams of correspondence detailing your sordid 'mentoring' arrangements with Craig Bell and his pimping syndicate."

A file was slapped onto the mahogany reading table. "Victims. Payments. Gloating bloody commentary on destroying lives!" George's hand shook as he stabbed a finger at the damning spreadsheets. "All leading back to you, the posh ringmaster of suffering!"

Garforth glanced at the papers, face hardening infinitesimally. But still, he shrugged, picking an invisible speck of lint from his cashmere sleeve. "Obvious fabrications. I host numerous youth programs. An easy matter for a disgruntled employee or some gutter press lackey to doctor records besmirching my good name."

His lip curled in disdain. "I'll not dignify this calculated character assassination with another word. You have vastly overstepped and will be hearing from my solicitors posthaste."

But George merely smiled grimly, a shark scenting blood in the water. From his inner pocket, he withdrew a clear plastic evidence bag and dangled it before Garforth's face.

Inside was a scrap of crimson fabric embroidered with the letter 'E' in black thread.

"Recognise this, Eugene?" George asked with deceptive mildness. "We found it in the rubbish at one of Craig Bell's rape pads." He leaned closer, voice dropping to a menacing purr. "Esme Bushfield was wearing this exact mini skirt when she disappeared from your estate."

The first hairline fracture appeared in Garforth's supercilious facade, an almost imperceptible tic at the corner of his eye betraying internal agitation.

"I'm sure I don't know what you..."

But George steam-rolled on, relentless. "Oh, let's not forget all about the young girls in your office. It was quite the special attention lavished on some random students, yeah?"

CHAPTER THIRTY-FOUR

George nodded at Luke, who hefted a laptop open to a particularly damning scene in his study.

"Amazing what nifty tech our data forensics team utilizes," George remarked with savage affability. He regarded Garforth through narrowed eyes. "Our team has forensically matched results between the illicit video footage found in Top Hall Pond and your private Brandling House office."

Eugene's breath hitched, composure unravelling further. A thin sheen of sweat glistened on his upper lip.

"And not only that, Eugene," George said. "We've found the stash of trophies hidden within your office at Brandling House."

"Really, detective, such prurient insinuation is beneath even—"

"Is that why you hid her away?" George interrupted, voice rising inexorably, the levee finally breaking on his tamped-down rage. "So you could control every aspect of her? Shape her to your warped desires?"

George seized the arms of Garforth's chair, caging him in with his bulk. His voice dropped to a lethal hiss. "Where. Is. She? What have you done with Esme?"

Eugene Garforth, scion of privilege and master puppeteer, crumpled like a house of cards before George's blistering onslaught. His face drained of colour and then splotched crimson as the magnitude of his downfall sank in.

"It isn't... She... She came willingly!" he sputtered, the words emerging strangled and panicked. Spittle flecked his chin as he beheld George's implacable, judging stare. "Such a ripe beauty, so eager to please. I was helping her reach her potential!"

Revulsion churned in George's gut. Eleven weeks. That's

how long this vile creature had Esme in his clutches to twist her mind and defile her body.

"Listen to yourself," he spat in disgust. "Esme is a child, you bastard! Groomed and trafficked by scum like you and Bell to sate your foul perversions."

A vein pulsed in Garforth's temple, eyes taking on a feverish sheen of madness. He giggled, a jagged, unhinged sound. "So prim and proper, the little prudes. But they all end up begging for more. Not so innocent flower, your lost lamb..."

George's vision tunnelled, edges tinting red. His gun hand twitched towards the evil bastard's sneering face.

"Last chance, Garforth," he said through numb lips. "Where have you stashed her?"

Eugene's gaze darted wildly about the room, the walls closing in. His tongue flicked out to wet, cracked lips. "Hidden her away, I have. Like a precious jewel. So delicate, yet so sturdy..."

George grabbed the front of Garforth's bespoke shirt, hauling the much smaller man halfway out of the chair until they were nose to nose.

"Where, damn you?" he roared. "What have you done with the lass?" Spittle flew from George's lips. After so long, so close, only to fail her at the very end...

"An atomic nuclear refuge built by the miners with the Atom Bomb in mind in the 1940s in the woods!" Garforth shrieked, the last vestiges of his urbane camouflage stripped away to reveal the quivering rodent within. "Been there for nearly a century, a family secret." A thin rill of mucus trailed down his chin as he hiccuped and rambled. "Perfect spot to keep my beauties hidden away until they ripen. She's waiting there for me now, my tasty little peach..."

CHAPTER THIRTY-FOUR

George wrenched his hands away from the repulsive creature, revulsion surging through his veins like acid. "Tell me exactly where this bunker is!" He had to get out and get to Esme before he throttled the mewling monster with his bare hands.

But Garforth simply shook his head. "Not without a deal."

"You piece of shit!"

"I want it put on record that because I told you where she is, I'll get leniency."

Grinding his teeth, George nodded.

"You word, Detective."

"Fine. You have my word."

"Excellent."

George pulled up a map on his phone, and Garforth pointed out the location.

"Luke, get the desk sergeant to book in this piece of shit," George barked over his shoulder, already striding towards the door.

Chapter Thirty-five

DCI George Beaumont sat across from Detective Chief Superintendent Mohammed Sadiq in his office, their mood tense as they discussed Eugene Garforth's unsettling revelations. Luke was in Middleton Woods with a specialist search team, and George was on tenterhooks.

A sharp rap at the door interrupted their brooding thoughts. DC Jay Scott entered, his typically buoyant features creased into uncharacteristic solemnity.

"Sorry to barge in, boss, but there's been a development," Jay announced.

George instantly sat straighter, radar attuned to his protégé's grave tone promising news, however grim. "Go on then, Jay. What's happened?"

Jay hesitated as if reluctant to voice the words. "It's Ashley Cowgill, boss. Her body's just been pulled from the river near Whitehall Road in the city centre."

George froze, blind-sided momentarily. Beside him, Sadiq bowed his head with a low oath. After a paralysed beat, George managed tightly, "What's the scene assessment so far?"

"Attending uniforms suspect suicide, given her recent trauma," Jay reported. "Currently being treated as a probable drowning until evidence indicates otherwise."

CHAPTER THIRTY-FIVE

George was already grabbing his coat, jaw set. "I want all the divers, footage collection experts, and forensics we've got down there, now. The priorities are on water and roadside cameras." He clasped Jay's shoulder. "And gently inform the family they have my deepest condolences."

Striding from George's office, DCS Sadiq called over his shoulder. "Inform me if any developments arise, DC Scott. I'll be taking point managing the media."

Settling heavily behind the wheel moments later, George sat motionless, blind-sided by the gut punch of news. Young Ashley, so full of complexity and creative passion, snatched forever by the hungry river's currents. The loss pierced George unexpectedly.

But he couldn't afford to feel, only act. Putting the car in gear, George navigated the bustling city streets towards Whitehall Road with hands that should not by rights be steady. Outwardly, he bore the news like stone, but inwardly, emotions threatened to breach the dam of discipline and duty.

Once this case was resolved, there would be time to process the gruelling toll it was taking. But not now, when the grief-stricken family needed his clinical clarity most. He clung to the slim chance this tragedy resulted from impulsive teenage despair rather than premeditated malice.

Approaching flashing lights marking the grim scene, George steeled himself.

Flashing his warrant card at the cordon, George strode past patrol cars to the river's edge. Ahead, divers continued scouring the oily water methodically while forensics specialists combed the muddy bank. The air hung heavy with grim purpose as personnel catalogued each piece of evidence with clinical precision, denying emotion's unproductive tides.

Spotting Sergeant Greenwood conferring with the search co-ordinator, George approached briskly. "Walk me through the circumstances, Sergeant."

Squaring his stocky frame, Greenwood summarised swiftly. "Emergency call came in forty minutes ago from a cyclist reporting what appeared to be a body snagged against a tree root downriver. First responders arrived to find the victim bloated and tangled in debris."

He grimaced. "It's pretty clear, even accounting for water damage, that it was Ashley. We've secured a perimeter, sir, pending your direction."

George nodded approval of the procedures followed. "And we're certain of the cause being drowning?"

Greenwood shifted his feet. "External assessment suggests so, but we've avoided undue handling or speculation before the post-mortem." He met George's gaze. "Never like to presume when kids are involved, sir."

"Too right," George agreed. He glanced downstream where the body was found, picturing poor Ashley jammed helplessly while the indifferent current battered her broken body.

Shaking off grim thoughts, George issued swift directives for canvassing river access points for witnesses and sweeping transport hubs for CCTV footage within a sizeable radius. He requested immediate retrieval of camera archives from the looming Whitehall Waterfront apartment complex overlooking this segment of the river. If Ashley entered the water here, multiple lenses likely captured critical evidence.

Briskly confirming search coordinates and protocols with Sergeant Greenwood, George allowed himself a brief moment of silence, staring out at the river's deceptively calm flow.

Turning from the lapping waters, George strode back up the

CHAPTER THIRTY-FIVE

embankment to confer with forensic technicians regarding preliminary samples and image documentation from Ashley's remains and the surrounding scene.

He kept his professional mask firmly in place, listening to the blunt catalogue of scrapes, bruises, and artefacts recovered from the body and adjacent riverbed. But the stark descriptions threatened to crack his composure with mounting implications this was no impulsive suicide plunge.

Signing off on evidence transfer to seal the chain of custody, George glanced toward Whitehall Waterfront looming above, its countless eyes surely hiding critical views of Ashley's final living moments. His jaw tightened in anticipation of whatever revelations the footage would yield.

Taking out his mobile, George quickly updated DCS Sadiq on initial findings, promising to liaise with media protocols once preliminary forensics analyses helped establish probable framing. Despite shock waves from these bleak developments, the public still deserved judicious information flow, not rampant speculation.

Ending the call, George surveyed the organised procedures underway by the riverbank. Satisfied the investigation began on the soundest footing possible given the circumstances, he headed for his car. The next phase now required verifying Ashley's mental state and relationships in her final days. He had a distraught mother to console while determining if cruel chance or calculated malice stole her daughter's fragile life.

Either way, the truth deserved uncovering, however painful its reckoning.

* * *

The grey, overcast sky matched the sombre mood as DCI George Beaumont pulled up outside the home of Johnathan and Sandra Cowgill. Beside him in the passenger seat, DC Jay Scott stared silently out the rain-streaked window, youthful features uncharacteristically grim. In the backseat, DC Tashan Blackburn flipped through notes with a scowl, shoulders rigid with tension. No one relished informing grieving loved ones.

The three detectives stepped from the vehicle into dreary rainfall. Trudging up the path, George mentally steeled himself for the wrenching task ahead.

With a fortifying breath, George rapped sharply on the faded front door. Muffled footsteps approached before Sandra Cowgill opened it, her wan features creasing in bewildered recognition. "Chief Inspector? Has there been a development in the case? Have you found Esme?"

"Can we come in, Mrs Cowgill?" George replied gently.

Brow furrowing in concern, Sandra mutely stepped aside. She led them down a dim hallway cluttered with shoes and coats into a cosy but careworn sitting room. Perching nervously on the sofa's edge, she clasped her hands tightly to still their trembling.

"Is it about Esme, then?" she asked unsteadily, searching their solemn faces. "You wouldn't all be here unless..." She trailed off hoarsely, eyes squeezing shut as if willing away reality.

Kneeling compassionately before her, George laid a bracing hand over Sandra's white-knuckled grip.

"I'm afraid we've received confirmation of your daughter's passing, ma'am. Her body was found in the river late this afternoon."

George watched Sandra absorb this sledgehammer of words,

CHAPTER THIRTY-FIVE

colour draining from her tortured features. As expected, she appeared more hollowed than shocked, the last frail fibres of hope crushed. When she finally lifted reddened eyes brimming with unspoken anguish, George squeezed her hands gently.

"I am so very sorry for your loss." He glanced briefly at the phone on the cluttered coffee table. "I understand your husband is not home currently?"

Attempting to collect herself, Sandra choked out tremulously, "No, he's... he's away on business. Ashley was found, so he decided to go." She seemed to fold in on herself then, face crumpling as wracking sobs overtook her slight frame.

At George's subtle cue, Jay crept into the cramped kitchen, returning with a box of tissues and a glass of water. Kneeling beside her, Jay offered both while murmuring an awkward but sincere condolence.

The simple gesture of comfort seemed to penetrate Sandra's haze of despair. Taking a deep shuddering breath, she dabbed at leaking eyes, regaining a fragile composure. "Thank you for your kindness, all of you," she rasped sincerely, though misery etched every line of her gaunt face. "I apologise for my outburst. This is just..." Her throat convulsed. "...just such a..."

"You've nothing to apologise for, ma'am," Tashan offered gruffly from where he stood, shifting his feet by the door. Beneath his characteristic brusqueness, authentic empathy resonated. "A parent's loss has no deeper or more terrible pain."

Gently squeezing Sandra's shoulder, George picked up the conversation's necessary thread. "We will arrange the release of... of Ashley once the post-mortem is complete to spare you further anguish." He hesitated delicately.

"How did she die?"

"We currently believe it was suicide."

Sandra said nothing.

"Can I ask your opinion on whether she seemed emotionally troubled or unstable lately?"

Sandra fiddled with a crumpled tissue, eyes distant. "What a stupid fucking question." Her voice caught raggedly. "But suicide? I struggle picturing that, despite recent trauma..."

She searched George's face. "Surely her death was a tragic accident? The river can be so treacherous." Sandra seemed desperate to cling to this possibility of a meaningless chance rather than a destructive choice.

Squeezing her hand consolingly, George answered truthfully, "We cannot rule anything out yet, ma'am. But rest assured, my team will uncover the full truth, however difficult." He held her tearful gaze with compassionate resolve.

Nodding gratefully, Sandra dissolved into silent weeping once more. Exchanging heavy looks over her bent head, the three detectives stood quietly and respectfully.

When Sandra's ragged sobs slowed to shuddering breaths, George murmured final condolences and assurances that their family liaison officer would maintain contact through arrangements ahead. He pressed his business card into Sandra's limp grasp should further questions arise.

Stepping out into grey rainfall, George felt the bleakness seeping deeper but shook himself sharply.

Young Esme awaited out there, relying on George to find her.

* * *

CHAPTER THIRTY-FIVE

The air in the basement mortuary was chilled and clinical as DCI George Beaumont stood facing pathologist Lindsey Yardley across the steel examination table where Ashley Cowgill's tragic young body lay shrouded. Despite years of investigating grim scenes, George still had to steel himself mentally entering this sterile realm of mortality. But duty propelled him forward without hesitation. Too much depended on unflinching resolve.

Dr Yardley glanced up from her notes, kind features creasing into a look of solemn compassion. "Apologies for the delay, Detective. I wanted to ensure I had substantive details for you regarding cause and timeline before we met."

"I appreciate you making this a priority, Doctor," George replied gravely. "Your insights will be crucial in determining factors surrounding the girl's death."

With a brisk nod, Dr Yardley launched into a bluntly factual overview of initial autopsy findings. "External examination of the body found only minor scrapes and bruises consistent with the trauma of rushing water. However, several fingernails were discovered broken or torn off completely."

She indicated the victim's ragged fingertips peeking from beneath the sheet. "Likely from her attempts to grasp at passing debris once in the river's grip." Dr Yardley sighed regretfully. "A reflexive desperation to survive, tragically in vain."

George nodded thoughtfully, filing details with a detective's keen ears. "Beyond the acute trauma of drowning, you found no other injuries or signs of struggle to indicate foul play?"

"None I can definitively substantiate at this stage," Dr Yardley confirmed, consulting her notes again. "Toxicology results are pending, but internal assessment suggests acute respiratory failure from water inhalation and aspiration. All other organs appear typically healthy for her age." She met George's eyes directly. "Based on preliminary findings, I see no conclusive evidence to indicate homicide or malicious intent. The poor girl's death appears consistent with a drowning mishap rather than a deliberate attack."

George kept his expression carefully neutral as he processed this sobering assessment. "And you're able to establish an approximate time of death?" he inquired briskly, mentally lining up events on his case timeline.

"Yes, initial liver temp analysis suggests she entered the water sometime between 4 and 5 pm today," Dr Yardley replied. "Died within minutes, most likely once immersed and incapacitated."

Refocusing on Dr Yardley, George asked pointedly, "In your expert opinion, would acute distress or suicidal mental state align with deliberately entering the freezing river in February without preparation?"

Dr Yardley frowned thoughtfully, absently twisting a necklace charm. "While I can't definitively rule out self-harm motivations given her recent trauma, the lack of a suicide note or history of attempts does cloud matters."

She tapped a pen on her clipboard musingly: "The broken nails do suggest a frantic fight for life once in the water. Not typically consistent with an intentional plunge." Shrugging helplessly, she conceded, "It's Impossible to determine absolute mental state without more context, I'm afraid."

George nodded, hiding his disappointment. He had hoped for concrete revelations, not more maddening ambiguity. But dwelling on frustrations served no purpose.

Thanking Dr Yardley sincerely for her diligent efforts,

CHAPTER THIRTY-FIVE

George headed out of the dreary mortuary into the bracing winter daylight. Pausing by the waiting Mercedes, he sucked in deep gulps of crisp air, clearing the crypt's stale morbid chill from his lungs.

Chapter Thirty-six

The Mercedes sped through the roads towards Middleton Woods, water spraying as DCI George Beaumont pushed the powerful engine to its limits. Beside him in the passenger seat, DC Jason Scott gripped the door handle, knuckles white as he relayed terse updates over the radio.

"Alpha team, what's your status on the nuclear bunker sweep, Sarge?" Jay barked.

A crackle of static preceded DI Luke Mason's brisk reply. "Negative so far, Jay. The dense brush is impeding access to the south-east quadrant." Frustration sharpened his tone as usual. "Requesting additional ground-penetrating radar support ASAP."

George clenched his jaw, mind racing. Every minute felt like an eternity with Esme's life in the balance. Who knew what atrocities that vile bastard Garforth subjected her to in his secret torture chamber?

"Get the helicopters providing thermal imaging assistance," George snapped to Jay. "I want eyes in the sky guiding the ground teams to any heat signatures."

"On it, boss," Jay affirmed, already relaying directives into his headset.

As the woods loomed closer, ancient trees reaching skeletal

CHAPTER THIRTY-SIX

fingers into the gathering dusk, George's gut clenched with dread. They were flying blind into hostile territory, innocuous ancient woodlands concealing untold horrors. The deceptively tranquil scenery mocked their frantic efforts to peel back shadows before another young life was swallowed forever.

Approaching the car park, teeming with police, George slammed on the brakes, tyres squealing as he threw the Mercedes into a bay. He and Jay were already sprinting towards the makeshift command centre erected in the visitor's centre, ringed by armoured response vehicles and swarming with purposeful activity.

Sergeant Greenwood intercepted them, thrusting a satellite map of the dense woods into George's hands. "Infrared scans have narrowed the likely location to this half-mile radius, which confirms the information Garforth gave you." He indicated an expanse of rugged terrain pockmarked with inactive mineshafts and bell pits. "But going will be slow on foot through that undergrowth."

"Christ," George breathed, calculating grimly. At this pace, they'd be lucky to reach Esme by dawn. He couldn't even let his mind venture into the vile violations she could endure in that yawning chasm of time.

Luke arrived out of breath and met his despairing gaze with staunch resolution: "We press on, son. We will not stop until we find her and nail that bastard Garforth's hide to the wall."

George clasped his friend's beefy shoulder, momentarily bolstered. Luke's dependability anchored him against the storm of hopelessness and fury. Falling apart served no one now, least of all the lost girl waiting for rescue from a monster's lair.

Turning back to Greenwood, George assumed an icy calm

belied by his racing heart. "I want the dog teams deployed immediately to aid the ground search," he instructed. Their noses might pick up a scent where our eyes fail."

Greenwood nodded sharply. "They're suiting up now, sir. Handlers are distributing scent articles from the Garforth estate as we speak."

Good. They needed every damn advantage technology and training could provide with time so perilously short.

Snatching up a radio, throat parched with stress, George issued clipped directives to the assembled search teams while poring over the ever-updating satellite imagery.

"Have the drones completed their sweep of the south-west quadrant yet?" he demanded, scrutinising the dense canopy for any sign of disturbed vegetation or heat signatures.

"Affirmative, sir," came the crackling reply. "No apparent bunker access points detected, but we'll keep scanning."

George exhaled raggedly, raking a hand through his hair. Esme had to be here somewhere, tucked away like Garforth's filthy secret.

Just then, Tashan's booming baritone exploded through the radio. "We've got a scent, sir! The dogs are going crazy near a hillside by the north-east perimeter."

George's pulse jack-rabbited as he shouted back, "Don't let them lose it, Tashan! Luke and I are inbound to your position now."

He was already motioning, barking orders as he ran. "Dispatch the crews to DC Blackburn's coordinates!"

"Roger that," Greenwood confirmed crisply, hot on George's heels.

Plunging into the shadowy underbrush, George forced his way through clawing branches and strangling vines, ignoring

CHAPTER THIRTY-SIX

the searing scratches criss-crossing his face. All that mattered was reaching Esme.

Breaking into a small clearing, gasping for breath, George zeroed in on Tashan restraining two snarling German Shepherds straining at their leads. The muscular detective's dark face shone with exertion but blazed with fierce urgency.

"They keep lunging at that area, sir," Tashan reported, indicating a dense thicket nestled against a sheer rock face.

The woods erupted into frenetic activity as personnel converged on the half-acre expanse Tashan indicated, tearing at underbrush and attacking stone with relentless purpose. George lost all track of time; eyes fixated on the steadily growing mound of dirt and debris that could conceal the passage to hell where Esme and God knew how many other victims suffered.

Suddenly, an excited shout pierced the dusk. "We've got something! Definite hollow space behind this boulder!"

George and Luke sprinted over, hearts in their throats, as the dig team frantically cleared soil from an odd seam bisecting an imposing granite slab. It was cleverly disguised, nearly imperceptible to the untrained eye. But now, the signs of human artifice shone through centuries of neglect.

After an eternity of tortured waiting, the heavy stone shuddered and then swung inward with a chilling whine of rusted hinges. Raising his torch, George peered into the yawning void, pulse roaring in his ears.

A crude spiral staircase plunged into the bowels of the hillside, rough-hewn walls glistening with damp and nitre. The stench of rot and human misery wafted up from the abyss, choking the throat. Ancient evil saturated the very stones of this subterranean labyrinth.

"Helmets and lights on now," Luke instructed sharply beside him, voice edged with revulsion. "Keep alert for any movement or sounds. Esme could be hidden anywhere in this warren."

Swallowing hard, George descended into the blackness, each wet step accompanied by the thundering of his own heart. The cold, fetid air pressed in like an evil force as if the weight of decades of atrocities lingered in the tunnels' mouldering depths.

At the base of the stairs, the teams fanned out, sweeping the twisting stone passageways with tense focus. George strained his ears past the dripping of water and his own harsh breathing for any trace of the missing girl.

Deeper and deeper, they forged into the dank innards of the hillside, playing their torches along crumbling brick and rusted iron gates set at intervals. The construction spoke of immense labour and resources poured into this devil's playground. Just how many generations of evil men had utilised this foul refuge to sate their jaded lusts?

* * *

George's head swam with exhaustion and disgust as they emerged hours later, filthy and bowed from the dungeon's mouldering corridors. The sinister honeycomb of cells and 'entertainment' chambers had disgorged obscene evidence of Garforth and his predecessors' vile pastimes—cruel instruments, soiled bedding, even macabre trophies suggesting victims stretching back decades or more.

An entire multimedia setup live-streamed the degradations to select audiences worldwide. Garforth hadn't just violated

CHAPTER THIRTY-SIX

but commodified innocence on an unthinkable scale. The depravity staggered George.

But there was no sign of Esme. Despair spiralled through George as he faced the grim probability that she wasn't merely hidden here but already trafficked far beyond reach. All their desperate efforts amounted to far too little, much too late.

"The lass is most likely already in transit to some godforsaken corner of Eastern Europe," Luke said, reading George's bleak expression. "We've heard whispers of pipelines snaking through Slovenia into Hungary and Romania via Slovenia once the girls are sufficiently broken." He shook his head with weary disgust. "Those bastards run an efficient business from procurement to resale."

George bowed his head, momentarily crushed under impotence. The knowledge Esme likely suffered alone in the clammy blackness while he fumbled sightlessly above tore his very soul.

Dragging George off to the side, Luke shook him roughly. "Now you listen here, mate," he growled. "We're making progress unravelling Garforth's network, however gut-wrenching each new thread proves." His grey eyes burned into George's with fierce conviction.

"We'll pursue every slimy tendril until justice is served. I swear we won't rest until we find Esme. No matter how long it takes or how far we must search."

George nodded mutely, but some vital spark had guttered within. As Luke pounded his back bracingly before moving off, he gazed into the middle distance, eyes unseeing.

This case had clawed under his skin from the start, a debt he'd sworn to pay as protector and avenger to lost girls. But as the sands slipped through his fingers, those promises turned to ashes.

With each passing minute, Esme drifted further beyond reach—a tiny boat on an inky sea without stars.

He had failed her.

The devastating realisation brought George to his knees at the bunker's edge, fists clenching handfuls of dirt as he struggled for composure. His mind reeled with the enormity of the evil operating unimpeded before him, devouring childhoods while the world turned a blind eye.

How would he face the trusting Bushfields or heartbroken Cowgills with news that not only were their daughters likely subjected to unimaginable violations beyond the estate walls but even now were disappearing down the maw of a relentless machine that chewed up beauty and spat out empty husks?

The burden of that unfulfillable promise threatened to suffocate George as he hunched in the shadows, ears ringing with imagined screams echoing from the depths below.

But into that maelstrom of torment and guilt, a cool, small hand descended on George's shaking shoulder. He jerked upright to find Candy Nichols kneeling beside him, blue eyes glinting fiercely in the torchlight.

"Come quickly, sir," she urged without preamble, ponytail whipping urgently. "We found something—or rather someone. You need to see this!"

Hope flared wildly in George's chest as he lurched to his feet. Could this be the breakthrough so desperately sought?

Without another word, he followed Candy's pounding steps back into the hillside's dank recesses, pulse roaring. Deep in the subterranean gloom, a knot of personnel clustered at the end of a cramped passageway previously obscured behind a cleverly concealed door.

CHAPTER THIRTY-SIX

Elbowing through the crowd, George skidded to a halt at the threshold of a tiny chamber rank with human misery. There, huddled against the clammy wall in a filthy nightgown, crouched Esme Bushfield.

But not the Esme of George's memories or case file photos. This wraith was barely recognisable as human, let alone a once vibrant teenager. All vestiges of lively innocence had been stripped away, leaving a shell quivering with terror, eyes sunken in a skeletal face.

She had shrunk against the far wall, whimpering weakly and shielding glazed eyes against the sudden light. Livid bruises and abrasions marred every visible inch of sickly pale skin. Ligature marks circled her bony wrists and ankles, testifying to interminable restraint. But worst of all was the emptiness in Esme's gaze, as if her very soul had been scoured away with systematic cruelty.

George's heart shattered at the sight of such abject brokenness. Esme had endured atrocities beyond imagining in this black pit. He couldn't even begin to fathom the trauma etched into every line of her ravaged body.

Approaching slowly, George knelt a cautious distance away, keeping his posture unthreatening.

Keeping his voice low and infinitely gentle, George said, "Esme? I'm DCI Beaumont. We're here to help you, to get you to safety." He swallowed hard, Adam's apple bobbing. "The ones who hurt you can never touch you again, OK?"

No response. Esme just stared right through him, features slack.

"It may not feel real yet, but this nightmare is over now," George continued, throat tight with emotion. "I promise we'll get you the care you need."

But Esme remained utterly unresponsive, gaze distant and limbs limp.

Exchanging an anguished glance with Candy, George knew they needed to extract Esme quickly but carefully to the waiting ambulance above. But he was terrified moving her forcefully could shatter her tenuous grip on reality entirely.

As he wavered uncertainly, a brisk movement in his periphery drew his gaze up to see paramedics entering bearing a stretcher. At their heels strode Maya Chen, clinical efficiency radiating from her petite frame as she shouldered through the crowd.

"Detective Chief Inspector," Maya greeted crisply, taking in the tragic tableau with professional calm. She nodded at Esme's crumpled form. "We'll need to assess her injuries and mental state to determine the best course of treatment."

She placed a gentle hand on George's tense shoulder. "I'll handle it from here. Please wait outside so we can stabilise her for transport."

"Right."

George watched helplessly as the medical team converged on Esme with gentle murmurs and coaxing hands, feeling the weight of every passing second. They had found her alive—but what quality of life remained after suffering mutely in this dank oubliette for nearly three months?

Stumbling from the suffocating cell, George shoved his way blindly back to the surface, lungs searing for air untainted by despair. He barely registered flashing lights painting the woods lurid shades as he staggered to his knees, retching violently into the undergrowth until his stomach emptied.

When the spasms finally eased, George wiped his mouth with a trembling hand, slowly rising to survey organised chaos

CHAPTER THIRTY-SIX

sprawling across the churned earth.

    Esme would get the help she desperately needed. But George knew her physical rescue was merely the first step in a long journey towards wholeness.

Chapter Thirty-seven

DCI George Beaumont sat hunched in a plastic chair under the harsh fluorescents of Leeds General Infirmary's trauma ward; head bowed as if under a physical weight. Endless hours had slipped by in a phantasmagoria of lights, alarms and terse voices as the emergency team laboured to stabilise Esme Bushfield's perilous condition.

Now, an uneasy hush cloaked the sterile hallway. Nurses moved between rooms with hushed purpose, nodding respectfully to the detectives keeping tense vigil. George scarcely dared to breathe lest the momentary peace shatter.

Across from him in matching chairs, DI Luke Mason and DC Candy Nichols murmured quiet strategies for their next steps. With Esme safe, their investigative momentum regained a crucial purpose—to bring the full scope of her abusers' network to swift, brutal justice.

But George barely processed their low discussion; eyes fixed unseeing on the scuffed lino. His mind churned in an endless reel of the horrors they'd uncovered below ground—the depraved torture chamber where Esme and untold others suffered unspeakable torment for the twisted pleasures of powerful men. He wanted to claw those images out of his head, to bleach away the soul-deep revulsion. But they remained

CHAPTER THIRTY-SEVEN

seared in his brain like a pulsating abscess.

The bleep of monitors and hiss of ventilators drifted from Esme's room, vital signs of life tethered to machines after so much had been ripped away. Fractured memories of finding her in that filthy dungeon cell kept battering George—her emaciated, battered body cowering from light and touch, once bright eyes deadened windows into unfathomable trauma. The Esme they'd lost had been devoured in that pit, perhaps never to fully return.

George squeezed his eyes shut against the despairing thought. He couldn't bear it—the magnitude of innocence defiled on his watch. Some vital part of him had cracked down in those clammy tunnels as comprehension sank in of the enormity thriving beneath his oblivious feet for so long. His very purpose had shattered with it.

Logically, he knew Esme's healing could only progress incrementally, her psyche carefully stitched back from the brink. But the gulf between that fragile, damaged girl and the laughing teen taken from them gaped like an open wound. They had taken too long to save her from the abyss...

A soft touch on his arm jolted George from his masochistic spiral. His head snapped up to see Candy watching him with compassionate understanding tempered by steel.

"It's not your fault," she said firmly, blue eyes flashing. "What happened to Esme is on Garforth and his circle of monsters alone. We can't let guilt distract from getting her justice."

George opened his mouth to argue, to growl that he should have seen the signs and moved faster. But Candy cut him off crisply.

"Esme needs you—needs us all—to stay focused on what

we can control now. Hunting down every last piece of scum involved and burning their foul empire to the ground." Her fingers dug into his forearm like talons. "So get your head back in the game, boss. Esme deserves our best, not wallowing."

George blinked at his usually exuberant detective's stern rebuke, so eerily attuned to his spiralling thoughts. But she was right. Stewing in useless self-flagellation dishonoured Esme's suffering and the vital work still ahead to dismantle the trafficking ring ensnaring her.

Drawing a shuddering breath, George forced his spine straight and nodded in gratitude to Candy. "Message received, Nichols. Loud and clear."

Candy smiled wanly, giving his shoulder a bolstering squeeze before turning back to Luke.

Just then, purposeful footsteps sounded down the corridor, accompanied by a familiar voice brusquely demanding access. George and his team shot to their feet as Detective Chief Superintendent Mohammed Sadiq rounded the corner, his habitually urbane features etched with urgency.

"Beaumont," Sadiq greeted crisply. "I came as soon as I heard. The entire force is breathing a sigh of relief you found the Bushfield girl alive."

His sharp gaze raked over George's dishevelled, dirt-streaked figure and pinched features. "Although I take it from your appearance, the conditions of discovery were grim indeed?"

"To put it mildly, sir," George replied hoarsely. He glanced involuntarily back at Esme's closed door. "She's endured unthinkable trauma. The medical team are still working to ensure basic stability."

Sadiq clenched his jaw at the weighted implication. "Walk

me through it," he instructed tightly.

As they made their way towards a vacant family room, George recounted in clipped tones the frantic search efforts leading to the underground dungeon's location. His voice shook imperceptibly as he described the dank horror of that mouldering prison and Esme's skeletal, violated form within.

Sadiq listened intently, dark eyes taking on a flinty cast as the sickening details sank in. When George fell silent, the DCS leaned forward, hands steepled.

"Obviously, this depravity reaches far beyond one man's crimes. Garforth is clearly the vile lynchpin to a much larger network of exploitation." Sadiq's lip curled with cold fury. "One, we will scorch the earth to dismantle, root and stem."

He pinned George with a piercing look. "Where do we stand with the evidence needed to crucify Garforth and his ilk?"

George took a fortifying breath, mentally rallying scattered thoughts. "We've computer equipment and paper trails linking Garforth financially to an organised trafficking pipeline," he reported grimly. "His 'youth charity' was a front to funnel vulnerable teens to high-paying clients. Bank records show the sums involved are staggering."

Sadiq's nostrils flared with disgust, but he motioned for George to continue.

"Tech is still decrypting the communications, but we've already confirmed key players as far as Hungary and Romania. They have a repulsively efficient process for procuring and transporting product." Bile scalded George's throat, uttering the clinical terminology. "All leading back to Garforth greasing palms and scouting fresh meat."

Sadiq closed his eyes briefly as if physically pained by the extent of the rot. "I want that digital footprint traced to the ends of the earth," he said in a deadly hush. "Every single name, every bloody transaction. We'll leave none of these cockroaches scuttling back to the shadows."

"Understood, sir," George acknowledged. He hesitated before asking delicately, "And what of Garforth's legal representation? I imagine his briefs will counter hard to suppress whatever evidence they can."

A glacial smile touched Sadiq's stern mouth. "You let me handle the politics and tape, Chief Inspector. Rest assured, no amount of solicitor double-talk will override the righteously enraged powers leaning on this one."

He stood abruptly, checking his gleaming Rolex. "I'm off to personally update Esme's parents. The media are already clamouring, so we need a coordinated front to control the narrative."

Sadiq gripped George's shoulder. "Your team have done exemplary work. Now get some rest, and let us keep the momentum to nail these bastards to the wall."

With that, he swept out in a swirl of expensive wool overcoat.

George watched him go, feeling a modicum of tension drain away. With the top brass and public baying for blood, Garforth's gilded cage had slammed shut. The beast would finally face the harsh light of justice—or die trying to slither free.

* * *

The atmosphere crackled with barely restrained tension as DCI George Beaumont once more faced down Eugene Garforth in Elland Road Police Station's Interrogation Room Four. The trafficking kingpin wore a sneer of pure contempt despite his

CHAPTER THIRTY-SEVEN

rumpled suit and haggard pallor from days in hospital and custody.

George leaned forward, voice deceptively soft. "Quite the busy boy, weren't you, Eugene? Procuring vulnerable girls to sate the perverse whims of toffs with more money than conscience."

Garforth's lip curled. "Baseless slander. My legal team will soon dismantle this tissue of lies stitched together by your crude provocations."

George smiled mirthlessly. "You mean Campbell? The briefs who have suddenly jumped ship now that your sordid enterprise is exposed?" He relished the flicker of unease contorting Garforth's patrician features. The rats scented a sinking ship.

Pressing his momentary advantage, George retrieved an evidence pouch from the stack before him. "Recognise this, Eugene?"

He dangled the bagged electronic device, its sleek gold casing winking obscenely under the fluorescents. Garforth's eyes widened a fraction before he regained his haughty mask.

"Just a bit of harmless kink," he scoffed. "Nothing criminal."

George's smile sharpened. "Our tech experts paint a different picture. This little beauty is positively stuffed with proof of your foul empire." He began implacably reciting damning highlights.

"Records of 'product' sales to international buyers. Meticulous notes ranking assets like cuts of meat. Even video clips of you sampling the wares." George spat the words like poison, knuckles whitening on the evidence bag. "Irrefutable confirmation you're the vile spider squatting at this wretched web's centre."

Garforth had paled further with each devastating bullet, realising his digital footprints wove an inescapable noose. But a flare of defiance coloured his papery cheeks.

"Even if your lurid narrative held a kernel of truth—which I categorically deny—nothing ties me concretely to criminal acts," he blustered. "Perhaps I moved in certain circles and witnessed unsavoury activities. But no hard proof exists that I personally violated any precious flowers." His sneer returned insufferably.

White-hot rage surged through George's veins.

But George merely leaned back, arms crossed and features an impassive mask. "If you're labouring under the delusion that splitting hairs could possibly get you off the hook, that ship has well and truly sailed," he said with terrifying calm.

"Perhaps you'd like to explain these recovered items to the court?" George plucked a stack of lurid photos from the file, fanning them across the scarred table like a perverse deck of cards.

Captured in nauseating focus sprawled Esme Bushfield's limp, battered form. In several shots, Garforth's smug face leered over her as he pawed at her exposed flesh. Others showed her bound and gagged in varying states of undress and consciousness, tear-stained face a rictus of despair.

The sickening images marched on relentlessly—different poses, different humiliating acts, but always Esme's broken gaze and Garforth's triumphant leer, a demon feasting on agony.

"I don't... it's not... you can't possibly..." Garforth spluttered, his composure unravelling as his depravity blazed forth in living colour. He swallowed hard, his tongue darting out to wet thinned lips. "This is all taken out of context!" The defiance rang hollow against visual proof of his base predations.

George merely raised an eyebrow, unmoved by the weak dissembling. "I was rather hoping you'd double down on denial, Eugene. Because that allows me to introduce my final nail for your coffin."

He fished the last item from the file—a standard drive, unremarkable except for the shattered lives chronicled within its digital bowels. George brandished it like a talisman against the loathsome beast across from him.

"This handy little device contains terabytes of high-definition video taken in the very dungeons Esme and your other victims suffered their darkest hells." The muscles in George's jaw ticked, voice tight with disgust.

"Multiple angles, crystal-clear audio capturing every muffled scream and smug direction from behind the camera. All starring you as the twisted auteur of suffering." He pinned Garforth with a stare that could cut glass. "Unequivocal proof that annihilates any claims of mere bystander misfortune."

As the blood drained from Garforth's slack face, the vestiges of his urbane veneer crumbled to reveal the quivering slug beneath. He opened his mouth, then closed it. No more grandiose bluster, no more weaselling half-truths.

Just the naked panic of a monster who'd finally glimpsed his own grotesque reflection and found it indefensible.

George could practically see Garforth's feverish mind churning through his shrinking options. Without his slick attack dogs to muddy the waters, the stark horror of his transgressions laid bare, undeniable...

The realisation settled in his eyes like curdled milk—he was well and truly fucked.

Sweat beading his upper lip, Garforth's gaze darted about the claustrophobic room, seeking escape from his inescapable sins. When he finally met George's merciless stare again, the fear poorly masked as affront had leached away.

In its place crept desperation as he calculated how to salvage his wretched hide.

"Perhaps... certain allowances could be made..." he stuttered, tongue flicking out to moisten cracked lips. "Consideration for... extenuating circumstances?" The oily plea turned George's stomach. But he merely smiled thinly.

"You want to bargain now, Eugene? A plea deal to wriggle free with a lighter sentence?" He leaned forward slowly, voice lethally soft. "After the abominations you've inflicted? The young lives your foul perversions snuffed out?"

Garforth stuttered and spluttered, but George cut him off with a sharp slash of his hand.

"Absolutely fucking not!" George's icy calm belied his seething disgust.

Swallowing hard at this ruthless dismantling of his delusions, Garforth hunched in on himself. "But surely my cooperation merits some consideration..." he whimpered, the words lacking conviction even to his own ears.

George gave him a ghastly parody of a smile, more snarl than a grin. "Cooperation?" He barked a humourless laugh that ricocheted harshly off the sullen cement walls.

"You're confusing cowardice with contrition, Eugene. Only now you've been caught do you deign to 'cooperate.'"

He stopped himself then, reining in the righteous rage to continue with terrifying control. "But even if you grovelled out every putrid detail in a bid to save your wretched skin, no

CHAPTER THIRTY-SEVEN

leniency will be granted. You crossed a line the moment you created those videos. Made your evil deeds a sick spectator sport." George took a deep breath. "Our earlier deal stands, but with this, you're more than fucked." George's voice dropped to a menacing purr as he leaned in closer, caging Garforth with his deadly intent. "So don't waste your breath bargaining with me, Eugene. You're utterly and completely finished."

Garforth had shrunk so far into himself that he nearly disappeared within the rumpled folds of his designer suit. All deception and pretence had been stripped away, leaving a pathetic, snivelling shell.

"Please..." he rasped desperately, his skeletal hands scrabbling at his collar as if it choked him. There must be something! I can give you names and locations! I'll do anything!"

As George watched dispassionately, Garforth seemed to crumple in on himself, shoulders slumping in devastating self-knowledge. "What about if I give you the name of the boss? The one at the top?"

Chapter Thirty-eight

DCI George Beaumont sat hunched at his desk, the harsh fluorescent lights casting deep shadows across his careworn face. The shared office outside hummed with muted activity as officers went about their duties, but inside George's glass-walled office, the air hung thick with a palpable tension.

Across from him, DS Yolanda Williams perched on the edge of her seat, a thick folder clutched in her slender hands. Her normally vibrant features were drawn, mouth pressed into a grim line.

"You said you had a development in Ashley's case," George prompted gruffly, impatience and dread warring in his gut. After the roller coaster of Esme's rescue and Garforth's capture, he wasn't sure how many more gut punches he could endure.

Yolanda nodded jerkily. "We finally managed to recover the CCTV footage from Whitehall Waterfront." She hesitated, uncharacteristically uncertain. "But sir... I need to warn you. What's on here, it's not easy to watch."

George's stomach clenched, a sick foreboding slithering up his spine. He had seen his share of horrors in this line of work and had stared unflinchingly into the darkest recesses of human depravity. But something in Yolanda's haunted eyes told him this was different.

Swallowing hard, George held out his hand for the folder. "Let's have it then."

With palpable reluctance, Yolanda passed it over, her fingers trembling slightly. George flipped it open, steeling himself for the worst.

Grainy black-and-white images spilt across his desk, time-stamped in accusing digital clarity. At first glance, they depicted an unremarkable stretch of the waterfront, the river a black ribbon winding through the heart of the city.

But as George's keen gaze skimmed the stills, two figures caught his attention. Though fuzzy with distance, he could make out Ashley's slight form, her body language tense and defensive. Across from her stood a taller figure wearing a baseball cap low, the shadows obscuring their face.

George's pulse quickened as he traced their silent confrontation frame by agonising frame. The baseball-capped figure gesticulated angrily, crowding into Ashley's space. She shoved them back, jaw jutting with familiar defiance.

But then the figure reached up and tugged their cap lower, further concealing their features. George cursed under his breath. "How are we supposed to identify this bastard if we can't see his face?"

Yolanda leaned forward, pointing to the figure's hands. "He's wearing gloves too. Clever prick didn't want to leave any trace."

George ground his teeth in frustration. Another dead end, another lead drying up like dust. He was about to toss the folder aside in disgust when Yolanda stopped him with a gentle hand on his arm.

"Keep going," she urged softly. "It gets worse."

Dread coiling in his gut, George forced himself to flip to the next series of images. What he saw there froze the blood in his veins.

Ashley and her capped assailant were grappling now, locked in a vicious struggle. As he watched in helpless, sickened fascination, Ashley reared back and delivered a stinging slap to the figure's face, knocking their cap askew.

And there, in damning digital clarity, was a face George knew all too well. Ishaan Sadiq, DCS Sadiq's cocky, entitled son. The same smirking visage that had slouched, oozing privileged disdain.

But now, that smarmy veneer had vanished, replaced by an ugly mask of pure rage. Ishaan's face contorted grotesquely as he lunged at Ashley, grappling her towards the river's edge.

"I need to see the video," he said, and Yolanda nodded.

George's heart seized as he witnessed the inevitable, hideous conclusion play out frame by frame. Ishaan, overpowering Ashley with sheer brute force. Her thin arms wind-milling desperately as she teetered on the brink. And then, with one final, vicious shove, her body plunging through the ice, swallowed whole by the black, freezing depths.

The video blurred before George's eyes, Yolanda's voice fading to an indistinct buzz. All he could see was Ashley's terrified face in those final, futile moments, her scream for help silenced by the river's icy maw.

Dimly, he registered Yolanda's gentle touch on his shoulder, her murmured words of comfort. But they couldn't penetrate the roaring in his ears, the white-hot fury searing his veins.

Ishaan Sadiq. That smug, arrogant little prick who had the world handed to him on a silver platter. George had known the boy was trouble and sensed the rot beneath the polished

CHAPTER THIRTY-EIGHT

surface. But this...

This was cold-blooded murder, captured in unflinching detail. And George would bet his last shilling that Ishaan's powerful daddy already had a battery of solicitors lined up to make it all disappear.

The thought made George physically sick, bile scalding his throat. How many more entitled monsters would slither free, their crimes buried beneath silk suits and family influence? How could he look Esme in the eye and promise her a world of justice and safety when beasts like Ishaan lurked in every shadowed corner?

Abruptly, George shoved back from his desk, the screech of his chair harsh in the suffocating silence. He couldn't breathe, couldn't think past the blinding rage and impotence. He needed air, needed to clear the stench of death and deceit from his lungs.

Ignoring Yolanda's alarmed queries, George stormed from his office, the door slamming like a gunshot behind him. He didn't know where he was going, only that he had to move, to outrun the tidal wave of failure and fury threatening to drag him under.

As he pushed through the station's double doors, the icy wind slapped him like a physical blow. George welcomed the pain, letting it scour him raw and aching.

* * *

DCI George Beaumont faced down a man responsible for shattering countless lives.

Across the scarred table, Ishaan Sadiq lounged with insolent ease, his once-pristine dress shirt rumpled from hours in custody.

Beside George, DI Luke Mason and DSU Jim Smith radiated matching coiled intensity, the weight of Ashley's brutal murder hanging heavy in the air.

"Let's cut the bollocks, Ishaan," George bit out, his calm fraying. "We know you murdered Ashley Cowgill."

Ishaan's lip curled, dark eyes glittering coldly. "Tragic, certainly, but nothing to do with me." He examined his nails, the picture of bored disdain. "I heard she committed suicide."

Beside him, his slick-suited solicitor, Niall Walsh, placed a warning hand on Ishaan's forearm. "My client has nothing further to say on baseless speculation—"

But Ishaan shrugged him off with a sneer. "Please. I'm not afraid of their theatrics."

George slammed his palm on the table, the sharp crack making Ishaan flinch. "Enough! We have evidence placing you at the scene." His eyes bored into Ishaan's, daring him to keep up the charade. "So drop the act and tell us what really happened that night."

For a tense beat, Ishaan glared mutinously before huffing and reclining back. "Whatever do you mean?"

His solicitor hissed in warning. "Ishaan! I must advise you to refrain from further comment until—"

"Oh, save it," Ishaan snapped, cocky veneer slipping. "I'm not playing their game."

"So you weren't at the river the night Ashley was murdered?"

"When was that again?" Ishaan asked.

George exchanged a loaded glance with Luke and DSU Smith. What an arrogant little prick. Then he told Ishaan the date when Ashley was murdered.

CHAPTER THIRTY-EIGHT

"Fine. Yes, I met Ashley that night, but I never murdered her." He grinned. "Must have been someone else."

"Like who?"

"You tell me, Detective."

"Well, I think it's you, considering we found your DNA on her body," George explained, sliding across a forensic report.

"Fine. Ashley and I had a row. Things got a bit heated. She slapped me, and I defended myself. It's as simple as that."

George exchanged another glance with Luke and DSU Smith. This little prick was arrogant enough to dig his own grave.

Carefully schooling his features, George replied evenly, "Interesting. And I suppose Ashley just magically ended up in the river after your little tiff?"

Ishaan rolled his eyes. "Guess the daft cow lost her balance. It's not my problem if she was too off her head to stand straight. You know she was an alcoholic, right?"

The tox report showed no alcohol in her system. George explained that to Ishaan and his solicitor.

"Dunno then, Detective," Ishaan said and leaned back, arms crossed.

"Well, Ishaan, let's see if the evidence agrees with your version of events, shall we?" George asked.

With that, he reached into a folder and withdrew a series of grainy black-and-white printouts, spreading them on the table like a perverse jigsaw.

Frame by damning frame, the truth of that awful night spilt out in harsh monochrome—Ishaan and Ashley squaring off by the river's edge. Ashley delivering a stinging slap. Ishaan's face contorting into a grotesque mask of rage.

And then the final, sickening sequence. Ishaan, brutally overpowering Ashley's slight form, shoving her into the icy depths. The images seemed to writhe with macabre life, Ashley's terrified expression searing itself into George's retinas.

Ishaan had gone deathly pale, all pretence of insolence drained away. "I didn't... that's not what..." He swallowed hard, eyes darting desperately to his solicitor. "Niall! Do something!"

But the solicitor was staring at the damning stills in mute horror, the colour leeching from his face. Clearly, this was not the narrative his gilded client had spun.

"I think these speak for themselves," George said, quiet menace thrumming in his tone. So how about we try this again, from the top?"

Ishaan licked his lips, fingers knotting in his lap. For the first time, genuine fear bled through the cracks in his armour.

"It was an accident," he replied hoarsely. It was manslaughter at most. I never meant it. She just made me so angry."

George sliced a hand through the air, cutting off his sputtering excuses. "Made you angry? So angry you battered a seventeen-year-old girl and shoved her into a frozen river to drown?"

Ishaan blanched, shrinking into his chair like a rat in a trap. "No! I mean, yes, but... it wasn't like that!"

"How exactly was it then, son?" DSU Smith asked quietly. It was the first time he had spoken, and the gravel of his voice made Ishaan jump. "Walk us through your version. Slowly."

But Ishaan's solicitor had finally found his tongue, placing a firm hand on his client's shoulder. "I'm afraid this interview is over. My client clearly is in no state to continue without further counsel." He stood stiffly, glaring at the detectives. "Ishaan will be exercising his right to silence going forward."

CHAPTER THIRTY-EIGHT

George clenched his jaw, fury simmering in his gut. Was this little snake really going to lawyer up and spin sob stories now that he had been caught red-handed?

But procedure was procedure. However much it galled him, George couldn't keep the smug prick without his briefs present.

"This isn't over," he growled, jabbing a finger at Ishaan's ashen face. "We have you, you little bastard. And I swear I will personally comb through every sordid second of your miserable life until I have enough evidence to bury you."

With that, George shoved to his feet hard enough to send his chair skittering. He stormed out without a backward glance, the door slamming like a gunshot in his wake.

Out in the hallway, George braced his hands on his knees, dragging in ragged breaths. The fury and disgust churned in his gut like battery acid, eating him alive from within.

That arrogant, dead-eyed monster had snuffed out a young girl's life as casually as crushing an insect. And now he dared paint himself the victim, just another spoiled brat acting out?

Dimly, he registered Luke and DSU Smith flanking him, their presence steadying rocks in the maelstrom.

"We'll nail the little gobshite," Luke growled, meaty hands flexing. "No posh git is above the law, no matter who his daddy is."

"He's not wriggling out of this one," DSU Smith agreed grimly. "We have him on camera, bold as brass. CPS will take it from here."

George shook his head, a bitter laugh scraping his throat raw. "You have met his father, right?"

He straightened, a muscle ticking in his clenched jaw. "Ishaan will be out by teatime, sharing stories at the country club while Ashley rots."

DSU Smith laid a heavy hand on George's shoulder, his craggy face lined with empathy. "Son, I know it feels like pissing in the wind sometimes. But we can't let the bastards grind us down." He held George's bleak gaze, eyes glinting steel. "If we stop fighting, stop believing that truth can prevail? Then they've already won."

George wanted to believe him. He wanted to trust that the scales could balance, that their tireless pursuit of justice meant something against the crushing weight of generational power.

"I need some air," George muttered, shrugging off the concerned hands. He couldn't bear their pity, their faith in a system so fundamentally broken.

He had to get out, to flee the cloying stench of conspiracy and corruption before it choked him entirely.

George didn't remember stumbling from the building, gulping lungfuls of icy air like a drowning man. He didn't remember driving aimlessly through the grey city streets; hands white-knuckled on the wheel as if he could outrun the sickness in his soul.

All he knew was that he couldn't keep doing this. He couldn't keep throwing himself into the breach only to be swallowed whole by the very monsters he had sworn to defeat.

George was a hollowed-out husk, bled dry by the unwinnable war against human wickedness. And he didn't know if there was anything left to fill the gnawing void.

Ishaan's smug, soulless face swam before his eyes, melding with Eugene Garforth's sardonic mask and Craig Bell's oily smirk. The predators and the powerful, forever circling, forever hungry.

CHAPTER THIRTY-EIGHT

And the innocents like Esme and Ashley, forever caught in their crosshairs, lambs to the slaughter.

George had dedicated his life to shielding the helpless. But now, he wondered if it had all been a futile self-delusion.

Chapter Thirty-nine

George stepped into his office, closing the door softly behind him. The space was a comforting cocoon, its walls adorned with accolades and photographs marking the highlights of his career. But today, those mementoes felt hollow, the trappings of a life's work dedicated to justice that seemed to mock him now in the face of recent failures.

Settling heavily behind his desk, George's gaze was drawn to the board dominating the far wall. Its once-pristine grid was now a chaotic collage of leads, evidence, and victim profiles—a tangled web with Esme Bushfield's angelic face at its centre.

Esme. The name tasted like ashes on George's tongue. They had found her alive, if only in the barest physical sense. But what kind of life could she hope to reclaim after enduring such horrors? The light in her eyes had been snuffed out; her spirit shattered into jagged shards. Putting those pieces back together would be a Herculean feat requiring far more than mere detective work.

Selfishly, George yearned to celebrate Esme's rescue as a hard-fought victory. To let the sheer relief of delivering her from that fetid dungeon wash away the accumulated layers of guilt and grime. But he knew her freedom marked a beginning, not an end. The real work of healing and restoration had only

CHAPTER THIRTY-NINE

just begun.

Sighing heavily, George let his eyes drift to the grainy photograph tacked up beside Esme—Ashley Cowgill's once-vibrant face now forever frozen in a rictus of youthful rebellion. George's chest constricted painfully, a familiar ache that had settled behind his breastbone and never quite abated.

Ashley—the whip-smart, troubled girl who had barrelled into their lives, challenging authority at every turn. In another life, George could imagine her spirit and tenacity channelled into leadership, artistry, and a force for change. Instead, her truncated story ended in murky waters, and dreams and potential were left to eddy in the uncaring current.

Staring into Ashley's defiant eyes, George felt the weight of her loss settle over him like a leaden shroud. They had been too slow, too blind to the rot lurking beneath the placid surface until it was far too late. For all of George's determination, he had failed Ashley most fundamentally, unable to deliver her from evil's devouring shadow.

But George recognised that Ashley's death was not his cross to bear. The blame lay squarely with the monsters who had manipulated and defiled her—Craig Bell and Eugene Garforth. But the knowledge did little to alleviate the guilt that scalded his veins, the insidious voice whispering that if he had just been better, faster, smarter, she might still be here.

Swallowing against the sudden lump in his throat, George forced his gaze away from Ashley's accusing stare to the final photograph on the board—Ishaan Sadiq, DCS Sadiq's son. The long arm of the law had finally trapped the cocky boy; his smarmy veneer stripped away to reveal the predator within.

But even that victory tasted like ashes in George's mouth. For Ishaan's sins, he would face a few paltry years behind bars under a manslaughter charge, coddled by family connections and an immaculate public façade. A slap on the wrist compared to the life sentence of trauma his victims would endure.

George's hand curled reflexively into a fist at the thought. The scales of justice always seemed to tip in favour of the privileged and powerful; their misdeeds cloaked in respectability until the stench could no longer be ignored. How many more hungry eyes were still out there, prowling for their next vulnerable prey while their upstanding families turned a blind eye?

The question haunted George. They had cut off one head of the Hydra in Eugene Garforth, but how many more vile tendrils lurked in the shadows, waiting to strike?

Staring at the three faces on his board—victim, casualty, perpetrator—George felt the familiar crushing weight of responsibility settle on his shoulders.

George had no easy answers, just the leaden certainty that he would continue to fight this battle with every ounce of his being for as long as he drew breath. He owed it to Esme, to Ashley, to every voiceless soul crying out for a champion.

But on days like today, when the losses weighed so much heavier than the victories, George couldn't help but wonder if it would ever be enough. If he would ever be enough to stem the tide of human wickedness.

Scrubbing a hand over his haggard face, George leaned back in his chair and exhaled slowly. The world kept turning, immune to his crisis of faith. There were still leads to chase, interviews to conduct, and a tedious but necessary mountain of paperwork to scale.

A knock on the door interrupted George's thoughts. Detective Superintendent Smith entered.

CHAPTER THIRTY-NINE

"Everything OK, sir?"

"No, son, it's not," Smith explained.

George narrowed his eyes. "Go on."

"Well," Jim said, "we've been looking into the attack on DC Candy Nichols last month in Beeston."

Jim Smith was referring to the incident where Candy was attacked outside The Bread Basket Case sandwich shop. They had assumed the attack to be the work of deceased Detective Chief Inspector Alistair Atkinson, the culprit in their last murder case.

"I've been looking at every piece of CCTV I could find," Smith said.

"OK."

"And it appears that Alistair was in the building at the time of the assault," Smith explained, "meaning Alistair couldn't possibly have attacked DC Nichols outside the sandwich shop."

Also by Lee Brook

Book 1: THE MISS MURDERER

Book 2: THE BONE SAW RIPPER

Book 3: THE BLONDE DELILAH

Book 4: THE CROSS FLATTS SNATCHER

Book 5: THE MIDDLETON WOODS STALKER

Book 6: THE CHRISTMAS HIT LIST - a completely new version of The Naughty List, entirely re-written

Book 7: THE FOOTBALLER AND THE WIFE

Book 8: THE NEW FOREST VILLAGE BOOK CLUB

Novella 1: MISSING: MICHELLE CROMACK

Book 9: THE KILLER IN THE FAMILY

Book 10: THE STOURTON STONE CIRCLE

Novella 2: A HALLOWEEN TO REMEMBER: THE LEEDS VAMPIRE

Novella 3: ECHOES OF THE RIPPER: THE LONG SHADOW

Book 11: THE WEST YORKSHIRE RIPPER

Book 12: THE SHADOWS OF YULETIDE

Book 13: THE SHADOWS OF THE PAST

Book 14: THE ECHOES OF SILENCE

Book 15: BENEATH THE SURFACE

More coming in 2024 - see https://www.leebrookauthor.com/ for more information

Printed in Great Britain
by Amazon